"Whoa!" Cooper looked in her rearview mirror. "What the heck did I hit back there?"

Slowing down, she eased the truck onto the farthest side of the shoulder. Though reluctant to leave the warmth of her cab, Cooper knew she had no choice. Grabbing a flashlight from her toolbox, she jumped out of the truck, and immediately saw that one of her rear tires had deflated like a spent birthday balloon.

"Great." Cooper's buoyant mood dissipated in the frigid air. Pulling her wool hat down over her ears, she retrieved her emergency road kit from the rear of the cab and unzipped it. After igniting two flares she unfastened the jack and spare tire from the inside of the truck bed.

As she watched, a motorcycle edged onto the highway shoulder. Its rider was a man, dressed in black jeans and a black leather jacket, whose features were completely obscured by his black helmet. Even when he tipped back the tinted visor covering his face and asked if she needed a hand, the moonless night cloaked him in shadow.

As he dismounted and began to walk toward her, Cooper's cell phone rang to the tune of the Beatles' "A Hard Day's Night." The man in black chuckled. "I recollect you mentioning the Fab Four, but I didn't know you liked them *that* much."

He stepped forward into the red glow of the flare and Cooper's jaw dropped as she recognized his face. "Get the phone, girl." He pointed at the device. "I'll jack the truck."

Answering the call, Cooper was at first too stunned to make sense of Ashley's frantic and garbled words. There was nothing coherent about the hysterical cries and pleas of *"Please!* There's a man! He's . . . he's dead! DEAD IN MY HOUSE! COME GET ME!" echoing down the line . . .

Hope Street Church Mysteries by

JENNIFER STANLEY

Stirring Up Strife

Path of the Wicked

The Way of the Guilty

Available from St. Martin's / Minotaur Paperbacks

THE WAY OF
THE GUILTY

Jennifer Stanley

St. Martin's Paperbacks

THE WAY OF THE GUILTY

Copyright © 2010 by Jennifer Stanley.

All rights reserved.

For information address St. Martin's Press, 175 Fifth Avenue, New York, NY 10010.

ISBN: 978-0-312-37684-0

Printed in the United States of America

St. Martin's Paperbacks edition / September 2010

St. Martin's Paperbacks are published by St. Martin's Press, 175 Fifth Avenue, New York, NY 10010.

10 9 8 7 6 5 4 3 2 1

For the amazing women of Circle #2,
Third Presbyterian Church, Richmond

And for Carol Booth,
who has taught me much about grace

Acknowledgments

The author is grateful to Jessica Faust of Book Ends for being a faithful cheerleader, Laura Bourgeois and Hope Dellon of St. Martin's / Minotaur Paperbacks for championing Cooper and friends, Frank Howarth for answering questions about car sales and documentation, Kim Faulker for providing the comfort cookie recipe, Mary Harrison for reading an early draft, and my family for reminding me that sometimes I just need to step away from the computer and play a little.

The way of the guilty is devious,
but the conduct of the innocent is upright.

Proverbs 21:8

1

The garden had hangings of white and blue linen, fastened with cords of white linen and purple material to silver rings on marble pillars. There were couches of gold and silver on a mosaic pavement of porphyry, marble, mother-of-pearl and other costly stones.

Esther 1:6 (NIV)

If Cooper Lee had known she would spend Friday night chugging champagne at an unfamiliar woman's mansion while a trio of busty coeds modeled lingerie, she would have come up with any number of creative excuses in order to avoid the whole thing. Unfortunately, Cooper had completely misunderstood her sister's invitation to accompany her to "a pajama party" being hosted by one of her church friends.

"Georgia Ferguson has such a *gorgeous* house! Wait 'til you see it!" Cooper's sister Ashley had shouted over the roar of Cooper's power sander the weekend before the infamous fete. "Can you turn that damned thing off for a second?"

After gently putting down the tool, Cooper slid her safety goggles onto the crown of her head, picked up a piece of sandpaper, and began working on the rough areas on a chapel-shaped birdhouse. "And why exactly should I be interested in Georgia Ferguson's house?" she asked her sister while gently stroking the wood smooth. "I don't even know this woman."

Stopping Cooper's hand with her own, Ashley announced, "Because *I'm* going to a party there next weekend and *you're* coming with me."

Imagining a room populated by Ashley's worldly acquaintances, Cooper grimaced. "In case you've forgotten, I repair office equipment for a living." She rubbed the tip of the steeple gently with a folded scrap of sandpaper. "Why would I want to go to Georgia's party? These are *your* church friends. I've got my own," she added happily.

Ashley drummed her fingers against the workbench and Cooper couldn't help but admire her sister's pristine French manicure. "You're going to this party because you're a mature, confident woman. That's just the kind of woman I need by my side to help me select an array of *fabulous* new night things with which I can seduce my husband."

Cooper's neck flushed as it always did when she was embarrassed. "I am well aware that you're trying to get pregnant, but I'd rather not have to hear too many details, okay? Some things are meant to be kept private."

"Some *things?* You can't even say the word!" Ashley giggled. "Go on, I dare you. Say 'sex.' Say it! Sex, sex, sex!"

"You talk about it enough for both of us, thanks very much," Cooper retorted. "I'm going to start calling you Dr. Ruth." She playfully elbowed her sister out of the way and reached for the power sander. Removing her safety glasses from the top of her wheat-blonde hair, she stared at Ashley with her intriguing, mismatched eyes. "Is that all? I'd like to get back to this."

"Don't you give me that blue-eyed, green-eyed glower," Ashley commanded and then began to push sawdust scraps around with her finger, forming the outline of a wobbly heart on the surface of the table. "The truth is that I could use Dr. Ruth's advice these days. Listen to me, Coop. I *need* to go to this party. I'm looking for a way to knock Lincoln's socks off. To make him sit up and take notice of me like he used to."

"Are you two having difficulties again?" Cooper looked at her sister with concern though she couldn't comprehend how a party could change how Ashley and her husband felt about one another. "Over the baby issue?"

Looking miserable, Ashley marred the sawdust heart with a sweep of her hand. "I think Lincoln's avoiding me. For the last few months he's been going to all these *late* meetings. Then there's the golf outings with his daddy and brother every weekend—not to mention the poker nights." Tears pooled in her lovely azure eyes. "I feel like I'm losing him."

Pulling off her gloves, Cooper put her arm around her sister's tiny waist and squeezed. "He loves you, Ashley. He'd be crazy not to."

Ashley sighed. "Love is hard work, isn't it? Harder than I ever thought it would be. I had my dream wedding, Lincoln carried me over the threshold of our perfect house, and for a while, everything was wonderful. A fairy tale. But then I was supposed to get pregnant and grow all round and cute and waddle and have that *glow.* I'd deliver the most precious beautiful little baby this world has ever seen and give it like five names and dress its precious little body in hand-embroidered smocks and Robeez booties. When we'd stroll around downtown, people would stop us on the street and just stare at my Gerber baby." She sniffed. "Instead I find out I have a bicornuate uterus and even after surgery will have a tough time getting pregnant. It's all I think about now!" She thumped the workbench and then eyed the sawdust on her palm in distaste. "I've never wanted *anything* so badly as I want this baby! Why did there have to be something wrong with me?"

Cooper cleaned up the sawdust using a small broom and dustpan. "Ashley, maybe you need to take a break from thinking about babies all the time. It obviously upsets you and if you're worried about your marriage, perhaps you and Lincoln need some time alone together."

"That's *exactly* what I'm planning!" Ashley's good humor immediately returned. "I've booked us a romantic cruise to the Bahamas as a surprise, but I need something *incredible* to wear when I tell him about the trip. Something that will ensure he won't say no to taking a week off work. That's why we're going to Georgia's party. I feel compelled to buy a whole bunch of things that'll be on display there."

"So it's like a trunk show?" Cooper asked, silently wondering if she had the name right.

"Exactly. And all the women attending are married and go to my church, so I doubt there'll be anything too scandalous for sale." Ashley added, "I know it's not your scene, Cooper, but it would really mean a lot to me if you were with me. And you might even find yourself picking out something to wear for that *magical* moment when you and Nathan are *ready*."

"So this is all about buying pajamas and nightgowns?" Cooper shook her head. *What a bizarre reason to have a party,* she thought.

Ashley scrunched up her lips as though stifling a smile and said, "Precisely. Nightgowns and robes and stuff. And whatever you set your cap on will be my treat. It's the least I can do since you've agreed to come." Shouldering her bright orange purse, Ashley flicked a wave of glossy blonde hair off her shoulder and smiled. "This whole plan has given me a fresh dose of hope, Coop! I'll pick you up at seven. Georgia always serves the most *unbelievable* desserts, but make sure you eat something for dinner." She straightened several gold bangles on her wrist. "You're going to need something in your stomach to soak up all the alcohol."

During the following week, Cooper forgot all about the Pajama Party. This was understandable, being that a manufacturer recall on one of Canon's most popular copiers had every employee from Make It Work! scurrying to replace drums and fuser units across the city of Richmond as quickly as possible.

Cooper was just returning from an assignment updating all the copiers at a pharmaceutical company's headquarters when she was accosted in the break room by one of her coworkers.

"Cooper!" She drew back as Emilio Calabria's bass voice with its heavy New York accent boomed in her ear. The dark-haired, square-jawed, muscular hunk grabbed her by the elbow. With his nut-brown eyes ablaze, he looked more like a romance cover model than ever, but Emilio was too arrogant and chauvinistic for Cooper's tastes. "You gotta help me!" he insisted without preamble. "I mean, *you're* a girl, so you must get how girls think."

"Glad you noticed," Cooper replied ruefully as she looked down at her ink-stained uniform top. "What's the problem?"

"It's our three-month anniversary. Me and Carla's. I need to think of something cool to do. Should I take her out to dinner? Buy her something? How much is it gonna cost for me to show her I'm better than all her ex-boyfriends? Do I have to get her some ice?"

"As in diamonds?" Cooper inquired after a moment's puzzlement. When Emilio nodded glumly, she tried to reassure him. "I don't think 'ice' is necessary. Unless you're preparing to propose?"

Emilio paled. "Hell, *no*! I like this girl, but I am *not* ready to wear the old ball and chain. No way, man."

Grinning, Cooper moved over to the sink and began to scrub her hands. It was too easy to push Emilio's buttons. Still, her coworker had earnestly sought her help, so the least she could do was take him seriously. "You don't need to buy anything. You could take Carla somewhere special. What does she like to do?"

"Same as me. Watch ESPN and reality shows on TV. Go out for big slabs of steak and cold beers. And when we wanna get our groove on, we go clubbin'."

"You could make her a mixed CD of her favorite dance songs," Cooper suggested.

He frowned and handed Cooper twice the number of paper towels she needed to dry off her hands. "No dice. Did that for our two-month anniversary."

Two months? This is so junior high school, Cooper thought.

"What about your man? Your church boy?" Emilio prodded. "What's he given you that made you go weak in the knees?"

Turning away from Emilio, she said, "Nathan bought me a bicycle for Christmas. It's the old-fashioned kind, with lots of chrome, a straw basket, and a big rubber horn. I love it." She smiled, remembering how Nathan had covered her eyes while he led her into his garage where he had hidden her shiny blue bike beneath a bedsheet. He had whipped off the sheet in a dramatic flourish, revealing the bicycle and the curled red ribbons hanging from the handlebars. She had thrown her arms around him in delight, kissing him fervently.

"Now for your gift," she'd whispered a few minutes later.

He'd pulled her close once again and stared at her intently. "I don't need anything else but you."

Eventually, Cooper had managed to disentangle herself from Nathan's embrace. She'd led him through his kitchen and out the back door. Standing in the small garden area behind Nathan's row house, she'd waited for his reaction upon seeing his gift. For the past month, she'd been busy in her father's garage making a birdhouse in the shape of a TIE fighter, the spaceship Darth Vader piloted in *Star Wars*, Nathan's favorite movie.

"Did you make this?" Nathan had been utterly delighted by the workmanship. When Cooper nodded, he told her that it was the best gift he'd ever received and then led her inside.

"I can thank you more properly in here," he whispered, kissing her lightly just below her earlobe. "No prying eyes."

But just when Cooper was wondering if this was the moment to indicate her readiness to make her way upstairs to Nathan's bedroom, the doorbell rang. Nathan's sister had stopped by with her boyfriend, and what was supposed to be a romantic evening for Nathan and Cooper quickly became an intense Monopoly competition between the two couples.

"Carla isn't gonna be bowled over by a *bike*," Emilio grumbled, bringing Cooper back to the present.

"Why are you freaking out about this gift, Emilio?" Cooper inquired as they headed for the employee break room. "Are you worried she's not, ah, as keen on your relationship as she was in the beginning?"

Emilio's thick brows creased in worry. "She's been hanging out a lot with the other mailmen. What if she's thinking about ditching me for one of them? I don't see why she would, seeing as they wear those dorky uniforms, but women don't make sense, most of the time."

Cooper decided not point out that Emilio was currently dressed in a rather lackluster uniform comprised of black pants and a gray shirt embroidered with the company logo in charcoal-gray script. "Buying Carla something for your anniversary isn't going to make everything better. You need to talk to her—find out how she's feeling about your relationship."

"Who do I look like?" Emilio spluttered indignantly. "That Dr. Phil clown? Ever since I told her how crazy I was about her she's been less into me. I sure as hell am not gonna do *that* again. Maybe I'll make her jealous—make her realize how good she's got it. Tons of chicks would thank their lucky stars to be able to get with me." He squared his shoulders and touched a lock of gelled hair.

Cooper pushed open the kitchen door. "That's not a good plan, Emilio."

"Pfahh! What do you know, anyhow? I can tell you and your man haven't even brought your relationship to the final level yet. You still get all embarrassed to even think about doing the nasty, don't you? What are you scared of, anyhow? It's not like you haven't done it before." He sat down in front of a foot-long sandwich and slung his arm around Angela, Make It Work!'s office manager. "Tell her what she's missing, gorgeous. I'm sure you know how nice it is to have someone keeping you warm in the winter."

"I like it downright toasty." Angela handed Cooper an Italian hero from Subway and winked. "That's right, darlin'. I've got the fire department on standby, just in case things get *too* hot."

As Angela and Emilio unwrapped their subs and bantered companionably, Cooper ate her lunch in a state of mute irritation.

I'll show them! I'm going to buy something at that Pajama Party that'll make Nathan weak in the knees. I'm going to tell him I love him and that I'm ready to spend the night in his arms. She tore open a bag of Sun Chips and bit down on one savagely. *Nothing is going to get in my way this time!*

"Why are you wearin' pajamas to the table? You sick?" Grammy scrutinized Cooper from top to bottom. "'Cause if you are, you need to turn right around and go back to your apartment. I'm goin' to the P. Buckley Moss Museum tomorrow and I wanna do some real damage at Golden Corral's breakfast buffet beforehand."

"I feel fine, Grammy." Cooper squeezed her grandmother's shoulders affectionately. "I'm going to a party with Ashley tonight and I'm supposed to dress like this."

"You're a little old for sleepover parties, ain't you? Unless you're havin' one with Nathan," she cackled.

Not Grammy, too! Cooper lifted her eyes to the ceiling in appeal.

Cooper's mother entered the kitchen and peeked into the oven. "Leave her be, Mama. She's a lady and ladies don't kiss and tell."

Grammy snorted, but mercifully remained silent. Cooper expected one of her grandmother's long-winded lectures on how to procure a marriage proposal from Nathan, but for the moment Grammy was more interested in Maggie's pot roast than Cooper's love life.

"You look cozy," Earl commented to Cooper as he took his seat at the head of the table. "I saw your latest birdhouse in the garage. What are you doin' with that one?"

"Donating it to Hope Street's winter bazaar. The church is raising money for a youth mission trip to Mexico," Cooper replied.

"Can they send your daddy and me to Mexico?" Maggie laughed. "Seems like we haven't been out of the state of Virginia since man walked on the moon."

"Don't stick around on *my* account," Grammy remarked

huffily. "I know my way around the coffeepot and the can opener. What else does a woman my age need?"

Maggie smiled indulgently at Grammy. "We all know how independent you are, dear. It's more about our empty piggy bank than us frettin' over you. After all, Cooper would look after everything if we went away, wouldn't you, honey?"

Cooper nodded—her mouth full of scalloped potatoes. She glanced at her father, who looked especially tired. As the head groundskeeper for one of Richmond's private schools, he performed physical labor that men half his age would find fatiguing. And her mother baked gourmet cookies for a dozen sandwich shops in the West End of Richmond, waking up at four in the morning in order to produce three varieties of her famous Magnolia's Marvels.

They've worked all their lives, Cooper thought. *They really deserve a special vacation.*

"He can retire in three years," Maggie had told Cooper one Saturday as she'd packed plastic baggies of fresh-baked cookies. "But we've put aside every spare penny in case Grammy develops a need for special medical care. We're not gonna have her rot away in some nursing home. She's gonna leave this earth with dignity—from her own bed—if it costs us the roof over our heads."

Fortunately, Grammy was still perfectly healthy and spry. Sharp-tongued and witty, the matriarch of the Lee clan spent her time caring for stray animals, hovering in the kitchen in hopes of receiving rejects from Maggie's cookie production, watching reality shows, and nagging her granddaughters about her desire to become a great-grandmother before meeting her Maker.

Cooper glanced at her grandmother, who was shoveling pot roast into her mouth as though it were her last meal, and then flicked her gaze to her mother, who was assessing her husband from the corner of her eye. Cooper was about to suggest to her father that he should get checked out by a physician and had just opened her mouth to speak when her first syllable was cut short by the blast of Ashley's horn.

"Ain't she even gonna come in and say hello to her family?" Grammy shot a cross look at Maggie. "You raised her better than that!"

Cooper noticed that her younger sister had been avoiding Grammy lately. Ashley wasn't trying to be rude, but she already put so much pressure on herself over becoming pregnant that she couldn't bear to hear anyone else raise the subject. Unfortunately, Grammy brought up the topic whenever she had the chance.

"We're probably running late is all," Cooper said hastily, covering for her sister. On impulse, she kissed her grandmother on the cheek and was warmed by the approval in her father's smile. "Maybe I can start selling birdhouses, Daddy. Send you two on a vacation."

"And go for days without seein' your pretty face? Now what fun would that be?" Earl stacked his fork with butter beans. "Better get a move on. If your sister lays on that horn again, Grammy might run out there and give her what for."

"Run?" Grammy laughed. She loved to be teased by her son. "You know I only pick up my pace when they're givin' away samples of chocolate at Costco."

Cooper put on a long wool coat, buttoned it up to the neck, and exited the toasty house. Stepping into the dark night, she hunched her shoulders against the brisk winter wind and trotted over to Ashley's Lexus. As soon as she opened the door, she was assaulted by the heady floral scent of her sister's perfume. Ashley was dressed in a knee-length fur coat and brown leather boots with sharp heels.

"Is this real?" Cooper asked and placed a hesitant hand on her sister's coat. "No wonder you didn't want Grammy to see you! She would've had your head on a platter."

"It's faux sable, actually, and it *still* costs almost as much as the real thing. Isn't that ridiculous? I should get a *huge* discount for being so humane. And you know why I didn't come inside." Ashley accelerated on the empty road leading through the rural county where Cooper and the rest of the Lees lived. Watching the stark trees pass outside her window, Cooper suddenly longed to be back in her tiny apartment, laid out on her sofa beneath a thick afghan while Masterpiece Theater treated her to a Jane Austen remake.

"I know what you're thinking over there," Ashley stated as though she were truly clairvoyant. "You're already figuring on not having fun. Just because these women are married with kids does *not* mean they're boring. And even though they have plenty of money in their wallets, they're not necessarily shallow. So don't feel intimidated by how they look."

"We can't look too different, anyhow," Cooper reasoned. "Since we're all wearing pajamas."

Ashley was too busy maneuvering the onramp to the interstate to answer right away. "What did you say?" she asked after merging directly into the center lane; she then proceeded to zip by a dozen cars while fiddling with her radio buttons. Ashley had always been a dangerously oblivious driver. "Who's in pajamas?"

Cooper unbuttoned her coat in order to reveal her pink flannel top. "I am, for one thing! Aren't you?"

At first, Ashley looked horrified and then she began to laugh. The sound of her laughter overshadowed the music coming from the car's speakers as well as the chiding honk delivered by the truck in the next lane. Ashley had been drifting again. "Oh, Coop!" she said after controlling herself. "You've already made this a night to remember! The girls are gonna *love* you."

Suddenly, Cooper reached over and yanked up the hem of her sister's coat, revealing a white skirt embroidered with black flowers and a pair of tights. "Uh-oh. I totally misunderstood." She gulped. "Turn around, Ashley. I need to change."

"Not a chance. We're late as it is and Georgia was *adamant* about people getting there before the show starts."

Visualizing Chippendale dancers, a fog machine, and strobe lights, Cooper groaned, but when they entered Georgia Ferguson's Spanish villa-style mansion fifteen minutes later, she was not surrounded by half-naked men, but by boisterous and cheerful women holding champagne glasses. To Cooper's relief, they were dressed quite casually in pressed khakis and cotton blouses or simple skirts and sweater sets. Their jewelry, shoes, and handbags were expensive and elegant, yet understated, and they welcomed Cooper warmly. Twice, Georgia offered to take her coat, which Cooper had thus far refused to unbutton.

"My sister's embarrassed because she thought she was supposed to *wear* pajamas tonight," Ashley explained, pulling apart Cooper's coat in order to allow her friend a glimpse of her sister's ensemble.

"I think that's a *fabulous* idea!" a woman wearing tight jeans and a lime-green turtleneck exclaimed. "I wish you had thought of that, Georgia! We could all be as comfy as this pretty thing is. Aren't you clever!" She beamed at Cooper. "Instead, we're all tossing back the booze and waiting for this show to start—about as comfortable as turtles lying on their backs in the middle of the desert!"

Another woman agreed with the metaphor. "Yes, what *is* the evening's entertainment, Georgia?"

"Wait and see," Georgia replied with a wink.

Suddenly, music began to pump through the speakers in the spacious living room. Cooper recognized the strains of Madonna's latest dance song and tagged along behind a handful of women as they made their way to a row of folding chairs. A young woman dressed in black pants and a black blouse snapped her fingers in time to the music as she ushered stragglers to their seats.

"Thank you for coming to my first Pajama Party!" Georgia beamed at her friends once they were all settled. "As married women, we sometimes need to shake things up a bit. It is our *duty* to please our husbands and for them to please *us*. So, in the name of marital bliss, I invite you to bring a little sizzle and a bit of *ooh-la-la* home to your hubby tonight. All purchases are private and will be conducted on a discreet, one-to-one basis in my kitchen. This is Lola." Georgia gestured at the woman in black. "She's provided you all with order forms and pens. You'll find them under your seats. Simply check off the items you'd like to buy as they are modeled for you. Now, is everyone armed with bubbly? Good, because this is no place for the timid!"

A glass of champagne was shoved in Cooper's hand. She took a grateful sip and, finally letting go of her coat, draped it over the back of her chair. The lights dimmed, the music was turned up a notch higher, and three voluptuous girls in their early twenties strutted into the room, wearing fishnet stockings and sexy silk nighties that fell to mid-thigh.

"Oh, my! I like the peach one!" A woman slid on a pair of reading glasses and uncapped her pen. "Would you look at that? They come in *plus* sizes, too. How nice! I can order one for my sister-in-law."

The models did a brief twirl and then handed some of the ladies in the audience packets of panties to examine.

"Edible underwear!" One of the partygoers giggled. "Chocolate, strawberries and cream, vanilla caramel, and mocha. Charlie *loves* coffee. Should I try one?"

"Go for it, Dolores!" another woman coaxed her. "You heard what Georgia said. It's our duty!" Both women laughed raucously.

The models returned wearing lacy bras and matching briefs. The women around Cooper muttered in approval over the ample coverage provided by the boycut briefs. "I thought this would be all about thongs and strapless bras. I could actually wear that outfit and not look too fat," declared a woman Cooper believed was surely a size zero.

Pens scribbled on order pads. Cooper glanced shyly at the models and gulped her champagne, accepting a second glass from a tray that seemed to magically appear by her elbow just as she finished her first drink. The models were busily handing out black and red boxes labeled *Dirty Girl, Lover Girl,* and *Naughty Girl.* Each box contained a minuscule pair of panties, breath mints, a toothbrush, a condom, flavored body oil, a perfume sample, and two energy pills. The *Lover Girl* box also included a red feather and the *Naughty Girl* package came with a silk blindfold.

Cooper handed the boxes to her sister. "Are you getting any of these things?" she asked her while trying to get a clear view of the order pad on her lap.

Ashley shook her head. "I'm not feeling inspired yet, are you?"

"Inspired? I am totally weirded out right now." Cooper guzzled more champagne. "I don't think I need edible underwear," she whispered, shifting uncomfortably as the models returned wearing thongs and push-up bras beneath sheer robes tied by a row of silk ribbons. "It's a timing thing for me—about how I'm feeling, not how I look. I want it to be just right and none of these . . . items are going to affect that." She gestured at her blank order pad.

Ashley scowled. "We're here for *me*, remember? You don't have to buy anything." She examined the *Dirty Girl* box and passed it to the next woman. "I'm just looking for a little inspiration, so sit back, enjoy the show, and tell me if you see something that will turn Lincoln into putty."

Wire baskets filled with massage oils and scented candles found their way to Cooper's row along with a serving tray loaded with truffles, bite-sized raspberry mousse cups, and strawberries dipped in white chocolate. Cooper helped herself to several treats, but nearly choked on a strawberry as the models sauntered in wearing latex bodysuits covered by zippers. They carried small riding crops and black boxes stuffed with hot pink tissue.

The women giggled and shrieked with amused laughter as the contents of the boxes were distributed around the room. When Cooper's neighbor handed her an object resembling a plastic cucumber, she took one look at the on/off switch and tossed it onto Ashley's lap as if they were playing hot potato.

Frowning, Ashley calmly picked up the device and passed it to the woman seated behind her, who squealed in embarrassment. Cooper noticed that the woman, who fanned herself in theatrical astonishment over being given such a toy, managed to turn it on for several seconds before delivering it to her neighbor.

Amid all this excitement, the models came into the room for their encore wearing flowing nightgowns trimmed in lace. The cream-colored silk combined with the tight, brocade bodices produced an ethereal effect. The models, who had looked little better than prostitutes a few moments ago, were now illuminated with an aura of alluring innocence. Staring at them, resplendent in their shimmery gowns, Cooper was sorely tempted to make a mark on her order sheet, but something held her back.

"*That's* what I want!" Ashley was thrilled. "Something beautiful, captivating, utterly romantic. With white candles, that nightgown and robe, and maybe a gardenia in my hair . . ." She made hasty marks on her paper.

"Where are you going to get a gardenia in the middle of winter?" Cooper inquired.

Ashley smiled. "I know an excellent florist. Besides, Lincoln loves that smell, so it'll be worth the cost. I'll look like a spring bride. Completely fresh and lovely. He won't be able to resist me." She reached over and squeezed Cooper's hand. "Thank you for coming with me tonight. It turned out to be a success. Cheers!"

Tapping the rim of her glass against Ashley's, Cooper realized that she couldn't recall whether she'd consumed three drinks or four. Her cheeks felt warm and the upbeat music and high-pitched laughter of the women seemed pleasantly boisterous.

Still, Cooper was glad that Ashley was more interested in placing her order and getting home than mingling with her friends. By the time the models had taken their bows and clothed themselves in jeans and sweatshirts, Ashley had already paid for her purchases and said her good-byes.

"Everyone was glad you came," she said to Cooper once they were back in the Lexus. "They all think you're really pretty. Georgia told me that her little brother's single and quite a catch—just in case things don't work out with Nathan—but I told her you were perfectly happy."

"Thanks," Cooper replied, her words slurring slightly. "I *am* happy."

Kneeling beside her bed a half hour later, Cooper folded her hands together. "Please guide me, Lord," she prayed. "I believe Nathan is a good and honest man, but after being hurt by another man I loved and trusted in the same way, I'm having a hard time giving myself to Nathan—body and heart. I want to, you know, love him in all ways, but I'm scared. Please take away my fear and replace it with trust. All things are possible through You. Amen."

Cooper crawled into bed and closed her eyes. She then opened them again. "Oh! One more thing, Lord. Let Lincoln see my sister with fresh eyes. If he's avoiding her, please guide him back home . . . before he wanders too far."

2

Trust in the LORD with all your heart
and lean not on your own understanding;

in all your ways acknowledge him,
and he will make your paths straight.

Do not be wise in your own eyes;
fear the LORD and shun evil.

This will bring health to your body
and nourishment to your bones.

Proverbs 3:5-8 (NIV)

Cooper was excited about starting a new Bible study with her friends from Hope Street Church. Except for Nathan, she hadn't seen any of them since the Christmas Eve candlelight service. Every member had left town in order to visit family. Savannah Knapp, the legally blind folk artist who led their small group, had stayed away even longer in order to conduct a painting workshop for an artist's colony, so they'd been unable to commence with a fresh study until she returned.

Feelings of pleasant expectation coursed through Cooper when she finally received a phone call from Quinton Enderly, the successful investment banker and talented amateur pastry chef, announcing that it was his turn to choose the next study. He'd picked *Directing Our Passion: Corinthians I and II.*

"Whoa!" she'd teased him. "Sounds steamy."

"I've been praying for a wife for over ten years now," Quinton had replied solemnly. "But suddenly I realized that I've got to have a clear relationship with God before I can even attempt to form one with a woman. This study just spoke to me."

"Trust me, Quinton. We could all use help in the relationship department. Besides, you're a real catch. Some girl is going to celebrate the day she found her way to your doorstep," Cooper told her kind-hearted friend and then sped off to LifeWay to buy the study guide.

She loved opening an unblemished, stiff workbook, uncapping her favorite purple pen, and rustling the pages of her Bible as she prepared to complete the first homework lesson.

"Sounds like the wings of a dove, doesn't it?" her mother had once said while flipping through her own Bible. "How the angels must rejoice over the music made by the turnin' of those pages."

Cooper had felt a bit lost during the break the Bible study group had taken. She'd gone to church, but her focus had wandered during each service, her eyes roaming the congregation in search of the faces of her friends. Now, on the third Sunday in January, it was time to reunite. The first to arrive in the Hope Street Christian Academy's biology classroom, Cooper set out a basket of her mother's meringue pecan bars, brewed a pot of coffee in the teacher's lounge, and placed a stack of snowman napkins alongside a plate of plump red seedless grapes.

"Now *this* is an interesting room," meteorologist Bryant Shelton declared as he entered, flicking a solar system model suspended from the ceiling into orbit. "I'm glad we got booted from the English classroom. I was getting kind of tired of being stared at by those Shakespeare and Virginia Woolf posters." He sidled up to the life-sized skeleton and slung an arm around its bony shoulders. "Sorry to keep you waiting for our dinner date, sweet cheeks. Why, you've practically wasted away!" He laughed, displaying his famous television smile. Twin dimples appeared in his tanned cheeks as he released the skeleton and walked over to embrace Cooper. "I've missed our meetings."

Cooper smiled at him, knowing that dozens of women longed to be the recipient of Bryant's attention and would have gladly locked her in the classroom's supply closet if it meant the gorgeous weatherman would hug them instead. Cooper cared deeply for Bryant, but only as a friend. The two of them had quickly bonded a year ago over their experiences with failed relationships. Bryant was a divorcee three times over, and Cooper's only serious boyfriend had left her for another woman. Together, they'd vowed to forgive those who'd hurt them and focus on the future instead.

"I smell cookies!" Jake Lombardi bellowed as he stepped into the classroom. "Yours or your mama's?" He stripped off a pair of worn leather gloves, dumped his aged barn jacket onto one of the student desks, and began to remove tissue-wrapped coffee mugs from a grocery bag.

"Magnolia's Marvels," Cooper admitted. "She made an extra two dozen for us this morning."

"Lucky us." Bryant pointed at the coffee mugs. "What are those, Jake?"

"I saw 'em online," Jake answered. "I wanted to get somethin' for our first meetin' of the year. I may be a plumber, but I got good taste. Check these out." He handed Cooper a mug. It showed a rising sun and the words: "Coffee Hour: The Third Sacrament."

"We're the Sunrise Bible Study group and we sure like our coffee," Jake explained. "Figured these were made for us."

"Did you come bearing gifts, Jake?" a mellifluous voice asked from the doorway. Savannah held a white cane in one hand and several books in the other. Quinton was guiding her by the elbow with Trish Tyler, an ambitious realtor and mother of two, following closely behind. Nathan took up the rear.

"These are cute, Jake," Trish said as she picked up one of the mugs. "Even if they're a tad cynical."

"Get your caffeine on and be grateful, lady." Jake grinned at her. "After all, I could've picked the ones that said 'God Only Loves You 'Cause He Has To'!"

Nathan chuckled. "Oh, man, that is *so* mean!"

The members exchanged small talk about their various trips and then settled down to begin day one of their study.

"The first book of Corinthians addresses the people of Corinth. Imagine that!" Savannah took a bite of one of the meringue pecan cookies and sighed in delight. "This Greek city was a bustling and wealthy port," she continued. "All kinds of exotic goods came in and out of this city and its people were as mixed as its goods. There was plenty of entertainment to be found there, including athletic competitions like the Olympics. According to my audio guide, there was also a tavern on *every* street corner."

"Sounds like Americans and our Starbucks," Bryant remarked.

"In this city filled with immorality, the apostle Paul appeared more than once to preach to the people," Savannah said with a smile. "Does this setting remind you of another biblical place?"

"Babylon," Nathan answered quickly. "Both cities have the lure of glamour, wealth, and greed."

Savannah nodded. "We live in a modern Babylon, so we face similar temptations every day. I don't know about you all, but I give in to these kinds of trappings on a regular basis." She held up her cane. "I can't even *see* and I've got a house loaded with stuff!" She laughed. "I admit to enjoying many material things. You probably didn't know that I listen to QVC even though I can't see the products clearly—only fuzzy colors! But I like how the hosts describe everything. It's a seductive show."

"My problem is a type of greed." Quinton spoke next. "I want more food than I need. I overindulge. I can't seem to get a grip on my cravings."

Jake patted the large man on the back. "I hear ya, man. Over the holidays I slipped and had a smoke. And then a second one. Now those cigarettes are callin' to me night and day."

"Boy, I know that feeling," Cooper sympathized with Jake. "Even though I quit months ago, anytime I get stressed the thought of taking a few drags is tempting. Hang in there." Glancing at her own workbook page, Cooper recalled that she'd written that her weekly pedicures were an unnecessary luxury, but that she had no intention of giving them up.

Savannah raised the next discussion point. "In verse nineteen of chapter one, Paul quotes from Isaiah. How do you respond to the phrases 'destroy the wisdom of the wise' and 'the intelligence of the intelligent I will frustrate'?" Savannah looked around the circle of faces, as though she could see everyone's features through her nearly sightless, navy blue eyes. Cooper noticed that she'd loosened her braid, allowing her dark brown hair to spill over her shoulders. The light from the windows caught a few strands of silver framing Savannah's unlined face. Once again, Cooper was struck by Savannah's loveliness.

Though only forty, their group leader possessed a level of grace, poise, and self-awareness that made her seem wiser than her years.

"I don't think Paul is trying to compliment smart people," Trish said and then paused to rub her glossy ruby-tinted lips with her pinkie. "Sometimes, the biggest brainiacs are the biggest atheists, too. Like they've figured out all of life's riddles and therefore have no reason to believe in God."

Bryant rubbed his chin thoughtfully. "Like Benjamin Franklin? I think he was the one who said, 'Lighthouses are more helpful than churches.'" He waved his hand around the room. "Here we are, in a place filled with the evidence of man's scientific discoveries, and they really are great, but even this level of wisdom doesn't give us what we *need*."

Quinton nodded. "Take Adam. He had everything he needed, but he wasn't satisfied. Look where *that* got us."

"Good point!" Jake exclaimed with a smirk. "That 'ole serpent knew what he was doin' when he told Adam he could know as much as God if he'd only take a little nibble of fruit." He nudged Trish playfully with his elbow. "Thanks a lot, Eve."

Trish scowled, her pencil-drawn eyebrows furrowing. "No one twisted Adam's arm. He made his own choice. Besides, women have paid for Eve's bad decision." Her voice rose. "You men don't have any idea what labor pains are like! That damned *fruit* cost us plenty." Her eyes dropped to her book and fixed upon the page as the rest of the group exchanged startled glances.

Savannah recovered first and steered the conversation back to the subject at hand. Cooper shared her thoughts that human wisdom was different from divine wisdom, for one had limits and the other had none, but felt that she needed to say something else to lighten the mood.

"I've definitely acted dumb when I thought I was being clever," she told her friends while trying to block out images of the Pajama Party. "When I started fixing office machines, I thought I was some kind of female da Vinci. One of my first jobs was to repair a printer in the nurse's office of a nearby grade school. I tried everything, but I couldn't get it to work. Then this seven-year-old boy comes in and tells me that it's not plugged in. Sure, there was a nest of cords and wires under the nurse's' desk, but I never even checked the most basic step because I *wanted* to solve a complicated problem." She shrugged. "Guess I needed a dose of humility."

" 'Arrogant' is not a word that I'd associate with you." Nathan winked at her. "And you're awesome at problem-solving. Do I have to point out that you've helped solve two murder cases?"

"Well, arrogant *is* a word people might use to describe me," Bryant commented with a self-effacing grin. "Once, when I was working at a station at the beach, I showed up too late for work to review the latest weather data before I went on the air at six a.m. Because of that, I failed to warn commuters that they'd be dealing with a serious fog. There were dozens of accidents that day and lots of people called the station to complain about my crappy forecast. My boss reamed me out with a hurricane-force lecture."

"At least you didn't punch a hole in somebody's septic tank." Jake screwed up his face in disgust. "On Fourth of July. Durin' a family reunion. Do you know what sewage smells like in the middle of a ninety-nine degree day?"

Quinton squirmed in his chair. "Ew! No more details, Jake, please. You'll put me off my cookies. Did I ever tell you guys about the time—?"

"ENOUGH!" Trish shouted and the Bible study members jumped in their seats. "*I* win the blue ribbon for being stupid! Hands down, no contest, game over! I win!" She hit the desktop with a closed fist, her crimson fingernails digging into the flesh of her palm. "I always thought I was the type of person who couldn't get sick. People who smoked or drank or never exercised got sick. Not *me*! I eat balanced meals, work out four times a week, and only drink a glass of Chablis when the mood strikes me. But I'm sick, all right. Look at this." She raked her fingers through her copper-colored hair and then showed her friends the red clump resting on her palm.

"What's happening?" Savannah pleaded, unable to witness the unsettling act.

"She's losing her hair," Cooper whispered, her eyes never leaving Trish's tormented face.

"I'll be lucky if that's all I lose," Trish muttered hoarsely and then her mouth began to quiver. "Do you remember that biopsy I had back in the fall? The one that came out benign?"

Her friends nodded fearfully.

"Well, I've had another one since then and it's *not* benign." She spat out the word as though it were an enemy. "I, Trish Tyler, have cancer. Right here." She folded her hands across her heart and then fanned them out across her chest. "I have breast cancer. The serious kind."

Jubilant music calling people to worship tripped down the corridors of the church wing housing the school, but none of the Sunrise Bible Study members responded to the enticing melody. The unhindered shrieks of children racing down the hall toward their Sunday School classes, the cheerful shouts of adults greeting one another, and the increasing volume of the drumbeat emanating from within the chapel produced a cacophony of joyfulness that seemed to mock the atmosphere in the biology classroom.

"I'm sorry." Trish hid her face in her hands. "I didn't

mean to let it out this way. I'm so mixed up right now. I go from brave to being scared out of my mind, to angry, to yelling curses in the privacy of my shower, to crying so hard I've got to pull the car off the road and park. Right now, I'm just really, really tired."

Savannah eased herself from behind her desk and walked carefully over to where Trish sat. Putting both arms around her distraught friend, she whispered, "Tell us everything."

"I've got grade two cancer, which means that they couldn't just cut the bad cells out and send me on my way. I had surgery right after Christmas—I didn't want to spoil things for the girls so I insisted on waiting a few days— and they removed the masses, but it's not enough."

Jake gave her a stern look. "You should've told us, you stubborn woman. Least we could've prayed for you while you were goin' through all that."

Surprisingly, Trish smiled. "I was in serious denial three weeks ago. I figured if I didn't tell anyone it would just go away."

"Do you need chemo?" Quinton asked with concern.

Trish picked up the loose strands of hair and began winding them around and around her index finger. "I've already started. Had my first dose on Thursday."

"Oh, Trish." Cooper's eyes grew moist.

"I get another dose next week. Through an IV. It takes about an hour. That should finish off what's left of my hair. And here I thought my auburn hair dye, the blow dryer, and the flat iron would be the ones to fry my gorgeous locks." Trish offered up a crooked grin. "Guess it's a good thing I had the photo taken for my Tyler Fine Properties billboard last summer."

"Woman, you're gonna look smokin' hot with no hair," Jake teased. "Like that singer, Sinead somethin' or other.

Or Demi Moore when she shaved her head for that *G.I. Jane* movie."

"I think you'd look nice in a wig, too," Nathan added kindly. "You could channel Princess Di one day and Cleopatra the next."

"Thanks, you two, but either way, the hair is going." She gripped Savannah's hand with sudden desperation. "I don't want to do it myself, though. I know I'm going to get upset when I see the results. Would you . . . ?" She faltered.

"We'll come over whenever you're ready," Savannah declared and gave Trish's hands a compassionate squeeze. "Though you might want to pick someone other than *me* to do the shaving!" She smiled. "We'll all be there to help you through this. Not just the losing your hair part, but every single moment of terror, anger, doubt, and grief."

Bryant also got up and walked over to Trish. "That's right. We'll cook for you—well, the rest of them will cook and I'll buy takeout—drive you places, go to the doctor's with you, and listen to you vent."

"Thank you." Trish sniffed and sat in silence for a moment. "Listen, I'd rather not talk about this anymore if that's okay. Let's go worship now."

"*After* we pray for you," Cooper insisted and everyone immediately reached out for a friend's hand.

Savannah closed her eyes. "I am too unsettled to come up with any words of my own, so I will rely on Scripture. Please turn to Isaiah forty-one, verse ten and read aloud with me." She pulled Trish's hands toward her own and bent over them, so that her breath fell directly onto the sick woman's skin.

> "'*So do not fear, for I am with you;*
> *do not be dismayed, for I am your God.*
> *I will strengthen you and help you;*
> *I will uphold you with my righteous right hand.*'"

One by one, the members of the Sunrise Bible Study stood up and placed their hands on Trish's body. They touched her shoulders, her back, her arms, her hands, the top of her head, and her face.

"You will not face this alone," someone whispered. "We are with you."

"Amen," Trish murmured through her tears.

3

Among my people are wicked men who lie in wait like men who snare birds and like those who set traps to catch men.

Jeremiah 5:26 (NIV)

The next Monday, Cooper found it difficult not to think about Trish. Like most people, she was aware that a great many people were affected by some form of cancer. She'd noticed the yellow bracelets made popular by Lance Armstrong, pink ribbons pinned to shirt collars, and the amusing *Save the Ta-tas* T-shirts, but the disease had never touched her personally.

Of course she'd met cancer survivors and friends whose family members had either beaten or succumbed to the affliction, but this was the first time someone she cared about was engaged in a battle for her life. In many ways, that's how Cooper saw Trish—as a soldier—an unsuspecting, preoccupied individual drafted to wage war upon a silent and potentially lethal enemy.

Cooper had no problem imagining Trish as a warrior. She could envision her red-haired friend hunched in some muddy trench, a rifle clenched against her chest—her violet eyes blazing and unafraid. If anyone had the willpower to overcome adversity, it was Trish. Cooper tried to focus on her friend's strength instead of the scary *what if* questions that crept into her mind.

The workday proved to be another long one and Cooper was grateful to be too busy to brood. All three of the Make It Work! employees—Ben, Emilio, and Cooper—spent the day completing the last of the Canon copier manufacture recalls. Just when Cooper thought she must have replaced the millionth faulty drum in Richmond, Angela rushed over to the work van and slapped another work order against the glass of the driver's window.

"I'm sorry, darlin'," she said when Cooper opened the door to receive the paper. "I know it's almost five, but a call came in from one of the higher-ups at the Bank of Richmond. He's fit to be tied. Seems the man came back from vacation in *Fiji* to find his executive secretary's copier broken." Angela rolled her eyes. "Could you imagine what would happen if he ran across a *real* emergency? Anyhow, I had the pleasure of speakin' to him and he was as rude as a rush-hour driver. If the bank didn't have such a big account with us, I'd tell him to go stuff himself like a Thanksgiving turkey, but someone's gotta tend to that machine." She shook her head. "I feel for the poor woman who's gotta deal with him day in and day out. There ain't a salary on this earth worth *that*."

"We can't all have bosses as great as Mr. Farmer," Cooper replied, knowing how much Angela adored their employer. The two had recently begun dating and now Angela's desk resembled the inside of a florist's refrigerator. "I doubt Mr. Bank of Richmond presented *his* administrative assistant with a bouquet of blue hydrangeas this morning."

Angela clasped her hands to her generous bosom. "Isn't Mr. Farmer dreamy?" She fluttered her false eyelashes and sashayed out of the garage, her patent leather heels clicking happily with every step.

"Dreamy?" Cooper asked her image in the rearview mirror, but her reflection was equally nonplussed. "If you're into middle-aged men who hole up in their offices drooling over *Popular Mechanics* and can easily double for Danny DeVito, then dreamy's pretty accurate, I guess."

Her amusement over the attraction between Angela and their boss didn't last long. The executive secretary at the bank's plush investment branch was the antithesis of Angela. A curvaceous platinum blonde favoring tight pencil skirts, snug sweaters with plunging necklines, dangerously high heels, and Bakelite jewelry, Angela greeted every person with a sincere and cheerful manner. The Bank of Richmond secretary neither smiled nor greeted Cooper, but grunted and tapped her watch the moment Cooper entered the office.

"I'm Felicia Hawkins," the reedy, thin-lipped woman announced to Cooper and eyed the nametag on her gray uniform shirt with disdain. "Cooper? Is that a person's name or a brand name?"

"It's a family name," Cooper replied politely, looking around for the copier. She spied the Canon in the hallway behind Felicia and moved to step around the stern-faced secretary so that she could complete her task quickly and call it a day.

"I assume you won't be charging the bank for this service," Felicia stated flatly. "Your faulty copiers have *greatly* inconvenienced Mr. Goldvolger."

The image of Ian Fleming's *Goldfinger* appeared in Cooper's mind. She could picture his meaty, ringed hand stroking a white, longhaired cat while he and his cohorts cackled in villainous mirth. Looking down at Felicia's black, squared-toed loafers, she grinned and wondered whether a blade had been built into its sole.

"Is something amusing?" Felicia growled and Cooper shook her head, hustling over to the copier. She rapidly unpacked her tools and began to unscrew the machine's back panel. She waited for the secretary to grow disinterested and return to her desk, but the older woman leaned against the wall, crossed her arms, and watched Cooper with a strange look in her eyes.

"How did you get into this line of work?" she asked, her tone laced with disapproval. "I've never seen a woman service our machines before. Are you certain you're capable of handling this assignment?"

Now Cooper understood why her coworker Ben routinely handled the Bank of Richmond account. "I'm good with machines," she answered modestly, refusing to be drawn into an argument. "Fixing them is kind of like putting together a jigsaw puzzle. You just need to see which piece is missing or damaged or dirty."

To Cooper's surprise, the woman pulled a cigarette from her shirt pocket and lit it. "Well, I'm good at crosswords. Does that mean I could repair jet planes?"

Why is she baiting me? Cooper thought and then felt inspired to say, "I bet you could, if you set your mind to it." She sat up and placed the faulty drum on one of her blue rags. Studying the other woman's face, she detected genuine unhappiness beneath the layer of foundation and the etchings of premature wrinkles. "What would your ideal job be, Ms. Hawkins, if you could choose one?"

At first, Cooper thought the secretary wasn't going to reply. The woman closed her eyes, puffed on her cigarette, and only opened them again in order to flick ash into the potted ficus. A cloud of nicotine-scented smoke floated Cooper's way and she immediately felt a pull of longing. It would be so easy to simply ask the secretary for a cigarette, but she rooted noisily around in her toolbox until she came up with a breath mint. Concentrating on the sharp peppermint flavor, Cooper picked up a pair of pliers, and prepared to finish her work on the copier.

The woman across from her remained mute for several minutes.

"This certainly isn't what I thought I'd end up doing," Felicia finally spoke. "I'm almost fifty years old and I've wasted my life waiting on men who've completely taken me for granted." She stubbed the cigarette out in the soil, twisting it back and forth as though she wished to singe the dirt. "Yet none of them could last a day without me. I prepare all their reports, research market trends, write their speeches, buy presents for their wives, their children, and sometimes their girlfriends, and I *never* receive a word of thanks." She sighed. "Do you know what I've always wanted to do?"

Cooper put down her tools and gave Felicia her full attention. "No, ma'am."

"Work at an auction house," Felicia whispered and then made a noise that might have been a suppressed laugh or a dry cough. "I even practice helping customers during my commute to work. The people who drive by and see me blithering to myself must think I'm not long for the psych ward."

"Sounds cool," Cooper said. "An antique auction? That kind of thing?"

Now Felicia did laugh. "No! I want to work at a *car* auction. I *love* cars! My father was a mechanic, so I guess it's in my blood. He and I used to spend every weekend at an auto auction, just reveling in the excitement. Have you ever seen a boy buying his first car?" Cooper shook her head. "The look on his face—pure bliss!" Felicia's eyes were bright and lively. "Oh, the pride of handing over a summer's worth of paychecks or a year's savings from having flipped burgers after school." Her voice rose as she grew more animated. "All the men talking shop, arguing about torque and rims and horsepower . . ."

As Felicia drifted off with her visions, Cooper was struck by the loss she saw in the other woman's face. "Listen, Ms. Hawkins, I'm all done here." She stood up and wiped her hands on a rag. "Would you like to grab a bite? My brother-in-law is in the car business. Maybe I could introduce you and he could give you some tips on how to get a job at one of those auctions."

"Why would you do that? I've been so rude to you," Felicia asked, clearly stunned. "Why would you want to spend another second with me?"

"Because I've felt stuck before. Pretty close to hopeless, actually, until someone told me that I could walk through life without taking any risks or I could actually *live*." She snapped her toolbox closed. "So what do you say? I'm starving and I'd love to hear more about your love of cars."

"That would be nice, thank you." Felicia smiled. "It's been a long time since someone asked me to dinner. And please call me Felicia. Only my boss calls me Ms. Hawkins!"

Later, driving home, Cooper questioned what had propelled her to offer friendship to such an unpleasant individual. After all, she was more of an introvert than not and preferred to work in quiet anonymity. Still, she had sensed a strong, almost urgent need in Felicia, and she couldn't ignore the inner voice prompting her to reach out to the unhappy stranger.

"I suppose that was Your doing? Sending me on that last assignment so I could meet Felicia Hawkins?" Cooper glanced at the black, starless sky out her window. She knew the answer, and even though it was nearly nine o'clock and bone-chillingly cold outside, and she was tired from such a long day, Cooper felt energized by the encounter with the secretary.

Feeling the need to sing for the remainder of the drive, Cooper switched her radio on. At the same moment, her truck tires crunched over an object in the road and her steering wheel pulled dramatically to the right. Though she didn't share Felicia's auto expertise, she knew enough to realize that the sudden and dramatic tug to one side was a telltale indication that a tire had gone flat. Really flat.

"Whoa!" Cooper looked in her rearview mirror. "What the heck did I hit back there?"

Slowing down, she eased the truck onto the farthest side of the shoulder. Though reluctant to leave the warmth of her cab, Cooper knew she had no choice. Grabbing a flashlight from her toolbox, she jumped out of the truck, and immediately saw that one of her rear tires had deflated like a spent birthday balloon.

"Great." Cooper's buoyant mood dissipated in the frigid air. Pulling her wool hat down over her ears, she retrieved her emergency road kit from the rear of the cab and unzipped it. After igniting two flares she unfastened the jack and spare tire from the inside of the truck bed. Just as she began the laborious process of jacking up the truck, the growl of a small but loud motor drawing nearer and nearer caused her to pause and look up at the dark highway.

Her truck had gone lame on a stretch of highway that only saw intermittent traffic at night. Truckers heading west toward Charlottesville were the most common sight, but the approaching engine did not belong to an eighteen-wheeler. It had the distinct, thunderous rumble of a motorcycle engine.

As she watched, a dark red and chrome Indian Chief motorcycle edged onto the shoulder. At first, Cooper had the absurd hope that a policeman had come to her aid, but it only took a brief glance at the fringed leather of the vintage motorcycle's seat and the rider's attire to transform her feelings of optimism into heart-racing alarm.

The Indian's rider was a man, dressed in black jeans and a black leather jacket, whose features were completely obscured by his black helmet. Even when he tipped back the tinted visor covering his face and asked if she needed a hand, the moonless night cloaked him in shadow.

As he dismounted and began to walk toward her, Cooper's cell phone rang to the tune of the Beatles' "A Hard Day's Night." The man in black chuckled. "I recollect you mentioning the Fab Four, but I didn't know you liked them all *that* much."

He stepped forward into the red glow of the flare and Cooper's jaw dropped as she recognized his face. "Get the phone, girl." He pointed at the device. "I'll jack the truck."

Answering the call, Cooper was at first too stunned to make sense of Ashley's frantic and garbled words. There was nothing coherent about the hysterical cries and pleas of "*Please!* The car! There's a man! He's . . . he's dead! DEAD IN MY HOUSE! COME GET ME!" echoing down the line.

"Slow down, Ashley!" Cooper shouted in an effort to make sense of her sister's shrieks. "I can't understand you! Take a deep breath and try not to yell. I'm right here, okay?" She waited silently while Ashley struggled to control her rapid breathing. As Cooper listened, her eyes were fixed on Edward Crosby, aka the Colonel, as he began to remove the lug nuts from the flat tire.

Cooper had met him a few months ago when he was still an inmate at Jail West, serving out the remainder of his sentence for the sale and distribution of narcotics. Her only communication with him had been through a telephone handset attached to a plate-glass divider, so she hadn't been able to appreciate his formidable physical presence at the time.

He wasn't tall, like Nathan, but Edward Crosby's figure reverberated strength. There was a sense of danger about him—something predatory. He stared up at her with his gunmetal gray eyes and waited, his wide hands gripping the wrench. She could see the shadow of the flag of Dixie tattoo that lay beneath the cropped hair of his scalp.

"There's a *dead* man in the trunk of my car! In my house!" Ashley wailed and Cooper was finally able to rip her gaze from Edward's intense stare.

Cooper made her sister repeat what she'd just said. After establishing that Ashley was unharmed and that a corpse had somehow materialized inside the locked garage, Cooper promised she'd be right over and told Ashley to call the police.

"I can't do that!" Ashley's voice cracked as it rose an octave. "What if Lincoln gets in trouble? I got this car— it's a rental—from his dealership to drive while mine's in the shop! What if there's something going on at the dealership and his name gets in the papers?" she yelled into the phone.

"Make the call, Ashley. If you don't, then I'll do it when I get there. Now turn on all the lights and fix a pot of coffee," Cooper directed firmly, even though her sister had begun to cry. "I'll be right over."

She slid her phone into her coat pocket and pulled the lapels tightly over her throat, as though she could block out the sharp air along with her sister's unbelievable story.

Seeing that her phone call was finished, Edward stood. "One of these lug nuts is stripped. It's gonna take time you plainly don't have. Tell me where you need to go and I'll get you there."

Cooper didn't hesitate. She grabbed the truck keys from her ignition and stuffed them into her purse. She then strapped on the extra helmet Edward had quickly produced and told him where Ashley lived. Standing in the cold, she felt foolish in her long, woolen coat, hand-knit mittens, and purse draped diagonally across her chest like some paranoid tourist, but Edward smiled and jerked his thumb over his shoulder.

"You best plan on holdin' tight!" he shouted. "I don't drive slow."

As the motorcycle lurched onto the pavement, Cooper gasped with surprise and threw her arms around Edward's waist. She'd never been on a motorcycle before and she was struck by the force of the icy air as it careened up her pants legs and slapped the exposed flesh of her neck. Edward shifted gears and the bike shot forward. Cooper tightened her grip on his leather coat, though she was actually more exhilarated by their speed than fearful.

Edward's body felt taut beneath his coat. It was as though every cell in his body was focused on getting Cooper to her sister's side as rapidly as possible. He was clearly skirting the line leading to reckless driving. Yet Cooper trusted his skill, even though she had never driven with him before. Instinctively, she felt she would come to no harm in his care.

She followed Edward's lead as he leaned his body into turns and hunched down further during moments of acceleration. He tore through intersections and soared under the pools cast by flashing yellow lights until they had reached the windy, dark corridor that was River Road. Slowing now, he waited for Cooper to tap him on the shoulder, indicating he should make a left or right turn. They had no other way to communicate, but they seemed to have a natural connection—their bodies engaged in a wordless conversation of trust.

Cooper was confused and shaken by the subtle feeling of loss she experienced when she released her hold on Edward in front of Ashley's Georgian mansion. However, she had little time to dwell on the sensation because her sister flew out the front door in a tracksuit and slippers and immediately buried her head against Cooper's shoulder.

"I'm here. I'm here," Cooper said soothingly. "Let's go inside." She hugged her sister tightly and then gently pushed her away. "I'll look in the garage, while you pour us some coffee, okay? We had a cold ride."

Ashley blinked and suddenly became aware of both the motorcycle and the silent man dressed in black. Her blue eyes widened and she shot a frightened, questioning glance at Cooper.

"He's a friend," Cooper said quietly and smiled at Edward. At this, he removed his helmet and fell in behind the sisters as they passed into Ashley's house.

The heat immediately wrapped itself around Cooper. Her fingers and toes tingled as feeling returned to them and her wind-chafed skin ceased smarting. She stripped off her mittens, but kept her coat and hat on as she moved through the kitchen and out to the garage with a greater show of calm than she felt.

The spot where Ashley's Lexus convertible was usually parked was occupied by a sleek, metallic gold Cadillac sedan. The trunk was fully ajar and several shopping bags were lying in disarray on the floor behind the right rear tire.

Cooper breathed in deeply, hoping to draw some courage from the still air and forced herself not to tiptoe to the back of the car.

Her first impression was that the body was in the fetal position. It was a man, but no one Cooper knew. He seemed small to her, almost childlike in his curled posture within the deep, spacious truck. She looked at his black hair and pecan-colored skin, at the pair of callused and grease-stained clasped hands that were bound with duct tape. His eyes were closed and he appeared to be asleep, though there was nothing serene or restful about the piece of silver tape covering his mouth and the lower half of his mustache.

The rest of the trunk appeared empty. There were no signs of a struggle. There was no blood or rents in the plush carpet lining the trunk. It was as if the man had been carefully placed inside, like a young boy being tucked into his bed.

"You know this guy?" Edward spoke softly beside her.

Cooper rubbed her arms, which had broken out in goose bumps the moment she'd looked inside the trunk. She shook her head, still staring at the coiled figure, trying to discern why a dead person looked so unlike a living person, even in a position of repose. There was something shrunken and diminished about this man, as though his chest had suddenly caved inward, his limbs had grown instantly thinner, and his face had become waxen and hollow once the energy—the presence of his spirit—was gone.

Bowing her head, Cooper muttered a quick prayer for those who'd mourn the stranger and then stepped back into the kitchen, gratefully accepting a cup of coffee from her agitated sister.

"Have you ever seen that man?" Cooper asked her.

"No." Ashley grabbed a tea towel and began to twist it around her fingers. "He could work for Lincoln. There are a lot of Hispanics on the lot. His hands are pretty dirty. Did you notice them?"

Cooper nodded as she sank onto a stool. She sipped her coffee automatically, her mind fixated on the image of the duct tape covering the man's mouth. Edward held his cup between his palms but did not drink. He simply stared at the sisters, his expression unreadable.

"We have to call the police, Ashley. Do you really think Lincoln tied that man up and put him in the trunk of a Cadillac?"

"Of course not!" Ashley responded heatedly and Cooper was pleased to see that her sister had settled down enough to listen to reason.

"We have no idea where this crime was committed or

who committed it, but that man"—Cooper gestured toward the garage—"deserves justice. I'm going to call the cops now. When they get here, I'm sure they'll want to speak to Lincoln." She made her voice very soft and gentle. "Do you know where he is?"

Ashley shrugged, but there was anger in the set of her shoulders. "He's at Morton's, having one of his three-hour steak dinners with his daddy and a few of the other managers."

"And he's not answering his phone?"

"He's at Morton's!" Ashley answered with her customary aplomb. "You couldn't hear a fog horn in that place. It's like some kind of conversation competition. Everyone talks louder than the next person. You're half deaf and ten pounds heavier after every meal at that place."

Edward's mouth twitched in amusement and Cooper was struck again by the sheer force of his presence. He hadn't uttered a single word and yet she felt clear-headed and confident just because he was in the room. As though predicting her next move, Edward handed her the phone from its cradle behind him. Cooper dialed 9-1-1 and provided what few details she could about the dead man in Ashley's garage, and then hung up. She exhaled in relief. Help was on the way.

"Well, ladies. That's my cue," Edward said and turned for the door.

Cooper followed him. "Your timing was heaven-sent. Thanks for stopping to check on me by the highway and for bringing me here."

Edward issued the briefest of nods. "I'm going to finish up the job on your truck. You can't leave it there all night," he said as he stepped out into the cold. "Have one of the cops"—he said the word with distaste—"drive you back there when they're done with you. It'll be ready to roll."

"Wait!" she said loudly as he strutted toward his bike. "I don't even know what to call you! Edward or the Colonel?"

Smiling, he threw a leg over his bike and prepared to don his helmet. "Depends on what company I'm keeping. With you, I guess I'm Edward."

Before she could reiterate her thanks, Edward had fired up the motor. With a wave of his black-gloved hand, he sped off down the drive.

Cooper stood outside, listening to the roar of his engine until the night fell quiet again.

By the time she returned to the kitchen, rubbing her cold-reddened hands together, Ashley had changed into a rose-hued sweater set and gray slacks. She'd even added a string of pearls and pulled her hair back into a silk headband. Cooper watched her apply a layer of pink lipstick using the toaster's reflection as though she were primping for a ladies' luncheon instead of preparing to meet a group of police officers.

"Are you getting gussied up for the cops?" she asked, startling Ashley. The lipstick slid across her sister's bottom lip and down her chin like a smear from a melting popsicle.

"I feel more comfortable this way." Ashley wiped her chin and eyed Cooper intently. "Do you mind explaining your Zorro on two wheels?"

"That's Edward Crosby." When Ashley responded with a blank look, Cooper explained further. "His father was murdered last year by the Door-2-Door Dinner killer. Remember?"

Her sister's eyes grew round in horror. "He's the *convict*? And he was in *my* kitchen?"

"He's not incarcerated anymore. Clearly," Cooper answered sharply. "I got a flat tire driving home and he pulled over to help me out. Then you called and I needed to get here as fast as I could, so he gave me a ride. Pretty nice for a *convict*."

"Edward." Ashley tried out the name. "He's got magnetism, that's for sure." She studied Cooper for a reaction and then yelled "Ha!" when the telltale blush crept up her sister's neck. "Just how tight were you holding onto him as you two sped over here?"

Fortunately, Cooper was saved from having to respond to Ashley's insensitive line of questioning by the arrival of the police. Answering the door, she was taken aback to see only a pair of men in blue standing on the welcome mat.

"This way, please." She stepped back to let them inside. As the younger officer closed the door, Cooper introduced herself and she led them through the kitchen into the garage. "And this is my sister, Ashley Love. She found the body."

Both sisters instinctively hung back as the officers walked to the rear of the Cadillac. The taciturn men exchanged subtle glances of surprise after looking inside the trunk, and suddenly, their doubtful expressions transformed their faces into visages of steely determination.

The trapped air inside the garage grew heavier in the silence. It was as though the presence of additional witnesses multiplied the number of unanswered questions surrounding the dead man's demise, making it hard to breathe in an atmosphere abruptly polluted by the taint of violence.

Cooper took Ashley by the elbow and drew her away from the garage and into her formal living room. There, the sisters sank into a deep sofa covered with a soft, olive-green chenille fabric. Ashley hugged a floral pillow to her chest while Cooper closed her eyes and tried to imagine what the policemen were saying to one another as they examined the bound corpse.

"When they come in, offer them coffee," Cooper whispered to her sister. "Remember—no matter what they seem to be implying by their questions—that we're on the same side. We all want to find out what happened to that poor man."

Frightened, Ashley nodded. She spent the following minutes chewing on her fingernails. Finally, when the ticking of the mantel clock seemed to increase in volume, she suddenly jumped up and announced her plan to call the maître d' at Morton's.

"I'll just inform him that there was an emergency at Mr. Love's home and he should call his wife immediately."

Satisfied by having decided upon a course of action, Ashley made the call. That done, she seemed to be in complete control as the officers tersely explained that a homicide investigation team was on the way. She smiled as though this was welcome news and then offered the two men not only coffee, but a plate of Magnolia's Marvels oatmeal raisin cookies, too. By the time three more policemen arrived, including a man dressed in a charcoal-colored suit, Ashley had covered the kitchen island with a hearty spread, including oven-warmed croissants, slices of cheddar and Havarti cheese, thick slabs of Virginia ham, small bowls of mustard and mayo, and of course, more of Maggie's cookies.

Somehow, the food miraculously softened the policemen's attitude toward Ashley. With the exception of the officer in the suit, who declined all offers of hospitality and remained in the garage, the officers all addressed her as *ma'am* and repeatedly thanked her for her kindness.

When the front door opened again, letting in a fresh burst of needle-sharp air, Ashley was too busy refilling coffee cups to realize that her stupefied husband had arrived. He was in the company of a burly, commanding figure Cooper hadn't seen for over a year.

"We meet again, Ms. Lee." Investigator McNamara took Cooper's outstretched hand and gave it a firm squeeze. "I believe your brother-in-law and I arrived at the same time. Does Mr. Love know what's happened here?"

Shaking her head, Cooper shrank a little beneath McNamara's penetrating stare. She noticed that his thinning salt-and-pepper hair was cut very short and that he needed to shave. A few of the hairs on his chin had already turned white and the skin beneath his eyes was bluish and puffy due to years of broken sleep and too much caffeine.

"You have a knack for discovering dead bodies, Ms. Lee." McNamara didn't smile, but his saddle-brown eyes softened as he spoke and Cooper relaxed.

"It wasn't me. I just—"

"Why don't you show me to your garage, Mr. Love?" The investigator cut off Cooper's protest, but he left her with a genuine smile before following Ashley's stunned husband deeper into the house.

"The garage?" Cooper heard Lincoln say and had to hold her sister back as a shout of shock and horror reverberated throughout the kitchen.

"McNamara had to do that, Ashley. He needed to make sure Lincoln was just as surprised as you were to find a body out there." She squeezed her sister tightly. "I know it's hard."

Lincoln entered the kitchen and sank, ashen-faced, into one of the chairs.

Ashley flew to him and put her arms around his neck. "Do you know who that is?" she whispered.

"He might work at one of the dealerships. He looks familiar, but Ash, with the way he looks, I can't be sure." He rubbed his eyes, as though trying to obliterate the image of the body, and then gently extricated himself from

Ashley's embrace and walked to the sink to pour himself a glass of tap water.

The night seemed interminable. Cooper, Ashley, and Lincoln were interviewed separately by McNamara and his partner, Investigator Wiser. Wiser, who was in his late twenties and had a mass of tight brown curls, espresso-brown eyes, and a face marked by a heavy shadow of stubble, did most of the talking while McNamara watched from a seated position on a wing chair, occasionally making notations on a pocket-sized notebook.

Cooper's testimony was the simplest, and after she'd gone over her version of events two times, McNamara informed her that she was free to leave. It was after eleven o'clock at this point, and Cooper was exhausted. All she wanted to do was crawl into bed, but she was reluctant to leave her sister. She had seen how Ashley had sent one pleading look after another Lincoln's way, and although he had hugged her upon his arrival, he didn't protest when the police forced them to separate during questioning.

"We're about to remove the victim," McNamara explained quietly as though he could sense her concern. "In another hour or so, your sister and her husband will be free to get some sleep." He paused. "That is, if they're able."

Reluctantly, Cooper asked for a ride to her truck, and McNamara responded by pulling one of the uniformed officers away from his ham and cheese sandwich. "You're to inspect Ms. Lee's vehicle until you're certain those tires are as full as your belly. Are we clear?"

The man instantly tossed his sandwich aside, stood a fraction taller, and said, "Yes, sir." He even helped Cooper into her coat and opened the front door for her with a flourish.

Ashley handed Cooper her mittens and the sisters embraced. "What's going to happen to us?" she whispered.

Over her sister's bent head, Cooper watched as two men from the Medical Examiner's Office exchanged a few words with Wiser before heading inside the garage. There was a lot of noise in the Love house for such a late hour, and the two sisters stood in their embrace, letting themselves get lost in the din. Radios crackled and tinny, disjointed voices mumbled unintelligible code from the policemen's utility belts; cell phones rang and were answered; water rushed through pipes as toilets were flushed or sinks utilized; and bass and baritone voices mingled together in a symphony of all-male voices. But the most forceful noise of the entire night had been the lack of sound—the dark vacuum of unalterable silence surrounding the body in the garage.

"You're going to be fine," Cooper promised Ashley and took comfort from her sister's warmth and the fruity smell of her hair. "But I think it will be awhile before things feel normal again." She touched Ashley on her smooth cheek. "I'm not saying that to worry you, but I want you to be prepared."

"What should I do?" Ashley clung to her sister's hand.

"Talk to your husband. You need to comfort one another." Cooper hesitated and then felt compelled to add, "And pray. For the cops, for the victim's family, for strength." She smiled tiredly. "Then rest. That's all you can do. Call me tomorrow, okay?"

After the sisters embraced again, Cooper stepped into the darkness. The clouds had thinned, allowing for a scattering of lonesome stars in the tar-black sky. Their weak twinkling seemed cold, standoffish.

Light from Ashley's open garage spilled onto the pebbled driveway in the form of a slanted square. The shadow of a gurney and of the two men lifting their burden into a white van fell upon the light and then, even the shadows were gone.

Within a few hours, the house would grow still, the lights would go off, and the silence would spread out and reclaim its dominion.

4

Cooper felt like a zombie the next day at work. After
briefly telling Angela what had happened the night before,
the office manager quickly restructured the daily schedule, giving Emilio the repair calls and putting Cooper on
shredder detail.

Moving through office after office as she emptied document bins stuffed with tight nests of white paper proved to
be the perfect occupation for Cooper's fatigued body and
restless mind. She called Ashley during her lunch hour but
barely recognized her sister's voice.

"What a nightmare!" Ashley croaked as though her
throat was inflamed. "I had to go to the police station and
give a formal statement this morning. Early!" she added
indignantly. "It's not like we got *any* sleep last night. When
we finally did crawl into bed, I told Lincoln that if he had
the *slightest* notion about what was going on, it was his one
and only chance to come clean with me."

"And?"

"He swore that he was as shocked as I was," Ashley
said through a yawn. "I believed him. But we still couldn't
sleep, so we talked about all kinds of stuff, Coop—the

way we used to when we were first married. I know this sounds awful, but that poor man in the trunk reunited us."

Taking a bite out of her Chick-fil-A sandwich, Cooper murmured tiredly, "I'm glad for you."

"The police tramped all through the house *again* this morning and those two investigators are at the West End dealership right now. That's where Miguel worked as the head lot attendant. The poor man," she repeated. "Now that I know his name I can think of him as a real person and not . . . the body in the car." She paused. "I can't stop wondering about him. Has his mama heard about what happened yet? Was he married? Does he have little children waiting for him to come home?" Ashley's voice cracked on the word "home."

"I've been thinking the same things," Cooper admitted and pushed her waffle fries away. She no longer had any interest in her lunch. "I feel like I've been moving through a fog bank today. I can't get the image of him out of my mind." She gazed around the eatery. Although she saw hassled mothers, raucous children begging for ice cream, and a group of old men in wool hats arguing about local politics as they stuffed their pockets with condiment packets, they left no impression on her. Not even the man making balloon animals could displace the sallow, waxen face and the tape-covered mouth of a lot attendant named Miguel.

Ashley sniffed. Cooper could hear her blowing her nose delicately in the background. When she spoke again, she was calm and clear-headed. "Thanks for coming over last night, Coop. I couldn't have handled it without you. Did you get home okay?"

"Edward had my truck ready to go, as promised."

"Ah, the mysterious Edward. The dark knight to the rescue," Ashley attempted levity. "And what does Nathan have to say about his competition?"

Cooper stuffed the remains of her lunch in the trash and tried to ignore the guilt stirring in her stomach. "I haven't told him yet. All I wanted to do last night was crawl into my warm bed and sleep for days, but I'll call him later. Maybe I'll cook him a nice dinner. It depends how tired I am tonight."

There was something judgmental about the way Ashley murmured, "Hmm."

"What are you not saying, Ashley?" Cooper demanded as she hurried out to the Make It Work! shredder truck, which took up four parking spots and released a noxious cloud of black smoke when the ignition was fired up.

"Nothing." Ashley's reply was nearly drowned out by the chugging of the truck engine. "It just sounds like you might have forgotten that today's Grammy's birthday and we're all having supper at Mama and Daddy's house. Including Nathan. You invited him weeks ago. *I* remember because I thought it was so sweet that he insisted on getting Grammy a present."

Slapping the steering wheel, Cooper moaned. "Her gift! I don't have time to pick it up now! Look, I've got to go. If I'm going to make it to the camera store before they close at five, I'd better get my work finished."

"Just don't mention our . . . unpleasant experience in front of Grammy. Mama doesn't want anything to spoil her special evening. I expect she'll be waiting for you with a pile of cookies when you get home."

"I wouldn't mind seeing her in the kitchen with some butterscotch squares." Cooper easily conjured an image of her mother engaged in a flurry of agitated baking as she waited for her oldest daughter to return from work. "But I doubt we can keep this from Grammy. She's mighty sharp and it's not going to be easy to act like nothing's happened."

Ashley sighed. "I know, but Grammy's a woman. *All*

women are easily distracted by pretty things, and I'm bringing her some jaw-dropping, eye-popping, let's-not-talk-about-babies-or-dead-men-named-Miguel pretty things."

Cooper disagreed with her materialistic sister about their chances of fooling their observant grandmother, but chose to remain quiet. She spent the rest of the workday emptying document bins as though she were engaged in a competitive sport and arrived at the camera store ten minutes before closing.

The clerk, a plump and friendly retiree named Janice, immediately recognized Cooper. Reaching below the counter, she proudly showed off the results of their joint planning. Once Janice was convinced that Cooper was completely delighted with the present, she wrapped it in tissue paper and then slid it into a gift bag decorated with birthday balloons.

"That's a beautiful pin you're wearing," Janice told Cooper as she rang up the sale.

Instinctively, Cooper's fingertips brushed the thin silver wings of the pin she always wore on her shirt, just above her heart. "Thank you. My grandmother gave this to me."

"I noticed it last time you were here. It's a lovely talisman." Janice smiled. "She's going to cherish your gift, too. I hope my grandchildren do something like this for me when I'm older." She laughed self-effacingly. "Oh, my, I guess *I'm* already older!"

"Ma'am, you've got the computer skills of people half your age. And an amazing eye for color," Cooper assured her. "I believe you're young where it matters." She tapped on her temple and the woman beamed at her.

"Thank you, dear. Come back sometime and tell me how the gift went over."

"I'll do that," Cooper promised and thanked Janice once more on the way out.

Gift in hand, Cooper relaxed for the first time that day. At the next red light, she slid her cell phone's earpiece onto her right ear and called Nathan. She wanted to tell him what happened the night before so he had time to compose himself before showing up at her parents' house for dinner. But that was only half the reason she decided not to tell him face-to-face. She didn't trust herself not to blush when she mentioned the role Edward Crosby had played.

Nathan, who worked as a Web designer from his home office, answered on the first ring. After exchanging greetings, Cooper hurriedly told her boyfriend what had happened and then apologized for not phoning earlier.

"I'm sure you're still in a state of shock. And exhausted, too," Nathan spoke gently once he'd had a moment to digest the startling news. "How's Ashley holding up?"

"As well as can be expected. The investigation's focusing on Love Motors's West End dealership, so by now she's probably glad her house is her own once more, though she may never step foot in the garage again." Cooper realized she was deliberately avoiding any mention of the dead man, but she wanted to push aside all thoughts of him until after Grammy's celebration.

"How many dealerships does the Love family manage?"

"Three. His father runs the original Love Motors downtown, and his younger brother has just been handed the keys to the new Cadillac/Hummer dealership on the Southside. Lincoln's is the only dealership that sells all makes of GM cars. It's a state-of-the-art facility. They even have a rotating dais inside to display special cars. Last time I drove by I saw a huge yellow Hummer spinning around."

Nathan huffed. "Who'd want a Hummer these days? You could take a week's vacation for the same price as a tank of gas."

"But you couldn't drive over a row of compact cars now, could you?" Cooper joked. "'Cause that could really come in handy during rush hour."

"I'm glad your sense of humor's still intact!" Nathan laughed. "Listen, why don't I show up a little early tonight? You can talk about anything you want and I'll listen while giving you the best shoulder rub in the world. My fingers are well-developed after years of flying over a computer keyboard. You can't let all this mad skill go to waste."

"No, I certainly can't. You made me an offer I can't resist." Cooper smiled into the phone.

Nathan was true to his word. Moments after Cooper welcomed him inside the small apartment above her parents' detached garage, he gave her a tender kiss and a lingering embrace. He then positioned himself on the sofa and gestured for her to sit on the floor in front of his feet.

As his long, nimble fingers worked her tight muscles, Cooper closed her eyes and began to talk. She rehashed every detail from the night before, beginning with the encounter with the truculent Bank of Richmond secretary, followed by her pickup going lame. She recounted how Edward Crosby had pulled over to help as succinctly as she could.

"What was he doing out in the country at that time of night?" Nathan asked curiously. "Didn't you say you'd just crossed the Goochland County line?"

Cooper leaned back into Nathan's strong hands as they kneaded the taut muscles beneath her shoulder blades. "I don't know. I never thought to ask. In all honesty, we didn't talk much. Once Ashley called, we tore over to her house and then, well, nobody felt like speaking."

Nathan dug his first two fingers into the tissue on either side of Cooper's spine and walked them from the top of her pelvis to the base of her neck and back down again. She moaned with pleasure.

"You're a magician, Nathan. I hadn't realized how tense I was and it's such a relief to let out all the things that have been bouncing around in my head." She closed her eyes and felt her body sinking into the floor, as though she were transforming from a solid state into a liquid one. "I can't stop thinking about the victim, Miguel. Why would someone do that to him?" She swallowed hard and immediately grew tense again. "They tied him up and put him in a trunk like he was a piece of luggage."

Just as Nathan put his arms around Cooper and embraced her from behind, there was a rapid tap on Cooper's door. Ashley burst into the apartment, calling, "I hope you two are decent, because I'm coming in!"

Nathan kept his hands on either side of Cooper's flushed neck, but after giving her shoulders a final, reassuring squeeze, he rose from the sofa in order to give Ashley a hug. "How are you doing?"

Ashley managed a thin smile. "I do declare—you are the sweetest man, Nathan Dexter." She patted him on the arm and then sank onto the sofa. After kissing Cooper on the crown of her head, she said, "I thought we'd better get things out of our systems before we go down for supper." Reaching into a zebra-striped purse, she removed a Love Motors newsletter and pointed to a boxed article on the inside page. "This is Miguel. He was the Employee of the Month last month."

Cooper stared at the photograph of the young man. Miguel Ramos looked to be in his early twenties. He had a round, friendly face and a shy smile, as though he was reluctant to look directly at the camera. Even so, Cooper believed she saw a glimmer of pride in Miguel's dark eyes and the tilt of his chin.

Miguel Ramos is a relatively new member of the Love

Motors team, the blurb began. *A former employee of Double A Auto in Norfolk, Miguel has been overseeing the West End lot since he started work this fall and our inventory has sparkled ever since! The first to arrive and the last to leave, Miguel says that he takes great satisfaction in a job well done. When he's not on the lot, Miguel enjoys going to nightclubs, singing karaoke, and playing video games.*

"He has a nice face, doesn't he?" Ashley said quietly. "His death doesn't make a lick of sense to me. Why would anyone kill him? He was a lot attendant who liked to sing and dance. He wasn't rich—no lot attendants are—he worked hard, and his hobbies were harmless enough."

"What happened at the dealership today?" Cooper asked as she continued to study the photograph. She was having a difficult time associating the image of a smiling, healthy man with the shrunken, lifeless form curled up in the back of Ashley's rental car. "Have the police come up with a motive?"

"That pair of investigators, Wiser and McNamara, questioned all the employees, made a copy of Miguel's personnel file, and went off to search his apartment." Ashley reclaimed the newsletter and folded it in half. "I don't think they got any leads, though. Lincoln talked to the same people afterward and all they had to say was that Miguel was a quiet, friendly guy. He took great care of the cars and everybody liked him. I hope his apartment gives the cops *something* to go on."

Cooper stood and walked over to the window. She could look down from this room and see her mother moving around in her kitchen. At the moment, she was setting the table using birthday-themed paper plates and napkins. "Did you find out about his family?"

"No wife or kids. I don't know about his parents," Ashley answered and began to fidget with her diamond tennis bracelet. "I kind of read through Miguel's file. Lincoln made a copy and brought it home. I think he was looking for an answer in the records, but Miguel didn't even list an emergency contact." She frowned. "There's one thing that seems kind of strange, but I don't want to mention it because I'll sound like a snob."

"You *are* a snob." Cooper pointed out.

After swatting her sister with her purse, Ashley turned to Nathan. "See how mean your girlfriend is to me?" When he shrugged helplessly, she sulked. "It's clear where *your* loyalties lie. Anyway, Miguel lived in one of those new apartment complexes right behind the dealership. They're supposed to appeal to up-and-coming yuppie couples who want to live within walking distance of shops and restaurants."

"The credit card generation," Cooper muttered. She knew all too well how easily one could be seduced by high-tech electronics and hip furniture. It had taken her two years to claw her way out of debt. "I know which apartments you mean. They've got access to the mall, the gym, two spas, five nail salons, and about fifty restaurants." She pictured the complex and realized what Ashley was implying. "You think the apartment would be too expensive for Miguel's salary?"

Ashley nodded. "It was bugging me, so I called over there. Go ahead and tell me that I'm a snob, but I couldn't picture a single guy working as a lot attendant living in that place. A one-bedroom costs over one thousand dollars a month and Miguel made less than ten dollars an hour. I'm no math whiz, but that seems like a lot of money to spend on rent. There'd be nothing left to live on!"

"Unless he had a roommate," Nathan suggested.

"Ah, I hadn't thought of that." Ashley ran her fingertips across her full lips and mulled over Nathan's theory. "I still think of a roommate as a college girl who blasts the Cranberries on her stereo and borrows your clothes without asking," she stated. "I guess the police will know everything about his private life within a few days. And everything about *mine,* too." She sighed. "I told them ten times about dropping off my Lexus at the service entrance sometime after six. Then someone drove the Caddy around front for me, and I sped on home. I only opened the trunk later because I was planning to return some clothes at the mall today. I could tell that younger guy, Investigator Wiser, didn't believe me when I told him I like to have my car loaded up the night before I go on errands."

"You always used to do that with your school stuff," Cooper recalled. "You'd put your book bag by the front door and lay out your outfit on that flowered chair in your room before going to bed." She gazed fondly at her sister. "I'm sure the police are just covering all the bases."

"But I *feel* guilty, even though I did nothing wrong," Ashley replied and rubbed her eyes wearily.

"At this point, it doesn't sound like they have a strong lead to follow. Do you know how Miguel died?" Nathan asked. "Have the police shared any information?"

Ashley shook her head. "It's a one-way street with those two. Lincoln couldn't be here tonight because he's got to provide them with records on the Caddy, Miguel's time sheet, and a mess of other documents." She crossed her arms over her chest. "I'm not stepping foot inside my house unless I know Lincoln'll be there. I'm scared to be alone now." Her voice wavered. "You're going to think I'm totally crazy when I say this, but I feel like there's a *presence* in the garage."

"That doesn't sound crazy to me at all." Cooper put her arm around her sister. "It's going to take time for you to recover from this, Ashley. If the police can find out what happened to Miguel, maybe you'll be able to let go of the fear."

"Maybe." Ashley didn't sound convinced. "But right now, my house feels haunted. *I* feel haunted. His face . . . I keep seeing it, Coop." Her eyes filled with tears. "I wish I could do something to help. I feel . . . responsible. There he was, in the trunk, with me driving around without a care in the world except for what I planned to wear to the Heart Gala. The whole time I was listening to music and sipping my mocha latté, he was back there . . ."

Cooper was just about to offer words of comfort when the sound of small rocks peppering her window caused her to turn away from her sister and peer outside.

"It's Grammy," Cooper informed Ashley and Nathan. "She's pointing at her mouth. Guess it's time to eat."

Nathan joined her at the window. "She's got some aim."

"You ought to see her shoot Daddy's rifle," Ashley replied, dabbing her eyes with a tissue. "You do *not* want to get on Grammy's bad side."

Nathan gulped. "Man, I hope she likes her present."

Grammy was so pleased to be served her favorite supper, Shake 'n Bake pork chops, macaroni and cheese, butter beans mixed with sweet corn, and white dinner rolls, that she was in high spirits from the moment her birthday meal began.

"Marryin' this gal was the smartest thing you ever did," she told Earl and toasted Maggie with a loaded fork. "If I go to my grave tonight, I'll be lickin' my chops when I stand before the Almighty."

"Now don't you go talkin' about joinin' the angels," Maggie remonstrated. "I've made a chocolate mousse cake big enough to feed the Gum Creek Volunteer Fire Department, so if you wanna eat leftovers, you'd best plan on wakin' up tomorrow."

Once decaf had been poured into the china cups given to Maggie on her wedding day, Earl carried out the birthday cake to appreciative claps from those seated at the table. Despite Grammy's threats that they'd be disinherited if they dared to sing, they serenaded her in exaggeratingly loud voices lacking any semblance of harmony.

"Doesn't look like you've got near enough candles on there," Earl commented to Maggie as Grammy inhaled a deep breath.

"Watch out, boy, or my birthday wish'll be that the *rest* of your hair falls out!" Grammy retorted and blew out the small flames perched on the tips of half a dozen pink-and-white striped candles.

As Nathan and the members of the Lee family dug into large slabs of the moist, rich chocolate cake, the doorbell rang.

"That must be Lincoln!" Ashley exclaimed, dabbed her lips with her napkin, and raced out of the kitchen.

Maggie watched her youngest child rush from the room. Shaking her head, she mumbled, "I don't know when that boy will learn to just come on in. We're his family, after all. He doesn't need to stand on ceremony."

Grammy shot Maggie a look of pity. "His folks are different stock. Just 'cause he married one of us don't mean he's gonna take up our ways. I reckon it's a good thing you broke out the fine china coffee cups tonight. I reckon the Loves don't drink from Dixie cups too regular."

Putting a finger to her lips, Maggie rose from the table and gave Lincoln a warm embrace hello as soon as he entered the cozy room.

"Always huggin'—the women of this family," Grammy grumbled, but Cooper knew she was secretly fond of being squeezed, kissed, and even patted by all members of the family. More than once, Cooper had walked into Grammy's room to find Little Boy, her enormous tailless tabby, licking her wrinkled face as she giggled with pleasure.

"Have you eaten?" Maggie asked Lincoln and, without giving him a chance to reply, placed the last pork chop onto a clean plate and loaded the empty spaces with scoops of macaroni and butter beans.

Lincoln accepted the laden dish gratefully. "Thanks, Mrs. Lee. I don't think I've had a bite since breakfast." He cast a sideways glance at Ashley. "It's been a real hectic day at work."

"Poor dear." Maggie shot both him and Ashley a warning look. "Sit down and fill your belly. Cooper? Get your brother-in-law a beer, would you, honey?"

Grammy cleared her throat. "I might've polished off the last one this afternoon."

"Mama." Earl's tone had a reprimanding edge. "Did you at least wait 'til five?"

"It's my party and I'll drink when I want to," Grammy answered evasively.

Cooper laughed as she dug through the refrigerator and then stood up, holding the last bottle of Budweiser aloft in triumph. Earl and Grammy drank their beer right from the bottle, but Cooper suspected Ashley would prefer her husband's beer to be decanted and served in a pint glass. Watching the foam crown the amber liquid as she poured, Cooper paused to scrutinize Lincoln, wondering if the effects of the last twenty-four hours were making their mark on his appearance.

Without a doubt, Lincoln Love was an incredibly handsome man. Cooper passed her eyes over the familiar all-American features—the sandy brown hair, bright blue eyes, and boyishly rosy skin—and thought he didn't look much the worse for wear. However, his conversation was more stilted than usual and his smile, when it appeared between bites of food, seemed forced.

Cooper often felt as though she didn't truly know the man her sister had married, but he had always treated Ashley like a queen. Now, Cooper placed a tentative hand on Lincoln's shoulder as she presented him with the cold glass of beer. He turned to her with a look of tenderness she'd never seen before. It was as if he were silently thanking her for coming to Ashley's aid when he'd been unavailable.

He'd barely taken a sip when Grammy slapped her napkin on the table and said, "Let's get this present nonsense over with. Imagine! A woman of *my* age gettin' gifts. It's damn silly. Y'all should be savin' your money, times bein' tight as they are."

"You're not gonna spoil our fun with that 'ole guilt song and dance. Anyhow, I *know* you'll want these." Maggie handed Grammy a birthday card. She sat back expectantly, but when Grammy opened the card and the strains of "Margaritaville" burst into the air, Maggie dug an elbow into Earl's side. "I *told* you to get her the 'Twist and Shout' card!"

Earl shrugged. "They all looked the same to me."

"Tickets to the Maymont Flower Show!" Grammy was thrilled. "Are you sellin' your cookies there?"

"Yes, ma'am. I was finally accepted into the *elite* group of vendors," Maggie answered proudly. "And I was hopin' one of your granddaughters might take you around durin' setup. Then you can see everything without bein' jostled by the crowds."

"I bet my gardenin' partner will take me," Grammy stated hopefully.

Cooper nodded in assent. "Of course I will. Maybe we can get some new ideas for the vegetable patch."

Not wanting to be excluded any longer, Ashley placed an exquisitely wrapped box on the table in front of Grammy. The gigantic bow was tied so tightly that she couldn't undo the knots, so Earl severed the beautiful satin with a quick stroke of his steak knife. Grammy placed the bow on her head, bowed jauntily, and tore the lovely floral gift wrap.

A delicate waft of perfume floated from within the box and when Grammy pulled out a rose-colored throw made from lush cashmere, everyone oohed and aahed. She'd also been given a pair of slippers and a scented neck wrap that could be heated in the dryer.

"You'll be warm and toasty for the rest of the winter," Ashley said.

Grammy smiled at her. "Thank you, darlin', even though you went overboard as usual."

Ashley preened, delighted to be told that she'd gone overboard. She was always too extravagant with gift-giving, but Cooper knew that her sister possessed a generous nature and truly enjoyed shopping for others. The sisters were polar opposites in that regard, for Cooper found the notion of spending hours in Richmond's over-priced boutiques as welcome as a root canal.

Nathan went next. He presented Grammy with a book on animal first-aid. She loved it and showed her delight by squeezing Nathan's cheek. "All right, granddaughter. Hand yours over and let's be done with this. I'm tired and I need a Tums." Grammy put her hands on her stomach.

Because it was heavy, Cooper pulled the scrapbook from the gift bag and set it on Grammy's lap. "Your wedding pictures and those from your childhood were faded and really needed to be restored, so I made you an album. It's got all those photos as well as some pictures of the animals you've saved over the years." She smiled as Grammy turned the pages. "There are a few of us, too, even though we're not as good-looking as that three-legged beagle or your blind raccoon."

Grammy flipped through the book in silence and then turned back to the cover, which showed her as a solemn bride. She ran her hands over the photograph, her eyes pooling with tears.

"I didn't mean to upset you." Cooper knelt down and covered Grammy's brittle, weathered hand with her own.

"You ain't caused me grief, girl. There are just so many faces here my heart's achin' to see again." She smiled and wiped her eyes with her thin forearm. "When you're old as dirt, it can be bittersweet to think of all those who've passed over before you." She tucked a lock of Cooper's ash-blonde hair behind her ear. "Don't you fret. I don't wanna leave you yet, and I will cherish this book until the day I do." She placed the album on the table and scraped back her chair. "Now, it's long past my bedtime. You young folks can keep the lights burnin', but I'm goin' to bed!"

Maggie refused to let Grammy go without a hug and a peck on the cheek. "We love you!" she shouted as the birthday girl shuffled down the hall.

Earl rose from his chair. "I'll tidy up, Maggie. You outdid yourself with that cake."

"No, Daddy." Ashley collected a pair of coffee cups. "You two go put your feet up. The kids will clean tonight."

As soon as their parents relocated to the living room and switched on the television, Ashley gestured for Lincoln to join her at the sink.

"So? Do the police have any idea what happened to Miguel now that you've handed over all the paperwork you had on him?"

Both Cooper and Nathan moved closer to the couple in order to listen to Lincoln's answer. "They talked to the girls in human resources the most," he answered while loading the coffee cups into the dishwasher. "I think they've got doubts about the authenticity of Miguel's official documents—his social security card and driver's license, for example."

"Was he an illegal?" Cooper whispered.

Lincoln nodded. "That'd be my guess. Other than

collecting the paperwork, they interviewed Jason, one of the mechanics. Apparently, he was the last person to see Miguel alive. Jason says that Miguel seemed totally normal yesterday. He came inside for a soda, chatted with him about an NBA game, and said he was going to gas up some demo vehicles before calling it a day." He closed the dishwasher and wiped his hands on a birthday napkin. "That's the last anyone saw of him."

"Until I opened the trunk." Ashley scoured Maggie's serving bowls over and over again with a bristly sponge until Cooper reached across her sister and turned off the faucet. Ashley continued to stare at the soapy water. "I don't want to sit around and wait for the police to figure this out." She gave Lincoln a pleading look. "Can't you start your own investigation at work?"

He quickly shook his head. "I'm leaving this to the professionals. We should stay out of their way, honey."

On one hand, Cooper agreed with Lincoln, but she also understood the sense of responsibility her sister felt. She, too, had seen how Miguel had been trussed up and stashed inside the dark trunk. It was an undignified and disrespectful ending to a life.

Ashley had mentioned feeling haunted. Cooper was experiencing the same sensation. She couldn't escape the image of the photograph in the newsletter. Miguel's reluctant smile. The light of pride in his eyes. The sense of expectancy in his young face. She wanted to act as well. It was torture to feel so helpless, to have no possibility for closure until the police informed them the case was solved.

While Nathan and Lincoln said their good-byes to Earl and Maggie, Cooper took out the garbage. She dropped the bag into the plastic can outside and shivered. Ashley's silhouette appeared in the doorframe. She hugged herself against the cold and stared expectantly at Cooper.

The two sisters came to a wordless understanding.

"We'll give the police a week," Cooper whispered as the clouds moved aside to reveal a white-sickle moon. "After that, I'll ask the Sunrise members to get involved. I have faith that they'll know just what to do next."

5

"Are not two sparrows sold for a penny? Yet not one of them will fall to the ground apart from the will of your Father. And even the very hairs of your head are all numbered. So don't be afraid; you are worth more than many sparrows."

Matthew 10:29-31 (NIV)

Savannah phoned Cooper on Saturday to inform her that their weekly Bible study would be held at Trish's house after worship the next day. Trish was so weak and nauseated from Friday morning's chemo treatment that she didn't expect to have the strength to make it to Hope Street to join her friends.

"So we'll bring Hope Street to her," Savannah said. "Quinton has graciously volunteered to feed us lunch and Bryant will do the hair-cutting honors. Trish wanted to give her locks one last week to hold on, but I think she's truly resigned to the idea of a wig now."

Cooper couldn't imagine how terrifying it would be to have entire clumps of hair coming loose from her scalp. "Poor Trish."

"She's a fighter," Savannah stated firmly. "When all is said and done, I believe she'll have taught us a thing or two about strength."

"I'm sure you're right," Cooper agreed, but still felt frightened for her friend. She was also tempted to keep

Savannah on the line and tell her about Miguel Ramos and the nightmares she'd had all week, but the moment passed.

In these disturbing dreams, she'd been the person tied up inside a car trunk instead of Miguel. Imprisoned in blackness, her body had pitched and rolled as the car hugged a curve or came to a sudden stop. With her mouth covered in duct tape, she struggled to breathe through her nostrils. Her lungs strained, burning for oxygen, and the little air she was able to take in was heavy with the stench of sweat and fear.

For the past few nights, Cooper had awakened abruptly, drenched in sweat, disoriented. She knew that only the resolution of Miguel's case would restore her peaceful slumber, but the police didn't seem to have much to go on.

Wiser and McNamara had repeatedly questioned the employees of Lincoln's dealership, as well as those working for the other Love franchises. As of this point, the only information they'd shared with Lincoln was that Miguel's Social Security card and driver's license were both forged and that he was likely an illegal immigrant.

Cooper didn't expect Investigator McNamara to provide Lincoln and Ashley with progress reports, but she assumed, perhaps unfairly, that their repetitious questions indicated a lack of progress. Cooper wondered if Miguel's murder had become less of a high priority now that the authorities were aware of his possible illegal status. She prayed this was not the case, but she was also conscious that gang-related crimes had escalated during the month of January, and the police had neither the funds nor the manpower to suppress the violence spreading throughout the city.

Her father was reading an article about the gang issue that very morning. As Cooper sat down at her parents' kitchen table, Earl slid over the *Richmond Times-Dispatch*.

"Your mama wants me to keep you close today," he

remarked over the rim of his coffee cup. "I don't reckon you're in harm's way, but it'll ease her mind."

Cooper had expected this. The day after Grammy's party, Maggie had called an emergency family meeting, forcing Cooper and Ashley to recount precisely what had happened Monday night.

"I've gotta listen to this story while both my girls are sittin' in front of me," she insisted. "A mother needs to look her children over after they've been through somethin' that awful. Besides, I wanna be sure that no one's out to get my babies."

The afternoon of their meeting, Grammy arrived at the kitchen table first, cold beer in hand, sitting with the expectancy of one awaiting a promising theatrical performance. "I knew you kids were actin' funny last night," she stated smugly. "You two didn't pick at each other—not even once. Only somethin' *big* could make sisters forget to squabble."

Despite their retelling of events, neither Ashley nor Cooper was able to provide their family members with a satisfying conclusion to their story.

"This case may never get solved." Ashley's hands shook as she reached for a paper napkin. "Some murderer is running loose out there!"

Earl put a strong hand on each of his daughter's shoulders and squeezed. "I'm right glad you two've come through this ordeal none the worse for wear." He then gave Maggie a tender look. "It seems like a sorry accident that the unfortunate young man ended up in your garage, Ashley, but I don't see that we have cause to get it fixed in our minds that anyone is after you." His gaze rested on Cooper. "In plain talk—this is now the business of the law. You stay out of the way and try to move on, ya hear?"

At the time, the sisters had murmured their unenthusiastic agreement. But even now, five days later, Cooper was just as troubled by Miguel's death as she'd been when she first peered inside the Cadillac's trunk. Whenever her mind roamed, it conjured the image of his newsletter photograph. Inevitably, that smiling, youthful face would mutate into the slack-featured visage she'd gazed down upon in the cold, weak light of Ashley's garage.

Cooper unfolded the paper and read the headline story on the strife in Richmond's East End. The reporter commented on the unusual number of shootings in January, stating that the amount of violent crimes committed that month were more like the statistics expected in June or July. The tragic exchange of gunfire by two African-American teens had made the front page of the weekend paper. The two young men, who had fought over the right to spray paint a few square feet of cement, both died at the scene. Theirs was not the only blood spilled, however, for a stray bullet also stole the life of a ten-year-old girl walking home from a friend's apartment.

The anguish felt by the residents of East End screamed through the black print.

"The police are never going to be able to focus on Miguel Ramos's case in the face of this horrible tragedy," Cooper muttered sadly while staring at the photograph of the East End crime scene. A dozen policemen were frozen in investigative postures, scrutinizing the ground, collecting spent bullets, interviewing bystanders. Crime scene tape was tied from every available tree and telephone pole. The image created both a feeling of industry and one of irrevocable waste, for no matter how much energy the men and women captured by the camera expelled, they could not reverse the results symbolized by the blood-stained asphalt.

Earl looked up from his crossword puzzle and tapped on the newspaper in Cooper's hand. "This scene is startin' to repeat itself. It's no good. No good at all. Little girls dyin' from stray bullets, young men killin' one another because someone spoke a sharp word, and drugs everywhere, poisonin' people's minds." He touched Cooper's fingers lightly. "I'm not sayin' Miguel's death isn't important, but it's not spreadin' fear like a wildfire." He put his pen down. "How 'bout we get outta here? Grammy wants me to take her to Wal-Mart, and you don't need to be readin' this stuff right now."

"Wal-Mart? On a Saturday?" Cooper was astonished. "It'll be a zoo."

Smiling thinly, Earl nodded. "Don't I know it. I reckon Grammy wants to get her kicks by ramming a few folks with her cart. Maybe she'll behave if you come along."

With Nathan away for the day visiting a former college roommate in Northern Virginia, Cooper had no plans, so she agreed to accompany Grammy and her father to the megastore.

From the moment they passed through Wal-Mart's sliding glass doors, Grammy was deliberately impish. She shuffled along behind her cart at a snail's pace, stopped abruptly in the middle of an aisle, huffed and snorted with impatience when another woman blocked her access to the pitted prunes, and spent undue amounts of time choosing the perfect bunch of bananas—only to rip them apart so that she ended up placing a single banana in her cart.

Earl bore her behavior in stride until they reached the women's underwear section. As Grammy held up bikini briefs in every color and fabric, demanding to know where the store was hiding the underwear meant for "normal, decent folk," his face grew redder and redder until he finally shouted, "I'll be in the hardware department!" and took off at a brisk pace.

Watching him tear past a display of slinky Valentine's Day nighties, Grammy smirked in satisfaction. She then held up a minuscule black pair of panties made of faux satin and spun them around on their hanger. "Tell me, granddaughter. Is this underwear or an eye patch?" she asked.

Laughing, Cooper managed to find the cotton briefs Grammy wanted. They moved through accessories, where Cooper was attracted to a colorful display of fleece hats, gloves, and scarves. Selecting a lavender cap, she stroked the soft material and then carried it over to a mirror and put it on. She was pleased that the material covered her entire head, obscuring her hair entirely.

Trish is going to get cold without her thick hair, she thought and placed the cap and the matching scarf and gloves into the cart. After a moment's hesitation, she selected a turquoise set for herself.

Her shopping completed, Grammy declared she was now in a great hurry to get back home. Apparently, one of her favorite Spencer Tracy films would be coming on TV at one o'clock and she wanted to eat her lunch and be "good and settled" on the sofa with her cashmere blanket and Little Boy before the movie started.

The second they reached the front of the predictably long checkout line, Grammy stamped her feet and sighed in annoyance over the cashier's inability to insert a fresh roll of register tape into her machine.

"I've seen slugs with more get-up-and-go," she complained too loudly.

Cooper shushed her and focused on unloading the cart. As she did so, Grammy reached out and grabbed the lavender fleece cap from her hand. "That ain't a good color for you. This is an old lady shade."

"It's not for me." As the cashier struggled with the register tape, Cooper quietly explained that Trish had breast cancer and, because of the chemotherapy, was losing her

hair. "She's asked us to come to her house tomorrow because she's ready to shave it all off. I figured she'd really
feel the chill without something warm on her head."

Grammy studied Cooper's face. "You're right worried
about your friend, ain't you? Don't worry, girlie. Love'll
see her through." She cradled the lavender cap gently in her
hands and then brought it to her face, murmuring into the
fabric. Cooper heard her say, "Oh, Lord, let Trish dwell in
Your shelter. Be her refuge, her fortress, her covering, her
shield. Command Your angels to guard her. Amen."

Cooper quickly looked away so that Grammy wouldn't
see her tears, but her grandmother had turned her attention to the eye-level candy displays lining the checkout
aisle. "I'm gonna have me a Baby Ruth. After all, you
never know when you're gonna draw your last breath."
She grinned and tossed three candy bars onto the conveyor belt. Slapping her purse on the bagging end of the
checkout area, she scrutinized the cashier until the young
woman withered beneath her gaze.

Once Grammy's plastic bags were packed in the cart
and she'd paid the cashier using a wad of mangled singles,
she dug one of the Baby Ruths out of the cart and handed
it to the surprised cashier. "Here ya go, sweet girl. If
you've gotta deal with folks like me, I reckon you deserve
a little treat."

Earl appeared in time to witness the exchange and gave
his mother an imploring look. "Got one for me, too?"

"No, I do not! With all the cookies you eat, it's amazin'
you've got any teeth in your jaw!" Grammy snapped and
marched through the sliding doors.

"Ouch." Earl clutched his chest as though he were
wounded and then smiled at Cooper. "She's a tough nut,
your grandma, but I love her more than my new socket
wrench."

"I'm glad Wal-Mart has proved to be so entertaining,"

Cooper commented wryly, but silently confessed that the errand had been exactly what she'd needed. Trailing her father to the car, she felt a rush of affection for her quirky family members.

She wheeled the empty cart to the closest collection site and paused for a moment, watching the other shoppers walk across the parking lot. She saw couples holding hands, adults helping their aged parents navigate the uneven ground, children raised on their father's shoulders, and toddlers riding on their mother's hips. Cheeks were flushed pink by the cold, plumes of cigarette smoke rose in the air, voices chattering into cell phones drifted over the cars, and here and there, the flash of a smile brightened the January day.

Cooper absorbed the signs of everyday living and felt that, suddenly, there was beauty all around. The cars gleamed in the winter sun. People waved to one another. Laughter was exchanged.

Heading back to Earl's station wagon, Cooper repeated Grammy's sentiment. "Love will see us through."

The next morning, Cooper's mood was buoyed further by Hope Street's worship service. After the opening hymns were sung to the accompaniment of hearty claps and quite of bit of hip-shaking from the congregation, Pastor Matthews announced that they'd begin the service by baptizing a six-month-old girl. As was his habit, he gently removed the baby from her mother's arms and walked her up and down the two main aisles, describing the act of baptism while members of the congregation, who simply couldn't help themselves, grinned foolishly or made cooing noises as the adorable infant passed by.

When minister and child approached the area where the Sunrise members were gathered, the child, whose name was MacKenzie Lynn, yanked Pastor Matthew's speaker from his ear and stuck it in her mouth. Her happy gurgling filled the auditorium and everyone burst out laughing. Finally, MacKenzie was returned to her parents, words of commitment were spoken, and water was drizzled in a halo pattern over the baby's head. This was the point in the baptism ceremony in which many children cried, but MacKenzie seemed to love the attention. In fact, when Pastor Matthews closed his eyes to murmur a closing prayer, she reached out, her dark hair still dripping, and grabbed the microphone affixed to his shirt.

"Oooooooo!" Her high voice warbled through the speakers and, though the minister smiled, he kept his eyes shut and finished the prayer.

Following another rousing hymn and a sermon addressing the afflictions of their city, the service concluded. The Sunrise members bypassed the beckoning table filled with donuts and fresh fruit and headed straight for their cars. As usual, Jake drove Savannah in his Mr. Faucet van. Cooper smiled as the plumber gallantly guided their study leader into the passenger seat but then nearly shut her cane in the van door.

Trish's husband, Phil, was loading their two daughters in the family Volvo as the Bible study group arrived at the Tylers' stately home. Trish's girls waved from the backseat and Phil smiled apologetically at his wife's friends and called, "We're off to Friendly's for lunch and then to *High School Musical 3*. Again!"

Cooper thought Phil and the girls seemed relieved to be leaving.

"It wasn't hard to chase them off. I've been horrible to live with this weekend," Trish explained from her position on the living room sofa—an enormous sectional in a soft cranberry material. Cooper felt like rushing to her friend's side and embracing her, for Trish truly looked sick. Her face was puffy and pale, her eyes dull and tired, and her legs were drawn up under her and obscured beneath a woolen throw. Cooper was used to seeing her made-up, attired in a skirt suit and heels, and displaying impeccable posture. Now, Trish was wearing a gray sweatshirt and a faded Richmond Braves baseball cap. She held the blanket against her chest as though it might offer her some protection.

"Should we have lunch and then review this week's lesson?" Savannah asked. "Are you hungry, Trish?"

"Not really," she answered weakly. "It's hard to eat with such a dry mouth, but feel free to bring your food in here. Make yourselves comfortable. I'm through with decorum." She gestured at the sweatshirt. "I've never allowed anyone to eat in this room before, but suddenly rules like that seem plain dumb."

"I'm serving comfort food today. Bologna and cheese on sesame-seed rolls with a side of Fritos." Quinton set a paper plate on Trish's lap. "And here's a big glass of water to help wash it all down."

Jake led Savannah to one of the wing chairs and offered to fix a sandwich for her. Bryant settled down next to Trish and put a hand on her shoulder. "How are you feeling?"

"Like total crap," she replied truthfully. "And I know I look awful." She picked up her *Directing Our Passion* workbook. "I didn't finish the homework, either. The question about Corinthians twelve—the one about spiritual gifts—I couldn't answer that one at all. Honestly, I don't know if I have any."

Nathan wiped Frito dust onto a napkin. "Of course you do. Look how many mission families you've found homes for. With all the support your company gives to the church for its East End housing project, your spiritual gift has been to put roofs over people's heads. That's no small feat."

"Yeah," Jake agreed. "*I* remember how you bullied me into takin' care of the plumbin' for a bunch of those houses.

Now *that's* a real talent—to get a plumber to work on a Saturday durin' football season."

Trish closed her workbook. "I'm sorry. I know this should be the one time to *really* focus on our study, but I cannot concentrate until we get this out of the way." She pointed to her baseball cap and then slowly removed it.

Cooper stared at the patches of pink skin peeking through the straggly, lusterless hair on Trish's head. "It's awful, isn't it? I look like a soccer ball." Her voice trembled and Bryant took her hand in hers.

"You're going to be the most gorgeous bald woman in all of Richmond," he teased.

Savannah leaned forward in her chair. "From what *I* can see, you're as beautiful as ever."

This statement, coming from a legally blind woman, made Trish grin.

"Bryant's Beauty Boutique is open for business." Bryant got up, fetched his electric clippers from the kitchen, and returned with one of the dining room chairs. Nathan and Jake spread out two large Hefty bags in the center of the floor and placed the chair on top of them. Quinton got a towel from the downstairs bathroom and motioned at the chair. "Your seat awaits you, milady."

Nodding, Trish threw the blanket from her legs and relocated to the chair. Quinton covered her shoulders with the towel and then kissed her on the cheek. He closed the towel at her neck using a plastic snack bag clip and then backed up, giving Bryant space to work. Not for the first time, Cooper thought about what a caring and wonderful husband Quinton would make.

"I'm scared!" Trish cried.

Cooper longed to remove her friend's fear. "Do you want me to read something aloud?"

"That would be nice. How about a little Samson and

Delilah? That seems appropriate." Trish's attempted laugh came out sounding like a strangled sob.

Opening her Bible to Judges, Cooper kept her voice soft and level as she recited Samson's victories over the Philistines. "Some time later," she read next, "he fell in love with a woman in the Valley of Sorek whose name was Delilah. The rulers of the Philistines went to her and said, 'See if you can lure him into showing you the secret of his great strength and how we can overpower him so we may tie him up and subdue him. Each one of us will give you eleven hundred shekels of silver.'"

"Damn those shekels of silver!" Jake called over the sound of the buzzer.

Cooper glanced up and was momentarily distracted by the locks of Trish's red hair raining to the ground. She returned to the narrative, bringing Delilah's passionate pleas to learn the source of Samson's strength to life with her voice.

"So the rulers of the Philistines returned with the silver in their hands. Having put him to sleep on her lap, she called a man to shave off the seven braids of his hair, and so began to subdue him. And his strength left him." Cooper paused, concerned over the negative wording of the latter phrase.

Nathan stooped down in front of Trish and smiled. "Good thing *your* strength is elsewhere, huh?"

Trish nodded.

"Sit still, woman!" Jake commanded. "Your barber ain't that skilled. He might buzz away one of your eyebrows."

While Cooper read about Samson's imprisonment, Bryant turned off the clippers and began to gently brush stray hairs from Trish's neck and shoulders. "Ready?" he whispered in her ear and then pressed a hand mirror in her palm.

The anxiety among the Bible study members was palpable. As Trish raised the mirror and stared at her reflection, they held a collective breath. Cooper dropped her voice to a hush. "Then Samson prayed to the LORD, 'O Sovereign LORD, remember me. O God, please strengthen me just once more . . .'" She trailed off after noticing the tears racing down Trish's cheeks.

Trish raised a shaking hand to her head and stroked the bristles on her scalp. Her lower lip trembled, but she could not hold back the force of her grief. "Oh, God!" she called out in pain and then buried her face in the hair-covered towel.

Jake jumped to his feet. "Come on now! You've got a fine pile of fancy wigs sittin' on this dining room table. Look!" He raced from the room and returned, modeling a strawberry-blonde wig that fell in shiny waves past his shoulders.

Hesitating, Trish raised her head and watched as Jake sashayed into the room, his hips swaying from side to side. "Y'all can just call me Jane Fonda." Taking Bryant's arm in his, Jake batted his eyelashes at the meteorologist. "*You* can call me *Miss* Fonda, you sexy thang." He then sauntered over to Quinton and sat right on his lap. Toying with Quinton's bowtie, Jake flicked a lock of hair over his shoulders and whispered huskily, "And *you* can call me Barbarella, big boy."

Nathan followed Jake's lead and popped on another long wig in a deeper shade of red. "Do I look like a Desperate Housewife?" he asked coquettishly, tying on an apron from Trish's pantry. "Come on, Jane. Let's aerobicize and then make us some cupcakes!"

"Good thinkin', Bree! We can stir a bunch of vodka into the batter!" Jake answered.

Suddenly, the two bewigged men were doing jumping

jacks and leg kicks. Their hair flew wildly about their faces as they grunted with exertion. Slowly, Trish's quivering mouth curved up into a smile. By the time the men began a series of frenzied abdominal crunches, everyone was laughing. Trish even put down the mirror and relocated to her former place on the sofa.

Cooper took the opportunity to remove the Hefty bags from the center of the room. She stuffed them into the trash can in the garage. As Nathan removed the "barber's chair," she handed Trish the lavender hat and scarf set she'd bought the day before.

"To keep you warm." She hugged her friend tightly.

Trish tried on the hat and examined herself once again in the mirror. She then wrapped the scarf in a fashionable knot at the base of her neck.

"I don't know what you all are up to," Savannah said. "But the elephant that was sittin' in the room is gone now!"

Jake scowled. "Who are you callin' an elephant? I've got thighs of steel!"

Savannah pulled a face.

"I knew you could get me through this moment." Trish smiled gratefully at the Sunrise members. "Laughter is definitely the best medicine, but knowing I can count on your friendship is what will carry me through the next round of treatments, the next dose of fear." She sighed. "Oh, I'm grateful that the rest of you haven't had to experience a week as bad as mine!"

Nathan and Cooper exchanged rapid glances, but they weren't quick enough to escape Jake's notice.

"What was that?" he demanded. "You two got somethin' to tell us?"

"Um . . ." Nathan hedged, leaving the decision to Cooper.

Knowing that it would be a great relief to share the

burden of Miguel's death with her closest friends, Cooper sat down on the carpet and quietly told them about what had happened Monday night.

"I take back what I said," Trish said apologetically. "Your experience was much worse, Cooper."

After her friends recovered from their shock and remonstrated with her over not sharing the news sooner, Cooper explained what was truly troubling her.

"It seems like the case is already growing cold," she said. "And I feel, because I saw Miguel's body, that I owe him something. He doesn't seem to have any family—there's no one to mourn him or to ensure that justice is done on his behalf!" She exhaled, realizing how forcefully she'd been speaking.

Savannah put both her hands into the air and reached out in Cooper's direction. "Bearing witness to this young man's death has taken its toll on you. I can hear it in your voice."

"Yes," Cooper confessed. "And on my sister, too."

Bryant helped himself to more chips, but didn't eat any. Instead, he pushed them around on his plate. "Maybe the police will come up with fresh leads this week?"

Cooper's eyes flashed. "*Maybe* isn't good enough. For a while I wasn't sure if I should get mixed up in Miguel's case, but now I'm certain that it's the right thing to do, and I'd like your help. We've conducted investigations before and have made a difference for the better. We can make a difference again, I'm sure of it." She searched the faces around her. "I'm asking you all to get involved."

"The first thing to do is to get to know who this Miguel fellow was," Jake mused. "Sounds like nobody has a real line on the guy."

"No man's an island," Quinton stated while rubbing his round chin. "If we could see where he lived, give his financial records a solid going-over, find out what his hobbies were . . ."

"We might discover who wanted to hurt him," Nathan finished.

Trish sat up straighter on the sofa, her violet eyes animated. "I can get you into his house, no matter where it is. I think that's where we should start. You can tell a lot about a person by going through their drawers." She flushed. "Not that I'd *ever* do that! I'm a professional realtor."

Bryant shot her a worried look. "Are you sure you're up to this?"

"I read the newspaper," she answered quickly. "And I listened to Pastor Matthew's sermons via podcast on saving our city. I think we're being called to act. This group. Right here. Right now." She jabbed a throw pillow for emphasis.

Cooper nodded. "That's exactly how I feel. Something outside of myself is telling me not to let this go. That this stranger, this man, was my brother and he was murdered. I just can't turn away."

Quinton turned the gold ring on his right ring finger around and around. "All right. I'm in. Just let me get some dessert before we start the planning and scheming part of the afternoon."

The others echoed his sentiments and joined Quinton in the kitchen in order to receive one of his succulent peanut butter cup brownies. Cooper was too full from the half bag of Fritos she'd consumed to make room for dessert, so she was the only person in the room when Savannah spoke.

"Cooper." Savannah stroked the worn, supple cover of her Bible. "I find it *very* interesting that Edward Crosby is part of this story. I believe you may have more than one calling when it comes to this case. His being there that night was no coincidence."

Reddening, Cooper gazed out the window into Trish's enclosed backyard where bowed forsythia branches leaned over the brown-speckled grass. Cooper could easily imagine how well the yellow flowers would show against the backdrop of red brick come springtime. She wondered if Trish had planted any bulbs, whether the eager faces of crocuses or the blushing pink of silky tulip petals would open beneath the shelter of the forsythia two months from now.

What will Edward Crosby bloom into? she wondered and then turned back to Savannah.

"I don't know why, but I have a feeling I'll be seeing him again, though how Edward can help us is a mystery to me."

Savannah smiled. "Have you ever considered that *you* might be the one helping *him*? Now go fetch yourself a brownie. We've got work to do!"

6

Trish was true to her word, and within two days had an appointment to view the empty apartment directly above Miguel's. Since they couldn't directly ask to see Miguel's place, Cooper had had to concoct an elaborate plan to at least get close to his unit. Ashley had made this much easier by providing her with Miguel's apartment number as it was written in his Love Motors personnel file. Ashley also agreed to hand over a copy of the young man's file, but with a reluctance that Cooper didn't understand. The two sisters met for lunch at their favorite Japanese restaurant in order to conduct the exchange.

After ordering the businessman's box lunch, a hearty sampling of sesame chicken, fried rice, vegetable tempura, six California rolls, and a halved orange, Ashley slid the file across the table, careful to avoid spilling the pottery tumblers of hot green tea. Cooper noted that her sister had elected to wear a lined trench coat instead of one of her warmer jackets. She wondered if the choice was deliberate or if Ashley was feeling subconsciously furtive.

"What? No sunglasses? No pen that shoots laser beams?" Cooper teased, but Ashley was not amused.

"Lincoln specifically asked me to butt out of this mess, and even though I can't forget about Miguel Ramos, I can at least feel rotten about deceiving my husband."

Cooper waited until their waitress had delivered bowls of salad in sweet ginger dressing before speaking. Breaking her chopsticks neatly apart, she rubbed the slim pieces of wood against one another to smooth away any splinters. "You need to tell Lincoln how you feel, Ashley. You two have been brought together by Miguel's death—don't let that fade away. Be honest with him."

Ashley shook her head. "It's not that simple. Lincoln's very stressed at work right now. Rumors are flying, sales are down, and his daddy's breathing down his neck over the salary he's paying the finance manager he hired back in October. What Lincoln needs is a quiet and secure home environment, and it's my duty to give him that. After all, he hasn't discovered shopping therapy." She opened the neck of her coat to reveal a stunning silver and turquoise necklace. The chunky stones highlighted Ashley's cerulean blue eyes and her halo of blonde hair. As usual, her skin was flawless and smooth—every attractive feature accentuated by the skilled application of costly makeup.

Her sister's head-turning beauty, which she possessed due to the endless hours and ridiculous sums of money she spent on a team of beauticians, aestheticians, physical trainers, and masseuses, suddenly incensed Cooper. She felt, even though she knew it was unreasonable to do so, that her sister's salubriousness was a slight to Miguel.

Pushing her empty salad bowl to the side, Cooper took a sip of hot tea and tried to wrestle down her anger. She failed. "Then do as Lincoln asks and forget about the case! Me and the Sunrise members will handle it. Go back to your stores and your tennis league and your benefits. Forget that you ever found a dead man in your garage." Cooper hadn't meant to be so harsh, but her sister's ambivalence was infuriating.

"If *you* were married, you'd understand that there's give and take involved between spouses!" Ashley snapped, jabbing at a tomato wedge with her chopstick and pointing it threateningly at Cooper. "I will help you any way I can, but I am *not* going to feel guilty for protecting my marriage or for moving on with my life! You might not approve of what I do, but at least I *have* my own life. I'm not living with my parents while I wait for someone *else* to define one for me!"

The sisters glowered at one another until the lacquered lunch trays arrived. It was difficult to remain cross when presented with such an artistic arrangement of delicious food. Cooper picked up the rose sculptured from paper-thin slices of ginger and brought it to her nose. "Let's call a truce. We won't get anywhere bickering." She inhaled the heady fragrance of the spice and then gazed at her sister. "Did anything in this folder catch your eye?"

"There's not much there," Ashley answered after a punishing pause. "The standard hiring documents. Interview notes. A glowing recommendation letter from Miguel's former employer. And all the identification papers which we now know are forged."

Swallowing a savory mouthful of potato tempura, Cooper frowned. "Doesn't sound very promising. I sure hope Miguel's apartment reveals a bit more about his life."

"There's one thing you *won't* find in the folder." Ashley sprinkled low-salt soy sauce over her rice. "Apparently, every mechanic and lot attendant gets a nickname within the first few days of working at the dealership. After talking to his employees, Lincoln found out that Miguel's was *abeja*, which is Spanish for 'bee.'"

"Why? Because he worked so hard?" Cooper asked.

"No. According to Lincoln, the veteran mechanics usually come up with the nicknames, but Miguel informed them that he already had one. He said that he used to be called *ardilla*, or squirrel, but that he had traded in his bushy tail for a stinger." She shrugged. "The guys got a big kick out of this and made so many lewd jokes over the whole stinger thing that Miguel got really mad. It was the only time they ever saw him riled up, so maybe his pride over this nickname is significant."

Cooper sat back against the booth cushion and tried to picture Miguel's kind face screwed up in anger. "Let's think about this. What's the difference between the two creatures?"

Ashley shifted rice around in the bowl. "Pretty much everything. One's an animal. One's an insect. Squirrels like nuts. Bees make honey. I don't see how this is important."

But Cooper felt that the nicknames meant something. "A squirrel is known for gathering up goods, for hoarding them away from sight. It's a harmless animal. A bee is hard-working and has the ability to sting—to cause pain. I think *that's* the significance, Ashley." She put down her chopsticks, thoroughly satiated. "The question is: Did Miguel want a weapon—the stinger—to inflict hurt, or as a defense against enemies? I don't know for certain, but what this nickname business says to me is that he wanted to erase a past identity. The *ardilla* was left behind. With his false documents, a new job, and a new apartment, Miguel had a clean slate."

"And became an *abeja*. The bee." Ashley waved away Cooper's offering of cash and placed her credit card on top of the check. "I'm impressed, Cooper." Her voice was sincere. "I think you're onto something. You must have eaten some real brain food during this lunch."

Ignoring her sister's remark, Cooper took a sip of green

tea. "What if someone didn't want him to change?" She stared unseeing at their waitress, who hustled over to collect the credit card. "What if someone from his old life killed him because of what he once was? Maybe he couldn't really get away."

Ashley's eyes were tinged with fear. "Do you think the murderer's still here? In Richmond? Do you think he's watching us—Lincoln and me? We have nothing to do with all this!"

"I don't know." Cooper pulled on her parka and examined her watch. "Look, I've gotta go, but I think Lincoln needs to tell the police about those nicknames. They might have some kind of underworld significance. Names are real important to folks in gangs, I know that from reading the paper."

Cinching her trench coat tight around her narrow waist, Ashley nodded. "Okay. And don't forget to look around for signs of a roommate in Miguel's apartment. *If* you can get in, that is. I know Trish is shrewd, but she's going to have to be mighty creative to get you inside a rented apartment."

"I've already cooked up a plan that you'd *definitely* call creative. Believe me, we're going in," Cooper promised and returned to work.

As soon as Cooper clocked out for the day, she drove the short distance to the leasing office of Short Pump Commons. She recognized Trish's black Mercedes SUV, which was plastered on both sides with magnetic signs promoting Tyler Fine Properties.

Trish was on the phone, but gestured for Cooper to sit in the passenger seat and enjoy the heat pumping out of the car's air vents while she concluded her call.

"I am perfectly capable of handling the closing!" she growled into her headset. "I've already assigned you *plenty* of lucrative listings. I'm not dead yet, you know!" Trish touched her paisley silk turban and then softened her tone. "I'm sorry. I know you're just trying to look out for me. You're wonderful and kind and I shouldn't unleash my insecurities on you. Of course. Yes. Thank you so much."

Trish closed her phone and sighed. "I'm trying to cut back on my workload, but it's tough." She smiled. "I'm such a control freak. Cancer's going to teach me a thing or two about *that* issue." Placing her headset on the dash, she turned to Cooper and said, "However, I am determined to do my bit to get us into Miguel's apartment today. I trust you have a plan?"

"A crazy one," Cooper responded while fidgeting with her purse strap. "But it kind of requires you to, ah, behave sicker than you look."

Eyeing herself in the rearview mirror, Trish made a small adjustment to her turban and grinned. "If we can use this disease for a good cause, then I'm all for it. Let's hear what tricks you'd like me to put up my sleeve."

As soon as they were ready, the two women walked up the cement path into the leasing office. Cooper had no difficulty acting nervous. She'd never been a skillful thespian and hoped she could pull off a personality so opposite from her own.

Trish, on the other hand, embraced the plan with her usual confidence and strode into the office as though prepared to rent every vacant apartment in the complex. She shook hands with the manager, handed him a business card, and then drew him aside for a quick word while Cooper pretended to be absorbed in the company brochure.

Short Pump Commons, she read. *A World of Luxury, Fashion, and Convenience.* Examining the arrangement of the four buildings, she realized the "common" area in the name referred to a small, treeless rectangle dividing Building A from Building B. Rent for a one-bedroom apartment was a thousand a month, but if Miguel had also rented a garage, he'd have to spend over eleven hundred a month. "Pretty steep," she said to herself and felt relieved that she had a free place to live while she paid off her credit card debt and added upon the small sum in her savings account.

"Delilah?" The manager, a portly man wearing a wrinkled dress shirt and a yellow tie speckled with ketchup stains, was addressing her. Cooper had almost forgotten her pseudonym. "Phil Burgess!" the man introduced himself. "I see you've already got one of our brochures. Terrific! Your realtor tells me that your company, ah, The Inner Eye, may be relocating to the Richmond area and that you and your employees might be interested in leasing *several* apartments?" His deep-set eyes gleamed.

Instead of accepting the man's pudgy hand, Cooper placed both palms over her heart. "Our futures shall be determined by *destiny*." She bowed a little. "My employees and I are all very sensitive about our *spaces*. In order to serve our clients, we have to obtain a state of *complete* peace in our home environment, so it may take me some time to determine if the *chi* in these apartments is well balanced. I hope you're open to this approach."

"Of course, of course." The manager nodded rapidly and Cooper was superbly relieved that he hadn't asked her to define *chi*. "Now, *I've* never visited a psychic before—no need—but my wife has. 'Course that was back before she met *me*. Ever since she snagged herself a hard-workin' man, she doesn't need to peer into a crystal ball anymore." He grinned smugly.

"The Inner Eye doesn't use crystal balls. Those are *props* for carnival acts," Cooper replied stonily and Phil nearly tripped over his tongue apologizing.

"Please, Mr. Burgess," Trish interceded in a clipped, professional tone. "Could we see the apartment now?"

"Yes, yes, yes." Phil grabbed a set of keys and pasted on a slick smile. "After you, ladies."

The threesome walked around the clubhouse, where they passed by a sheeted, rectangular pool, a row of empty bike racks, and a putting green. These public areas were landscaped with neatly pruned evergreen shrubs and clusters of purple and yellow pansies. There were no signs of litter and the grass aligning the sidewalks looked as though it had been hand-trimmed with a pair of sharp scissors.

As they headed toward Building B, Phil chattered about the complex's amenities, the quality of its residents, the awards it had garnered over the past year, and how unique Short Pump Commons was for being the first complex in the area to own a state-of-the art tanning bed.

"Costs a pretty penny, too," he added proudly. "The sign-up list is full every evening."

Murmuring their approval, Cooper and Trish followed Phil up a few flights of stairs to the third floor. He unlocked the first door on the left and stepped inside. Before he finished switching on the lights, Cooper pushed her way past Phil, walked resolutely to the center of the living room, raised her hands to her forehead, and closed her eyes.

"She's gauging the aura of this unit. We should be quiet," Trish whispered to the leasing manager in a conspiratorial fashion and then made a big show of dabbing her forehead with a tissue.

"Oh?" Phil seemed flustered by the idea that he should remain silent instead of proceeding with his sales pitch.

Acting completely relaxed, as though she were accustomed to such bizarre behavior from her clients, Trish strolled around the living room assessing the peach-colored walls, a grouping of oil paintings featuring sickly-looking sunflowers, an overabundance of brass torchiere lamps, and the kind of sofa that uncomfortably encases one's body in overly deep polyfill cushions.

"Do all the units have security systems?" Trish asked softly, indicating the device attached to the wall next to the front door.

"Ye-es!" Phil answered enthusiastically. The man was clearly unable to speak in a volume lower than that used by a circus ringleader.

Trish approached her client and touched her on the arm. "How does this place feel?"

"I need to be a level lower," Cooper pronounced after opening her eyes. "The vibes are *almost* balanced here and I'm sure most of my employees would be perfectly happy with this apartment, but *I* must be one floor lower."

"We have some lovely units on the second floor in Building C," Phil replied.

Cooper shook her head. "That won't do. You see, I have to be facing north and I must have my rear windows positioned over a natural area. Also, I've got to have an even number in my address. Odd numbers conduct negative energy."

Phil's mouth hung slack in befuddlement.

"Is the apartment on the second floor available?" Trish inquired innocently.

Phil fidgeted with his tie, obviously stalling for time as he tried to think of a way to dissuade the women from focusing on the apartment below. "It *will* be soon, but at the moment it's not in showing condition. The, ah, current resident's possessions have not yet been removed."

Cooper brightened. "That's excellent! I'd rather get a sense of the presence of the person who inhabited the space *I'll* be living in before I move! People leave their signature on their homes, you know. *Please* let me spend a few moments in that apartment. I only need to stand in the heart of the unit—the living room—just as I'm doing now."

Both women gave Phil their most winsome smiles until the poor manager had no choice but to agree. He resumed his sales pitch as they walked down the stairs and then insisted on poking his head into the apartment before opening the door wide enough for them to enter. Cooper noted that the unit had not been sealed off by the police or, if it had, Phil had received permission to enter the apartment again. The front door bore no posted warnings and there was no sign that they'd dusted for fingerprints inside, either. They must have searched the premises and, having found nothing useful, left instructions for Phil and moved on to the next step of the investigation.

"This resident was quite neat," Phil said and Cooper thought she detected a hint of nervousness.

Forgive us for deceiving this man, Cooper silently prayed and then quickly examined Miguel's living room.

Unlike the model apartment, Miguel's stark white walls held no artwork. The monotone brightness was interrupted only by the presence of an enormous flat-screen television. Mounted to the right of the fireplace, it was the focal point of the room. A leather sectional was positioned so that no matter where a person was seated, one could view the screen with ease.

The glass-topped coffee table was not used to display pictorial books or sports magazines, but was a holding area for an X-Box unit and dozens of games. The only other piece of furniture in the room held a complex stereo system and a karaoke machine. Speakers were attached on either side of the balcony doors as well as in the kitchen.

"Could I take a quick peek down the hall?" Trish whispered as Cooper began her statue act for the second time. "I'm feeling a little unwell, but maybe if I splash some water on my face . . ."

Nodding, Phil held out his arm and gestured toward the bedroom. As soon as he moved off, Cooper examined the contents of Miguel's refrigerator. The produce drawer contained the rotten remains of several mangos, and the

meat drawer held a pair of rib eyes that had turned a repulsive gray-brown shade. Moldy cheese, a half gallon of
milk, coffee grounds, the usual condiments, and a case of
Corona rounded out the contents.

When Cooper heard a moan echo down the hall from
the bedroom, she knew that Trish was initiating the part
of the plan they hoped would rid them of Phil for a few
minutes.

"If I could just get some fresh air!" she cried weakly.
"The chemo makes me so nauseated!"

Trish was leaning on Phil so heavily that he could
barely walk, but as the pair passed by Cooper, she closed
her eyes and pretended to be completely absorbed in her
psychic reading.

Once they were safely removed to the balcony, Cooper
slipped down the hall into Miguel's bathroom. A quick
look in the medicine cabinet revealed a bottle of Advil,
shaving cream, aftershave, and a surprising collection of
costly skin-care products.

She hesitated until she heard Trish call out, "Thank
you!" before entering Miguel's bedroom.

Part of her felt indecent for entering the room without
an invitation. After all, the bedroom was a haven for most
people. It was the place in the home that bore witness to
hopes and fears, doubts and dreams. This was the space
where people talked to themselves in the mirror, hid away
in times of sickness, and whispered prayers into the darkness. It was a reflection of one's inner self and it made Cooper nervous to think that she might meet the real Miguel
Ramos for the first time once she crossed the threshold.

Miguel's sanctuary was presided over by half a dozen
posters of bikini-clad women draped erotically over the
hoods of luxury cars. The furniture was a matched set—
the kind found at all the giant furniture chains—consisting
of a queen bed, two nightstands, and a chest of drawers.

The pieces were made of dark mahogany veneer and had ornately carved skirts and feet. Another flat-screen television rested on top of the bureau and a cigar box next to the bed contained a TAG Heuer watch with diamonds on the face.

Normally, Cooper wouldn't have had the faintest idea of the watch's value, but Ashley had bought Lincoln a similar timepiece for Christmas, so she knew that it sold for over three thousand dollars.

"How could you afford this watch?" Cooper quietly accused the room. "The TVs? Steaks from Whole Foods? And the rent?"

"Have you found anything?" Trish asked as she walked into the room. "Phil's gone to the office to get me orange juice, but I don't think we'll have more than ten minutes to search."

"Miguel *had* to be living beyond his means." Cooper opened the closet, examining the divide between Miguel's Love Motors work shirts and a colorful array of silk button-downs, tailored slacks, and expensive leather footwear.

Trish whistled. "He must've maxed out a few credit cards on this wardrobe alone. Those loafers are Moreschis. Italian leather. Cost almost two hundred and fifty dollars a pair."

Cooper fingered the shimmery material of a black-and-yellow collared shirt. The colors reminded her of Miguel's nickname. "The bee," she whispered and then looked over at Trish, who was producing a strange, strangled noise in the corner of the room.

Joining her in front of the nightstand pinned between the bed and the wall containing the room's only window, Cooper bent down over an open drawer filled with lewd magazines.

"It's not the porn that's got me winded," Trish breathed heavily, "but what's underneath."

Removing a pen from her purse, Cooper lifted the oft-used pile of magazines until she could see what was hidden below. She saw three neat stacks of money held together with rubber bands. The bills on the top were hundreds. Trish reached inside the drawer and quickly flipped through the nearest brick of cash.

"They're all hundreds," she stated in awe.

Cooper shut the drawer. "He could have gotten credit cards with his fake documents, but not cash. Miguel *must* have had another source of income besides his paycheck from Love Motors."

"The cash is definitely odd. And have you noticed that there's nothing personal in this apartment? No photographs, no letters—none of the paperwork we all have stuffed into drawers." Trish walked out of the bedroom and Cooper followed her into the kitchen. "No catalogues, nothing's taped to the fridge, there's no calendar. Why is it our young man made no imprint on his own home?"

"Maybe he was afraid to," Cooper suggested and then jumped as she heard the sound of footsteps in the hall. Expecting Phil, Trish hustled to the sofa and slumped against the cushions.

The footsteps halted at the door and someone knocked tentatively.

Cooper's heart began drumming loudly, but she opened the door to find an attractive Asian woman in her early twenties on the other side.

"Oh!" she squeaked. "I'm sorry! I heard people in here and wondered . . ." She leaned to the left in order to peer around Cooper. Spying Trish, she apologized again, yet was too curious to leave. "Are you Miguel's friends?"

Cooper answered vaguely, "We're visitors."

Confused, the young woman peeked at Trish again. "Are you with the police? They interviewed me last week. Miguel liked to play his music too loud sometimes, but other than that, I hardly ever knew when he was home." She sounded regretful. "I tried to get to know him. He seemed to like to go clubbing, so I invited him out with me and my friends, but he never came." She pushed a wave of glossy black hair back from her face and studied Cooper's mismatched eyes. "I'm Lisa. Who are you?"

"Feel free to come in," Trish hailed her from the sofa. "I'm Trish Tyler. I'm a realtor. This is Delilah, my client."

Lisa tiptoed into the apartment. "They're already leasing this apartment? What are they going to do with all his stuff? Once, when I was opening Christmas cards by the mailboxes, I asked Miguel if he'd gotten any, but he said he had no family. Isn't that *so* sad?" Her eyes grew wistful. "He was really sweet. I had a crush on him, big-time, but he wasn't interested."

"His loss, I'd say." Trish gave the girl's arm a maternal pat. "What happened to Miguel?"

"You don't know?" Lisa's jaw dropped. "He died. No one knows how. The police were here for hours. I know because I was home with a nasty virus. They even had those *drug* dogs, like you see at the airport." She seemed pleased to be performing for a captivated audience. "But I heard one cop tell another cop that the place was clean." She crossed her arms. "*I* could have told them *that*. Miguel was no drug dealer! He was polite and nice and shy. And he never had anyone over, either, so if *was* selling drugs, he must have been doing it somewhere else."

Cooper looked around at the pin-neat living room. "I'm surprised the cops left this place so neat."

"Oh, I straightened up," Lisa admitted. "They let me. I told them I just wanted to do *something* for Miguel. I know that sounds dumb since he wasn't ever coming back here." She sniffed.

Touched by the young woman's gesture, Cooper smiled

at Lisa. "That was very thoughtful of you." Then, a thought occurred to her. "Does this unit come with a garage?"

Lisa shrugged. "Got me. Miguel drove some clunker he bought from Love's. *I* wouldn't bother renting a garage for *that* car."

Cooper suspected Lisa spent a good deal of time observing Miguel's movements.

"This whole thing must have been quite a shock for you." Trish gazed at the girl sympathetically and they chatted for a few more minutes, but Lisa didn't seem to know anything more about her neighbor than she'd already told them. Casting a longing look around the room, she eventually returned to her own apartment.

A few moments after Lisa left, Phil returned with a small tin can of orange juice. It was the kind stocked in hotel minibars and Cooper wondered where on earth he'd found it. She thought she caught a whiff of vodka as he reached over to hand Trish the juice. It seemed as though Phil helped himself to a screwdriver now and then in the privacy of his office.

Again, she felt guilty for deceiving him. "I like this complex, Phil. This unit seems sad to me, as though there's been some kind of loss here."

"Wow, you're good," Phil uttered in astonishment.

Trish rose from the sofa on wobbly legs. "Does this unit come with a garage?"

"We have several garages available at the moment," was Phil's cryptic answer.

"Well, we're sure there are plenty of suitable apartments for Delilah's employees, even if she hasn't found the perfect one today." Trish wiped the can lid with a tissue and took a small sip of its contents. "I would be glad to take a few brochures along with me, Phil. You've been so kind. An angel, really."

Phil beamed.

Back in the Mercedes, Trish and Cooper reviewed their findings.

They'd walked back past Miguel's parking space and had noted his aged Chevy Cavalier. The car's exterior was dented and scratched in several places and the interior appeared to be empty. It told them nothing about its owner.

"Time to pass the buck to Quinton, I'd say. I'm sure the police went over Miguel's car carefully, so that's of no help," Cooper said. "We need to get a financial picture now. Even though Quinton will be researching a person that doesn't officially exist."

"Well, Miguel's false identity enjoys watching TV, playing video games, singing karaoke, and looking at naked women," Trish remarked with a sigh. The two women watched as Phil moved about inside his office. "I do feel kind of rotten about putting on that act for Phil Burgess. The guy's just trying to do his job. To make it up to him, I'm going to go out of my way to send him clients." Her mouth formed a small smile. "Even if The Inner Eye isn't one of them."

7

"I know that nothing good lives in me, that is, in my sinful nature. For I have the desire to do what is good, but I cannot carry it out."

Romans 7:18 (NIV)

The next step in Cooper's investigation was to deliver the documents in Miguel's personnel file to Quinton. After completing her last repair job of the day, she drove to Wawa to fill up her truck and buy a hazelnut decaf. As her truck gulped down over seventy dollars in gas, Cooper called Quinton at home and asked if he was free in the immediate future.

"Meet me tomorrow," was his cheerful answer. "Let's go to Jimmy's on West Broad and order breakfast. I could do with a three-egg omelet stuffed with mushrooms and provolone."

"A pound of Japanese food today and a pile of pancakes tomorrow?" Cooper laughed. "I'd better go on a mighty long run after work this afternoon. See you at Jimmy's."

She turned and waved at the line of drivers waiting to use the pump. At five-thirty, Wawa was even more crowded than usual. With the lowest gas prices in town, people were willing to spend extra time idling in line, but Cooper knew she'd be risking her life if she left her car at the pump in order to go inside for a cup of coffee. She moved her pickup to the only available parking spot at the rear of the convenience store. As she paused to toss yesterday's newspaper into the Dumpster, she noticed a familiar figure jump down from the passenger seat of a RoomStore furniture truck.

Their eyes met over a row of industrial-sized trashcans. Edward Crosby smiled and strutted over to where she stood.

"You following me?" he demanded, popping a stick of gum in his mouth.

Cooper looked over his khaki pants and blue long-sleeved polo bearing the RoomStore logo.

He pointed at the embroidered letters on his chest. "Do I look better in this than in the last uniform you saw me wearing?"

Remembering the beige scrubs he'd worn in jail, she nodded. "Blue suits you. How do you like the job?"

Edward shrugged. "The money's crap compared to what I made before." He snorted. "I could make this kind of paycheck in a single day without moving a muscle. Now I gotta carry entertainment centers up three flights of steps while some woman warns me not to get her carpet dirty." He shrugged. "But I've got another job I like better." Without elaborating further, he gestured at the store entrance. "If you're going in to buy something, let's go. This man needs a coffee and I gotta be back on the clock in thirty."

Inside, Cooper poured coffee into the largest cup Wawa sold. As she fitted on a lid, Edward leaned toward her and whispered, "What happened with that dude? The one in your sister's crib?"

Cooper avoided looking into Edward's shimmering gray eyes as she passed him the coffee. "No one knows. Or at least *I* don't. Neither Ashley nor her husband have received an update from the police."

"Pfft!" Edward blew away a curl of steam escaping through a hole in his cup lid. "The men in blue ain't gonna report to your sister or to you. Shoot, girl. They forgot about you before the sun came up the next day." He shook his head in disdain. "Probably stuffed that Mexican boy's file into a drawer and moved on to bigger and better cases. They got things going on in *my* part of town and folks are *watching* them. That's what's important. You following what I'm saying?"

"They're all important!" Cooper retorted heatedly. "*Justice* is important!"

Edward stared at her, his jaw clenched and his eyes flashing. "Whatcha gonna do with that anger, girl? Let it go to waste? Or are you gonna use it? Change the world with it?"

Cramming a lid onto her own cup, Cooper shot back, "I'm doing something, don't you worry!"

"Glad to hear it." Edward's hard look instantly softened and he gave her a satisfied smile as they joined the check-out line. "That's what's so amazing about you," he continued, his smile dissipating. "You felt that kind of anger on behalf of my daddy. When he died, nobody else gave his death a second thought. Nobody gave a damn, but you wouldn't let it go." He put his hand on her shoulder and turned her toward him. "Because of what you did—the way you fought for righteousness—I've got your back 'til the day I die. I owe you, and a Crosby never forgets his debts."

Cooper didn't know what to say. She dropped her eyes and murmured her thanks.

"What was the Mexican boy's name?" Edward inquired as he picked up a package of Hostess cupcakes. "I could ask around—see if he was in my old line of work."

"This is a fake name, but it's what he went by." After scribbling Miguel's full name on a napkin, Cooper passed it over to Edward. "Shouldn't you avoid those places?" she asked carefully. "What if . . . you get drawn back in?"

"Nice to know you care." Edward returned the napkin to her. "Put your digits on here, too. In case I dig up anything in my spare time."

Cooper added her cell phone number to the napkin. She held it out to Edward and his hand shot out and closed around hers, forcing her to lose her balance and careen into his chest. "Of all the people in this town," he whispered into her hair, "I need *you* to believe I have the power to change. Understand?"

Once again, Cooper felt as though she could simply melt into Edward's chest. She wanted to linger in the moment, his breath stirring her hair, his hands capturing hers in a warm, strong grip. "I believe in you, Edward," she whispered back, her voice more husky than she'd intended.

"Now *that's* worth the price of coffee." Edward laughed and handed money to the cashier. "And maybe one of my cupcakes." He paused, as though debating the issue. "Nah. I'm keeping them both. I need the sugar rush."

He walked Cooper to her truck and held open her driver's-side door. "Be careful poking under rocks, girl. You never know what kinda creepy insect is hiding underneath. I can't watch you *all* the time."

"Watch me?" Cooper's heartbeat accelerated wildly. "What do you mean?"

"Like I said. I got your back." Edward winked and slammed her door shut. Without looking back, he jogged across the parking lot and climbed into the delivery truck's cab. The truck reversed to the accompaniment of high-pitched beeping and, after issuing a burst of noxious gray smoke, merged into one of the westbound lanes.

At home, Cooper listened to the message on her answering machine with relief. It was Nathan, imploring her not to go out of her way to cook him anything fancy for dinner as he'd had a filling lunch. Distracted by her run-in with Edward, Cooper doubted whether she could produce anything more complex than a BLT, but after taking an hour-long jog along the serene country road leading from the Lee house to the hamlet of Gum Creek, she felt settled enough to blend together eggs, vegetables, and cheese. She poured the mixture in a prebaked pie shell and took a deliciously hot shower.

Nathan arrived just as Cooper had finished drying her hair. He hung up his coat and the oven's timer went off. "Something smells good, though it doesn't seem possible that I could ever be hungry again after lunch at Grandpa Eddie's." He leaned against the counter and watched Cooper gather her hair into a ponytail. "My client and I split an okra basket and a barbequed rib and hot wing basket. After that, I *still* managed to eat an entire pig sandwich *and* peanut butter pie." Nathan washed his hands and began to chop the two tomatoes positioned on the cutting board.

Drawing the asparagus and Swiss cheese quiche from the oven, Cooper scrutinized the browned crust and smiled. "You'll get your fill of vegetables tonight. The menu is quiche and tossed salad. And all I have for dessert is a box of Junior Mints."

"The perfect movie snack. If you don't have Milk Duds, that is."

Nathan placed the salad bowl in the center of Cooper's table and poured the wine. Over dinner, Cooper described the state of Miguel's apartment.

"Stacks of cold hard cash? Just sitting in a drawer?" He was intrigued. "Maybe Miguel's illegal status caused him to feel safer having his money at home instead of in a bank. A savings account means more paperwork."

"But he must have written checks," Cooper argued. "How else would he pay his bills?"

"With a credit card. He could charge his rent, his utility bills, food, gas, and anything else to the credit card and then send them a cashier's check each month to cover the minimum payment." Nathan helped himself to a large wedge of quiche. "This looks fantastic."

Cooper cut a smaller slice and lifted it toward her plate, leaving a trail of melted Swiss on the tabletop. "I hope Quinton comes up with a major lead. If he doesn't, you and I are going to have to visit some of Miguel's favorite karaoke clubs this weekend in hopes of finding *someone* who really knew him."

Nathan twirled a length of cheese around on his fork. "Um, I might have to drive back to Arlington this weekend." He studied his laden utensil intently. "Rob could use a hand painting his basement, so I'll probably drive up Friday afternoon, before rush hour."

Rob was Nathan's college roommate, and though Cooper knew he was a close friend, she was surprised that Nathan planned to spend two weekends in a row in Arlington. Cooper contemplated another Saturday night without her boyfriend and frowned.

How can Nathan believe that helping his friend paint is more important than helping me investigate Miguel's murder? she thought crossly. *Well, I'm not going to let Nathan's absence stop me. If I have to visit Miguel's haunts without a date, so be it.*

Aloud, she simply said, "I'll be thinking of you while sampling neon-colored drinks and listening to people sing 'I Will Survive' and 'Summer Nights' over and over."

"'Summer Nights'? The song from *Grease*?" Nathan shivered. "I hope the songs are more contemporary than that!" He laughed. "Better bring some ear plugs. If those folks sing like Rob or . . ." he trailed off and shoved another bite of quiche into his mouth.

Cooper was disappointed and more than a little miffed

that Nathan seemed perfectly willing to turn her loose in a crowded bar so that she could question a bunch of strangers while he painted his friend's basement walls. Growing grumpier by the minute, she cleaned up the dinner plates in relative silence and then dumped the Junior Mints into a bowl.

The couple got comfortable on the couch and, after quickly devouring the chocolate-covered mints, watched a lackluster comedy in which a jilted wife exacted revenge upon her husband and his girlfriend (who turned out to be their son's science teacher). The final confrontation between husband and wife was especially slapstick and Cooper had never been so relieved to see the end credits appear on screen.

"That movie was a total flop," Nathan declared as he ejected the DVD from Cooper's machine. "I'll drop this off at Blockbuster on my way home. Thanks for a great dinner, Coop. Without you, I'd never eat my vegetables." He planted a brief kiss on her lips, squeezed her tightly, and then jogged out to his car.

Cooper watched his pea-colored BMW back out of the driveway. Long after the cylindrical beams from his headlights had been swallowed by the darkness, she stared out the window.

"Something's up with him," she muttered to her reflection. With a sigh, she turned away from the blue-black sky and pulled her flannel pajamas out of a drawer. When her mind recalled the sensation of Edward Crosby's breath in her hair, she pushed the memory aside and knelt down beside her bed to pray.

"Why am I thinking about the wrong man, Lord?" she whispered into her hands. "Why can't things just move forward with Nathan the way they're supposed to? And this whole thing with Miguel . . . am I looking in the right places? I feel like nothing is clear, but I sense danger up

ahead. Lord, I really could use Your help. Guide me and
protect me. Amen."

When Cooper walked into Make It Work! the next morning after catching an early breakfast with Quinton, Angela
met her at the door. Dressed in a tight red pencil skirt and
a snug black sweater made from an enticing fuzzy material, Angela's ample curves were accentuated by a wide
leather belt cinched tightly at the waist. A chunky bead
necklace encircled her neck and her nails and lipstick
were of the same tomato red as her skirt. Her platinum
hair had recently been touched up at the roots and her fake
eyelashes were especially dark and lush. Today, she'd applied her beauty mark just above her right cheekbone.

"You're a vision," Cooper complimented her friend.
"Are you celebrating a special occasion or are you and Mr.
Farmer going out on yet another hot lunch date?"

"This most certainly *is* a special occasion!" Angela
drawled. "We've landed a *major* shredding account." She
grabbed Cooper's arm. "We're gonna need a new truck
and a new employee to drive it, 'cause the *entire* office
park that opened off the interstate has signed up for our
complete shredding service package. And they want us to
start in *two weeks!* I can't wait to tell Mr. Farmer! We've
got to get an ad in *Job Finders* as of yesterday!"

"Get him to hire a woman. Even up the numbers around
here." Cooper pointed toward the front doors. There was
Emilio, leaning against the hood of a Trans Am as he
flirted with one of the employees of the Sun Goddess Tanning Salon located in the next building.

Angela shook her head. "You got a point there, darlin'.
Look what happened when he signed on that Yankee
Doodle Hunk."

Up until that moment, Make It Work! had remained
small enough for Cooper and Ben to handle all the mainte-

nance and repair requests. Then, Mr. Farmer had branched out into the document-shredding business and Emilio was brought on board. Cooper recalled how Emilio's arrival had disrupted the peace and camaraderie between the current employees and hoped the next new face wouldn't upset the group dynamic in the same manner.

"Mr. Farmer's not in yet?" Cooper was surprised. She glanced at the clock behind Angela's desk. "I don't think I've ever beaten him to work. He usually likes to pore over the latest issue of *Wired* first thing in the morning."

"Don't I know it." Angela popped open her compact and puckered her lips in the mirror. "Do you have any idea what it's like to compete with a bunch of gadgets and gears? It's enough to drive a gal mad!"

"Come on, no machine could hold a candle to you," Ben stated gaily as he picked up the day's work orders from Angela's desk. "The boss man's parking his car. I think this is the only time I ever gotten to the office before him."

Mr. Farmer entered the reception area with an audible sigh and a listless wave. He slowly pushed a ski cap off his head and stuffed it into his coat pocket. Static cling caused the remaining strands of his salt-and-pepper hair to stand straight up, like soldiers saluting a superior officer. He then removed a handkerchief from his other coat pocket, honked twice into its folds, and sighed again. His nose was pink and his eyes were bloodshot and watery.

"Sounds like you've got one heck of a cold," Ben remarked sympathetically.

Their boss nodded and allowed Angela to take his briefcase so he could use both hands to sneeze into the handkerchief. "All made worse by lack of sleep," he grumbled and walked back to his office without saying another word.

The employees exchanged perplexed looks.

"Don't look at me! I stayed home to watch a Cary Grant marathon on AMC last night." Angela trotted behind her desk, sprayed a curtain of perfume into the air, passed through the fragrance with her eyes closed, and clasped Mr. Farmer's briefcase against her bosom. "I'll take care of him. Emilio!" she shouted as their coworker sauntered through the door. "You're late! Y'all hustle off and get on with your work orders! We need some peace and quiet 'round here!"

As Angela sailed past, cloaked in a heavy layer of scent, the phone at her desk began to ring. She ignored the chimes and continued down the hall and into Mr. Farmer's office. When a second line began to ring, Emilio turned to Cooper and asked, "What gives?"

Cooper shrugged. "No clue. But I'm not sticking around or I might have to answer those." She gestured at the flashes of red lighting up on Angela's phone. Their consistent blinking conjured up images of irritated callers. When the third line lit up, all three employees sprinted to the locker room to change into their uniforms.

Quinton called Cooper's cell phone soon after she arrived at her second assignment—a small advertising firm located in the Fan District. A girlish secretary led Cooper to the room where the copier was kept. She eased opened the door and flicked on the lights without actually looking inside.

"I apologize for the mess," she whispered as her smooth cheeks flushed red. "Um, I believe some of the executives were celebrating in here last night." She cleared her throat. "Mr. Bowman has this . . . tradition. He likes to make Valentine's Day cards of his . . ." She stopped and then began again. "Let's just say he's gained some weight since last Valentine's. You'll see what I mean when you get a load of the copier. Uh-oh! I've got to bring Mr. Bowman his cappuccino. Excuse me."

The sound of men's voices caused her to hustle off, patting her hair into place as she returned to her desk to greet her superiors and distribute the carton of Starbucks beverages she'd been busy labeling when Cooper appeared.

The room Cooper entered gave evidence that the evening's festivities had been quite raucous for the higher-ups at Bowman and Peters, Inc. Empty wine bottles were toppled across the surface of a polished conference table, a whiskey bottle was overturned in the sink, and the detritus of vegetable crudités and a fruit and cheese platter filled the room with the odor of rotting food. Kicking aside an empty cardboard bucket from KFC, Cooper noticed that a collection of stripped chicken bones were heaped in the exact center of the table. Balled-up napkins littered the floor and, to Cooper's horror, a pair of ladies panties dangled from the light fixture above the conference table.

The sudden vibrating of the cell phone in her back pocket was a welcome distraction from the sight of the ruined copier.

"Are you busy?" Quinton asked as Cooper approached the machine.

"That depends," she answered with a smile. "I'm responding to a repair call. But they should have called a garbage disposal service instead. This copier is toast. Not only did some drunken VIP break the glass by sitting on it, but it looks like he proceeded to give it a good beating with a seven iron." Retrieving the offending weapon from beneath the closest chair, she examined the scuffed metal surface and shook her head.

Quinton laughed. "Oh, man! That must have hurt! I've heard of people my size busting the copier glass, but I thought it was just an urban legend. An office myth."

"I'd take a photo and post it on YouTube, but that goes against Make It Work! ethics." Cooper leaned closer to the top of the copier. "Yuck. There's blood on a lot of these shards. I feel really sorry for the ER nurse who had to pick out the *rest* of the glass with her tweezers."

"Or *his* tweezers!" Quinton added with an amused snort. "I like the idea of some bulky guy named Angus or Hans pulling them out. Roughly."

"I doubt the patient felt a thing. You should see all the empty liquor bottles in this room." Cooper examined the copier's battered paper drawers. "Any luck following Miguel's paper trail?"

She could hear a rustling on the other end of the line. "Let me dig out my notes. Miguel had been using his current set of credit cards for less than a year. I can't find any financial records for this guy before that time. No bank accounts, tax refunds, nothing."

Cooper was confused. "But he had another job before this one and needed forms to get paid. Wouldn't he have had a W-2?"

Quinton was silent for a moment. "Not if he got paid under the table. What was the name of his former employer? I'll give them a call and pretend to be with the IRS. Perhaps I can discover his previous salary and position."

"Double A Auto. In Norfolk." Cooper kicked aside a shard of glass with her work boot. "Though the recommendation letter might be a fake, too. I doubt Miguel is his real name."

"It could be," Quinton countered. "The documents aren't real, but he could still have had them made showing his own name. He didn't steal anyone else's identity. I already checked that out."

Somehow, Cooper was pleased to learn that Miguel wasn't guilty of identity theft, even though he'd clearly committed a minor crime by purchasing false documents. "I wonder where you can buy a fake Social Security card?" she wondered aloud. "It must have been good enough to fool the human resources folks at Love Motors and the DMV as well."

Quinton took a sip from something and exhaled. "Can't help you with that one. I'm fresh out of underworld contacts."

Cooper picked up a sliver of glass and touched its jagged point. "But *I* may have one," she mumbled and pictured Edward leading her into a shadowy alley. There, between a Dumpster and the rusted fire door of some vacant store, he'd slip a folded bill into the hand of a figure wearing a hooded sweatshirt in exchange for a whispered name.

Unintentionally, she gripped the piece of glass more firmly and the edge bit into her finger. The brief flash of pain jerked her back to reality. Cooper thanked Quinton, got off the phone and told the embarrassed secretary that the damaged copier would have to be replaced. She then headed off for her next assignment.

Cooper returned to the office shortly after noon bearing ham and cheese sandwiches on pumpernickel for herself and Angela. Ben and Emilio opted for Buffalo Wild Wings for lunch, but Angela refused to dine there on the grounds that she'd spend the rest of the day smelling like hot sauce.

As she approached the reception desk, Cooper was greeted by the sound of high-pitched barking, and she smiled as Angela's Yorkshire terrier slipped and skidded across the laminate floor in order to reach her.

"Why, Betty Boop! You look mighty sweet!" Cooper scratched the tiny dog behind the red-and-white polka-dot bow between her ears and admired the terrier's matching polka-dot sundress. "Angela, you and Betty are quite the pair of fashionistas. Did you spray her with your perfume?"

Angela swatted Cooper's arm with an unopened letter. "What kind of mama do you think I am? She's just come from the groomers." She scooped up her dog and planted a series of kisses on her small black nose. "I wanted to show Betty off to Mr. Farmer, but he hasn't come back from lunch yet."

A pout began to form on the secretary's mouth as she sat down across from Cooper in the break room.

"Is anything wrong?" Cooper asked as she handed Angela a sandwich and a bag of Rold Golds.

"Mr. Farmer's actin' real funny today. He said it was awful timin' to have a cold because he's gonna need every spare drop of energy to face his one o'clock appointment."

Cooper waved her pickle spear at the clock. "Who's he meeting?"

Angela frowned. "Hell if *I* know! I'm just his office manager—the person who books each and every meetin' he's had in the past *five* years. I don't know a single thing about this *appointment,* and do you know what? I'm not too happy about that!" Angela angrily bit a pretzel in half.

Hoping to distract her friend, Cooper told her about her plans to invite Edward Crosby to join her for a night of club-hopping on Saturday in hopes of discovering new information on Miguel.

"And Nathan doesn't mind?" Angela's pencil-drawn eyebrows shot up her forehead.

Cooper fiddled with her sandwich remains as her neck flushed.

"Oh, my word, you're not going to tell him!" Angela shouted and then leaned toward her friend. "Why, Cooper Lee, I do believe you have the hots for a drug dealer!"

"Former drug dealer. And I do *not*!" Cooper retaliated and then tore one of her bread crusts into shreds. "Actually, I don't know what I feel about him. But every time I'm near him, my body turns into jelly and it's as though someone's turned up the thermostat. I can barely breathe."

Angela shook her head. "Girlie, you are in a fix! This

boy's got a hold over you and you'd better figure out what you're gonna do about it before you see Nathan again."

"I know, I know." Cooper sighed.

Just as Angela launched into a string of questions regarding Cooper's weekend plans, a woman's voice called out, "Hello? Does ANYONE work here? HEL-LO!"

Cooper indicated that she'd take care of the lunch debris and Angela hustled out to her desk. By the time Cooper approached the area in order to collect the afternoon work orders, the visitor was roaring at Angela.

"YOU DARE TO TELL ME THAT HE'S NOT BACK THERE *AND* THAT YOU HAVE NO IDEA WHERE HE IS? ARE YOU A *SECRETARY* OR A CALL GIRL?"

Though she wanted to retreat in the face of the woman's overt hostility, Cooper had no intention of abandoning her friend. Taking one look at Angela's crossed arms and pursed lips, Cooper stepped in front of her.

"Can I help you, ma'am?" she asked the grim-faced matron who responded by tapping the toe of her boot in impatience.

The woman, who was short and pudgy but carried herself with authority, closed her eyes, exhaled loudly, and looked Cooper over. "Well, perhaps *you* understand the Queen's English." She spoke very slowly, as though addressing a simpleton. "I am here for an appointment with Mr. Farmer and this *secretary*," she spoke the word as though referring to something incredibly distasteful, "*insists* that he is *not* in the building."

"I'm afraid our employer isn't here at the moment," Cooper assured her softly.

The woman pushed back her coat sleeve in order to examine the face of her gold watch. "Well! *I* am a busy woman and I'm also a *tired* one, so I shall now march back to his office and wait for him there. No need to show me the way." She raised a gloved hand at Angela.

Angela shook her head defiantly. "I'm sorry, but I can't allow visitors in Mr. Farmer's office without him being there."

"You can let *me* in, blondie!" She opened her Gucci purse and dug out a silver flask from within. "After all, I *own* half this joint."

Scowling, Angela took a step toward the stranger. "What did you say your name was, Ms. . . . ?"

"It's *Mrs.*!" the woman snapped, flicking the tail end of her cashmere scarf over her shoulder. She waddled down the hall toward the office and then paused to call over her shoulder, "Mrs. *Farmer*! You got that, blondie?"

8

"For whoever keeps the whole law and yet stumbles at just one point is guilty of breaking all of it."

James 2:10 (NIV)

Cooper stood in front of the full-length mirror in Ashley's bathroom. She wore a leather mini skirt, black leggings, knee-high black boots with formidable heels, and a T-shirt covered with the design of a Chinese dragon.

"Add a tight suede jacket to the ensemble, and you're ready to hit the clubs," Ashley pronounced. She stood behind her sister and held an enormous pair of silver hoops beneath each ear. "Perfect. These give you a little ghetto edge. Now you need to tease your hair. And make it high. I'll loan you some gel and some decent holding spray. I'm sure you're still using grocery store junk."

Pivoting slightly, Cooper frowned over the amount of leg protruding from the short skirt. "There's nothing wrong with Suave. If you read the labels, you could see they're all made out of the same chemicals. Isn't this skirt a bit too short? How will I be able to sit down?"

"You're not going to be sitting down, remember?" Ashley laughed. "Jeez. It hasn't been *that* long since you were on the scene with Drew. You're only in your thirties, Coop."

"My *ex* and I went to mainstream hangouts, like the club inside the Sheraton. They played Top 40 music and didn't stay open past midnight. After I described Miguel's clothing style to Edward and a little about his taste in music, he told me we'd be meeting at a dance club downtown. And not until ten-thirty."

Ashley yawned. "Good Lord, that's late! I'll be in bed with Nora Roberts by then!" She slid an arm around Cooper's waist and squeezed. "You're doing the right thing. I admire your tenacity."

"Even though I'm going out with Edward?" Cooper asked.

"It's not a date." Ashley handed her sister a tube of garnet-hued lip gloss. "He's helping you investigate, that's all."

When Cooper remained silent, her sister stopped rifling through her makeup drawer. Their eyes met in the mirror. "Oh, my word, you've got a thing for him, don't you?"

"Edward's just more exciting because I don't know anyone like him." Cooper focused on applying the lip gloss. "He's intriguing. But you're right. It's *not* a date."

Ashley sat on the granite countertop and rubbed moisturizer onto her cheeks. "I saw the way he looked at you, Coop. Be careful. You'd better tread lightly around that man. He's like a caged tiger that's been released back to the wild." Her eyes flashed as she warmed to the metaphor. "On the *prowl*. And he's picked you, big sis, as his prey."

"You've got some imagination, Ashley. Let's go downstairs. I need to drink twelve cups of coffee if I'm going to survive this night."

"*Rrrrrrrr.*" Ashley made a rumbling noise deep in her throat and curved her hands into mock claws. "Come here, you sexy little rabbit."

"Knock it off, Tony." Cooper grabbed her sister by the arm and pulled her out of the bathroom. They stepped over the trail of deflated shopping bags littering the bedroom floor and headed downstairs. Ashley tiptoed on the carpet and continued to growl like a tiger.

"Why don't you save that act for Lincoln? I'm sure he'd find it appealing."

Upon hearing her husband's name, Ashley immediately ceased her play-acting. "He's going to be late *again*. I'm sure I'll be sound asleep by the time he gets home."

Cooper scooped fragrant grounds into Ashley's coffee maker. "Another dinner at Morton's?"

"With the finance manager. His name is Alex, or something that sounds like that. It's their second after-hours meeting this week."

Watching the steam rise from the top of the carafe, Cooper asked, "But why so late at night? Can't they have a conference during the day?"

Ashley removed a pint of rocky road ice cream from the fridge and began to burrow into its flat surface with a tablespoon. "That's what *I* wanted to know, but Lincoln got mad at me when I asked. He said Miguel's death has got everyone unsettled at the dealership right now, but strangely, sales are still at an all-time high considering it's wintertime."

"So he and Alex are working on promotions or inventory changes or what?" Cooper persisted.

"Heaven only knows!" Ashley shoveled the ice cream into her mouth. "I've never been too interested in the nuts and bolts of his business before, so Lincoln doesn't really go into detail with me."

Cooper poured herself some coffee and then turned to her sister. "One of his employees has been murdered. Your husband is attending a bunch of late-night meetings, and in the middle of winter, during a recession, sales are going up?" She stirred milk into her coffee and then wagged the spoon at Ashley. "You'd *better* get interested in the details, starting tonight! Something's going on at Love Motors."

Ashley nodded glumly. "You're right. In my heart, I've been wondering the same things, but I've been too scared to look any further. I have a feeling that I don't want to hear the answers to my questions. My life might never be the same again."

Touching her sister's hand, Cooper said, "I'm scared, too, but now's the time for us to dig deep in search of that inner strength. I know it's in you and I pray it's in me."

The sisters stared at one another, their hands clasped tightly. Ashley broke contact first.

"You'd better fix me coffee, too." She slapped the lid on the ice cream container and stuffed it back into the freezer. "I'm waiting up for my husband. And when he walks through that front door, that man's going to tell me *exactly* what his meeting was about. Or else." She smiled. "I can be a tigress when I need to be." And she issued a serious and completely menacing growl.

At ten thirty-five, Cooper waited by the front door of *The Flood Zone,* a downtown dance club located a block away from the James River. Hugging herself against the cold, she turned her head each time the club's metal door swung open. The blast of loud music and the scent of stale beer and cigarette smoke escaped as the bouncer waved couples and small groups of friends into the club.

Suddenly, someone slipped an arm around her waist. It was Edward, dressed in jeans, a black T-shirt, and the same leather jacket he'd worn the night they rode to Ashley's house on his motorcycle.

"You've let your hair grow in," she remarked over the thumping of her heart.

Edward ran a hand over the spiked bristles of dark hair covering his scalp. "My tat didn't go over so well at work."

He jerked his head toward the club. "Besides, my old crew would recognize me too fast if I didn't do something different." He glanced around the street. "I wanna have the advantage. Only talk to them if I need to. You brought the picture?"

Cooper handed him the Love Motors newsletter. Edward moved beneath the grainy pool of light cast by the streetlamp and examined Miguel Ramos's photograph. "Man, I've seen you somewhere before." He rubbed his hands over his prickly scalp again and frowned. "He wasn't a user, but he was in it. Somewhere, somehow, he was playing the game." Edward clucked his tongue and shoved the newsletter into his front pocket. "You played with matches and you got burned. What did you do, little man?"

Sensing that Edward had momentarily forgotten her presence, Cooper remained silent, but when a gust of frigid wind smacked her cheeks and slipped down her neck to chill her entire torso, she tugged on Edward's coat.

"Yeah, we're going." Edward placed his hand on the small of her back and steered her toward the bouncer. After the two men exchanged cryptic nods, Edward opened the heavy front door and escorted Cooper into a steam bath of strobe lights and gyrating bodies.

In such a crush of people, the pair could not make their way toward the bar walking side by side, so Edward took a firm grip on Cooper's hand and carved a path through the diverse crowd using his shoulder and a resolute expression that caused many a larger man to step aside. Women eyed him appreciatively and Cooper felt an unanticipated flush of pride that she should be the woman he turned to and asked, "What'll ya have, sweetheart?"

Flummoxed by the use of the endearment, which he uttered with just enough humor to make her doubt its sincerity, Cooper stared at the rows of liquor bottles, beer taps, and rotating drink machines containing frozen cocktails in tropical red, yellow, and tangerine hues, and tried to make a decision.

"Two Coronas," Edward shouted his order and then smiled at Cooper. "You gotta act fast or they'll serve somebody else." He pointed at the margarita and daiquiri machines. "'Sides. You're a tough chick tonight. No sissy drinks for you."

The beer came in chilled bottles with slices of lime tucked into the necks. Edward slapped a bill on the bar and turned around, relaxing his shoulders and taking a small pull of beer as his eyes surveyed the room.

"Damn," he muttered and his words were drowned out by the music, but Cooper had been able to read his lips.

"What is it?" she shouted and then took an unfeminine swig from her Corona bottle.

Edward turned toward her. "The fuzz is in the house. That's good, 'cause it means there's a deal going down, or one's *supposed* to go down. But it's bad, too."

For a moment, Cooper was confused. Then she said, "Because no one will want to talk about Miguel once the cops make their move."

Nodding, Edward smiled. "Brains and beauty. You can't beat that."

Cooper followed him as he edged around the dance floor. She had no idea that he was heading for a tall, black-haired man with light coffee-colored skin. Without making eye contact, Edward spoke casually to him. The only word Cooper caught was "papers."

The man gave Cooper a licentious stare and then jerked his head toward the restrooms.

"Stay here!" Edward commanded and disappeared with his new acquaintance.

Suddenly stranded beneath the flashing lights, Cooper distanced herself from the nearest speaker and tried to strike a nonchalant pose by leaning against a wall and taking lazy sips of beer. She pretended not to notice an attractive man in his late thirties smiling at her, but her lack of interest didn't deter him from approaching her.

"Your beer's almost empty. Can I get you a refill?" he shouted and then added, "My name's Rich."

"Nice to meet you!" Cooper replied loudly. "And thanks, but I'm fine. I'm actually waiting for someone!"

"Aren't we all?" Rich smiled again and Cooper felt herself warming toward the stranger. "I think I saw you two come in. Guess I'm not your type—seeing as you like guys with rough edges."

Cooper gave the stranger a sideways glance. There was something about him that struck her as incongruous. Like most of the other men in The Flood Zone, Rich was wearing acid-washed jeans and a T-shirt. The males on the dance floor seemed to opt for the colorful silk button-downs Cooper had seen in Miguel's closet. Those lingering around the fringes—settled at the bar or openly assessing the females closest to them—wore tight T-shirts with a variety of graphic designs. Rich's shirt was gray and featured a box of Good & Plenty candy on the front. He saw her grin at she stared at it.

"Says it all," he said cheerfully as the DJ paused the music in order to announce drink specials and future Flood Zone events. "I'd offer to hook you up, but your boy's probably got you covered."

Having no idea what Rich was talking about, Cooper murmured in agreement and wished Edward would finish up whatever business he was conducting in the bathroom so she could escape from her neighbor's penetrating stare.

"I've never seen you here before," she said, deciding to challenge him.

A shadow passed over his face but he recovered quickly. "I keep late hours. You're probably snug in bed before I even walk through that door."

Suddenly, Cooper knew why Rich seemed to carry himself as though he were on guard. "You're a cop, aren't you?" she asked, and before he could argue, added, "It's cool. I won't grab the mic and tell everyone."

Rich took a step closer. "You seem like a nice young woman. Stay away from the Colonel. I can see he hasn't roped you in yet, so you can still get out. Go now!" He had to shout again as the frenzied rhythm of music recommenced. "Before he comes back!"

At that moment, Edward emerged from the restroom—sans the tall Hispanic man—and made a beeline for Cooper. Smirking, he walked straight up to the undercover cop and pointed at his shirt. "Nobody calls them that anymore. Get yourself some updated threads, my man."

Unperturbed, Rich toasted Edward with his empty beer bottle. "Word has it that you've cleaned up your act. Working two jobs. Paying your taxes like any other true-blooded American." He fixed his gaze in the direction of the restrooms. "Maybe you can't believe everything you hear."

Edward shrugged and grabbed Cooper's hand. "Thought you knew that already, dog. How many bad tips have you chased down?"

"A lot!" Rich replied in a good-natured bellow as the music peaked in volume. "But some of them work out, like the one that led me to you! No hard feelings, Colonel?" He held out his hand.

Edward searched the man's face and then clasped his hand. "I might wanna trade favors with you someday. Off the record. You cool with that?"

Rich rubbed his freshly shaven chin and then winked at Cooper. "Sno-cone cool."

It was impossible not to like the good-humored officer. Cooper smiled at him before following Edward out of the club.

Edward didn't speak again until they'd walked several blocks east of The Flood Zone to a public parking lot. He marched up to a white sedan painted with the text *After Dark Taxi* and below, in smaller letters, *6 p.m—2 a.m.* and a phone number.

"Your second job?" she asked, breaking the silence. "And who was that guy back there?"

"A cop." The usual derisiveness was missing from Edward's use of the word. "The special drug task force, undercover, pit-bull kind of cop. The guy's a machine. I don't think he ever sleeps. He's like Batman. Shows up outta nowhere and takes no prisoners."

"Sounds like you admire him."

Considering this, Edward fiddled with his keys. "I respect the man. He gets results without treating people like they're scum. He reads them their rights, makes sure none of his buddies get the chance to slip in a few right fists or kicks to the ribs, and takes them in for booking." He unlocked the doors and he and Cooper quickly escaped the winter air. "When Rich Johnson shows up, something big is going down." Edward started the car. "The night *I* got busted, he wasn't even after me, but I told him I wasn't gonna rat anybody out and he just signed the papers and sent me to Jail West. No threatening or yelling or blowing smoke in my face. He gave me a choice and I picked doing time over getting chopped up into tiny pieces and being tossed into the James. So yeah, I respect him 'cause he plays fair."

As Edward started driving, Cooper checked her watch. It was well after eleven. "Um, where are we going?"

"There's a video store a few blocks from here. Let's just say they have a back room and it's *not* full of porn."

As a flush crept up her neck, Cooper drew her thin jacket tighter over her chest. "Fake IDs?"

"Yeah, and you're gonna buy one. Got any cash?" Edward had warned her previously that she might need to spend some money if she wanted to uncover a clue about Miguel's death.

"Two hundred. It's really all I could spare."

"It'll do. I'll make sure of that."

Edward parked in front of Doc Buster's Video, and Cooper had to smile at the name. Her grin quickly dissipated as she looked around the ill-lit street and noticed several hulking shapes conversing in the shadows. Shattered glass was strewn on the sidewalk, the streetlamps cast a bruised, purplish light, and the store's filmy windows displayed water-stained posters of movies that were popular a decade ago.

Inside, a man with a weathered face obscured by thick eyebrows and a scraggly beard barely looked up from his laptop as they entered. Edward strolled through the action section until the only other customer in the store paid a few dollars for a previously viewed DVD and then disappeared into the night.

Edward leaned on the counter and pretended to watch the *Law & Order* rerun for a few moments. When a commercial appeared onscreen, the proprietor took a drink from an insulated mug and licked his lips like a sleepy cat. "What you want?" he asked in accented English.

Taking out his driver's license from his wallet, Edward stated, "*Mica*." And then pointed at Cooper. "For her."

The man shook his head. "We got videos," he said, turning his attention back to the television.

Unfolding the Love Motors newsletter, Edward shoved the photo in front of the storeowner. "Miguel Ramos *recommended* you, bro. You trying to tell me he sent us to the wrong place?" Edward inserted an element of hostility into his tone and it came out sounding like a low growl.

Without taking more than a brief glance at the photo,

the man said, "You got hundred big ones, then you can go to the back. If not, go find ATM."

"I've got it," Cooper answered and strode through a set of pink bead curtains as though she'd shopped for a fake ID dozens of times before.

The back room of the video store was filled with scanners, printers, computers, and a camera on a tripod facing a blank screen.

"I'm Hector. You pay me first." A young man looked them over. "A license costs a hundred bucks. Social Security card will be another seventy-five. Both of you?"

"Just me." Cooper handed Hector the money and followed his instructions as he tinkered with the camera. Reaching behind him, the fingers of his right hand flew over a computer keyboard while he adjusted the camera lens with his left. Edward took an interest in a state-of-the-art laser scanner.

"Don't touch anything!" Hector ordered sternly.

Cooper tried to relax, to act like she belonged in the back room of a decrepit video store purchasing false documents. "So, do you know Miguel?" she inquired. "He told me about this place."

"I know fifty Miguels," was Hector's neutral response.

"This one worked at a car dealership," Cooper elaborated.

A shadow crossed Hector's face and then quickly disappeared. "Haven't seen that little *cabrón* for a while. His *cojones* too big to hang out with his old posse. Miguel and his . . ." he muttered something under his breath and Cooper thought he mentioned China and the word *blanco*, but she couldn't be sure.

"Well, I'm looking for him, too," Cooper pressed on. "Bastard owes me money." She put on her best indignant frown.

Snapping a few photos, Hector laughed. "Man, you

look pissed! They wouldn't let you look like such a she-devil down at the DMV. I should know—*mi tía* works there. Give Hector a smile, *mamacita*."

Cooper did as she was told and within twenty minutes, she was handed a new driver's license and Social Security card for a woman by the name of Erica Rollins.

"You're good," she blurted in astonishment and Hector grinned.

"Top-of-the-line equipment," he said, his chest puffed out with pride. "'Cept for the Social. I didn't have to make that one and Erica won't even know someone else is usin' it." He smirked.

So he's got stolen IDs, too, Cooper thought and did her best to look impressed by the variety of Hector's wares.

As she and Edward made to leave, Hector grabbed her by the coat sleeve. "You tell Miguel I'm ready to whip his ass on the court again." His dark eyes met Cooper's and then he glanced back over his shoulder toward the beaded curtain. "You'll never see a single buck of what Miguel owes. Forget about the money. I'm telling you this because I like you. You try to get paid, you get snuffed. You hear me?"

Suddenly, there was a distinctive throat-clearing sound behind Miguel. The store clerk was giving Hector a ferocious stare.

"You come back if you need more of Hector's perfect papers, *sí*?" The young man gave her a little shove toward the front room.

It was clearly a dismissal.

Climbing into Edward's cab, Cooper suddenly felt exhausted. The press of bodies in The Flood Zone, the conversation with Rich Johnson, the harshness of the winter air as they'd walked to Edward's car, followed by an illegal transaction in the rear of a grimy store had left her drained.

"You did okay in there," Edward spoke to her for the first time since they'd entered Doc Buster's.

Cooper was warmed by his praise. "What's *mica*?"

"Spanish slang for IDs. I greased that guy's palm in the club bathroom and he told me about the video store. I've seen him around. He's kinda the go-to guy for this part of the city. You want something—he knows where you can get it. He gets paid by the customer *and* the seller."

"Did he know Miguel?" Cooper asked hopefully. She hated to think that the evening's efforts were fruitless.

"Just that he remembered sending him to the same video store about six months back. Says he never forgets a face."

Edward pulled into the parking lot behind The Flood Zone. He kept the engine running but released his seatbelt. Cooper had been wondering how the night would end and what demands Edward might make on her for assisting with the investigation. Part of her wanted to bolt from the car, but her body betrayed her and she turned to him— fearful, uncomfortable, and yet filled with desire.

At that moment, there was a knock on Edward's window and Cooper let out an involuntary cry of alarm. A face appeared on the other side of the glass. It was Rich Johnson.

The undercover officer slipped into the backseat and popped a stick of gum into his mouth. He was as refreshed as Cooper was drained. "So what movie did you kids rent?" he questioned casually, as though it weren't after midnight and they weren't sitting in an idling car in the middle of a dark parking lot.

"Nothing looked good," Edward replied flatly, but Cooper's heart was in her throat.

Am I going to get arrested? she wondered and held her breath.

"Nobody's made a decent movie since *Forrest Gump*."

The policeman leaned forward and handed Cooper a business card. "In case you ever need to reach me."

He clapped Edward on the shoulder. "Colonel. I'll spread the word about your cab service. I know some women who'd feel safer calling a stand-up taxi service late at night. I'm certain they'd be in good hands with you. Have a nice evening."

Cooper exhaled and dug her truck keys out of her purse. "That's it? He's just going to let us go?"

"It's how he works." Edward gazed out into the starless sky. "And he hasn't let us go. He's going to show up again without us even knowing. I told you, he's freaking Batman." He sighed. "And now the Dark Knight has got his eye on you."

9

"He was given authority, glory and sovereign power; all peoples, nations and men of every language worshiped him. His dominion is an everlasting dominion that will not pass away, and his kingdom is one that will never be destroyed."

Daniel 7:14 (NIV)

During worship service the next morning, Cooper could barely keep her eyes open. She'd arrived late, missing the first set of praise songs, and tried to sneak in as the music leader paused to introduce a new band member.

As Cooper peered around in search of a vacant seat, Jake stood up and waved her over to his row. The empty chair was situated between Jake and Quinton, but Quinton didn't even glance in her direction. His eyes were fixed upon the plus-sized woman onstage as she smiled at the congregation and accepted the microphone from the lead singer.

"Thank you so much for welcoming me to Hope Street. My goal is to integrate a few Spanish hymns into our eleven o'clock service so that our Spanish-speaking friends feel at home." She indicated a cluster of dark-haired worshippers seated in the first ten rows. "So let's start with one that you all know. 'How Great Is Our God,' which translates to 'Cuan Grande es Mi Dios.' Please stand and sing with me!"

Jake had to elbow Quinton in the side in order to bring the big man back to reality.

"She's the most beautiful woman I've ever seen!" Quinton breathed in awe as he rose to his feet.

Cooper studied the woman. She had a large bosom and a full, high rump encased in a chestnut-colored skirt suit. When she turned to the side, moving forward with small, dainty steps, Cooper thought she bore a close resemblance to a hen. Her hair was full-bodied and glossy. It flew out around her face in rows of brown corkscrew curls. The most remarkable thing about her was the joy that seemed to fill her body and burst forth from her throat as she sang. Her dimpled cheeks and radiant smile were infectious and her voice rolled over the congregation like a river of milk and honey.

"You're right. She's beautiful," Cooper agreed and couldn't help but smile. The woman's rapture was contagious and the congregation sang the unfamiliar Spanish words with delight, grinning up at their music leader.

When the song finished and the congregation resumed their seats, Quinton followed the woman's every move as she walked off the stage. "She teaches Spanish in Church Hill," he informed his neighbors. "She even bought a house on one of the most rundown streets so she could truly be active in the community."

"What's her name?" Cooper asked.

"Gloria May." Quinton spoke the name with relish, as though each letter melted on his tongue like a piece of fine chocolate. "Sounds like poetry, doesn't it?"

Cooper waited to respond until Pastor Matthews finished his opening prayer and began reviewing the morning's announcements. "How did you know she was a teacher?"

Quinton pointed at the back of the program. "Her bio's

listed here. No mention of a husband, either," he added brightly and then finally tore his gaze away from the back of Gloria's head and looked at Cooper. "Did you have a rough night?"

"Yes, and I didn't have time to put cucumbers on my eyes, so you're stuck sitting next to a zombie." She yawned widely. "Not that I have any cucumbers."

"Did you stay up 'til midnight *painting* with Nathan?" Quinton nudged her playfully in the side.

Cooper dropped her eyes. She'd barely thought about Nathan until she heard his voice on her answering machine earlier that morning. "No, I was doing something *much* more interesting." She yawned again. "Tell you about it later. And Nathan won't be joining us for Bible study. He decided to spend the whole weekend with his friend."

Both Jake and Quinton yawned shortly afterward. "Stop that!" Jake hissed. "Don't you know yawns are contagious? The whole row'll be doin' it in a minute. 'Cept for Savannah."

"You can make people react just by saying the word," Quinton informed Jake. All three friends leaned over to watch Savannah as Jake described how tired Cooper looked and mentioned that she'd been yawning over and over again since her arrival. Sure enough, Savannah's hand rose up to cover her mouth as it stretched into an elongated oval.

"Where's Bryant?" Cooper inquired as she stifled a giggle.

"On the far side by the door." Quinton subtly pointed in that direction. "He brought his coworker—that single mom he's mentioned a few times. I think they're officially dating now."

Cooper clapped silently. "I remember him talking about her in the fall. Her name's Jane, right? She's in her thirties *and* has two children. Quite a difference from that grad student he was dating before. Maybe Bryant's growing up."

At that moment, the band returned to the stage to lead the congregation in the offering hymn and Quinton's focus was again entirely on Gloria. He sang without taking his eyes from her face, as though willing her to see only him. At one point, Cooper was certain their gazes met and Gloria's sunny smile shone a fraction brighter.

The four friends paid careful attention to the sermon, which was titled "Nothing Is Impossible for God." Twenty-five minutes later, Pastor Matthews issued a benediction and the service was over, but Cooper longed to remain, to hold fast to the feeling that her prayers could be answered if she only had enough faith. To walk outside meant rejoining a world filled with uncertainty. Cooper wanted to carry the sermon's theme inside her where she could use it like a weapon against whoever had hurt Miguel Ramos.

Trish had insisted on having lunch prepared for them since they were meeting at her house for the second Sunday. Once again, she'd sent her husband and children on an excursion, but when she described the outing they'd planned, her voice was stronger and more energized than it had been the week before.

Over a salad of mixed greens with cranberries and goat cheese, and sandwiches made with grilled chicken, red roasted peppers, and a cilantro mayonnaise (courtesy of a local café that catered), Trish explained the changes she'd experienced since the group had seen her last.

"The homework reading for this week couldn't have been timelier," she began. "The second book of Corinthians begins by describing the God of All Comfort. After I was done with Thursday's chemo treatment, I went to a Breast Cancer Support Group meeting. One of the women told how she'd recently written letters to her husband and her three sons. She called them 'just in case' letters and read one aloud to us."

Savannah knit her hands together. "Oh, my goodness. There couldn't have been a dry eye in the room."

Trish shook her head. "No, there wasn't, but the loudest sobs came from me. I never cry! And I didn't even realize I was until the woman stopped reading, got up, and put her arms around me." Trish picked up her Bible. "When Paul refers to the pressure he and the other Christians were under in Asia, he says, 'Indeed, in our hearts we felt the sentence of death. But this happened that we might not rely on ourselves but on God, who raises the dead.'" She tapped on the page. "After reading that, I realized I've been praying all wrong."

"What do you mean?" Jake asked.

"I've been asking God to deliver me from this cancer, when what I should be doing is trusting in Him and praying to enjoy my life *in the present*. Right after I adjusted my prayers, I looked around and saw my husband and my girls so clearly. I knew that I'd been given such riches in them, yet I couldn't remember the last time I'd told them how precious they are to me."

Bryant nodded. "Our study reminds us to be aware of the gifts we've already received. Paul also says that no matter what we ask, the answer, given through Christ, is 'yes.' I love that!" He smirked. "Pray big, right? I wouldn't mind taking Al Roker's spot on *The Today Show*."

Everyone laughed.

Quinton held out Hope Street's worship program and pointed at Gloria's name. "I'm going to be praying to meet *her*."

Savannah turned toward Jake. "Let's move on to the next homework question. Trish already touched on the first point, but what about the author's discussion on scent? Why do we smell like death to non-believers while giving off the sweet perfume of life among ourselves?"

"I don't think there's a soul on this earth who'd describe a plumber as sweet-smellin'!" Jake stated with a grin and then consulted his workbook. "I guess I do some things that make my scent kinda rotten. Paul would tell me that if I could forgive my dad for leaving us when I was a kid, I'd smell sweet to the Lord above. I keep tryin', but I'm not there yet." He shrugged. "Reckon I'm gonna be smellin' like a regular workin' man for a bit longer."

Smiling indulgently, Savannah said, "Perhaps Paul was saying that some people will find us unattractive because of what we believe, but to those who have similar faith, we emit a heavenly, life-giving fragrance. I'd like to think that we all smelled like that Clinique perfume, Happy."

Bryant scribbled a note in his workbook. "Happy, huh? That would make a nice present for Jane, the woman I brought to church today." His cheeks turned a bit pink. "First lady I've ever sung in front of. I think that's a good sign. She didn't flee the building, anyway."

The friends shared a few more of their homework answers and then Cooper requested they spend their remaining time figuring out what action to take in the Miguel Ramos investigation. She told them about her adventurous evening and then opened her Bible to a passage she had circled earlier in the week.

"Ever since I was a little girl, I've heard this verse in chapter four, but it never meant so much to me as it does now. Paul says, 'But we have this treasure in jars of clay to show that this all-surpassing power is from God and not from us.' " She traced the verse with her fingertip. "Here we are—these fragile, breakable vessels, and yet we're filled with God's power." She glanced at her friends, her mismatched blue and green eyes afire with intensity.

"Pastor Matthews reminded us that nothing is impossible through Him. Until this morning, I felt pretty certain we'd reached a dead-end over Miguel, but maybe we can tap into that power, pray for something impossible, and sincerely believe that it will happen."

Savannah leaned forward in her seat. "Tell us what you'd like to pray for."

"Guidance!" Cooper answered passionately. "If it's His will for us to solve this case, we need direction! We need to be shown a path to travel down, because *I* sure don't know the way."

Trish moved closer to Cooper's spot on the couch and touched her on the arm. "We all seem to be learning something about what happens to the plans we make for ourselves compared to those God has for us." She removed her hand and fussed with her indigo turban. "He sure changed *my* direction."

"Well spoken, Trish," Savannah stated enthusiastically. "Now let's pray together. And we won't forget to include Nathan, who we've missed today." The friends took one another by the hand and bowed their heads in unison. As always, Savannah began the prayer with thanksgiving and then spoke of the needs expressed by the Sunrise members.

When Savannah was finished, Cooper said a hearty "Amen!" and then exhaled in relief. She felt buoyed by hope. Her confusing feelings for Edward, the possible troubles in her sister's marriage, Nathan's odd behavior, Trish's illness, and Miguel's murder were nearly impossible for her to handle alone. To have lifted them up to a higher power allowed her an incredible sense of calm.

"Since there's no tellin' if we're gonna be detecting next weekend, let's do somethin' else to change our world." Jake began to dig around in his coat pocket.

Bryant watched him with keen eyes. "What did you have in mind?"

Jake answered by showing them a flyer announcing a community clean-up in the East End, the area of the city that had seen such an outburst of violence over the past month. "They need a paintin' crew to freshen up the elementary school on Saturday. Who's in?"

Everyone volunteered but Trish. "Sorry, but I'm going to be selfish next weekend. Phil and I are going to read the paper in bed like we did when we were first married and then my girls and I are planning to work on our scrapbooks and watch our favorite Disney movies while eating all the junk food we can stand."

"It's not selfish to take that time," Cooper replied. "It's a gift to your family. Would you like to adopt me for a day? I love pajamas and junk food."

"Don't worry about us, Trish." Quinton rose and collected his coat and books. "There's a certain new member of Hope Street I could ask to help out." His hands ran over the text of Gloria's name in the worship program. "I wonder what kind of cake is her favorite. I could bake something to take to her as a welcome gift."

Jake shook his head. "You got it bad, boy. Real bad."

Cooper looked closely at Jake, speculating whether he and Savannah were still close friends or had progressed to something more romantic. He continued to gaze at Savannah with pure adoration, fetched her food and coffee, and chauffeured her wherever she needed to go, but nothing else in their behavior toward one another seemed markedly different.

As though reading her mind, Quinton slung an arm around Jake and laughed. "Looks like we all have it bad! Trish and Phil, Cooper and Nathan, Bryant and Jane, and hopefully, me and Gloria . . ." he trailed off, his cheeks flushed with anticipation. "I just have this *feeling* about her, like my prayers are being answered this very day! I'm going to call her the second I get home."

Cooper mulled this over and then responded, "Edward doesn't really know me. He sees me as this Angel of Justice or something. But I feel capable of anything when I'm with him. Like I could rise above myself."

"And Nathan?" Grammy queried, reaching for another candy.

"He goes to church, cares about his family, and works hard. He's educated, funny, and . . . safe."

Grammy cackled. "You know, men used to say that all women were either Marilyn Monroe or Jackie Kennedy, but the perfect woman would be a bit of both. Damn fools. We've *all* got two sides. Edward isn't some beguiling demon sent from below just to raise your body temperature any more than Nathan is some choirboy who drifted down on a cloud from heaven." She wagged her finger and her expression turned stern. "Either way, you gotta straighten your feelings out right quick before you lose 'em both and end up marchin' down the aisle with Little Boy. So get busy with your soul-searchin', you hear?"

"Yes, Grammy."

"Go on and sneak me some of your daddy's sliced ham first. I'm feelin' peckish."

Even though she knew full well that the ham would end up in Little Boy's belly, Cooper agreed to the request.

She'd barely fished the deli meat from the refrigerator when Ashley appeared and hung from the open fridge door. Fascinated by how she was making bottles of ketchup, mustard, and dill pickle spears quake, she peered into the refrigerator's interior and slurred, "Isfereanyjuish?"

"What?" Cooper's eyes dropped to the bottle of vodka her sister's left hand.

"Juish! Juish!" Ashley bellowed in a most unladylike fashion and then hiccupped.

Quinton waved good-bye and hastened out to his car. Cooper watched his jaunty gait and laughed when he turned to blow a kiss over his shoulder. As the rest of the Sunrise members departed, she collected her purse from its hook on the hall tree. Spying an unopened package of Valentine's Day cards featuring Miley Cyrus, she groaned inwardly. Sooner or later, she was going to have to sort out what she felt for Edward. In the meantime, she owed Nathan a confession that she was feeling tempted by another man.

We need to talk, she thought. *V-Day is creeping up and that'll only put more pressure on.*

She inserted the demo CD that Quinton and Jake had recently completed and allowed the first song on their *Songs of Our Father* collection to wash over her. Quinton sang back-up and plunked out some simple chords on the piano. Jake had taken over the role of lead singer. His gravelly speaking voice was utterly transformed by devotion— made smoother and deeper like a rock softened by the power of flowing water. His classical guitar echoed the melodies while a Mr. Faucet coworker handled the percussion.

Cooper sang along to the title track, her heart swelling with pride as her voice joined in with those of her friends.

Songs of Our Father,
Lift high on the wind,
To the edge of the oceans,
And where the rivers begin.

She had just begun to sing the second verse when her phone signaled a new text message. Lifting the phone to eye level, she glanced at the screen. The message was from Nathan.

WILL DROP BY 2NITE. MUST TALK. OK?

Paused at a red light, Cooper responded by typing

"OK," and then hit the send button. A second later, her phone beeped again. Assuming she'd received another message from Nathan, Cooper gave the screen a casual glance and then frowned in confusion.

SEND ME YR ADDY. WE NEED TO TALK. E.

E? Cooper thought and then realized who had sent the message.

WHEN? she typed back and then jumped as the driver behind her laid on the horn. She waved at the vexed motorist and shot through the intersection, where she'd clearly been holding up a long line of traffic.

She almost drove off the road when she read Edward's reply.

2NITE.

"What's wrong with you, girl?" Grammy asked as Cooper returned from taking Columbus out to the field for a rodent snack. "You've been runnin' like my pantyhose today. Barely two words at supper and you've taken the bird out three times. He's gonna think it's Christmas all over again."

Cooper sat down on Grammy's bed and stroked Little Boy's soft, orange fur. The rotund tabby purred in gratitude and rolled on his back, winking at Cooper with contented, amber eyes. "I've got men problems."

"Men?" Grammy's eyes gleamed. "Oh, this is gonna be better than Rachael Ray's cookin'. Lemme get in position." She settled down next to Cooper and popped a butterscotch candy in her mouth. Little Boy heard the slurping and slipped out from beneath Cooper's fingers in order to sniff at the discarded wrapper.

"Well, you know Nathan. He's sweet, smart, and cute, and everyone likes him," Cooper began.

Grammy crushed the butterscotch between her molars. "I believe I've met the man a time or two. Don't beat around the bush, child. What's wrong?"

"It's Edward. The man with the motorcycle
me to Ashley's house when my truck got a fl
wound a loose thread from Grammy's bedspre
her middle and index fingers. "I went out with
night. We were just trying to find out more abou
since the case is still unsolved, but we went to a da
and—"

"I'm *old*, girl!" Grammy slapped the thread from
per's hand. "Git to the meat of the matter before
ninety!"

Cooper flushed and blurted out, "I'm tempted by l
I keep imagining what it would be like to kiss him,
have his arms around me." Her face burned. "I try not
but I can't get him out of my mind!"

Pressing a butterscotch into Cooper's hand, Grammy
eased back against the pillows and closed her eyes. "Lemme
tell you about this lady from church this mornin'. She and I
were waitin' to use the bathroom—you know they've only
got two stalls for *all* us women in that church—and I asked
her how she came by the sling she was wearin' over her
shoulder. What do you think she said?"

"I have no idea." Cooper wondered where her gran
mother was heading with this anecdote.

"Turns out, she was tryin' so hard to fit into a girdle
she pulled her shoulder. She had a date, see, with a fe
she knew about forty years back and she wanted to lo
finest for this man." Grammy glanced over at the f
wedding photograph on her dresser. "But she wa
same girl. We all change, granddaughter. There ar
ent seasons to our lives."

"Sorry, Grammy, but I'm not following you."

"What I'm sayin', child, is not to wrench lo
tryin' to fit yourself to one man or the other
barked good-naturedly. "Which one fits *you*
low wants you just as you come—flaws and

Cooper tried to take the bottle away but Ashley hugged it to her chest. "Thass mine! Get yer own!"

Placing both hands on Ashley's shoulders, Cooper steered her inebriated sibling to the nearest kitchen chair. "What the hell, Ashley? I've never seen you drink liquor straight. In fact, I've never seen you drink *anything* right out of the bottle and, in case you haven't noticed, it's the middle of the afternoon! What's going on?"

Ashley put her arms on the smooth planks of the family's farm table and allowed her forehead to fall onto the makeshift pillow. "Dizzy," she muttered.

"You need some fresh air." Cooper hoisted her sister back to her feet and nearly dragged her out onto the patio. They stood there for a few moments as Ashley groaned and Cooper wondered if her sister was going to be sick. "If you're going to puke, turn to the right," she ordered. "That empty plant pot will do just fine."

As though inspired by the suggestion, Ashley uttered a single, guttural moan and then emptied her stomach into the container that would be filled with fresh basil come summertime.

"Ugh." Cooper made a mental note not to partake of Maggie's first batch of pesto sauce. When Ashley had finished purging her stomach, she sank to the ground and pressed her face against another flowerpot. Cooper gathered her sister into her arms and wiped the sweat-dampened hair away from her cheeks. "What happened?"

Ashley's body had gone limp. Through closed eyes she whispered, "I asked Lincoln a *whole* mess of questions and I found out about that guy, Alex." She sighed and Cooper tried not to pull back as she caught a whiff of her sister's breath. "'Cept his name's not Alex, it's Alek. And he's *not* a guy."

"Alek is a woman?"

"Yeah. Go figure." Ashley pushed a strand of blonde hair off her forehead. "Alek*sandra*. That's who Lincoln's been with all these nights." Her mouth curled into a snarl. "*Aleksandra, Aleksandra, Aleksandra.*"

Cooper was losing feeling in her toes. Ashley's skin was cold and both sisters had come outside without coats. "What you need is coffee and a shower, but not in that order." Cooper wrinkled her nose. "Come on, Ashley, we'll figure this out."

"I've *figured* it out," Ashley sneered but then sagged, the fight gone out of her. An hour later, she was clean and a good deal more lucid. Cooper had loaned her cotton sweatpants and a University of Richmond sweatshirt. She then helped her get comfortable on the sofa, covered her with an afghan crocheted by Grammy, and placed a giant mug of black coffee in her hands.

Cooper sat down next to her and muted the television. "Feel better?"

"No," Ashley replied and Cooper was pleased to see the return of her sister's customary pout.

"It'll help to talk about it. Start from the beginning."

Ashley nodded blankly. "I waited up for Lincoln last night and just as he tiptoed into our room I switched on the lights. He froze like a deer in front of an eighteen-wheeler and I told him it was high time he came clean about these extracurricular meetings."

"Go on," Cooper prodded and handed Ashley one of their mother's iced almond cookies.

Wolfing down the sugary treat, Ashley gestured at the plastic baggie and Cooper handed it over, staring in fascination as her sister consumed three more cookies within a matter of seconds. "Sorry," she said in between swallows. "I don't remember eating today." She dunked a cookie into her coffee cup, bit it viciously in half, and then licked the icing from her fingertips. The latter action made her appear so vulnerable and childlike that Cooper had to refrain from embracing her again.

"Lincoln tried to convince me that the meetings were Alek's idea," Ashley continued. "That she's been working overtime to figure out how to make *his* dealership rise above all the area dealerships, including the other Love franchises. Apparently, she's worked at six different car places and knows more than Lincoln does about trends and cost effectiveness and all the rest of that junk."

"Is it her ideas that have made winter sales figures so high?" Cooper asked hesitantly.

"That's the picture Lincoln painted. Said she'd convinced a whole bunch of customers to purchase the most expensive cars their credit could buy. Talked them into the costliest warranty packages, too. The dealership makes a nice bundle on those." Ashley sneered and continued, "Plus, many of those customers brought family members in within a month or two. Husbands and wives, parents and kids, brothers and sisters. Customer-loyalty purchases out the yin-yang."

Cooper was impressed. "And here I thought the whole country was broke. She must have some incredible business savvy."

Scowling, Ashley tossed the rest of the cookies on the coffee table. "That's great, Coop. Why don't *you* join them the next time they go out to P.F. Chang's or Morton's or Bookbinders or"—her voice rose with every restaurant name—"or for a quickie at the Holiday Inn Express!"

"Did Lincoln *admit* to having an affair?" Cooper winced, expecting her sister's tirade to escalate.

Ashley shook her head. "He says it's all business—that he's been trying to get out from under his daddy's thumb for years. I guess he's cooked up bunches of schemes to change the business but was afraid to swim against the tide without proving himself first. *Alek's* smarty-pants ideas have let him do that now." Her face was infused with sadness. "He's so happy, Coop, and I had nothing to do with it."

Now Cooper did take hold of her sister's hand. "Then be happy *with* him, Ashley. Since things are going so well, ask Lincoln to spend more time with you. Have Alek over for dinner. Then the two of them can talk business and you won't miss out on seeing your husband. Get involved. Share your opinion. Show both Alek and Lincoln that you're not just a pretty face. You've always helped *me* out when I'm in a tight spot." She gripped Ashley's fist and forced the fingers to uncurl and relax. "Close the space between you and your husband."

"Easy for you to say," Ashley grumbled. "I checked out this woman's picture on the dealership's website. She's gorgeous. Auburn hair, blue eyes like a Husky, and judging from how much of the doorway she fills, she must be about six feet tall." She snorted. "And in case you forgot, I'm not much of a cook."

"But I'm decent," Cooper answered. "I can prep some Dijon lamb chops for you and Mama can whip up a fancy-looking tart."

Ashley giggled. "A tart for a tart. Perfect!" Despite the rueful remark, she'd brightened considerably over the idea of inviting the finance manager to dinner. "You're right. I'm not going to play the desperate housewife. I'm going to be part Martha Stewart, part Oprah, part Angelina Jolie. I'll do exactly as you said—close the space between us. Thank you. Thank you for making sense of this mess." She reached over and gave Cooper a hug.

At that moment, there was a knock on the door. Cooper checked her watch and wondered if Nathan had arrived early for their dinner date.

But he usually knocks and then comes in, she thought curiously as she opened the door.

It wasn't Nathan.

"Edward?" It was so incongruous to see his black-clad form standing on the top stair. She blinked dumbly, wondering how he'd found her house when she'd never replied to his text message.

He held up a bottle of red wine and a loaf of crusty Italian bread. "You didn't tell me when to come over, but this seemed like as good a time as any." He pushed the bread into her arms and she had no choice but to accept it and invite him inside.

"You remember my sister, Ashley?" Cooper said as they entered her tiny living room.

"Who could forget?" Edward answered with an enigmatic twinkle in his gray eyes.

Ashley flushed prettily and gathered up the afghan so Edward could sit beside her.

"Good thing you're here, too," Edward stated decisively to Ashley as though he was calling a board meeting to order. "We gotta go over this thing again. Right from the night you found Miguel. A detail's been missed. I feel it in here." He pounded on his muscular chest with his right palm and then examined a colossal stainless-steel watch. "It's after five. Let's pour some sour grapes, break some bread, and make headway on this case."

When Cooper didn't react, Ashley cheerfully replied, "*I've* had enough alcohol for the rest of this decade, but I'll take some bread. Got any cheese, Cooper?"

Cooper nodded and walked slowly into the kitchen to unwrap the small wedge of Havarti she'd bought the day before. As she cut the cheese into thin slices, her hands trembling around the knife hilt, she listened to the blending of voices as Edward and Ashley fell into easy conversation in the next room.

In the midst of arranging the bread and cheese on a platter, another knock sounded on her door followed by a burst of cold air flowing into the kitchen. Someone else had just entered the apartment.

"Hi," Nathan greeted her as he stepped into the room. He placed another bottle of wine onto the counter and removed his coat, only pausing briefly to look at Cooper.

"What?" He looked perplexed. "Am I too early?' He gestured toward the kitchen window. "Looks like you're having a party up here. I recognize Ashley's car, but whose motorcycle is that?"

Cooper swallowed and gripped the cheese plate. "Come on into the living room. There's someone you need to meet."

10

Cooper wriggled her toes in the bubbling water of the foot spa and sighed deeply.

The morning had not gone as planned. First, she'd listened to the curt voicemail Angela had left on Cooper's cell phone saying that she wouldn't be showing up for work. As a result of her friend's truancy, Cooper had been forced to man the phones and rush out during her lunch break in order to complete two repairs as well.

At five-fifteen in the afternoon, the nightmarish ringing of the phone finally fell silent and Cooper knocked on Mr. Farmer's closed door with plans to inform him that she refused to repeat the miserable experience of being Angela for a day. She felt as though she'd said, "Thanks for calling Make It Work!, how can I help you?" one thousand times. She didn't want to see a telephone for the rest of the week.

As a result, she banged on Mr. Farmer's door with more force than she'd intended.

"Come in," her boss mumbled lugubriously. Cooper

entered to find him staring fixedly at his computer screen. When she approached the desk, he clicked his mouse and a wallpaper image of M.C. Escher's merging black and white fish replaced whatever image he'd been gazing at with such mournful longing.

"Sir, I know it's none of my business, but have you spoken to Angela since your, um, since Mrs. Farmer was here?"

Her boss rubbed his temples. "No. She won't return my calls. I've even driven over to her house, but I don't think she's staying there. Betty Boop likes to be taken out at regular intervals when she's not in doggie daycare and there hasn't been a Yorkie in sight." He shook his head. "Nobody's home. I can tell."

Hesitating, Cooper spoke softly. "Sir, you must have known she'd be upset to discover the existence of a *Mrs.* Farmer."

Mr. Farmer's forehead creased into unhappy wrinkles. "Bea can be quite abrupt, I know. That's why I've waited so long—" He gripped his mouse and leaned forward in his chair. "Did she say something rude to Angela? Something horrible?"

Cooper knew she should tread carefully. After all, the woman in question was the boss's wife. On the other hand, Angela was a cherished friend and hadn't deserved the scornful, patronizing tone Mrs. Farmer had used to address her. "She was pretty impolite, sir. Kind of looked down her nose at us. Angela didn't take that well, but it was hearing that there was a *Mrs.* Farmer *and* this *Mrs.* Farmer owned half the business . . . now *that* really got to her."

Her boss's eyes bulged from their sockets and he eased himself to a standing position. He placed his balled fists on the desktop and hunched forward, looking like a crazed ape about to launch an attack on an intruder. "Do you mean . . . ?" He swallowed, his face drained of all pigment. "Angela believes Bea is my *wife*?"

"Yes," Cooper stated flatly. "What *else* would she think?"

Unexpectedly, Mr. Farmer began to laugh. It started as a wet rasp deep in his throat and then rose, like a gurgling water fountain, until he was holding his round belly and chortling with mirth. "Bea . . . is . . . not . . . my . . . wife!" he said in between guffaws. Cooper waited mutely for her unpredictable employer to calm down.

After an interminable minute, Mr. Farmer grabbed a tissue from the top drawer of his desk, blotted his eyes, and blew his nose with a loud honk. "Mrs. Farmer is my *sister*." Collapsing into his chair, he released an audible sigh. "Bea was married when she was very young. Like many gals these days, she hyphenated her name to Allen-Farmer. After her divorce, she just went by Beatrice Farmer, but everyone kept calling her Mrs. and she didn't bother to correct them. I think she liked being a Mrs. without being married! But it's confused a lot of folks, including you and Angela, it seems."

"It was logical to assume she was your wife, sir," Cooper pointed out.

"Sure it was." Mr. Farmer nodded. "Bea's also a silent partner in the business. When our folks passed on, she and I put every dime of our inheritance into Make It Work!" He shook his head. "Bea and I . . . we've been one another's main source of company for a long time. I think it's been hard for her to see me . . . fall in love."

Cooper thought, *If only Angela could have heard him just now!*

Giving Mr. Farmer her warmest smile, she said, "I'm sure it's difficult for your sister, sir. I know I've been envious of my sister's happiness before. Maybe when you and

Angela get together again, you can invite Bea along. Give the two women a chance to get to know one another."

"*If I* can find my sweet Angela, that is!" her boss exclaimed. "It's bad enough that I miss her on a personal level, but I can't have my best repairperson manning the phones, either. Ben would quit if I asked him to fill in and Emilio has that horrible accent *and* can't spell. You're the only employee capable of running the whole show."

Flushing at the compliment, Cooper eyed the wall calendar behind Mr. Farmer's head. It was unlikely Angela had fled too far from Richmond. Cooper knew her friend was fastidious about keeping the roots of her platinum hair touched up and would never trust anyone but her regular beautician to do the job. A stickler to schedule, Angela always visited her stylist on the second Monday of the month. She'd be due for an appointment that very afternoon, in fact.

"Why not write Angela a note explaining everything and allow someone else to give it to her?" Cooper suggested. "This way, she's bound to read it—especially if she's trapped under a dryer hood. As soon as she realizes that you're still a bachelor, and a bachelor who's sorry to have caused her pain, she'll call you right away."

Mr. Farmer grabbed a piece of paper and a green Sharpie and pushed it across the desk. "Write down where and when, please." He looked up at Cooper. "But before I rush off to get this situation under control, there's something I'd like to talk about with *you*."

Cooper penned the name and address of Angela's salon. "Anything serious, sir?"

Without glancing away from the letter he'd immediately begun composing on his computer, Mr. Farmer shook his head. "Only if you consider a new title and a significant pay raise serious. It seems that I need to divide our company into two divisions: Document Security and Leasing & Maintenance. I've approached Ben about running the shredding operation and now I'm asking you if you'll be my department head in charge of repairs and service. Ben gets Emilio and the new hire of his choice and you'll have to bring two more folks on board to complete your team." He patted a stack of paperwork with his left hand without pausing in his scribbling. "The contracts are flooding in, Cooper."

"Why now, sir?" Cooper was as perplexed by this as she was by the increase of sales at Lincoln's dealership. "The economy is so weak."

"Because Reliable Office Solutions hasn't been so reliable lately." Mr. Farmer grinned in amusement. "In fact, our main competitor may be going out of business any day now. Several of their employees have informed me that they're ready to jump ship."

Cooper pondered the impact of expansion. Their company would be the frontrunner in repairs and service, they'd own a small fleet of repair vans, new coworkers would populate the break room, and there'd be an influx of funds. Mr. Farmer had mentioned a significant raise. Perhaps she'd knock off her credit card debt once and for all. "My salary, sir? What would that be?"

Mr. Farmer spoke a number fifty percent higher than Cooper's current salary. Holding on to the door handle for support, she nodded. It took her a moment for the reality to sink in. Her employer seemed to have forgotten she was there until Cooper said, "I accept, sir."

"Excellent." He paused long enough to get up, walk over to her, and shake her hand. He then placed a manila folder bursting with disheveled papers in her arms. "See to the needs of our latest clients and sort through these employee applications. Your role as department head starts now."

"Thank you, Mr. Farmer!" Cooper clutched the paperwork as though it contained national security secrets. "I won't let you down."

"The thought would never cross my mind," he replied with a smile. "You're the best I've got and I know a good thing when I see it. Now go on and spend some of that new, bigger paycheck."

Taking her boss's advice, Cooper drove straight to the nail salon and plucked a shade of dark burgundy polish called Royal Rajah Ruby from the shelf. It was from OPI's India Collection and was cited as being the hue for "the prince's princess."

I'm feeling quite regal at this moment, Cooper thought as she slipped her feet into the warm scented water.

"How you been?" inquired Minnie, her regular technician.

Cooper thought, *I feel like my life is a big Tilt-A-Whirl ride. Things are spinning out of control and I'm just trying to hold on. I'm cooking dinner for my sister and her husband this evening, and my boyfriend and an ex-con I've got the hots for ate pizza together in my apartment last night. On the other hand, my good friend Angela's love life is back on safe ground and I just got a promotion and a killer raise.*

"Busy," she replied instead.

Minnie squirted a generous splotch of green lotion onto a rough sponge and got to work on her client's calluses. "You pick bold color! Always pink or beige for you before. You feel kinda wild today?"

Laughing, Cooper nodded. "Yes, I do! It's been a crazy few weeks."

A look of skepticism passed across Minnie's smooth face. "I no believe you. You church girl. Nice boyfriend. Fix machines. How *you* get wild?"

Cooper was accustomed to Minnie's broken English, but she knew there was no way to communicate to this sweet young Vietnamese girl that she was investigating a murder in her spare time. "Let's just say that when my vacation week comes up in March, I'll be good and ready for it."

An hour later, refreshed and reinvigorated as a result of Minnie's strong and skillful hands, Cooper drove to Ashley's house in order to commence with dinner preparations. As she washed plum tomatoes for the field greens salad, she couldn't help replaying the scene in which Edward and Nathan had introduced themselves, shook hands with one another, and gotten down to brass tacks on Miguel's case as though they were old friends.

It was only when Cooper recounted the exact comments made by Hector during the creation of her forged documents in the back room of Doc Buster's Video that they realized an important detail had been overlooked.

"And then he muttered something that sounded like *China blanca* but I couldn't be sure," Cooper had said as she'd finished relating her final words with Hector.

Edward had been steering a wedge of pizza toward his mouth, but he dropped it back on his plate with a wet thud. "*China Blanca*? That's China White. And he wasn't talking about a country, either."

"What is it, then?" Ashley had demanded.

"Black tar, diesel, smack, brown sugar, chiva, junk." Edward picked up his pizza and began to eat, his gray eyes distant. "Heroin. Good sh—ah, stuff, too. China White is pure as Arctic snow."

Nathan had gaped at Edward in astonishment, but Cooper's only reaction had been to say, "So we can assume that Miguel's extra money came from being involved in illegal drugs. Great. Time to tell McNamara and Wiser what we know."

Edward had shaken off the idea immediately. "What do we know? That Miguel Ramos might've been a runner. He didn't deal. He was small-time. A little fish. Doesn't help the cops a bit. They don't know who the kingpin is or where he's at. I gotta go to a shooting gallery and find out who's importing the China White."

"A shooting gallery? You're going to fire a gun?" Ashley had been nonplussed. "Like for target practice?"

Wiping his hands on his napkin, Edward had stood and indicated that it was time for him to leave. "No, darlin'. This kind of gallery uses needles, though there's plenty of heat there, too. Folks pay to shoot up in a protected environment. Sometimes they buy the drugs there, too." He rose and clapped Nathan on the back. "Nice to meet you, man. Catch you later, ladies."

Once he'd gone, Nathan had turned to Cooper and said, "Interesting fellow," and then he'd also departed, claiming he needed rest from three straight days of physical labor.

"They're fleeing from you like flies from the swatter," Ashley had teased on her way out the door.

Now, twenty-four hours later, Cooper was in Ashley's kitchen rubbing olive oil into a fortune's worth of lamb chops while her sister trimmed a bouquet of long-stemmed, winter-white roses. Cooper didn't regret her offer to cook dinner for Ashley, but she desperately wished she could spend the evening in quiet reflection instead. The last few weeks had been tumultuous, and if she could just focus on something uplifting, like her Corinthians Bible study assignments, she knew the ongoing drama of Miguel's death wouldn't seem all-encompassing.

Several times throughout the day, Cooper had removed Rich Johnson's card from her wallet and smoothed her fingers over the embossed black letters. He headed up the city's special drug task force unit, so it made sense to tell him about Miguel's connection to the heroin known as China White. True, she had nothing more to offer than a mumbled Spanish phrase, but perhaps it would be enough of a lead for someone as dogged as Officer Johnson to follow. However, she'd promised to give Edward until the end of the week to come up with a more definitive clue and was now forced to keep her word, despite the fact that she worried about his safety and his proximity to the vices of his former way of life.

"Didn't I buy lovely chops?" Ashley asked, breezing into the kitchen with all the glamour of a movie star. She wore a cashmere sweater in a rich indigo hue, a shimmering gray skirt, and a diamond and pearl necklace that would have made Liz Taylor jealous.

Cooper nodded. "You look gorgeous, sis. What's your pre-dinner game plan?"

"Cosmos in the living room." Ashley removed chilled martini glasses from the refrigerator. "The fireplace is lit, the roses will be in the Waterford vase Lincoln gave me for our second anniversary, and I've got the cutest little cocktail napkins to set out." She handed Cooper a pink and green napkin showing a cartoon woman seated in front of a line of liquor bottles. The caption read, "Some people call it a problem. I call it a hobby."

Laughing, Cooper turned her attention to mashing potatoes in one of Ashley's stainless-steel mixing bowls. She blended sautéed garlic, melted butter, and a scoop of sour cream into the steaming starch and then transferred the fragrant mound into a celery-colored porcelain bowl. At that point, the doorbell rang and the two sisters heard Lincoln's voice in the hallway welcoming his coworker to his home.

"Showtime," Ashley whispered with a playful wink and scooped up the cocktail shaker. "See you after you've got the chops in the oven."

"Remember to put on the oven mitts when you carry the platter into the dining room!" Cooper called after her. "If you're going to pretend to be the chef, you've got to look the part."

Setting the oven to broil, Cooper arranged asparagus spears into a symmetrical fan and drizzled Hollandaise sauce over the green stalks in a zigzag pattern. By the time the French baguette was sliced and placed in a lined basket and the chops had finished broiling until a fine bark of Dijon mustard had formed on the surface of the tender meat, Cooper assumed the threesome in the living room had had ample time to finish their first round of drinks. She washed her hands, put on her wool coat, and walked out through the garage and to the front door. Knocking, she entered the house and hung her coat on the hall tree. Pretending to follow the sound of voices, she meandered into the living room where Ashley greeted her warmly and pressed a martini glass into her hand.

"Aleksandra Jones, this is my big sister, Cooper," Ashley informed the statuesque beauty standing to the side of the fireplace.

The woman, who had translucently pale skin, icy blue eyes, and dark auburn hair shorn in a sharp razor cut just below the ears, reached out a slim arm and offered Cooper her hand. Every finger but the thumb held a gold and gemstone ring, and one of the jewels took a nip of Cooper's flesh as the two women shook hands.

Taking a calculating sip of her cocktail, Aleksandra reminded Ashley that she was accustomed to being called Alek. She used the clipped formal tone of a member of the aristocracy remonstrating a household servant. Her voice was deep and low and was punctuated with authority.

"Of *course*," Ashley responded to the reprimand with equal haughtiness, her tone pure Scarlett O'Hara. "*Do* forgive me. It's just that Alek sounds *so* masculine and you are the very *picture* of all things feminine."

The battle has begun, Cooper thought and took a generous swallow of her Cosmopolitan.

"I am in a business dominated by men," Alek stated,

ignoring the barbed compliment. "It is best to fit in so that your ideas are not dismissed. Don't you find that to be true in your line of work?"

Momentarily flustered, Ashley paused. Cooper filled in the silence by saying, "Charity work is often dominated by women, but Ashley knows how to organize a group like a five-star general. Because of her devotion and leadership skills, thousands of dollars have been raised to benefit local charities."

Alek produced an unimpressed frown. "Isn't that a great deal of effort to put forth for strangers who will never know of your sacrifice?" She gestured at the photos of her hosts on the mantelpiece. "And you have no children to fill this big house?"

This time, Lincoln intervened. "Honey, I think I hear a bell going off in the kitchen."

After calmly indicating that everyone should proceed into the dining room, Ashley darted off for the kitchen.

Cooper filled in the silence by telling their guest about her career. "I'm in a line of work traditionally occupied by men," she said, and told Alek about Make It Work! until Ashley reappeared wearing a Vera Bradley apron and matching oven mitts. Pushing open the swinging door between the kitchen and dining room with her hip, she proudly deposited the platter of warm lamb chops in front of her husband.

"Would you serve, darling, while I collect the rest of our meal?"

Lincoln admired the entrée for a moment and then asked Cooper and Alek to hold out their dinner plates. "These are some gorgeous chops!" He smiled at Ashley as she reentered with the potatoes and asparagus. "What a feast. Sweetheart, it's better than any restaurant!"

"I even made that honey butter you like. Let me just fetch the bread and your *homemade* butter. Be back in a wink."

Ashley didn't notice Lincoln's appreciative glance at his wife as she disappeared through the swinging door, but it hadn't gone unnoticed by Cooper or Alek, and while Cooper was thrilled for her sister, Alek appeared rather displeased. However, the second Lincoln passed his co-worker the bowl of potatoes, she plastered on a smile that would have made a jester proud and launched into a diatribe on climbing interest rates.

She was well into her monologue when Ashley took her seat. Lincoln listened politely to his guest and murmured in agreement a time or two, but his eyes kept returning to his wife's face. The couple exchanged knowing smiles while Ashley repeatedly praised Alek for her business acumen. Then, she began to make gentle inquiries regarding the other woman's personal life.

"Those brains *plus* the figure of a supermodel—you must have a dozen boyfriends!" Ashley exclaimed. "I bet you can even change a light bulb without standing on a stool. Men just *adore* tall, powerful women such as yourself."

Alek waved off the suggestion. "I have no time for such indulgences. My job is my life."

"So are you from this area originally?" Cooper asked in hopes of keeping the conversation flowing.

"No. It's such a pity I don't have the *charming* accent of those born here." Alek cocked her head as though seeing Cooper for the first time. "Do you have the opportunity to travel much doing your, ah, copier repair work?"

Cooper paused in the act of cutting a piece of her lamb chop. "I haven't even crossed the Atlantic. All of my jobs are in the metro Richmond area." Staring into the flickering candlelight, it was difficult not to turn wistful. "I'd like to go to another country. I could drive to Mexico, but I don't speak Spanish, so I'm not sure what the experience

would be like. Do you speak any foreign languages?"
Cooper pushed the wine bottle in Alek's direction.

"Four, actually. Including Spanish," Alek stated flatly
and poured herself a second glass of wine.

Ashley shot Cooper a questioning look and then began
to clear away the dishes. "Irish coffee and miniature
chocolate crème brulée for dessert. Be right back!"

"Let me help," Cooper said, quickly rising to her feet.
She hadn't prepared any dessert, but when she saw the
bakery box on Ashley's counter, she was relieved. "I was
worried there for a sec. There are limits to my culinary
skills, you know."

"You've done enough, Coop, and *I* can actually make
Irish coffee." Ashley giggled, the flush on her face indicating a slight inebriation combined with the satisfaction of
having successfully played the charming hostess. "Why
did you ask her about whether or not she spoke another
language?"

Cooper shrugged. "I don't know. I just wanted to see if
she'd react at all when I mentioned Mexico, but either she's
a great actress or my remark didn't serve as a reminder that
she'd murdered Miguel and thrown his body in the trunk of
a rental car."

Ashley poked Cooper in the ribs with a teaspoon.
"You're so naughty! I think Alek's lethal, all right, but not
in *that* way." She took the individual ramekins of crème
brulée out of the oven. "Come on, I don't want to leave
Lincoln alone with that tigress. *Not* that I'm afraid he's attracted to her, but because she might poison my wine glass
while he's not looking!"

It took the two sisters several minutes to warm the dessert and pour the coffees into tall glass mugs. Alek's seat
was empty when they returned to the dining room.

"She's powdering her nose," Lincoln whispered and

then pulled Ashley down into his lap. "Thank you for inviting her tonight, honey. I think, deep down, she's really lonely. You're too sweet and I don't deserve you. I am a lucky, lucky man." He kissed her on the cheek and she nuzzled against his chest.

Cooper busied herself by refolding her napkin until it was a perfect square. When the married couple's kisses grew more ardent, she cleared her throat. "I'll just go and see what's keeping your other guest."

The plush carpet in the hallway muffling her footsteps, she quietly approached the bathroom. The door had been left slightly ajar and as Cooper raised her hand to rap on the frame, Alek leaned into the mirror and applied a fresh coat of lipstick. At such an angle, Cooper had an unobstructed view of the other woman's face.

"Who could ask for a more perfect boss?" Alek puckered her lips and scrutinized the monogrammed hand towels. "And his silly little wife? *She's* no threat to me." This remark was followed by a derisive snort. She appraised her reflection with satisfaction, and then her mouth formed a twisted smile and her shoulders shook in silent mirth.

Cooper backed away from the door and retreated to the dining room. Ashley and Lincoln had separated and were sipping their coffee while talking softly to one another. It was time to leave the married couple alone.

"I'm going to call it a night, you two." She gave Ashley a kiss on the cheek and squeezed Lincoln's shoulder as Alek entered the room. "Thank you for a lovely dinner." She smiled at Alek, though she felt more like tossing a glass of red wine in the woman's face instead. "It was a pleasure to meet you."

Confident that the arrogant and thoroughly unpleasant woman wouldn't linger much longer, Cooper showed herself out.

11

Flowers appear on the earth;
the season of singing has come,
the cooing of doves
is heard in our land.

Song of Solomon 2:12 (NIV)

Angela was back at her desk the next day, surrounded by such an abundance of red, pink, and blush-colored roses that Cooper had to part the blooms in order to see her friend's face.

"Looks like Valentine's Day came early," she commented as Angela's mouth curved into an illuminating smile.

Jumping up from her chair, Angela raced around her desk as quickly as she could in four-inch, patent leather pumps and threw her arms around Cooper. "Cupid sure found me, thanks to you!" She dropped her arms and tugged on her form-fitting, bubble-gum pink sweater, which had snaked up over her curvy hips. "There I was, at my hairdresser's, busy lookin' at the latest pictures of Britney and Lindsay and that *delicious* George Clooney, when Ginny hands me a letter."

"Written by a plump cherub with wings?" Cooper teased.

Angela wiggled a red, manicured talon at her. "My man's a little round, but then again, so am I. That's why we fit so well together when we're snugglin' in bed." She raised and lowered her eyebrows impishly.

Cooper put her hands over her eyes. "I do *not* need that kind of visual of my boss, thank you very much."

"Anyhow," Angela continued, "I open the thing, read it, and leapt right outta my seat. Well, not *right* out, seein' as I was under the dryer. I smacked my head on that thing like nobody's business, but it knocked a lick of sense into me. How could I have assumed the worst without even askin' my man for an explanation? I never even gave him the *courtesy* of hearin' his side of the matter."

"The important thing is that you're back together and that *you're* the one answering the office phones again." Cooper pointed at the apparatus. "I don't know how you do it, Angela. You're sweetness and courtesy all day long, no matter how crazed or demanding our clients act."

"Oh, I draw nasty pictures of the ones who are mean to me. Why do you think I burn through notebooks so fast?" Angela winked. "Now. I've got a little gift for you for covering for me *and* for bein' such an *amazing* friend."

Cooper gathered the day's work orders. "You didn't have to get me anything. I'm thrilled to see you and Mr. Farmer happy. That's reward enough."

"I knew you'd say somethin' silly like that, but you can't return this gift, so you're gonna have to accept it!" Angela grabbed Cooper's hand and led her to Mr. Farmer's unoccupied office.

There, huddled in a shallow basket lined with a green gingham blanket, were two black and white kittens. Judging from the pink and blue rhinestone collars Angela had placed around their necks, Cooper concluded the tiny cats were brother and sister.

"You need company in that apartment of yours," Angela whispered. "These guys are too young to go outside 'til spring, so all three of you can snuggle away the rest of the winter. Or, all *four* of you, if Nathan's there, too." She reached into the basket, removed the male kitten from within, and placed him in Cooper's arms. "Or is it Edward you're gettin' cozy with these days?"

The kitten opened his yellow eyes, yawned, and began to knead her chest with his little claws. Cooper nuzzled her face against the fur of his chin and he immediately began to purr.

"Precious thing," she murmured. "You smell like clean clothes fresh from the dryer." Reluctantly, she placed the kitten back into its warm nest and gently stroked the top of his sister's head. The little cat wriggled a bit in her sleep and the black line of her mouth curved into a contented grin, but she did not open her eyes. Cooper turned to Angela. "I can't believe you got me kittens! That's a pretty high-risk gift! What if I was allergic or didn't like cats?" she teased.

"*Please!* Your Grammy's practically a reincarnation of Noah. You could *never* turn away a homeless animal." Gloating, Angela crossed her arms. "And I knew you and these furry treasures *needed* each another. Mr. Farmer will keep an eye on 'em today and I've got a carrier for you to use to bring the sweet darlin's home, but I imagine you'll be off to Food Lion durin' your lunch break. Good thing you got that raise and can support your new family. Take it from me—gourmet pet food's more expensive per ounce than filet mignon!"

Cooper caressed the kittens again and then sat still for a moment, watching the rise and fall of their sides as they slumbered. "Thank you, Angela. Aside from my pin," she brushed her fingers against the silver butterfly attached above her nametag, "this is the most unexpected and wonderful gift ever!"

"Just like the *love* Mr. Farmer and I share." Angela smiled dreamily.

Rolling her eyes, Cooper collected the work orders from the floor. "It's a good thing the office is empty for most of the day. You and Mr. Farmer can flirt with one another right until the whistle blows and no one's going to overhear your sweet nothings."

"That won't be true for long!" Angela replied cheerfully as she examined her reflection in the compact that never seemed to be out of reach. "*I'm* gettin' an assistant. I can't handle the phones, the incoming orders, the inventory, *and* the books, so Mr. Farmer's lettin' me hire a part-time girl to do the stuff I don't have time for."

"Are you putting an ad in the paper?" Cooper asked.

"Yep. I only wish I could write 'cute girls need not apply!' I'm not lettin' any hot-blooded young things around my man. I aim to be Mrs. Farmer by this time next year—and I'll be a helluvalot more pleasant than the *other* Mrs. Farmer!" With that, Angela sashayed down the hall to her desk.

Over the course of the morning, Cooper visited her favorite elementary school to perform a quarterly service on their leased copier, tweaked the drum of a finicky Hewlett-Packard at the Bank of America, and completed a roller replacement in a laser printer at a podiatrist's office. She gulped down an Italian sub and an orange for lunch and spent a tidy pile of money buying food, litter supplies, and toys at PetCo. After that, she dashed to Mr. Farmer's office to cuddle her kittens before settling down in the small Make It Work! conference room to await Bobby Weller, the first of the day's three interviews.

Cooper reviewed the questions on her legal pad and tried to still the butterflies in her belly. She'd never been on the hiring end of a job interview before and was surprised to find the reversal unnerving. After all, the two new hires would be working on her team, and her decisions would determine the overall success of her department. Not only that, but Cooper wanted to be worthy of the position and the praise Mr. Farmer had given her.

After reviewing Bobby Weller's application once more, Cooper decided to peruse the *Times-Dispatch* until he arrived. As usual, the front page was filled with gloom. The text decried a sinking stock market, a senator caught cheating on his spouse, and the emotional funeral service given for the young girl killed in the East End shooting the week before. It was quite a pessimistic montage.

Cooper sighed and turned the page, hoping for a shred of uplifting news, when a column detailing the slaying of a Hispanic man named Hector Gutierrez caught her eye.

Could it be the Hector that made me my fake license? she wondered, her heart thumping more quickly as her anxiety mounted. She read the sparse account of the twenty-one-year-old's death. According to the reporter, Hector had been shot, execution-style, in the back of the head, and his body had been dumped at a construction site near one of Richmond's upscale shopping centers. The police were quoted stating they were actively following several leads but had no further information to share with the public at this point in their investigation.

Cooper was frustrated by the lack of detail given in the article. "It's like Miguel's death all over again." She closed her eyes and whispered a brief prayer for Hector's family and for the members of the police force. As she concluded, she heard Angela's voice in the hall and jumped up from her seat in order to meet Bobby Weller at the door, but not before tearing the article from the paper.

I've got to find out more about this victim, she thought solemnly and then turned to greet her first candidate.

Bobby was in his mid-forties and had grease-stained fingers, an honest, open face, and a generous paunch. As he shook Cooper's hand, his eyes crinkled with good humor and, after holding out her chair, proceeded to answer her questions with a relaxed and confident air. Having repaired televisions, computers, and most recently, motorcycles, Bobby informed Cooper that he was ready for a job with consistent hours and more growth potential.

"I've got six kids, so the benefits package you're offering is mighty attractive, too." Bobby produced photographs from his wallet and passed them across the table. Cooper looked over the smiling faces of the Weller brood and then pointed at what appeared to be a prom photo of Bobby and a woman who could have doubled as his sister, so similar were their builds and round, smiling faces. "Is this your wife?" she asked him.

"Yep, that's the missus. We were high school sweethearts. Went to the prom and never stopped dancin'."

Cooper returned the photographs, told Bobby she'd let him know her decision by the end of the week, and wished him a pleasant day. She made a few, quick notes on his application and wondered if the rest of the applicants would be as personable and qualified as Mr. Weller. "This could be tougher than I thought."

The next candidate was a man named Frankie Kepple. Cooper expected him to be waiting outside by the time Bobby left, but she had time to read the paper's movie reviews and complete the crossword before Angela knocked on the door again. The man she invited into the room was not the tardy Frankie Kepple, but Edward Crosby.

"I think your two o'clock's a no-show," Angela remarked while overtly ogling Edward. "But *this* man insisted he see you *and* he comes bearin' gifts, so I had to let him in." Angela winked and walked out of the room.

Edward produced a sheepish smile and laid a bouquet of stargazer lilies on the conference table. "I tried to come off as the FTD guy, but that woman sized me up in two seconds and gave me the full *Law & Order* interrogation. Damn. I told her my name, how I know you, and all about my jobs." He shook his head. "The CIA should recruit her. She's *good*."

Cooper grinned. "It's true. Angela's our gatekeeper and a woman of many talents, but you might have gotten past her had you not been dressed in your RoomStore delivery uniform."

He looked down at his embroidered shirt. "I tried to cover the letters up with the flowers. Shoulda bought a bigger bunch."

The conference room seemed to have grown smaller in size now that Edward was there. Cooper shifted on her feet and did her best to appear relaxed and in control. "So, other than pretending to work for FTD, what are you doing here?" She gestured at one of the vacant seats. "Did you find out who's dealing China White?"

Edward nodded smugly. "I got the name of the big fish. Guy named Albion. I've heard of him before, but since he operates in a different part of the city than I used to, we never butted horns." He laced his fingers together and stared at Cooper. "But I know where he spends his time. That's why I'm here. Check your calendar, 'cause we're goin' to Club Satin to pay him a visit Saturday night."

Cooper blanched. "Club Satin! That's a *strip* club!"

"Sure is." Edward seemed to revel in Cooper's discomfort. "But there's a pool tourney there this weekend, so there'll be other girls there besides the ones with bills hanging out of their panties. Can you shoot pool at all?"

"Yes." Cooper was angered by Edward's dismissive remark concerning the dancers. "I'm pretty good, actually." She cleared her throat. "But I've never played in front of drug dealers and half-naked women before, so I might be a bit off my game."

"Or you'll focus so hard we'll beat the tar outta the other players and go home with a wad of cash," Edward countered and then stood up. "The competition is our cover.

You're gonna have to be the one to approach Albion. Word is he likes good-looking blondes. I'm afraid that rules me out."

Gripping the arms of her chair, Cooper shook her head. "He'll know something's fishy if I talk to him. I can't fool him into thinking I'm a heroin user!" Her heartbeat accelerated as she pictured the scene. "This is totally crazy, Edward. If this man *is* responsible for Miguel's murder, we could get killed too! It's time to bring in the police."

"No cops!" Edward was at her side in seconds. "They'd blow our cover and then things *will* turn bloody. If we can get close enough to Albion to be sure he's dealing China White, then we know where the kill order on Miguel came from. Albion can be the cops' problem after that." He reached out and touched the tip of her chin. "Trust me, Cooper. No one's gonna harm one hair on your head." He exhaled and backed away. "I'll pick you up at nine. And wear what you had on last time we went out. Albion's sure to like that teeny, tiny skirt. I know I did." With an amused smile, he left the room.

Cooper stared at his empty chair for a moment, and then hastened to the locker room where she dug Mr. Johnson's card from her purse. "Sorry, Edward," she murmured as she opened her cell phone and began to dial. "I guess I don't trust you quite that much."

Afterward, she crossed Frankie Kepple off her list of potential candidates and awaited her last interview of the day. Josh Whitaker arrived out of breath, rumpled, and full of apologies.

"It's okay. You're not late," she assured him.

He smiled in relief. "That's good, because this old lady's radiator was smokin' and I just couldn't pass her by. I know I look a right mess, but I just had to stop."

Despite the oil stain on his tie and the strong smell of cigarette smoke seeping from his wrinkled sports coat,

Josh was also a strong candidate for the job. He was able to present a glowing recommendation from his current employer—a mom-and-pop copier repair company that would be closing its doors by the end of the month—and colored with embarrassment when Cooper read select passages aloud.

"I'm sure gonna miss Mr. and Mrs. Peterman. They've been working for thirty years," Josh explained. "And their kids both live in Florida. They wanna move while they can still pick up their grandbabies and bounce them on their knees."

"Well, even though this is your first job since graduating high school, you sure have picked up a lot of skills working for the Petermans. They've written you a truly amazing letter." She smiled. "In fact, I wouldn't be surprised if they were waiting outside right now."

Josh's young face flushed. "They fuss over me like I'm one of their kids. I'm sure gonna miss Mrs. P's home-cooked lunches. I don't even know how to scramble my own eggs."

Cooper laughed. "You're probably a lot healthier for not eating Subway and Burger King and Mexican takeout like the rest of us. And my mama's a gourmet cookie baker, so I eat cookies every single day on top of all that junk."

"They're not Magnolia's Marvels, are they?" Josh asked.

When Cooper informed him that Magnolia was indeed her mother, Josh fairly leapt from his chair.

"When Mr. P. was sick last year, he lost so much weight you could practically see through the man. For a whole week the only thing he'd touch were Magnolia's Marvels oatmeal raisin and butterscotch clusters. Tell your mama she saved Mr. P's life!"

Cooper promised she would pass the anecdote on and then wrapped up her interview with the enthusiastic young man. The last thing she did before packing her kittens into the new carrier was to call and confirm appointments with the three remaining candidates. If those men turned out to be as talented and friendly as Bobby and Josh, Cooper knew she'd be faced with some difficult decisions. Still, she left the office with a newfound confidence that made her feel ten feet tall.

"I *am* cut out for management!" she informed her mewling kittens as she eased the carrier onto the passenger seat. "I hope you two like the Beatles," she said, pressed the skip button on her CD player until it reached 'With a Little Help from My Friends,' and motored toward home.

She'd barely released the kittens from the carrier and changed into jeans and a periwinkle sweater when she heard a car pull into the driveway. Seeing that it was Nathan's car, she quickly brushed her hair and applied frosted pink lip gloss. By the time he knocked and entered the apartment, she was out of the bathroom and in the kitchen, filling a bowl with water for the kittens.

"Oh! More flowers!" she said by way of greeting when he presented her with a bouquet of fragrant white orchids.

"More?" Nathan looked confused. "I haven't given you any for ages."

Flustered, Cooper pictured Edward's grinning face above the bunch of stargazer lilies. Pushing thoughts of Edward's visit away, she touched Nathan on the arm. "I'm glad you're here. I really need to talk to you."

She placed the orchids into a glass pitcher and popped the tops off two bottles of Miller Lite. After clinking rims, Nathan and Cooper sat across from one another at the kitchen table. Cooper put her bottle on the table and began peeling off the label as she talked. "Nathan, I don't know how what I'm about to say is going to affect our relationship, but I cannot keep this from you another second." She met his concerned eyes and hesitated. "Oh, I don't want to hurt you! I'd never intentionally do that! But Nathan, I've been feeling drawn away from you lately. I didn't plan it, but it happened." She gulped. "I feel tempted."

"By Edward?" he asked softly.

Cooper nodded and was about to explain that she and Edward didn't even know one another and that the attraction was of a baser kind, but decided that such a qualifier wasn't helpful and might only serve to wound Nathan's pride.

He reached across the table and took her hand. "Don't be angry with me, Cooper, but I'm going through the same thing. I came over Sunday night with the intention of telling *you* everything I've been feeling, but Ashley and Edward were here and then we ended up talking about Miguel . . ." He trailed off and took a swallow of beer.

"You wanted to tell me about the weekend painting party?" Cooper guessed as a mixture of jealousy and disappointment began to stir in her heart.

Nathan's gaze never left her face. "Yes. I ran into an exgirlfriend from college while I was up there. Her name's Melissa. She just, um, has some hold over me. Always has. In college she only paid attention to me when it suited her, but now she seems to be much more interested." He squeezed Cooper's hand as tears began to pool in her eyes. She balled her free hand into a fist as she tried to picture Melissa as some gorgeous seductress, languidly raising and lowering a paintbrush as she ran her tongue over her lips and gazed at Nathan with naked lust.

"But that's all it is, Coop." He gently shook her hand to reclaim her attention. "A temptation. A pulling toward something shallow, impermanent. My heart belongs to *you* and it took this stupidity on my part to realize it."

Cooper brushed away a tear. Nathan's words had penetrated through every ounce of confusion she'd been feeling as of late. "You're right." Suddenly, the fog surrounding her heart evaporated. "This stuff with Edward . . . it's not *real*. I mean, he's an ex-con, a guy who's lived in the shadows and moved in circles I only read about in the newspaper, but he's also someone trying to lift himself above his past. I think I just wanted to witness his transformation. I was in awe of him." She looked down in shame. "I also think I wanted to take some credit for his change and because he sees me through a very favorable lens." Sighing, Cooper took a fortifying sip of beer. "But it's a false image. He doesn't *know* me. You do, Nathan. You see *me* and want me for who I am."

Nathan shoved back his chair and lifted Cooper out of hers with a brute strength he'd never exhibited before. It was so sudden that Cooper forgot to breathe.

"I do see you." Nathan's voice turned husky. "And I want you." He cupped her face in his hands. "But it's more than that. I love you. You're everything I need. Now and always."

As his words washed over her, warming her through and through, she recalled how they had first met. On a beautiful early spring day, she had run headlong into Nathan in the hall of the high school where Hope Street Church held its worship service.

The man she loved stood before her just as he had on that day. His eyes were filled with the same tenderness, humor, and kindness. His hands steadied her just as they had a year ago. Grammy was right. She'd known precisely what her granddaughter needed most when she'd told Cooper to reach for the man who loved her for who she was, not who he wanted her to be.

Nathan was that man.

"I love you, too," she whispered. "Please forgive me. You've been here all along, but I didn't realize how much I cared for you until now."

He kissed her cheeks, her mouth, her forehead, the lids

of her eyes, all the while murmuring, "Apology accepted. Please forgive me, as well. I'll never make such a foolish mistake again. There's only you." His lips sought her mouth. "Only you." His breath mingled with hers.

Later, as they lay on Cooper's bed, talking softly, she introduced Nathan to the kittens. She'd named the male cat Moses, as the clumsy feline had fallen into the toilet within the first few hours of entering the apartment. Cooper had had to rapidly scoop him out of danger, for which he'd repaid her by shredding the skin of her hands and arms.

"Moses means 'drawn from the water'," she informed the mewling bundle of wet fur after he'd slipped into the toilet. "Suitable, don't you think? And since you've got an Old Testament name, your sister shall be called Miriam." She drizzled some water over Miriam's forehead and then gave the kittens a saucer of warm milk and a jar of Beech-Nut chicken baby food to celebrate their new names.

Moses and Miriam took to Nathan immediately. They scaled up his chest and pounced on the strings of his sweatshirt hood while he stroked them behind the ears. They attacked his long graceful fingers with their tiny teeth and claws, purring in contentment when he pushed them off his belly and dangled one of his socks just out of reach.

"This is one of those times I regret living out in the sticks," Cooper said after her stomach grumbled for the second time. "We can't just run out for a quick bite to eat."

Nathan tucked a lock of Cooper's disheveled hair behind her ear. "I'll go out and get anything you want. Just name it and it's yours."

Cooper laughed. "You sound like a genie. But it's freezing and I'm too hungry to wait another minute. Luckily," she grinned, "I know of an excellent restaurant within walking distance. I'm sure Mama would love the company.

I'll just call to make sure she's got enough for the two of us."

Maggie was delighted by the request. "I had the strangest notion I oughta roast a big chicken tonight. Good thing I heeded that inner voice. Come on down. You and Nathan can set the table while I make the gravy."

Nathan was meticulously placing forks and knives on top of paper napkins covered with designs of conversation hearts when Grammy shuffled into the kitchen. She stopped in her tracks when she saw Nathan and a smile blossomed on her face. She quickly regained control of her features and pretended to be assessing him with disapproval.

"Now, now, young man. You stop that women's work and come over here and give me a hug!" she commanded, her eyes twinkling.

Nathan instantly obeyed. "I figured Mr. Lee wouldn't mind sharing his three generations of lovely ladies with me," he stated while Grammy grinned at Cooper around Nathan's shoulder.

Cooper's father materialized behind Grammy and clapped Nathan on the shoulder. "I'd be right thrilled to have you join us for every meal. It sure is nice to even up the numbers a bit."

Maggie served Nathan first, piling his plate so full of food that his eyes grew wide at the sight. Earl spoke a short grace and then there was a lengthy silence as the diners focused on Maggie's roast chicken, greens, and wild rice. Grammy took most of the canned cranberry sauce for herself, but when she tried to pick up a thick slice of the jellied stuff with her fork, it slid onto her chest and down to her lap, leaving a red stain as it oozed down her sweater.

Grammy examined the mess nonchalantly. "Shoot, I never liked this snowman sweater, anyhow," she remarked wryly, plucking the wayward jelly from her lap and popping it into her mouth. "Why old ladies wear clothes with cutesy puppy dogs and snowmen is beyond me. I guess somebody thought it was a good idea to dress us gray-hairs like babies. Reckon it's 'cause we kinda eat more like babies as we get up in years." She swallowed. "Do we have any more cranberry sauce, Maggie?"

Cooper volunteered to get more from the pantry, and as she shuffled through sundry canned goods, the phone rang. Maggie and Earl had a strict rule about refusing to accept telephone calls during mealtimes, so the speaker volume was turned down low. However, Cooper could hear Ashley's stricken voice through the answering machine. Her sister cried, "If anyone's listening, *please* pick up!"

Cooper leapt for the phone.

"I'm here!" she quickly assured her sister and carried the receiver into the dining room.

"Oh, Coop!" Ashley exclaimed sorrowfully. "You'll never believe this, but someone *else* connected to Lincoln's dealership has been killed!"

Stepping into the dining room, Cooper closed the door leading to the kitchen and leaned against the solid wood for support. "Who?"

"Maria's son. She's the title clerk at the dealership and just the sweetest soul on this earth! Always a smile for everyone, always a kind word to me whenever I stopped by . . ." Ashley sniffed. "Her son was *murdered*, Cooper! Shot in the back of the head like some—"

"I'm so sorry, Ashley." Cooper didn't want her sister to complete the image. "What was his name? Maria's son?"

"Hector Gutierrez. You might have seen the story about him in today's paper." Ashley was quiet for a moment. "Those policemen were back. McNamara and Wiser. Lincoln told them he'd only met Hector once or twice and very briefly, but that the young man had never worked for any of the Love dealerships. He couldn't think of a single thread that could tie Hector and Miguel together, but apparently the investigators are certain there must be a connection."

"Except they were Hispanic men of about the same age and both met violent ends," Cooper surmised unhappily. "Do you know where Maria's son worked?"

"No, but Maria and Hector were from Mexico. Just like Miguel," Ashley confirmed. "Now the police have *two* unsolved cases! But it's almost worse this time because we know that Hector has a family—someone will definitely mourn him and want answers about this senseless killing!" Ashley's anger fueled Cooper's desire to take action immediately. "Poor Maria! What can I do to comfort her? What words can I offer to a near stranger whose only child has been murdered?"

Cooper could hear the sounds of Nathan and her family continuing their dinner. Laughter mingled with the clinking of silverware and Ashley's subtle weeping seemed incongruent with the companionable murmurs emanating from the next room.

"You'll do what women do during times like this," she counseled, keeping her voice strong in order to soothe her sister. "You'll bring Maria food and flowers, you'll sit with her and look at photographs of her son, and you'll pray for her." Cooper gripped the phone tightly in her hand. "And I haven't forgotten Miguel, Ashley. Edward and I are going in search of answers this weekend. We're on the right track with this China White stuff. I can just *feel* it."

"Will you come to Maria's house with me on Saturday?" Ashley asked hopefully.

"I can't. The Sunrise members and I have committed to sprucing up a school in the East End." She paused. "Bring Lincoln. Comfort Maria together."

Her sister sighed. "All right. Can you put Mama on now? I want her to teach me how to cook her famous beef stew so I can bring Maria something I've made with my own hands." She chuckled once, dryly. "But I want it to be edible and for that, I need Mama."

"Sure. And Ashley? I'm not going to give up," Cooper said. "Miguel. Hector. I won't let their deaths go unexplained. They will not be lost in some police station file cabinet. I promise."

Ashley whispered, "I believe you, but I also want you to be really careful. This killer, whoever it is, places *no* value on a human life. If he killed both Miguel and Hector, then he did something unspeakable and then tossed them away like they were bags of trash. Didn't even bother to hide their bodies." She paused for a moment. "Maybe those boys were supposed to serve as warnings, I don't know, but promise me you'll guard yourself. Promise me you'll be smart enough to stay out of danger."

Thinking about her recent conversation with Rich Johnson, Cooper was able to infuse her voice with confidence. "I promise. I'm not going in there alone, Ashley. Someone will be watching from the shadows."

12

"Remember this: Whoever sows sparingly will also reap sparingly, and whoever sows generously will also reap generously. Each man should give what he has decided in his heart to give, not reluctantly or under compulsion, for God loves a cheerful giver."

2 Corinthians 9:6-7 (NIV)

Saturday was Valentine's Day. Maggie had risen earlier than usual in order to make heart-shaped Linzer cookies, hazelnut meringue sweetheart cookies, and squares of raspberry truffle fudge. Her special treats had been custom-ordered and had to be delivered to half a dozen sandwich shops by mid-morning, so the house had been replete with the scents of baking cookies since dawn on Friday.

Cooper joined her mother a few minutes after seven and spent an hour packaging the cooled and decorated confections. By the time she had entered the kitchen, Cooper knew Maggie had already been up for three or four hours and would be in need of a break. Her kindness was rewarded with a tired but grateful smile from Maggie and an entire tray of raspberry truffle fudge.

"You take this to your Bible study friends. Y'all are gonna get mighty hungry fixin' up that school today." She drew Cooper into her pillowy bosom and squeezed her tightly. "Do you and Nathan have special plans for tonight?"

After breathing in her mother's familiar perfume of warm dough and cinnamon, Cooper released her and returned to the task of applying the gold-foil Magnolia's Marvels labels to each two-pack cookie bag. "We decided to celebrate tomorrow. The restaurants are so crowded tonight and I can't stomach the price inflation . . ."

"In other words, y'all didn't make any plans and now you're left out in the cold!" Maggie laughed.

Cooper's laughter mingled with her mother's. "In a nutshell!" After a brief pause, she said, "You know, Mama, Nathan and I kind of had a falling-out. This space started growing between us. Neither of us saw it coming, but we started drifting away from each other and toward people who weren't really a good fit. The great news is that we worked things out, but not in time to celebrate Valentine's Day."

"I wouldn't let all those commercials for rings and roses and candlelight get you down," Maggie said as she carefully filled a cardboard tray with Linzer cookies. "Your daddy and I've been married longer than most of those fancy restaurants have been in business, and we're not goin' out for a six-course meal or bottles of wine that cost as much as a whole week's worth of groceries. We're gonna do what we do every year."

"Watch *Roman Holiday* and drink homemade apple wine," Cooper stated mechanically.

"It's a fine date, too!" Maggie waved a wooden spoon at her daughter as though warning Cooper not to mock the event. "My point is this: Make your own tradition with your man. You don't need to spend a lot of money or get stuffed into some teeny-tiny table at a five-star café to prove that you're sweethearts."

Cooper kissed her mother on the cheek. "That's good advice, Mama," she said, wondering what Maggie would think if she knew that her oldest child would be spending a romantic evening at a strip club. "I'm going to carry a few of these boxes to your car and then I'm off. Will you check on the kittens today?"

Maggie clicked her tongue. "Those two are gettin' mighty spoiled! You're worse than your Grammy." She hesitated for a moment and then peered into the pantry. "Bein' that it's a *special* day, I'm gonna give those little darlings a nice tuna-fish lunch. Your daddy had a hankering for tuna but he'll have to settle for grilled cheese and bacon."

Noting that her mother was lost in culinary-related thought, Cooper filled a thermos with coffee, put on her coat and hat, and carried two loaded trays out to Maggie's gold minivan. The sky was heavy with low, gray clouds and Cooper wondered if the warning Bryant gave during his Friday evening forecast about a Valentine's Day ice storm would come to pass.

"Just hold off until we fix up this school," Cooper commanded the ominous clouds. During the forty-minute drive to the East End, she noticed a lightening above the horizon—the odd, pinkish glow that typically preceded snow. Switching off her *Best of the Beatles* CD, Cooper scanned several radio stations. All the weather reports sounded dire.

"Better plan on snuggling with your Valentine at home today," one meteorologist warned.

Another said, "Get your errands done this morning, folks. We're expecting the precipitation to hit the Richmond metro area sometime around noon."

"This storm is going to be nasty," a third promised, sounding rather gleeful. "The western parts of the state are already experiencing power outages by the thousands. Have extra blankets and battery-operated lanterns ready, and remember to use caution when burning candles."

The charcoal-gray sky had lightened to a silvery pewter by the time Cooper's truck bumped across the elementary school's pot-hole marred lot. She alighted and sniffed the air, which was tinged with a sharply cold, clean, and wet scent. Already, the outside seemed to have fallen silent, as though the city was holding its breath before the oncoming storm.

Jake, Savannah, Bryant, and Nathan were waiting for Cooper inside the school, making plans to bring Savannah's vision of painting vibrant murals to life. They decided to start with the main corridor, which was currently a shade of industrial beige. Several other volunteers and school employees listened to Savannah's proposal, and the principal, a tall African-American man with round spectacles, was clearly enthused by her ideas.

"Imagine stepping into a garden scene every day." Savannah swept her arms around the hallway. "These students deserve brightness and beauty in their environment— not just another coat of monotone paint. Let's stimulate their senses as soon as they walk through the front door!"

"I'd love to see the long wall in the library painted with storybook characters, too," a small, elderly lady said. "Quite a few of our fifth-grade students will be joining us this morning. I'd like to let them loose on that wall if we have enough supplies."

At that moment, Quinton arrived with Gloria May on one arm and a gallon of paint on the other. "Don't worry about supplies! The sky's the limit! My company agreed to sponsor our labors here today. My car is so full that Gloria had to bring our snacks in hers." He turned to the woman on his arm with an adoring smile. "No one will go hungry while we labor, because Gloria and I baked late into the night."

"I listened to Quinton and Jake's CD and thought it was *just* marvelous! Between the music and all the cooking, the hours flew right on by!" Gloria giggled.

As Quinton received thankful handshakes and thumps

on the back from the grateful schoolteachers and staff for the supplies, Gloria quickly introduced herself to the other members of the Sunrise Bible Study.

"Someone's missing, right?" she asked, looking around for Trish.

Bryant waited until his friends were gathered close together before he whispered, "Trish is feeling *terrible*. She's been receiving chemo treatments for a month," he explained to Gloria. "And she's got good days and not-so-good days." He looked pained. "This last round has made her awfully sick. I only talked to her for a minute, but it truly upset me. I've never heard her sound so weak. It was . . . scary."

Cooper squeezed Bryant's hand. "We'll check on her later today, after she's had a chance to rest. Maybe we can bring her some food before the storm arrives. That way, her family can focus on taking care of her without worrying about what to have for dinner."

The friends nodded in solemn agreement.

"No more frowns!" Jake clapped his hands. "If we're gonna do all this good before we get covered by a layer of ice, then we'd better get crackin'!" He began to distribute brushes and rollers to Gloria and the Sunrise members. "We're gonna make Savannah's garden come to life and after that, we'll paint pictures of healthy food in the cafeteria." He lowered his voice. "Just as long as I don't have to paint the broccoli. I sure hate that stuff! Used to hide it in my cowboys boots durin' supper. I always wore my boots when I smelled Mama cookin' beets or broccoli."

Savannah chuckled. "Never fear, Jake. We won't make you paint such traumatic veggies. You can make a smiling carrot instead."

Looking visibly relieved, Jake followed Nathan, Bryant, and Quinton outside to collect supplies.

"This is quite a palette you've brought," Nathan said as he gestured at four gallons of different shades of blue. "These walls won't know what hit them."

For the next three hours, the Sunrise members transformed the entrance hall into a verdant paradise. Sunflowers, poppies, tulips, lilies, and daisies lifted their faces toward a glorious sunrise in the middle of an azure sky. Cotton-candy clouds formed the backdrop for a host of soaring birds and butterflies.

Nathan placed the final dot on a ladybug's wing just as Cooper painted a curling antennae on a grinning inchworm. Quinton and Gloria's hands met as they completed the violet stripe of their rainbow arch. As one, the friends stood back to admire their handiwork.

"Would you look at this?" Gloria made a sweeping gesture down the hall. "I am *convinced* the Almighty Creator guided our brushes this morning."

Cooper had to agree. Except for Savannah, none of them were known for possessing drawing or painting talents, yet the mural they had created together sparkled with color and shimmered with liveliness.

"Imagine what we can do to the cafeteria next!" Cooper exclaimed.

"Nothin' yet! At least not until we fill our bellies!" Jake declared and dumped his brush into an open can of corn-yellow paint. "I gotta refill the well. Especially if we're gonna paint a bunch of food."

Quinton rubbed his round paunch. "I second that motion. How does beef stew sound to you? One of the women's groups from Hope Street provided us with crock pots full of stew and trays of homemade cornbread."

"It's a good thing we don't have to drive anywhere for lunch. Look!" Bryant pointed toward the double doors leading outside. Just as he'd predicted on television the night before, the ice storm had arrived.

Gloria and the Bible study friends walked to the entranceway and watched transfixed as pellets of ice struck the cement walkways and ricocheted off the asphalt parking lot.

Above the barren trees, the sky was tinged a strange gray-pink.

"Looks a bit like birthday cake icing," Quinton murmured and took Gloria's hand. "I think you picked the perfect cupcake design for today."

Intrigued by this comment, the Sunrise members followed Quinton down the hall with the expectant gait of first-grade students being led to recess. Once they'd gathered around the cafeteria table, Quinton carefully eased back the lid of a bakery box and waited for the cries of surprise and delight.

"Wow!" Jake shouted and leaned toward Savannah so that he could describe what he'd seen. "Gloria made penguin cupcakes. The wings are chocolate cookies, the snow's made of shredded coconut, and there's even little candy fish tucked in their yellow mouths."

"How'd you made the beak and the feet?" Nathan asked.

"Laffy Taffy," Gloria answered. "And the penguin's head is a donut hole dunked in melted black frosting." She giggled and her bosom shook. "I figured we'd need some sugar and coffee by mid-afternoon. Painting is serious exercise! No wonder the Karate Kid had to paint Mr. Miyagi's fence."

Quinton closed the box and indicated a row of similar boxes. "She made enough for everyone." Again, he gazed at Gloria with rapture. "If you're still hungry after the stew, I've made a simple cake and my finely tuned nose has detected the smell of fudge."

Cooper laughed. "Oh, you're good! Mama sent raspberry truffle fudge. And I doubt you made a *simple* cake, Quinton." She winked at Gloria. "He's being modest."

"It's just a cinnamon sour cream cake with a vanilla glaze," Quinton argued, his boyish face rosy with pleasure.

"I'm gaining weight just listening to you all!" Savannah said. "Let's eat and then brainstorm about how to spruce up this room. It *feels* gloomy in here and if this place is anything like other school cafeterias, these kids are eating Mystery Meat and Nameless Noodle Casserole, so the least we can do is give them something fun to look at."

"Limit the pictures of cakes and candy, if you will," one of the teachers sitting nearby pleaded. "Paint more of what the students *should* be eating, like dairy, fruit, and vegetables. If you saw some of the lunches these kids bring from home, you'd wonder if their parents were food shopping at the 7-Eleven."

"Fresh fruits and vegetables are expensive," Gloria pointed out kindly. "Perhaps we could start a fund drive to provide the students with healthy lunch sides during the week. I'm sure the area churches would band together to help . . ." The two women excitedly exchanged ideas.

Cooper nudged Quinton, who was staring at Gloria's profile with a faraway smile. "So, Romeo, what are you doing to celebrate V-Day?"

"I'm cooking for her, of course. Fondue. And then we're going to play some board games while we listen to Sinatra." He sighed happily. "The ice and snow can pile up outside. It doesn't matter to me because wherever Gloria is, the sun will be shining." Quinton slung an arm around Nathan. "What about you two? Any big plans?"

"Oh, you know, your run-of-the-mill Valentine's Day activity," Nathan replied sotto voce as he buttered a piece of cornbread. "We're meeting Edward Crosby at Club Satin, where Cooper's going to play in a pool tournament and then attempt to buy heroin from a dangerous drug dealer. After that, the three of us will try to stay alive long enough to discover Miguel Ramos's connection to said drug dealer."

Jake, who was about to take a bite of cornbread, dropped the square back onto his plate. "Hold the phone! Three of you ain't gonna stand a chance! Don't you think a plumber with a pipe in his back pocket might come in handy?" He gesticulated at Quinton and Bryant. "These two can't blend in with a rougher crowd, but I can."

"And I could be your ears," Savannah said, clearly not happy over being excluded.

"You can't hear yourself think over what passes for music in that kind of joint. And even though you couldn't see what was goin' on in there, it's no place for a lady." Jake looked appalled by the idea. "I don't know a thing about this adult club *personally*," he added for Savannah's benefit, "but you're not goin' within miles of its pink front door. This is a mean, dirty club filled with mean, dirty people." He squeezed Cooper's forearm. "You're made from tough fiber, my friend. I just pray this turns out like you want it to. This is a mighty big risk you're takin'."

"Have you read the paper lately? There are so many bad things happening in our city," Cooper answered with quiet passion. "I can't just sit around when there's a chance I can stop someone else from being hurt."

Quinton looked abashed. "I wish I'd been more helpful. I placed several calls to Double A Auto to try and discover something fishy about Miguel's employment history, but no one would believe I was with the IRS. As such a terrible actor, I don't think I'd be any good to you in that club."

"Me, either, my friend." Bryant slapped Nathan on the back. "I'd be right by your side, but my face is too famous and I've got a date with Jane that includes playing Pictionary with two kids."

Nathan grinned. "We'll be okay. Just send any extra guardian angels you run into our way." He brushed cornbread crumbs from his hands and picked up a clean paintbrush. "I think I'll start by painting a pizza slice. I know it's not the pinnacle of nutrition, but I've never met a kid who didn't like a slice of cheese pizza."

"Pepperoni's better," Cooper playfully countered. "If I could choose my last meal, it would be pepperoni pizza."

"Don't talk about last meals," Nathan whispered. "I want mine to be manlier than a cupcake shaped like penguin!"

13

Because Cooper had planned on the ice storm's arrival, she'd brought two changes of clothes with her. One to wear to Club Satin, as well as a pair of dress slacks, underwear, and a twin set to wear to Hope Street the next morning. A second, smaller case held a custom cue for use in the pool tournament. She and Nathan had agreed the night before that it made more sense for Cooper to drive straight to his house after their day of painting and then sleep over at the conclusion of their late-night adventure.

They spent what was left of the afternoon snuggled up on the sofa as the fire crackled in the grate. Afterward, they ate a quiet dinner and then tried to while away two hours watching *When Harry Met Sally.*

"I cannot focus on this movie," Nathan said as he returned to the living room with a bowl of popcorn. "I never thought it would take so long for ten o'clock to arrive."

"I can't relax, either." Cooper ate a few handfuls of popcorn but her stomach was too unsettled for much more.

She passed the bowl back to Nathan. "Come on, let's go upstairs and figure out what you're going to wear."

He touched his blue and white checked button-down and frowned. "What's wrong with this?"

"Not seedy enough," Cooper commented and turned the television off. Upstairs, she searched through Nathan's closet until she found dark, acid-washed jeans and a black sports coat. "Add a black T-shirt and your loafers and you're set."

"Those shoes pinch my feet." Nathan sighed and began to unbutton his shirt.

Cooper placed her hands over his. "Leave that to me," she whispered. She kissed him as she pushed each button gently through its hole and then slowly lowered the shirt off his shoulders. "I'm so glad you'll be with me tonight."

"As if I'd let you be alone with Edward. I'm done sharing you," he murmured into her hair and slipped his hands beneath her sweater. "Your turn."

Nathan's arms tightened around Cooper's bare back and their kisses grew in hunger. It took an intense effort for Cooper to detach herself from the embrace. "We don't have *that* much time." She smiled and turned away to finish dressing. Groaning, Nathan followed suit and then sat on the edge of the bed and watched as Cooper zipped up her knee-high black leather boots.

"You're beautiful. No, you're downright sexy. And those boots?" He ran his hand up her leg. "Do I get to take them off later?"

Cooper swatted him. "Stop it! I still have to put gobs of makeup on and tease my hair until I look like the frontman for an eighties rock band."

Holding his hands up in surrender, Nathan laughed. "That's a surefire way to stop me from trying to seduce you. Now I'm thinking about Jon Bon Jovi."

"Good. Keep him in mind until we're alone again."

* * *

The roads were slick and treacherous, and Nathan maneuvered Sweet Pea through the nearly deserted downtown streets with care. Club Satin wasn't far from his Fan District house, but the prevalence of black ice forced him to drive with extreme caution. By the time they arrived in the public parking lot where Cooper had planned to meet Edward, they were fifteen minutes late.

Nathan parked alongside Edward's cab, which was idling beneath one of the lot's few streetlights.

"I see you brought back-up," was Edward's only comment as he opened the passenger door and held out a hand for Cooper. Before she could answer, he pointed at the black carrying case on her lap. "Is that your own cue?"

"I told you I used to play," she answered cryptically.

Edward studied her for a moment. "We'll keep an eye on Albion and his crew as we shoot. If things go well and we kick ass on the pool tables, we'll end up talking to our big fish."

"Anything I can do to help?" Nathan inquired. "I admit to being out of my league here, but an extra pair of eyes might be useful."

"Our friend Jake's coming, too," Cooper added. "He's probably inside already."

If Edward was surprised or displeased by this revelation, he didn't show it. "You go in separate from us and hang out with Jake," he told Nathan. "Buy some drinks, get some food, and pay attention to the girls. Pick one to spend some money on and tell her you were a friend of Miguel's and that he always talked about the club. See what she's got to say." Edward unzipped his leather coat, revealing a tight shirt emblazoned with a smoking pool cue and the text, "Shut Up and Shoot."

"What if she gets suspicious?" Nathan asked.

"Then she'll squeal to Albion and we'll know for sure

Miguel was one of his runners. It'd be a lead, but not a good one, so you should try to play it cool and leave the tricky stuff to me. We don't want Albion paying attention to *any* of us until the time is right," Edward explained. "If the girls blow you off, we'll find a way to send Cooper into the viper's pit. Albion likes blondes. You get what I'm saying?"

Nathan nodded and Edward seemed satisfied. "If I need to tell you something, I'll approach you. Just be regular Joes in there. Watch the women and drink your beer."

"Be careful," Nathan told Cooper and then kissed her on the mouth as though Edward wasn't watching. "Listen to your gut. If something feels wrong, then leave. Finding Miguel's killer is important, but don't risk your own safety tracking him down."

"I'm not backing down now," Cooper insisted firmly. "But I promise not to do anything stupid. You'll have to settle for that." She softened the strength of her words by squeezing his arm reassuringly.

Once Nathan was out of sight, Cooper was forced to face Edward's dark, questioning gaze. "He's my boyfriend, okay? He wasn't going to sit at home while I hung out at a strip club."

Edward shrugged. "I wouldn't think he was much of a man if he did. Now, get your game face on. Here we go."

Hands clasped for support, Edward and Cooper picked their way over the slippery parking lot. Twice, Cooper lost her balance and had to cling to Edward, but she no longer yearned to linger in the crook of his arms as he held her upright. The temptation had passed.

"You're different tonight," he murmured as they made it to a portion of the sidewalk lit by the pink neon arrows pointing the way to Club Satin. "Why?"

Cooper stopped and turned to him. "I have been trying to figure out what I felt for you, Edward. You're intriguing.

You've got a background that's so foreign to me and ever since you've been released, I've been in total awe of your courage and determination."

"Here comes the 'but' . . ." he said, his eyes unreadable.

"You've been like some kind of shadow guardian since the night Ashley found Miguel. I am *very* grateful to you for looking out for me." She hesitated. "But I love Nathan and I can only offer you friendship. And whatever you think you feel for me . . . it's not real. You see me through a tinted lens that makes me better than I actually am."

Edward reached out and touched her cold cheek. "I may not know your favorite color or book or damned ice cream flavor, but I see *you*. I'm not the type of guy you're used to and I get that. I get that you've got a man and you're gonna stick with him." He smirked. "But let me be straight. I'm not here tonight because I've got a thing for you. I'm here to see that right's done, because I owe you one and I'm looking for a way to even the score, so let's go in before they start the contest without us."

Tongue-tied over Edward's abruptness, Cooper followed him past a stretch Hummer limousine. The elongated side of the ridiculous vehicle had been painted with the figures of two bikini-clad women with full lips and enormous eyes. One girl was stereotypically Scandinavian with her round, blue eyes and white-blonde hair while the second was distinctly exotic in appearance. She had fathomless dark brown eyes, shiny cascades of black hair, and nut-colored skin. Both women were positioned so they seemed to be crawling toward the viewer. Cooper had a hard time tearing her gaze from their open mouths and come-hither expressions.

"It's false advertising," Edward told her. "Trust me, the girls inside aren't that hot."

Club Satin was housed in a brick building that had once been inhabited by a small hardware company. The business had folded and the Club Satin owner had tacked on a cheap addition resembling a prefab trailer. Now the storefront windows that had once been used to display drill sets and power saws were painted black and covered with electric-pink awnings emblazoned with the club's name. Tubes of pink neon lighting accentuated the roofline and two spotlights had been erected on top of the highest portion of the roof. The pair of strong beams signaled to traffic passing overhead on I-95 that something exciting was occurring below and travelers need only take the next exit to discover what it was.

Cooper had only seen strip clubs in movies, so she expected to encounter the raucous members of bachelor parties, zealous fraternity boys, and businessmen in town for a dull convention. But Club Satin's clientele was a marked degree shadier than her *Risky Business* visions, and as soon as Edward paid the cover charge and she stepped past the unsmiling bouncer, Cooper felt her anxiety level rise.

"You look like Bambi in a forest fire," Edward hissed in her ear. "You gotta play this like you go wherever you want, whenever you want. Act like there aren't any rules for you. Own it, girl!"

Nodding, Cooper pointed at a chalkboard announcing the pool tournament and the night's food specials. "Just steer me to a table. I'll be ready to play."

Edward drove her through a knot of men whose attention was focused on a woman dancing on a small, elevated stage in the shape of a circle. A brass pole protruded from the center and the dancer was hanging upside down using the incredible strength of her legs.

"Wow," Cooper murmured.

Dodging sloshing beer bottles and lit cigarettes, Edward pulled Cooper toward the purple-felt pool tables located in the middle of the main room. A gargantuan man dressed in a lime-green tracksuit waved a clipboard at them, indicating they needed to stop before approaching the tables. "You registered?" he growled.

"Yeah." Edward appeared irritated by the question.

The man flicked his eyes at Cooper. "Team name?"

Deadpan, Edward replied, "The Ball Busters."

The man chuckled. "At least one of you, anyhow. Rack 'em up on table two. You're playin' the Pick Pockets."

Cooper wasn't happy about their team moniker, but decided not to criticize her partner right before their first game. Instead, she focused on assembling her custom cue. As she chalked the tip, she took a moment to take stock of the environment. The six purple-topped pool tables were aligned against the club's far wall, opposite the long bar. The area near the entrance was reserved for those wishing to dine while viewing the dancers, and smaller tables meant to hold drinks and ashtrays were scattered around the remainder of the open floor. In the center of the room, an elevated catwalk with a dance pole at each end jutted out into the sea of tables and chairs. A fog machine was pumping out a veil of mist at the base of the runway and pink, purple, and yellow strobe lights sent confusing pulses of color through the air.

"I hate this techno music," Edward snarled in Cooper's ear and handed her two ibuprofen tablets. "Trust me. You're gonna need these. It's only gonna get louder as more girls take the stage." He swallowed several pills. "We won the coin toss. You any good at breaking?"

Cooper nodded, stuck the Advil in the back pocket of her skirt, and stared intently at the tight triangle of billiard balls on the table. For years, she and her ex-boyfriend Drew had played pool against each another, in lighthearted games with friends, and in local competitions. After only a few games, it became clear that Cooper had a natural talent for the sport, and Drew encouraged her to hone her skill whenever they went out.

"I just visualize where the ball needs to go before I move the cue," Cooper had once explained to a group of admirers. "Everything else fades away right before the shot. It's like being in a tunnel and seeing only that circle of light ahead."

Now, she leaned over the table, gripped the cue with a firm yet flexible hand, and exploded her right arm forward. The sound of the cue ball cracking against the hard cluster of solids and stripes brought a smile to Cooper's lips. She felt more at home in the strange setting the moment the burgundy seven-ball and the sun-yellow one-ball slipped into separate corner pockets with satisfying thuds.

"Guess we're solids," Edward remarked to the Pick Pocket males. He watched in admiration as Cooper proceeded to sink the cobalt two-ball and the mango-colored five-ball before missing an attempt to put the forest-green six-ball into a side pocket.

The Pick Pockets looked like strong contenders at first, but the leadoff player was much more skilled than his partner, who missed his first shot by a mile.

When Edward's turn came around, he swept the remainder of the solids as well as the eight-ball from the table in three shots. She and Edward shook hands with their opponents, collected pint glasses of cold beer, and prepared to begin round two.

"Dicks with Sticks?" Cooper repeated the competitor's team name. "Charming." Her attention was divided among the roughness of their challengers' appearance (the two men were clad entirely in black leather and had tattoos of flames licking up the sides of their necks), the exotic dancers who had eased out of their costumes and were now gyrating clad only in minuscule thongs, and an attempt to spot Nathan somewhere in the crowded club.

"I've been checking up on him," Edward said, following her gaze. "He and Jake have been chatting up one of the lady bartenders. They're doing their job. You focus on yours."

"And what is my job again?" She placed her hand on her hip and frowned. "You never made that quite clear to me."

Edward put his lips against her ear. Pointing at the table as though strategizing their next game, he whispered, "We win this tourney and the big fish will have us to his table for a drink. One of his associates will give us a pile of cash as our reward. That's how we get close to him. I'll disappear and you try to spend some of our prize loot on China White."

"What if I'd been a horrible pool player?" Cooper was stunned by the riskiness of Edward's plan.

Edward shrugged. "I've been racking and whacking since I was a kid. In clubs, in jail, at people's houses . . . As long as you didn't scratch or shoot the wrong balls every time, I figured we'd win this thing easy enough. I just let you go first to see what you were made of." He smiled. "Turns out, you got game."

Edward was right. While the second-round players possessed a crude name, their skills were also equally unrefined. After Cooper and Edward sent the glowering men packing, they next defeated a pair of big-bellied bikers. Only the reigning champions, the Snipers, barred their path to victory.

"Good team name," Edward commented to no one in particular as he placed the loose balls in the wooden triangle. The Snipers, swarthy young men in their early twenties, wore dress shirts unbuttoned far enough to reveal tanned, hairy chests and thick ropes of gold chains hanging down from their necks. Cooper could smell their musky cologne from across the table. As she studied them covertly, she realized that their outfits were very similar to the clothing in Miguel's closet and decided that it might be worthwhile to flirt with whichever player wasn't currently shooting in hopes of discovering a more tangible connection to the dead man.

"That's a hot shirt," she said, leaning against one of the Hispanic men as she stroked the smooth material.

The man, who had introduced himself as Jorge, responded immediately. "You like what you see, huh, baby? Nothin' but silk. I got silk sheets on my *big, big* bed, too. You wanna come over and see?"

Cooper pretended to consider his offer. "I dunno. I kinda came here with another guy."

"So?" he practically spit out the word. "He can't do for you what I can do for you!"

"Yeah, you Latino men are *supposed* to be talented." She did her best to form a sultry pout. "But I've only been with one and *he* wasn't that great."

Jorge began to laugh, slapping the leg of his pressed trousers. "Shut *up*! One of my brothers couldn't get the job done! Who *was* this loser?"

Shrugging, Cooper said, "You probably don't know him. Name's Miguel Ramos."

"Oh, but I *did* know him." Jorge scoffed and chalked the end of his cue stick. "He got clipped, girlfriend, so he won't be disappointin' any more hotties like you." He licked his lips. "You can count on me to light your fire."

"He's dead?" Cooper interrupted while trying to act skeptical. "He seemed like a nice guy. Who'd bother killing him?"

"*Nice* don't cut it on the street. You can be as nice as you want, but you better not get greedy or you get cut down," Jorge preached importantly and then stood back in order to examine Cooper's buttocks. "Let's have a little side bet, huh? Make things more interestin'. I win, you come home with me."

"And if I win?"

Jorge grinned lecherously, his white teeth gleaming

beneath the neon lights. "Then you get to come home with me. See? You get to be happy either way!"

Just then, Jorge's partner missed a shot and it was Cooper's turn. If she could sink the thirteen-ball followed by the eight-ball, she and Edward would win the tournament. As she leaned over the ball, her hand didn't feel as steady as it should. She backed away from the table and reached for her beer, trying to shut out Jorge's derisive laughter and lewd tongue gestures.

"Get your brain in the game," Edward suddenly hissed in her ear. He then tapped her gently on the side of her head. "Take yourself out of this bar and to a place of peace before you pick up that stick again."

Cooper heeded his advice. She gazed at the floor for a long moment, picturing herself in the backyard of her parents' house. There, in the shelter of a rear wall, was an aviary custom-built for Columbus, the wounded red-tailed hawk Grammy had adopted several years ago. It was one of Cooper's delights to take the injured raptor to the large field bordering their property so that the bird could use his crippled wing just long enough to hunt for a meal. In her mind, she left the noise and stale air of Club Satin, opened Columbus's cage, and invited the majestic bird to alight onto her gloved arm. She visualized walking with him to the field behind her house, seeing the thistles and buttercups waving in the breeze. Only when she truly believed she could feel the heat of the sun on her face did she reclaim her stick. Leaning over the table, she took the shot. The thirteen-ball floated into the side pocket.

"Eight-ball, left corner pocket," she announced and sank it with a perfectly aimed and definitive strike. The crowd gathered around the table burst into applause.

Smiling, Cooper gave Edward a celebratory embrace. Jorge and his partner were markedly aggrieved over their loss and began to insult Cooper and Edward using a stream of English profanity punctuated with angry words in Spanish. Fortunately, the giant in the lime-green tracksuit quickly intervened, pushing the foul-mouthed pool players away with one shove of his massive paw.

"Boss wants to congratulate you," he informed Edward and then leered at Cooper. "Especially you."

"Who *is* the boss?" Cooper asked before Edward could stop her.

"He's at his table in the corner. Call him Mr. Albion." His mouth twitched into a twisted smile. "That's all you girls need to know."

The crowd parted for the man in green and Cooper and Edward followed him to the back of the club. The dancers onstage had been replaced by a batch of fresh, fully clothed girls, and while Cooper pretended to observe their risqué cowgirl and squaw costumes, she spotted Nathan and Jake. The men were eating hot wings and laughing with their waitress, who was displaying a large amount of cleavage as she leaned over the bar and wiped a spot of blue cheese dressing from Nathan's chin.

Suppressing a surge of jealousy, Cooper looked ahead and focused on the figure of the man in white. Seated at a large table with a view of the entire club, he was obviously Albion. The big fish. The boss. He was dressed in a translucent white shirt and cream-colored linen trousers. Like Jorge, his shirt was unbuttoned at least three buttons in order to show off gold necklaces bearing diamond-encrusted pendants, one of which was a cross. He had a neatly trimmed dark beard, ice-blue eyes that protruded rather eerily from their sockets, and very pale skin. As the giant in green introduced Cooper and Edward, Albion smiled, revealing a mouthful of nicotine-stained, jagged teeth.

He looks like a vampire, Cooper thought and did her best to conceal her fear.

"Congratulations, my friends." To Cooper's untraveled ears, Albion spoke in what sounded like an subtle, Eastern European accent. He openly assessed Cooper and pointedly ignored Edward. "You are pretty and talented, my sweet. How do you want your prize money? I assume cash is good, yes?"

"Thank you, Mr. Albion," she replied and dipped her head in a slight bow. This act of subservience seemed to please Albion and put him at ease as well.

"Some champagne." He snapped his fingers at the man in the tracksuit and then turned to the brunette seated beside him. "Go powder your nose," he ordered. "I wish to talk to the pool sharks." His toothy smile, pale skin, and cold eyes recalled the underwater predator precisely.

The girl sent Cooper a hostile glare but obeyed without comment.

"If you'll excuse me for a minute," Edward told Albion. "I see an old Army buddy of mine by the bar."

"Please. Take your time." Again, the tone was unmistakably commanding.

"Where are you from?" Cooper asked him once they were alone. "Your accent is *so* attractive."

"Russia," Albion answered as his gaze traveled from Cooper's breasts to the edge of her short skirt. "And I enjoy your accent, too. You Southern girls. You sound so innocent, but can be quite wild in private, is that not so?"

Luckily, the arrival of the champagne precluded Cooper from answering. Albion poured and raised his glass to toast her victory. After a single sip, she removed the Advil from her skirt pocket and placed them on her tongue, turning her back slightly away from Albion as though attempting to hide the action.

"What are you taking there?" he asked curiously.

Cooper decided to go on the offensive. "That's *my* business." Now she studied *him*. "After all, you could be an undercover cop or something."

This made Albion laugh for several seconds. He wiped his eyes with a napkin and exhaled in contentment. "That's a good one! You truly do not know who I am, do you?"

"I live out in the country. In Louisa County," she said by way of explanation.

Albion digested this information and continued to gaze at Cooper with his icy eyes. "If you want to have some fun, you should come to me. I'm a famous man in the city. For *fun*."

Cooper indicated the envelope of cash sitting in the middle of the table. "What will *that* get me?"

A greedy light washed over Albion's face. "Some excellent product. Tell me what it is you want."

Here it was. The moment she'd been working toward all night. Now that it had finally arrived, Cooper was nearly frozen with fear. To cover up her anxiety, she gripped her champagne flute until her knuckles turned white. She sipped, pretending to mull over his question.

"If I could pick anything, I'd choose China White," she replied, looking out into the crowd instead of his face. "I've heard it's the best there is."

Albion was silent so long that she was forced to turn to him. "What's wrong?" she scoffed at him playfully. "I thought you were famous for fun. What could be more fun than China White?" She reached for the envelope. "Don't sweat it, though. I can get hooked up later. It's a big city." She smiled at him. "Thank you for the champagne. You have great taste in bubbly."

His pale hand shot out and closed over hers, flattening her palm and the envelope against the table.

"Relax, baby." He smiled again, though no pleasantness permeated the coldness of his eyes. "Drink your champagne. Order some food." Waving expansively, he snapped his fingers at the man in the tracksuit. "We have plenty of time for business."

"No, thank you. I'm keeping an eye on my figure." Cooper glanced at Albion from under her lashes.

"And what a figure it is." He moved his chair closer to hers. "I'd like to show you the inside of my Hummer."

It took all of Cooper's restraint not to guffaw at such an inept come-on. "Look, you seem like a cool guy, but I'm not ready to get close to anybody. This guy I was seeing . . . he died recently. I'm still not over that."

Albion toyed with his champagne glass, his expression one of boredom.

"I met Miguel when I brought my car in for service. We'd only been out on one date, but he treated me nice." She continued even after she felt Albion's body stiffen beside her. "Even though he tried to get me into bed right away and I knew nothing about him at *all*, I liked him. I guess you *men* are all the same. Always after the same thing!" She giggled slightly as though the baser nature of the opposite sex was genuinely amusing. "But I'm holding out for the real thing this time." Feeling daring, she traced a finger down Albion's upper arm and looked at him with intensity. "Are *you* the real thing?"

"You should stop playing with squirrels, my pet, and spend some time with a wolf." His crooked, yellow grin was repulsive. "First, you come to my Hummer. Then, we'll have more fun."

"And you'll get me my China White?"

Albion slid his hand up her thigh. "As much as you want, baby."

Cooper drained her champagne. She didn't want to be alone with this man, no matter what it might prove. "That sounds fun, but I need to tell my partner I'm leaving first. Be right back." She reclaimed the envelope and stuffed it in her purse, her heart hammering. Would this predator even let her walk away without permission?

He said nothing as she turned from the table and headed for the bar, but his expression confirmed his belief that she was utterly under his spell. As soon as Edward, Nathan, and Jake spotted her, they immediately got to their feet.

"We can go now," Nathan stated firmly. "Jake and I have learned enough."

"But you can't *prove* anything," Edward argued.

Jake placed his hands between the two men and spoke hastily. "Proof ain't our job. That's for the cops. We've got a lead for them and it might be all they need. I'm a plumber. Nathan's a computer guru. We can fight the good fight by helpin' out the men in blue. We don't have the muscle to take this guy on."

Edward opened his mouth, but Cooper clamped a hand onto his arm. "What we've got will have to do! I am *not* getting trapped in a limo with that creep and that's exactly where he plans to take me. Take my arm, Edward, and pull me out the door like you're *seriously* pissed at me. NOW!"

"No problem." Edward reacted immediately. As he yanked her forward, Cooper acted surprised and angry but made sure to wave to Albion and mouth *"I'll be back"* on her way out.

Outside, the foursome hastily retraced their path toward the parking lot. Despite the cold, Cooper was relieved that the lot was a safe distance from the club and that no one had followed them there. A maroon sedan obscured Edward's white taxi, and as their little group drew alongside the red car, a man opened the driver's door. Head bent, he lit a cigarette and then held the lighter in front of him.

The small flame illuminated his face.

Edward stopped in his tracks. "Batman."

If Rich Johnson heard the comment, he chose not to react to it, but smiled at Cooper with genuine warmth.

She handed him the case containing the pool cue. "How'd I do?"

He exhaled a funnel of smoke into the black sky. "Not bad for a first-timer. He's got the product, but he didn't say anything incriminating regarding Miguel. There's no proof that he even knew him."

"Your pool stick was bugged?" Edward butted in, sounding angry.

"Not the stick, the handle of the case," Rich Johnson answered.

Cooper tried to mollify Edward. "If this was going to be our only shot at Albion, I wanted it to count, so I phoned Mr. Johnson and told him we were coming here tonight." When Edward didn't respond, she turned back to the policeman. "And there's *no* doubt he knew Miguel."

"What makes you say that?" the policeman inquired as he flicked ash onto the shimmering pavement.

"He called Miguel a squirrel. And when Miguel started working at Love Motors, he told his coworkers that he was 'done being a squirrel.' He wanted them to call him *abeja*. The bee. Someone capable of stinging."

For a moment, Johnson forgot about his cigarette. "Nobody stings Albion and lives. You found a connection, albeit a tenuous one. Still, well done. All of you."

"What now?" Cooper asked.

"Go home. And keep your distance from this place until we've built our case against Albion. We've picked him up before on possession of a concealed weapon, assault and battery, and prostitution charges, but he's got a slick lawyer and he's always slipped out of our net. The guy's an eel. One hundred percent slime."

"Don't worry, one visit to Club Satin was more than enough for me," Cooper replied.

Johnson unzipped the bugged cue case and handed Cooper the polished stick. "You earned this. I'd like you to keep it as a token of my gratitude for placing your trust in me."

Cooper thanked him and then offered the envelope to Edward. "And you earned *this*. Your idea to enter the tournament was brilliant."

Edward made no move to take the money. "I wouldn't touch that. I told you what tonight was about and now we're even. G'night." He saluted the group irreverently, got in his cab, and slowly pulled out of the lot.

Once the taxi turned the corner and disappeared from sight, Jake pointed at the envelope. "What'd you score, anyhow?"

"Three thousand dollars," Cooper answered as she counted out the money. "But every bill feels dirty."

"Then wash it clean," Nathan whispered and closed his hand over the envelope. "Think about those school kids and our hope that they might eat healthier foods."

Cooper beamed at him. Nathan's generous heart had steered her right once again. "Three thousand dollars could buy a lot of apples," she said and linked her arm through his.

Undercover officer Rich Johnson waited until the three civilians were safely out of the parking lot before he crushed his cigarette against the sole of his shoe and zipped his coat. He stared at the spotlights piercing the night sky and his eyes flashed with a determined zeal. "I'm coming for you, Albion," he whispered. "And this time, you will not get away."

14

"So, if you think you are standing firm, be careful that you don't fall!"
1 Corinthians 10:12 (NIV)

Nathan and Cooper were nearly late for Bible study the next morning. Armed with travel mugs of strong coffee, they drove separate cars to Hope Street Church and hurried into the classroom, jostling one another in the doorway to be the first inside. They elbowed each other like a pair of flirting teenagers and giggled, but Nathan's good humor dissipated the moment he crossed the threshold.

"Oh, no!" he exclaimed. "It's my turn to bring refreshments!"

"Phil's got a dozen bagels in the car," croaked someone from behind them. Cooper swiveled around to see Trish leaning heavily against her husband. "These are for this morning's Leadership Team meeting, but I'm sure he wouldn't mind running out to get more. Would you, honey?" She smiled tenderly at her husband and he kissed her on the top of her head.

"No, really. I can go out," a shamefaced Nathan argued but Phil waved off the protest.

"The girls didn't eat much breakfast this morning. They'd love a bacon, egg, and cheese bagel before worship. Let me just get Trish settled and I'll be back before you know it."

The rest of the Sunrise members watched as Phil helped his wife slide into one of the student desks. He then put a flat, square pillow behind her back and propped her legs up using the teacher's chair and another pillow. After depositing a tote bag containing a pink crocheted blanket, a water bottle, and a box of tissues within her reach, he cupped Trish's cheek against his palm, smiled at her with his eyes, and then walked out of the room.

"I have a confession—a dog ate my homework," Trish joked, but Cooper could see that her friend's recent chemo treatment had really taken its toll. A raw, bright red rash covered Trish's hands and face, her forehead was shiny with sweat, and there were several painful-looking sores on the chapped flesh of her upper lip. Her body looked diminished, and in her loose cotton pants and an oversized sweater, she seemed much older than her years. Yet her violet eyes were more luminous than ever and the light Cooper saw there spoke of hope.

"It's so great to have you here today," Cooper told her friend with a warm smile. "We missed you last week."

Trish readjusted the pillow behind her back. "I almost didn't come this morning. Look at me! I own twenty-five skirt suits, a closet full of designer shoes, and drawers of accessories. If you told me a few months ago that I'd be coming to church dressed in yoga pants and tennis shoes with my face covered in Neosporin, I would have asked you what drugs you were taking, but here I am. No pantyhose, no pearls, and no makeup. My mother would be appalled!"

"Then she'd be missin' the point. You dragged yourself to church, even though you'd rather be in bed. Still, your husband seems to be takin' real good care of you," Jake said.

Cooper noticed that he had dark shadows under his eyes and wondered if her lack of sleep had created similar

discoloration on her own face. She'd been too sluggish earlier that morning to bother with foundation or eye shadow
and had settled for applying mascara and lipstick and pulling her dark blonde hair into a headband. But Nathan had
told her more than once that she was beautiful, and between his compliments and the pleasure she felt over having aided the police to move forward in Miguel's case, her
skin seemed infused with a contented glow.

Trish nodded. "Like I said before, cancer is teaching
me quite a few lessons. Phil and I and the girls have never
been closer." She picked up her Bible and held it to her
chest. "And Paul has taught me *so* much over the course
of this study. As a family, we are all trying to be as hopeful as Paul is in chapter five of the second book of Corinthians. We get on our knees every day before we go to bed
and pray to be released from the fear of death, to fully
believe that if 'my earthly tent is destroyed' that I 'have a
building from God.' "

"It seems to me," Savannah spoke softly, "that you're
growing brighter in the Spirit every time we see you. You
may feel physically weak, Trish, but your faith is burning
like a lamp on a stand."

Bryant said, "That's true! And I've been inspired by
you, Trish." He opened his thick study Bible. "In verse
seven, Paul says, 'We live by faith, not by sight.' For me,
that's easy to *say*, but hard to *do*. When something unexpected comes up, something that disturbs the peace
of my world or my plans, I kind of shake my fist at God
and question whether He knows what's right for me." He
reached over and squeezed Trish's shoulder. "You remind
me that faith requires trust, that we can't have one without the other."

At that moment, Phil tapped on the open door of the
classroom and entered carrying a cardboard box from Ein-
stein's bagels. "A baker's dozen, one plain cream cheese,

and one tub of honey walnut cream cheese for the more adventurous." He put the treats down and wagged an index finger at his wife. "Send someone for me if you get too tired."

Quinton jumped out of his seat and rubbed his hands together over the box of bagels. "Let me take orders. I'll prep the bagels and hand them out so we have enough time to go over all our homework questions. I admit that I'd like to hear what happened last night at Club Satin before we go to our morning service. Even though I was with Gloria," his boyish face tinged pink at the sound of her name, "I was thinking about you guys."

"Let's begin our discussion with the definition of *agape*," Savannah suggested after giving Quinton her bagel order. "Any volunteers?"

"*Agape* means 'God's kind of love,'" Jake answered.

Savannah continued. "How does Paul use the word in the second book of Corinthians, chapter seven?"

Cooper checked her answer, which she'd written down several days ago and had already forgotten. "Paul calls his audience 'loved-people.' He's addressing those who believe what he believes. Those first church people."

The Sunrise members went on to discuss false apostles and Paul's sufferings, and then Bryant shared his homework answer concerning Paul's reference to the "angel of light."

"Paul's description reminds us that evil people can present themselves as holy, church-going people. Even Satan was an angel once." Bryant concluded, "Personally, I prefer terms like the Father of Lies or Prince of the World over Angel of Light. It sounds like someone too pure and beautiful on the outside to be corrupt on the inside."

"I know," Nathan concurred. "I hear that title and I immediately picture someone in a white choir robe."

Cooper's mind conjured the image of Albion in his

translucent white shirt and cream-colored pants. She thought of his pale face illuminated beneath the harsh white lights of the fixture hanging above their table. A shiver ran up her torso. If Albion was responsible for Miguel's death, for drug trafficking, and for the other charges he'd managed to acquire acquittal over, then he was truly one of the Prince of the World's ministers.

She looked up from her workbook and noticed that Trish hadn't taken a single bite from her sesame seed bagel. Cooper had wolfed down her own cinnamon sugar bagel in mere minutes and had also drained her coffee cup completely dry. Surrounded by her friends, it was almost easy to forget about the trials of others.

For example, she hadn't spent much time thinking about Maria Gutierrez, the woman who worked for Love Motors and whose son had been murdered a few days earlier. She hadn't even called the video store to find out if the Hector working there was the same young man who'd been killed. She hadn't prayed for Trish lately, uttered many prayers of thanksgiving, or taken the time to complete the last few homework questions as she'd been too busy focusing on her new job and Saturday's events.

"List some ways Paul suffered for his beliefs," Savannah prompted.

"*I* got this one," Jake volunteered. "The poor guy was beaten with thirty-nine lashes, hit with a rod, stoned, shipwrecked, spent a night and day in the open sea, feared bandits, rivers, and his own countrymen. He was hungry, thirsty, and sleep-derived. *Plus*, those Corinthians called him weak and made fun of him because he didn't look physically tough or charge them a pile of money as a speakin' fee." He snorted. "Paul was more patient and gentle than I woulda been, that's for damned sure." Jake's hand touched his lips as he glanced at Savannah. "I mean, darned sure."

"Yet in his letter, Paul still calls the Corinthians his dear friends," Quinton said as he fixed himself a second bagel. "Even though he fears they're going to sink back into a pit of temptation, he doesn't give up on them."

"Remember the Corinth we discussed during our first session?" Savannah's question was rhetorical. "It was a place of anger, envy, gossip, boasting, lust, and debauchery. Paul writes this letter before visiting Corinth for the third time in hopes that the Corinthians have been practicing faithfulness and self-examination. I think we could all benefit from receiving such a letter. Every once in a while, we need to take a pulse—to stop and consider how our faith walk is progressing. Are we all talk or are we all action?"

The group fell silent, reflecting on Savannah's words. She allowed the silence to settle on them for a while and then smiled. "For what it's worth, I've been a witness to the growth in faith of everyone in this room. It has been a great joy to accompany you through another study. You enrich my life with each meeting."

"And I know you've fed me strength through your prayers and your love," Trish whispered weakly.

Several of the Sunrise members blinked away tears. They joined hands as Savannah led them in a closing prayer, and then exhaled in unison as they raised their heads and opened their eyes.

"Guess what? Gloria will be joining us for our next study!" Quinton proclaimed happily as though he couldn't refrain from sharing the news another second. Turning to Bryant, he said, "Why don't you invite Jane?"

Bryant blanched. "Um, I'm not sure about that. This is kind of my safe place. I totally let my guard down with this group. That would be a pretty big step—to have her here."

Trish jabbed his forearm with her pencil. "Haven't you learned *anything,* you big oaf? Bring that woman to this circle and show her who you really are! You're ready, Bryant. Take the plunge! At the very least she'll find out that you're not the type to go hanging around Corinth-like places like Club Satin." She winked at Cooper. "Now tell me everything that happened last night. You've got this *glow* about you today. I've seen you like this before, but only after we'd had some big breakthrough in one of our investigations."

"It's that superhero, good-triumphs-over-evil kind of glow," Quinton added.

"Well, I did look at the face of a devil and he *was* dressed in white," Cooper began. "And I hope I never have to do that again." While refilling her coffee cup, she began to tell those members who hadn't been present at Club Satin what had happened. As she spoke, she encouraged Nathan and Jake to fill in details and it wasn't long before her friends knew the full story.

"But how will we know if the police can pin Miguel's murder on this guy?" Quinton asked, troubled. "He seems to pull himself out of hot water all the time."

"We'll have to settle for reading about the case in the newspaper," Bryant answered. "Frankly, I'm relieved that we're not going to be involved. This Albion sounds like a dangerous character."

"He is," Cooper assured them. "Fortunately, none of us will have to lay eyes on him again."

She'd used her arms to emphasize her point, but her left hand knocked into the ceramic coffee cup perched on the edge of Bryant's desk. It fell to the floor and smashed into pieces, startling everyone.

Cooper looked down at the jagged fragments and the rivulet of steaming brown liquid that seemed to slide, snakelike, along the tiled floor. Swallowing, she felt a prick of dread.

Perhaps she had spoken too soon.

* * *

Later that evening, Cooper had completely forgotten about the broken mug. While mouthwatering scents emanated from her parent's kitchen, Cooper helped her father insert a leaf into the dining room table. Nathan, Ashley, and Lincoln would be joining them for Sunday supper, so Maggie decided to celebrate Valentine's Day for the second day in a row. She'd even made place cards out of red paper hearts and hung up paper streamers. Tiny red, pink, and silver cupids hung from each streamer.

"I don't think we've used this table for a meal since Grammy invited all the church ladies over for a luncheon about ten years back." Earl chuckled. "She crammed them in this room and then paraded in all her orphaned animals."

"That must have been quite a sight," Cooper remarked with a smile.

Earl picked up the folded tablecloth and held it to his chest, lost in the memory. "You shoulda seen those women. They thought Grammy was servin' them *real* turtle soup and was tryin' to show 'em just how fresh it was by bringing in a live turtle. Your mama advised her to start off by bringin' in a dog or cat first, but Grammy wouldn't listen!" Earl rubbed the polished oak leaf. "You could hear a pin drop when Grammy carried that thing in here. I never heard twenty-five women go so quiet in all my life."

Cooper laughed, picturing the group of women dressed in their church finery expecting to share in a pleasant meal, and perhaps some harmless gossip. Instead, Grammy had thrust skittish bunnies, mangy cats, and flea-ridden puppies into their white-gloved hands. Looking around the room, Cooper could almost hear the women's shrieks of surprise and dismay.

"You two speakin' ill of the nearly departed?" Grammy asked crossly from the next room.

"Your hearin' seems to be just fine now!" Earl responded with a smirk. Lowering his voice, he leaned toward Cooper. "It wasn't ten minutes ago that I begged her to change the channel so I could hear the spring-trainin' news, but she pretended her ears weren't workin'."

"Well, who wants to hear a bunch of men yappin' about baseball? I like to watch those boys in tight pants as much as the next woman, but not when Cary Grant's on TV. No sirree!"

Earl threw out his hands in surrender.

As Cooper set the table, she hummed the Beatles' "Do You Want to Know a Secret." All day long, she'd been feeling as though a burden had been lifted from her heart. Now that her encounter with Albion the drug lord was over, she felt as though she could truly trust Rich Johnson and his task force to put the devil clothed in white behind bars.

I wonder if anyone knows Albion's last name. No one ever mentioned it, she thought briefly but the ringing of the doorbell banished further thoughts of the sinister criminal.

Cooper opened the door to find Nathan standing on the welcome mat, his face partially obscured by a spray of pink roses.

"How beautiful!" she declared and reached for the flowers.

Looking sheepish, Nathan held them out of reach. "Sorry, lady. These are for your mother."

Maggie made a big deal of her gift, hugging Nathan against her generous bosom while she chastised him about spending too much money. "I'm glad enough just to have you here, dear boy! You don't *ever* have to come bearin' gifts, you hear?"

"Of course I do," he argued pleasantly. "I'm being fed dinners that would put Emeril Lagasse to shame! The least I can do is find a way to show my gratitude to the master chef." Nathan extricated himself from Maggie's warm embrace in order to remove his overcoat.

"Master chef, huh?" Maggie mused. "I like the sound of that." She elbowed Earl as he removed a pitcher of sweet tea from the refrigerator. "I think *you* should start callin' me master chef from now on."

Deadpan, Earl replied, "We all know who the master of this house has been since day one. I'm just grateful to bask in your light, my love."

Ashley and Lincoln arrived amid the laughter. The married couple had their arms linked and seemed to be leaning against one another for support. Suddenly, Cooper remembered that they had spent several hours with Hector Gutierrez's bereaved mother the day before. The experience must have taken its toll on them both.

"How did your visit with Maria go?" Cooper asked softly while she and Ashley hung up coats on the hall tree.

"It was really hard, but I'm glad we went." Ashley unwrapped a chenille scarf from her neck and draped it over her coat. "You were right about her just needing to talk. We just sat there and listened. Every now and again I'd pat her hand. Lincoln's decided to set up a scholarship fund in Hector's name. When Maria heard that, she smiled for the first time since we got to her apartment." Ashley sighed. "After we left her place, I kept thinking about how someone can go on living after they've lost a child. I'd just crawl into my bed and give up."

"That's not true," Cooper replied softly. "You haven't quit trying to have a child, even though things have gotten rocky. You didn't give up on your marriage and you've always stuck by me through thick and thin. You're made of tougher stuff than you think."

Ashley ran her hands through her silky, blonde mane and grinned, pleased by the compliment. "Maybe. And now you've given me just the opening I was looking for." She glanced down the hall to make sure no one was nearby. "I'll tell you a secret." She paused for effect. "I'm late."

Cooper shrugged. "What else is new? You're always late. Shoot, I had to hold the schoolbus for you for years!"

"No, no!" Rolling her eyes, Ashley pointed at her belly. "*This* kind of late."

"And?" Cooper grabbed Ashley by the shoulders, longing to shake the news out of her.

"It's too early to take a home pregnancy test. I'll have to wait a few more days." Ashley put her finger over her lips. "Don't say anything to anybody about this, but Coop, I already *feel* different."

Examining her sister's hopeful face, Cooper felt a rush of excitement course through her body. She hugged Ashley and whispered into her hair, "I pray it's true, sis."

"Just think," Ashley murmured happily. "It'd be a Halloween baby."

"A treat for all of us," Cooper said with an affectionate smile and the two sisters rejoined the rest of the family.

Over dinner, Nathan and Cooper told a filtered version of their Valentine's Day activities. They completely omitted all mention of Club Satin and instead focused on the revitalization of the East End elementary school.

"Wait until that principal finds out you've got three *thousand* dollars to spend on healthy snacks for those kids!" Maggie stated buoyantly as she served Nathan a second helping of beef burgundy.

"We may have more than that," he replied, happily eying the squares of wine-soaked meat served over egg noodles. "There was a special collection at church yesterday and I believe folks dug real deep. That school might be receiving a year's worth of fruit as well as a crateful of new books for the library *and* a computer or two. We're going to let Quinton tell the principal the good news because he convinced the execs at his company to match the donations penny for penny." Spearing a piece of meat with his fork, Nathan added, "I'm so glad he found someone who'll appreciate his big heart."

"Hrmph! He's likely to get hitched before you two do," Grammy issued an irascible mutter while chewing on a mouthful of glazed carrots. "Nice girls really *do* finish last."

Refusing to rise to her baiting, Cooper reached across the table and took her grandmother's hand. "I'm doing just fine, Grammy. I've got a new position at work, a loyal group of friends, a wonderful boyfriend, and the folks around this table—my precious family."

"Oh, please!" Grammy scowled. "I ain't talkin' about *you* here. *I* don't wanna be in a wheelchair by the time you two get yourselves into the church to take your vows! I do *not* wanna be wearin' a diaper when y'all say 'I do!' "

"Let's just enjoy the here and now," Ashley cut in as the rest of the diners tried not to laugh. "What did you whip up for dessert, Mama? I'm *still* hungry."

Maggie's eyebrows shot up in surprise. "I declare, Ashley! I've never seen you put away so much food!" She observed her daughter thoughtfully and then collected several empty dishes. "I was in the mood for somethin' pretty, so I made a triple-berry lemon trifle. *That* oughta coat your Grammy's sharp tongue with a layer of sugar." She leaned over and kissed her mother-in-law on the cheek.

"You shoulda had sons," Grammy growled at Earl, who rose to assist with clearing the dishes.

Earl walked to the sink, deposited a few dinner plates into the basin and returned to the table for more. Before refilling his hands, he placed one on the top of each daughter's head. "Not only did the Lord bless me with these two jewels, but he's brought me sons in His own way."

Lincoln and Nathan smiled shyly over being included

in Earl's blessings. Maggie, who was prone to tears at the slightest provocation, dabbed at her eyes with her apron corner and placed a trifle cup under Grammy's nose. "Dig in, darlin'. We all know you're grumpy because that handsome boy you liked got voted off *American Idol*. You've been seein' red since Thursday!"

"And why not? That Simon doesn't know what he's talkin' about!" Grammy remarked heatedly, lifting a loaded spoonful of trifle toward her mouth. "I'd like to put him over my knee and give him a sound spankin'."

Lincoln laughed. "I'd pay money to see that!" He then turned to his wife, who was shoveling down spoonfuls of fruit and custard as though she were a participant in a trifle-eating competition. "Slow down, honey! You're going to have an upset stomach if you keep up that rate."

Pausing for breath, Ashley sat back in her chair, looking rather green. Suddenly, she put her hand over her mouth, whispered, "Too late," and jumped up from the table.

The sounds of her being sick echoed down the hall from the bathroom.

"I sure hope she ain't got the flu," Grammy muttered and continued to eat her trifle with salubrious gusto. "But I'll finish her dessert if she can't."

Cooper met Lincoln's eyes. "I hope she isn't contagious."

Brother- and sister-in-law exchanged covert smiles.

Monday came and went in a flash. Cooper interviewed the final three candidates for her new division and was now going to have to reach a decision over whom to hire. She felt that the day's first two interviewees were too inexperienced when it came to working with machines, but the third candidate was highly skilled in not only the repair of office machines, but of all makes of computers as well. Minutes before he'd arrived, Cooper had just been mulling over the possibility of expanding her division to include computer repair and tech support, thereby turning Make It Work! into a comprehensive remedy for all the problems Richmond businesses might encounter. So it seemed as though Donny Mahanoy, a good-looking, clean-cut twenty-eight-year-old, was exactly what she needed.

But I don't like him, she thought, frowning as she reviewed the young man's application once again.

Donny had sauntered into the conference room, taken her hand with unnecessary firmness, and had then proceeded to brag about his "nimble fingers." Cooper had had a tough time asking him any pertinent questions because he'd continuously interrupted her. He also stated that he preferred to work alone because he'd never met a coworker who could comprehend his "mathematical mind" or keep pace with his "Einstein-like problem-solving abilities."

"You're arrogant, rude, and are definitely not a team player." Cooper made notes on Donny's application. "To summarize: Your nimble fingers, mathematical mind, and Einstein-like intelligence aren't worth it."

It was a delightful task to be able to phone the two men she planned to hire and welcome them to the Make It Work! team. Bobby was especially happy and thanked her effusively while his wife issued jubilant screeches in the background.

By five o'clock that afternoon, Cooper had finished all her work for the day and was in the middle of buttoning her coat when she looked up to see Angela leading a troupe of people down the hall.

"We were just lookin' for you!" Angela trilled. "This here is Mrs. Weller and her children. They've brought you a goodie."

"You're such a blessing!" Mrs. Weller cried and thrust a pie into Cooper's hands. The warmth of it soaked right into her palms and the smell of cooked apples and cinnamon permeated the tea towel wrapper. Cooper's stomach gurgled audibly. "Did you know Bobby was let go on Friday?" Mrs. Weller asked.

Cooper shook her head, but didn't get a chance to speak.

"Yes, indeed!" the woman declared breathlessly. "The garage had to make cutbacks and the other employee was the owner's son-in-law, so guess who got fired? We've spent a good part of the weekend on our knees and our prayers were answered by your phone call today." She crossed her hands over her heart. "I know this isn't professional, to come down here like this, but my heart was burstin' with joy and relief and I just *had* to bake you somethin'. Bakin's all I'm good at, aside from makin' babies."

Cooper ran her eyes over the Weller brood. The children were all sandy-haired, freckled, and polite. They also looked hungry. "Would you come into the conference room and share this pie with me? I'd love to get to know you all a bit."

Angela treated the children to Cokes from the vending machine while Cooper brewed coffee for the adults. For the next half an hour, she and Angela listened to the Wellers as they talked, laughed, and argued with the boisterous harmony of a large family.

Later, her hunger stifled by a thick slice of pie and two cups of coffee, Cooper left the office and drove to the nearest grocery store in order to pick up yet another bag of cat litter and a six-pack of tuna fish. She was surprised, upon taking her place in the long express line, to find Investigator McNamara standing directly in front of her.

He seemed lost in thought, so Cooper tapped him lightly on the arm and he swung around abruptly, knocking the cans of tuna from her hands and spilling the baggie of red grapes he'd been carrying.

"Clean up on aisle ten," he joked and scrambled to collect the cans and capture the errant grapes before anyone could step on them. "Sorry about that. My mind was far away."

"Were you thinking about a case?" Cooper inquired, her eyes lit with curiosity.

"Indeed." He turned away in order to place his items on the conveyor belt and then, once his order was bagged, stepped aside to wait for Cooper. "May I carry that litter to your car?" the policeman offered gallantly.

"Yes, please," Cooper accepted and the pair stepped into the dark February evening together. "Can you tell me if there's been any progress in Miguel's case? Have you been in contact with . . . Mr. Johnson?" She'd almost called him Batman and had caught herself just in time.

The ghost of a smile crossed McNamara's face and Cooper wondered if he was aware of his fellow officer's nickname. "Can we sit inside for a moment?" He gestured at Cherry-O. "This is a fine truck. An oldie but a goodie."

"She prefers the term *vintage*," Cooper whispered in collusion and unlocked the doors. She turned on the engine and directed one of the dashboard heating vents toward McNamara.

"You played a dangerous game Saturday night," he began without preamble. "Ivan is sure to suspect you. Even though he's been brought in for questioning in regards to Miguel's murder and may be detained overnight, he's got plenty of minions available to carry out his wishes." His eyes grew dark as he turned to Cooper. "One of his wishes might be to find and punish *you*."

Cooper felt anger, not fear, sparking inside of her. "Just like he snapped his fingers and had Miguel killed? He doesn't know a thing about me."

Shaking his head in disgust, McNamara said, "Do *not* underestimate him. I believe you were one of the last people to see Hector Gutierrez alive. It wouldn't take much for Ivan to discover you were snooping around the video store and Club Satin."

Cooper blanched. "So that *was* the Hector from Doc Buster's? That man, that boy, was shot in the back of the head! He was Maria's son!" She felt sick to her stomach. Fumbling with the window crank, she fought back nausea while inhaling a rush of cold air.

McNamara nodded. "Miguel, possibly Hector Gutierrez, and many others have been Ivan's victims. We're building a case against this scum. Very carefully. If there's a hole in it, Ivan will slither through it and escape. Again."

Ignoring the warning behind that latter bit, Cooper focused on his first sentence. "What *is* the connection between Hector and Miguel?"

"Forged IDs and Love Motors," McNamara answered. "Investigator Wiser and I found their common denominator in Hector's room."

"Club Satin?" Cooper guessed.

"Yes. They visited frequently. To get paid, to run product, we don't have hard proof yet. We believe Miguel was a squirrel—a drug runner for Ivan. He probably skimmed from the take and was murdered because of his theft." He sighed. "We're not sure why Ivan would rub out Hector."

Cooper grabbed the policeman's arm. "Because of me? *I* brought up Miguel's name. He mentioned the words China White. He said them in Spanish but he also warned me not to go near Miguel's boss." Tears filled her eyes. "Hector's boss overheard the warning, I'm sure of it. It's because of me that he's dead!"

"No, Ms. Lee," McNamara told her firmly. "Hector Gutierrez was killed because he was involved in the criminal underworld. He was an underling and his superior was disappointed with his job performance." After gently patting Cooper's hand, McNamara shifted in his seat, making it clear that the discussion was nearing an end. "These young men were dependent on Ivan. I can't prove that yet, but I will. They were small-time crooks, both looking to make it rich quick by serving a fickle master."

"Who clearly viewed them as expendable," Cooper said sadly, still distraught over the idea that she'd had something to do with Hector's demise.

McNamara's tone matched Cooper's as he muttered, "There are dozens of young men just like them waiting to fill their shoes."

"But why Hispanics? Is there something special about their ethnic background? Hector wasn't an illegal, was he?"

The question seemed to force McNamara into silence. Placing both hands on the dashboard, he stared out through the windshield. "I've only told you this much because I don't want to receive a call in which I learn that a beautiful, young woman has been murdered. I want you to hear me when I tell you to lie low until we've got what we need to put Ivan behind bars for good."

"It sounds to me as though you don't have enough proof against him. He's going to get away with murder, isn't he?" Cooper's anger grew hotter.

McNamara's jaw muscle tightened. "I'm warning you to stay out of this. You've helped, yes, but that's enough. Do *not* jeopardize our case." He opened the door, stepped out of the truck and then leaned back into the cab. "If you *truly* want to see justice done, let us do our jobs. Show some faith." With that, he slammed the car door.

Cooper immediately backed out of her parking spot, drew alongside the policeman as he walked to his cruiser, and opened her window. "Tell me one thing."

The investigator said nothing.

"Is Ivan this guy's first or last name?" she asked.

"Last. His first name is Albion." He turned his back in dismissal.

Cooper wished him good night and drove away.

"Albion," she said and the name felt despicable on her tongue. As she thought about the vile man and the unspeakable acts he'd either committed or had set into motion, an idea suddenly took hold in her mind. At the next red light, she pulled out her cell phone and dialed Ashley's number.

"You need to pay another visit to Maria Gutierrez," Cooper informed her sister. "Immediately. And this time, I'm coming with you."

15

"For I am about to fall,
and my pain is ever with me.
I confess my iniquity;
I am troubled by my sin."

Psalm 38:17-18 (NIV)

Ashley called Cooper on Wednesday to report that Maria Gutierrez wasn't answering her phone, so she'd been unable to schedule a visit with the grieving mother.

"It just rings and rings," Ashley stated in befuddlement. "I guess she doesn't have an answering machine."

"I can understand her not wanting to talk to people right now. Could you imagine fielding calls from telemarketers in her state?" Cooper finished cleaning the dirt from a copier drum and then set the soiled rag onto the floor. "Still, I *must* talk to her. We'll just drive over there after I'm done with work today. This can't wait any longer."

"Where's the fire?" Ashley whined. "I've got special plans with Lincoln tonight and I've just *got* to be waiting for him when he gets home from work."

"Why? Did you take the pregnancy test?" Cooper asked breathlessly.

"*That's* part of my plan. I'm going to take it while he's changing out of his work clothes. If it's good news, I'll

serve him nonalcoholic champagne and we'll celebrate."
Her voice held a smile. "I've even got a little baby plate to
put on the dining room table."

Cooper paused and then said quietly, "And if the test is
negative?"

Ashley sighed. "Then we'll just have to drink the real
bubbly and try, try again." Her tone suddenly lightened.
"Really, Coop, I'm not going to be upset. Well, maybe a
little, but I won't wallow in self-pity again, don't worry.
After visiting with Maria, I know there's greater suffering in this world than me not being pregnant."

"I'm proud of you, Ashley." Cooper wished she could
express her admiration more clearly, but she couldn't stop
thinking about the task at hand. "Can you at least come
with me to Maria's house and introduce us? You can leave
right afterward, I promise. Please, Ashley, this is important. I believe Ivan either killed Maria's son or had him
killed and I need to know why. You see, I don't think
Hector stole from him like Miguel did." Cooper struggled
to verbalize her confused thoughts. "There's a specific
reason Ivan uses Hispanic men to do his dirty work. If I
can find out why, then maybe the lives of other men like
Hector and Miguel can be spared their fate."

"Don't you think the police would have gotten that information out of her?" Ashley argued.

"Hector lived with his mother. Maria must have known
how he made money and who he worked for, but maybe
she was ashamed. She probably just told the police that he
worked at a video store," Cooper reasoned.

"Then why would she tell *you* the truth after lying to
the authorities? You're a total stranger. Maybe you need
to work on your humility, Coop."

"There's no guarantee she'll tell me anything," Cooper
admitted. "But I'm going to ask her to think of the *other*
mothers that could lose *their* sons." Hearing Ashley's in-

take of breath, she hurriedly added, "It's not a kind thing to say, I know, but this is not the time for delicacy."

Ashley sighed again, but this time it was mostly theatrical. "I don't think Emily Post would approve of how you've decided to pay your condolences, but you're my sister, and I'll give you thirty minutes of my time. But if Maria's not home this afternoon, then you've got to drop this until I can get her on the phone and arrange a *proper* visit. Deal?"

"Deal," Cooper answered. "I'll be at your place by twenty after five."

Back at the office, Cooper hustled into the break room, hoping Ben and Emilio hadn't polished off all the egg rolls and fried wontons from the office's celebratory lunch. It had been Mr. Farmer's idea to treat the incoming staff members to a decadent takeout lunch from Peking Restaurant, and Cooper was nearly drooling at the thought of succulent sesame chicken served over a pile of fried rice.

Her new hires, Bobby and Josh, welcomed her with a smile. They had spent most of the morning filling out paperwork but would accompany Cooper on her afternoon maintenance rounds. As soon as the two men became familiar with the Make It Work! clients and the machines included on each service contract, Cooper would send them off on their own. Until then, she decided to mentor them for a week first.

"Where's the female addition to your team?" she asked Ben while pulling out a chair between him and Bobby. "And where's Angela?"

"Both chicks are in the locker room," Emilio answered through a mouth stuffed with egg roll. "Brandi said she needed to fix her lipstick before lunch and Angela's coolin' off."

Cooper raised her eyebrows. "Who made her mad?"

"Boss's sister—the freakin' Wicked Witch of the West End," Emilio muttered and then, mercifully, swallowed his food. "Told Angela she was bringin' Mr. Farmer down. That they were from different worlds and she should back the hell off." He popped a fried wonton onto his plate and stabbed it with the end of his chopstick. "I heard the whole thing. It's like a damned soap opera around this place." He swallowed and then slapped Bobby on the back. "Welcome to Make It Work!, pal!"

Bobby smiled. "I've got three daughters, my friend. *Every* day's a soap opera in our house. Keeps things lively. I wouldn't change a thing."

Cooper threw him a grateful look. "Things are usually pretty quiet here. Excuse me, would you? I'm going to go check on Angela."

She nearly knocked Brandi over as she rushed into the locker room. More accurately, she nearly collided with Brandi's hair, which was as long as that of a pop princess, and dyed blonde with black tips. Brandi was bent over with her head facing the floor as she pumped copious amounts of holding spray through her locks. Sensing that someone else had entered the room, she flipped herself upright and smiled. She wore generous amounts of black eye shadow and liner and vamp-red lipstick.

"Hi!" Brandi extended a hand. Cooper tried to reach around her coworker's black and silver acrylic nails and, failing to do so, ended up shaking the other woman's index and middle fingers instead.

"Are you having a good first day?" Cooper inquired politely.

"It's totally awesome! Who *wouldn't*, like, wanna tag along after Emilio?" She giggled and Cooper couldn't help but smile. If Emilio and Carla had truly called it quits, Brandi was exactly the type of woman he'd be quick to pursue.

"Ben's great, too," Cooper said, feeling as though the person responsible for hiring Brandi shouldn't be omitted.

"Oh, yeah! He is, like, soooo sweet." She lowered her voice. "I met him and his wife at an A.A. meeting. During our refreshment break a few weeks ago, I told him I wanted out of Reliable Office Solutions before they went under. I knew he worked here and even though it took me, like, three meetings to work up the nerve to ask, I finally asked him if y'all were hiring." She scratched her chin with her thumbnail. "He already knew me inside and out from our meetings. All my secrets, good and bad, and he still gave me a chance!"

Something Brandi had said triggered a thought in Cooper's memory about Miguel's case, but she needed quiet to figure out what it was.

"I'm sure you're very skilled and Make It Work! is lucky to have you," she told Brandi kindly, though she was impatient to find Angela. "Now you'd better get some lunch before there isn't so much as a fortune cookie left!"

Brandi jerked a thumb toward the bathroom stalls and lowered her voice. "I tried to talk to her, but I figure I'm, like, the new girl on the block. Still, she's pretty torn up about something."

"Angela's just experiencing a little bump on Relationship Road." Cooper guided Brandi out the door. "She'll be just fine."

"I'd like to run over that *bump* with a tractor trailer!" Angela shouted from deeper within the locker room.

Cooper waited on the bench in front of the employee lockers until Angela had composed herself enough to be seen. The office manager sat down next to Cooper and examined herself once more in her compact. Next, she removed a travel-sized perfume bottle from her purse and sprayed her wrists. After inhaling the fragrance on her skin, she exhaled loudly.

"Mr. Farmer gave me this scent for Valentine's Day." She sniffed and blinked back fresh tears. "It's called

Petite Cherie and it came in this *beautiful* glass bottle with two angels on the stopper. Breathin' this in, I'm tryin' real hard to focus on him at this moment and not on that shrew who shares his DNA! That harpy in high heels! Medusa in a fur coat!"

"What is she after you about?"

"Oh, nothin' much!" Angela spat. "She just wants me to find another job and never talk to her brother again. That's all."

"But you and Mr. Farmer make one another happy. Is she jealous of that happiness?" Cooper asked.

"'Course she is! Who'd wanna date her, no matter how much money she's got! Oh, I simply *cannot* let her see how she can get under my skin! Time and time again I have ignored her nasty little remarks. Why, I've cooked supper for that woman for the past two Sundays and she has yet to thank me. Instead, she makes snide comments about my butter beans or my garlic bread or what-have-you!" Angela touched a shellacked lock of platinum hair to be certain that it was where it was supposed to be. "I'm just afraid that she'll turn my man against me, Cooper. The woman is grass-green with envy, and folks like that are capable of real cruelty." She threw her purse on the ground. "Just when I was feeling so secure, I stand to lose everything!"

Cooper took Angela's hand. "Mr. Farmer is *not* going to stop loving you because his sister wishes it. I'm sorry she's making life hard for you both, but you're doing everything right. It's up to Mr. Farmer now. She's his sister and she is out of line."

"But Bea's his *whole* family. He'd never cross her— even for me! So I've gotta bite my lip and smile when what I'd really like to do is smack the woman clear into next week!" Angela's bubble-gum pink lips formed a pout. "And she's right about me not bein' a college graduate or a world traveler and all that, but nobody's gonna love her brother like I do. Not ever!"

"And she'll come to realize that eventually. Her envy will fizzle out, you'll see. It is simply impossible not to like you, Angela." Cooper put an arm around her friend. "Come on, you can't be angry when there's a plate of lo mein with your name on it close by."

"Truer words were never spoken." Angela managed a thin smile. "Thanks, sugar. I just needed to vent a spell. Love can be so complicated sometimes."

"But it's worth it," Cooper said and linked her arm through her friend's.

Five hours later, Ashley led the way as the two sisters drove south over the Willey Bridge. Cooper always slowed down during the brief crossing in order to take in the vision of the James River moving in dark, gray-blue ripples beneath the overpass. Even in the dead of winter, flanked by spiny trees and shrouded by a dull, charcoal-colored sky, the water's movement was a reminder that the world was alive and animated, despite the impression that it was in a state of deep hibernation.

Ashley took the exit from the highway south of one of Richmond's two mega-malls and continued driving east toward the Richmond City line. Without bothering to use her turn signal, she abruptly veered into the entrance of Stony Point Village. She drove toward the first cluster of brick townhouses and parked next to a cargo van with its rear doors left open wide. As Cooper pulled into the space next to her sister's car, a Hispanic man came out of the closest townhome carrying a large cardboard box. He slid the box into the van and then headed back inside without giving the unfamiliar women a second glance. Something about his somber expression and brisk pace made Cooper feel uneasy.

"Looks like Maria's moving," Ashley remarked casually. "I hope she's not leaving her job. Lincoln didn't mention a thing about that, but I know she's a dedicated and responsible employee and would be hard to replace."

"If that turns out to be what she's doing, it's hard to blame her. I think I'd want to leave everything behind and start over, too," Cooper stated sympathetically as the man reappeared bearing a suitcase in each arm. He called something over his shoulder in Spanish and two women materialized in the front doorway.

As Ashley waved in greeting, Cooper was certain she saw fear flash across their faces. The women were nearly identical in appearance—black hair streaked with hints of gray; soft, stocky bodies clad in sweatshirts and snug jeans; round faces; chestnut-brown eyes framed by black lashes.

"Are you moving?" Ashley asked the woman on the right.

Maria Gutierrez nodded. "Yes. This is my sister, Nina. She and her husband are loading the last of my things." Her tone was polite, but it was clear that she wasn't in the mood for a social call at the moment.

Courtesy dictated that Ashley and Cooper make their excuses and leave. When it seemed as though Ashley was about to do just that, Cooper clamped a hand firmly on her arm. "We don't mean to trouble you, ma'am!" she called over the space of the tiny front yard. "I know you're busy, but do you think you could spare me just a few minutes of your time? It's very important that we speak."

"Well . . ." Maria began, but her sister was quick to respond on her behalf.

"Maybe tomorrow," she said in flawless English. "That would be a more convenient time. We need to finish loading before nightfall."

"I don't think you'll be here tomorrow," Cooper stated softly, locking eyes with Maria. She held out her hands in what she hoped was a gesture of supplication. "Please. It's about Miguel and Hector. And other boys just like them."

Maria grabbed onto the doorjamb for support and Nina's eyes turned dark with indignation. "You have no respect! Leave my sister alone! Isn't she in enough pain?"

Ashley was also staring at Cooper, her mouth ajar in horrified embarrassment, but Nina's reaction confirmed what Cooper had suspected. The family knew about Hector's illicit activities. Did that knowledge now endanger them? She sensed it did.

"I'm begging you, Mrs. Gutierrez," Cooper whispered plaintively. "Help me prevent Albion Ivan from hurting another boy." She used the word "boy" deliberately.

It seemed as though time slowed to a crawl as Maria made up her mind. Nina's husband squeezed between the two sisters in order to fetch more items from inside the townhouse. As soon as he passed them by, the women instantly reclaimed their positions, standing shoulder to shoulder as though guarding the abode against invaders.

"Go ahead, Ashley," Cooper said loud enough for the other women to hear. "Ivan might be coming after me, too, so I've *got* to stay."

Ashley opened her mouth to protest, but seeing the steely determination in her sister's face, nodded, and turned away with an apologetic smile for Maria.

Cooper took a step forward. Maria's reluctance to talk, her sudden decision to move, and the panic written in her eyes confirmed Cooper's suspicion that the older woman had withheld information from the police. "Other boys will be killed. You know this is true. Don't walk away from them." Cooper kept her voice as gentle as she could, despite the urgency she felt. "Please. Just tell me what you know so I can do *something* to stop him."

Maria looked at the ground, her face contorted as different emotions—fear, anguish, and anger—manipulated her features.

"Do you want more mothers to know your grief?" Cooper asked, allowing her own anxiety to show. "To be in agony?"

Covering her face with her hands, Maria began to cry. Nina instantly advanced on Cooper and pointed at her. "Have you no shame? Go away from here!"

"No!" Maria called out, her voice cracking. She spoke quickly to her sister in Spanish and then vanished into the house. As no one had invited Cooper inside, she waited out in the cold, hugging herself against the air and the sharpness of her own words. After a few minutes she sat down on the edge of the curb, her back turned toward the Gutierrez house.

Maria joined her there, coatless and shivering. Her eyes were raw from crying and her nose red from being rubbed over and over again with a tissue. She handed Cooper a photograph. "This is my son. I came to this country for Hector, so that he would have chances I never had. I was a single mother and an illegal, but I got papers and a job. Nina had immigrated before me and had become a true citizen by then. But there was never enough money."

"What was your first job?" Cooper asked to keep the other woman talking. Maria's answer took her by surprise.

"I was in charge of human resources at Double A Auto in Norfolk," she said.

That's where Miguel once worked! Cooper was stunned by the revelation. *But what does the connection mean?*

Maria touched the picture of her son, tracing the curve of his face with her fingertip. "I had nothing when I got that job, but both Nina and I spoke good English and we were quick to learn computers."

"Did Nina work at Double A, too?"

"No. She got a government job, but like her, the people who hired me taught me everything I needed to know." She fell silent and Cooper was afraid that she'd heard all Maria was willing to say. But finally, she began to speak again. "As long as I stayed quiet, my son and I would have a good life. I knew what I was agreeing to and for his sake, I did everything they said. After a while, I convinced myself I was doing nothing wrong—just taking a shortcut to the American Dream."

Tears streamed down her cheeks and Cooper handed her a tissue. Maria stared at the object and then, as though unwilling to antagonize the chapped skin on her nose any further, dabbed gently at her face and then balled the tissue inside a clenched fist.

"But Hector . . . he wanted more and more as he grew into a man. He wanted a car and expensive clothes and video games. I couldn't give him all of these things, so he started working for *them*, too. He was foolish, to steal from these people. Him and Miguel. Those silly boys wanted to live like movie stars, to forget that they were still foreigners here and might be for the rest of their lives."

She carefully reclaimed the photograph. "Envy. One of the deadly sins. It's what truly killed them." A tear plopped on the image, then another, the water distorting Hector's grinning face. "The Bible says, 'A heart at peace gives life to the body, but envy rots the bones.'"

Cooper had never heard that line of Scripture before. She touched the other woman's hand. "I am sorry for what you've lost."

Maria placed a small cardboard box in front of her. "*My* heart has not been at peace since I came to this country, no matter how much I tried to deceive it. May God forgive me, forgive Nina, and forgive my son. This," she pointed at the box, "will serve as our confession."

Assuming Maria intended for her to look inside the box, she reached for it. Suddenly, her hands were seized.

"Swear to me you will not open this until tomorrow night!" Maria's brown eyes were wide with dread. "By then, we'll be gone. I can't let any harm come to my sister! Nina is all I have left and I'm the one who talked her into . . . Just make me this promise. And if I don't believe you I won't give you the box!"

"I swear," Cooper assured the woman, meeting her frantic gaze and squeezing her hands to show her earnestness. She had no choice. "I swear to honor your request."

"After tomorrow, you can show it to the police. But I beg you—do not let Mr. Love take away the scholarship in Hector's name. It is the only good to come from all of this wickedness."

"No matter what, there will be a scholarship. Lincoln doesn't go back on his word." Cooper prayed she was speaking the truth. After all, if he discovered Maria was also a criminal, he might feel too betrayed to establish such a fund. Shaking her head, Cooper knew she couldn't think about such things now. "Are you going back to Mexico?"

Without answering, Maria rose and looked at the box at Cooper's feet with disdain. "Do not let envy spoil your life. Be grateful for what God has given you." Her lips trembled as she clasped Hector's picture against her chest.

"I will," Cooper promised and felt a wave of sorrow as Maria trudged across the dormant grass toward her house. Her posture was stooped, as though a heavy weight pressed down upon her back and the load was too much for her to bear. She shuffled forward like an old woman into the outstretched arms of her sister, who glanced at Cooper accusingly as if to say, "Look what you've done."

Though Cooper's throat was tight with grief, she recognized that Maria's exhaustion partially stemmed from speaking the truth. It had taken Maria's last bit of strength and courage to entrust a stranger with her secrets. Cooper stared at the box. She knew the police would pry open the flaps within minutes and whisk Maria straight to the station for questioning, but Cooper had made a vow. She had accepted the transfer of the bereaved mother's burden and it was now hers to carry.

Glancing backward, Cooper saw the two older women locked in an embrace. Their shoulders shook as they cried in one another's arms. ·

Whatever you're guilty of, Maria Gutierrez, Cooper thought, *you deserve to be comforted*.

Collecting the box, she climbed quietly into her truck and drove off into the descending night.

16

"Why did you run off secretly and deceive me? Why didn't you tell me, so I could send you away with joy and singing to the music of tambourines and harps?"

Genesis 31:27 (NIV)

To avoid temptation, Cooper put Maria's box under her kitchen table. She didn't even touch it before heading out the following morning. Its presence had haunted her all night, preventing her from falling asleep until well after the stroke of twelve.

She'd tried calling Ashley to tell her about her conversation with Maria, but only succeeded in speaking to her answering machine. Nathan had offered to come over and take her mind off both Maria and the mysterious package, but Cooper had politely declined. What she most wanted was to sink into a tub filled with hot, lavender-scented water, and then bundle up in her flannel coffee-cup pajamas and read a book on the sofa with Moses and Miriam curled into twin balls of vibrating fur at her feet.

Her attempts to lose herself in the pages of Oprah's latest book-club pick had failed, so she'd turned on the television and watched *American Idol* mainly so she could discuss the strengths and weaknesses of the remaining contestants with Grammy.

After the episode was over, Cooper flipped channels

in search of something humorous or romantic, but every show seemed to be a crime drama. Forensic techs in pristine lab coats exchanged information with detectives in tailored suits on one channel. Uniformed policemen led a prisoner to his cell in another. There were historical crime shows, legal-themed crime shows, and paranormal crime shows. If Cooper wanted to watch anything else, she'd have to settle for an infomercial about a butt-toning machine or a Western. Neither choice was appealing.

Cooper had switched off the TV and lay in silence for a moment. Moses yawned, stretched, and walked up the length of her body. He'd wiped his small face along her jaw line, his affectionate way of indicating that while he loved her, he would love her twice as much if she'd get up and serve him a snack.

Kissing the top of the kitten's soft head, she'd smiled. "I suppose you'd like a nice can of tuna?"

At the word, Miriam's head had whipped up from where it had been burrowed partially beneath Cooper's slippered feet. Laughing, she'd scooped the kittens into her arms and carried them the short distance to the kitchen. Knowing she was fostering a bad habit, she placed both cats on the counter and dumped a small can of tuna onto a saucer. As they mewed in anticipation and nuzzled one another in excitement, Cooper drizzled tap water over the tuna and set the treat in front of the little cats.

She'd listened to their contented lapping for a moment and then turned toward the kitchen table, as though lured by a powerful magnet.

"Don't worry, I'm not going to open the box," Cooper had announced to her preoccupied felines. "But I can give it a little shake, right? That won't hurt anybody." Grasping the cardboard box in her hands, she'd shuffled it back and forth very gently. It sounded like the edges of a thin book banging against the sides.

Whatever this is, she'd thought, *it's close in size to the box. It could be a book, or a bunch of standard-size papers, or an envelope of photographs!* Her mind conjured numerous possibilities.

"I'm not going to stand here and blindly guess!" she'd informed the object before returning it to the table. After brushing her teeth and putting on some moisturizer, she'd reentered the kitchen, picked up the box, and put it under the table out of sight. She'd then whiled away the rest of the evening working on a two thousand-piece jigsaw puzzle showing the various wares sold in an old-fashioned general store. After completing the edge pieces and a large chunk of the penny candy display, Cooper had finally gone to bed.

Nestled under a down comforter and a soft, cotton blanket, Cooper had expected to drift off immediately, but her thoughts wandered. She recalled walking through Miguel's apartment, touching the silk shirts hanging in neat rows in his closet, and discovering the drawer filled with cash. Images of Club Satin followed, then the newspaper article's title about Hector's execution-style murder, and finally, Maria's hunched shoulders and weary gait as she walked into her sister's waiting arms.

Exasperated and exhausted, Cooper had thrown back the covers and stumbled in a groggy haze between sleep and wakefulness to the bathroom for a glass of water. As she'd filled the tumbler, Maria's box seemed to call to her from the kitchen. Fortunately, she'd been too tired to be enticed by its contents and had shuffled back to bed. She'd eventually drifted off to sleep, only to be plagued by fragments of unrelated but frightening images such as Miguel's body in the trunk, a shark exposing its rows of daggerlike teeth, a pair of headlights in the rearview mirror.

The final sequence had been downright scary, for it involved a lurking shadow in an empty, ice-covered parking lot. In her dream, Cooper had tried to open the door of her truck, knowing that she had to get inside and quickly. But no matter how hard she pulled and yanked at the handle, which was covered by a thick crust of unrelenting ice, the door would not budge. She knew, without turning, that someone was coming for her, hunting her like some silent panther. Crying, she pleaded for the door to give way, struggling with all her might to get it open. When she felt the stalker's breath on her neck, she woke up.

Never had the weak light of a February morning been so welcome.

Cooper was thankful to be so busy at work that same day. Make It Work's main competitor, Reliable Office Solutions, had officially closed its doors and, as a result, the phone rang insanely all morning. Angela had been talking so steadily that she hadn't even had time to reapply a fresh layer of lipstick.

"I thought you were going to hire an assistant," Cooper whispered while Angela wrote down a prospective client's information in her bubbly script.

Covering up the mouthpiece, Angela snarled, "Her *Highness* doesn't think I need any help. She's talked Mr. Farmer into waitin' another two weeks to see if we're really gonna stay this busy."

Cooper frowned. "That doesn't make any sense. We're obviously expanding. My department already has more than enough work and so does Ben's. I believe you're getting a raw deal."

Angela thanked the client sweetly and hung up. Ignoring the steady blinking of the other three phone lines for a moment, she took a long drink of Diet Coke and sighed wearily. Despite the flashing lights, the phone remained silent.

"How'd you get the lines to stop ringing?" Cooper asked, recalling how maddening it had been to listen to the blaring of the multiple lines during Angela's brief absence a few weeks ago.

"When I heard the news about Office Solutions, I ran right out to Costco and bought a new phone. This one's got a mute button." She answered line two and pleasantly asked the caller to hold. "See? I'm not as dumb as Mrs. Farmer thinks."

Cooper watched as Angela returned to her momentous task. She noted the pile of paperwork threatening to fall out of her friend's overflowing inbox as well as the stack of manila folders occupying the corner of Angela's desk customarily occupied by a vase of fresh flowers.

This is not good, Cooper thought and vowed to speak to Mr. Farmer during the lunch hour. However, her boss was nowhere to be found when she returned to the office at quarter after twelve, though Angela was exactly where Cooper had left her. Replacing the receiver, the office manager put her head in her arms in exhaustion. The phone continued to twinkle like a Christmas tree.

"I haven't so much as gone to the ladies' room *all* mornin'!" Angela wailed. "I used to love my job, but frankly, I'd rather be gettin' a root canal than spend another minute in this place. Least I wouldn't have to talk at the dentist's!" Angela gestured at the blinking telephone base. "See? It never ends!"

"I thought you put on a voicemail recording during lunch," Cooper stated in surprise.

On the verge of tears, Angela cried, "*She* thinks we'll lose our potential new clients if they don't get to talk to a friendly, professional Make It Work! employee right away. I don't dare leave my desk in case she calls, pretendin' to be a client! Cooper, I'm a prisoner!" she cried.

"Come on, Angela." Cooper didn't like the futility in her friend's voice. "What's going to happen if you don't listen to Mrs. Farmer? She's never been involved in the daily operations of this office."

"Well, she sure is interested *now*! And if I make *one* false move, she'll have a reason to convince Mr. Farmer that I'm not worth my weight in salt. I'll be out of a job. After that, she'll make sure I'm out my man, too!"

Cooper grabbed Angela's hand as she moved toward the telephone receiver. "Don't let this woman hold such power over you!" Without asking for permission, Cooper opened Angela's top desk drawer, knowing that her appearance-conscious friend kept a variety of beauty products there, and held up a small mirror. "Is this the face of someone who can be intimidated?" She tried to sound stern. "The face of a woman who agrees to be glued to a chair for five hours straight? Or is willing to surrender without a fight?" Pushing the mirror into Angela's hand, she selected one of three lipsticks from the drawer. "For goodness sake, Angela. Your lipstick has completely worn off! I haven't seen your bare lips since I started this job!"

This realization seemed to shock Angela into action. She snatched the cotton-candy gloss from Cooper, deftly applied it to her lips, and slammed the mirror back into the drawer. "Thank you, darlin'! I needed someone to slap me on the cheek and you cared enough to do just that! *Two* hours with naked lips! What next? No nail polish? No perfume? No trips to the restroom to powder my nose?" She exhaled slowly and then punched a few buttons on the telephone.

"I believe you've earned a break," Cooper said.

Angela smiled broadly. "Yes, indeed. I see a nice, sit-down lunch in my crystal ball, charged to the Make It Work! expense account. After that, I'm gonna march into

Mr. Farmer's office and demand an assistant. If he back-pedals, he's gonna be all alone in his bed tonight! *I've* got my own kind of power!"

After a lunch hour that stretched well beyond its sixty-minute limit, Angela reapplied her makeup, brushed and sprayed her puffy platinum hair, and doused herself with magnolia-scented perfume. "I'm goin' in!" she trilled and walked into Mr. Farmer's office without knocking.

Pleased to see Angela regaining control of her future, Cooper and her team headed to her next appointment in one of the work vans. As they drove out of the garage, she suddenly stopped mid-sentence during her conversation with Bobby.

"You okay?" Bobby inquired.

"*I* am." Cooper nodded and then pointed at the figure alighting from a black Mercedes. It was Mrs. Farmer. "But I think there's about to be a gladiator match in Mr. Farmer's office."

"Between that lady and someone in our office?" Bobby inquired.

"Yes. Angela," said Cooper.

"Then my money's on Angela," Bobby stated loyally and once again, Cooper felt glad that she'd hired him.

She slowed the van in order to observe Mrs. Farmer's determined march into the Make It Work! building. "We'd better pick up some roses on our way back later on."

"What for?" Josh asked in confusion.

"That's what the Roman spectators would have thrown into the arena. It was their way of rewarding the winning gladiator," Cooper replied with a grin. "I believe red will do quite nicely."

Cooper had asked Nathan to meet her at her apartment after work so they could open Maria's Mystery Box together. She felt a twinge of guilt for not having informed him that Maria was probably in a different country already and that they were now responsible for the box's contents. As she drove home, Cooper felt hopeful that she and Nathan would discover enough proof to put Ivan away until he was stooped with age.

Upon turning off the narrow, country road onto the gravel driveway leading to her parents' house, Cooper was surprised to see Nathan's old pea-green BMW parked in front of the garage. He didn't have a key to her apartment, so unless he was waiting in the car, he must have felt comfortable enough with her family to seek shelter from the winter afternoon's bite inside the Lee house. Pulling alongside his car, she noted it was empty, so she entered Maggie's domain through the back door.

As usual, the kitchen was filled with delicious aromas. A stew pot gurgled on the stovetop, releasing the scent of simmering tomatoes, garlic, and basil. The comforting smell of baking bread leaked out of the oven and Cooper inhaled deeply. She smiled at her mother, who was washing leaves of iceberg lettuce in the sink.

"Did you make your Key lime cookies today?"

"I sure did! What a nose you've got on you, girl! And I was *just* puttin' a few in a bag for you and Nathan to have for dessert." Maggie beamed at Nathan, who was sitting at the kitchen table cradling a mug of tea in his long, graceful hands. "Now, my darlin' girl. I hope you have somethin' upstairs to feed this boy. If not, I've got plenty of spaghetti to share."

"We're having pasta, too, Mama. It'll never be as good as yours, but I *am* using homemade pasta sauce. Homemade by the organic grocery store, that is."

Maggie smiled, her cheeks flushing pink as she removed the lid from the pot on the stove and gave the sauce a perfunctory stir. "Do you need some bread? Salad? Grated cheese?"

Earl walked into the kitchen and, after greeting Cooper, slipped an arm around his wife. "Stop givin' our food away, Magnolia. Our eldest knows how to fix a fine supper on her own. You know Grammy and I don't wanna share our meatballs or garlic bread."

"Earl!" Maggie chided and slapped her husband with a potholder. He leaned in and kissed her on the cheek, squeezing her thick waist with his strong, weathered hands. Maggie's cheeks turned a shade redder.

Cooper cleared her throat. "Um, we'll see you later. I've got to start cooking and Nathan and I have some detective work to do, too."

Following her cue, Nathan rose and accepted a bag of cookies from Maggie, who had detached herself from her husband's embrace and was holding him at bay with a pair of tongs.

"Thanks again, Mr. and Mrs. Lee." Nathan smiled.

"Please! It's Maggie and Earl!" Maggie waved her wooden spoon at Nathan. "Go on, you two. I know you're itchin' to have some time alone together."

"Are they talking about us or themselves?" Nathan whispered as they closed the back door behind them and trotted up the short flight of stairs to the apartment.

Cooper unlocked her door. "They've always been like that. I was embarrassed by their little displays of affection when I was growing up, but now I realize how lucky I was to have such openly loving parents. In these days of so many divorces, it's nice to know that it really *is* possible to live happily ever after." Moses and Miriam rushed the door, nearly tripping both Cooper and Nathan as they mewled for attention and dinner, winding around both pairs of human feet. Cooper obliged the kittens immediately by popping open a can of cat food.

"Let me get supper started before we deal with *that*." She pointed at the box under her kitchen table and then removed her coat. "I want to be able to concentrate on the contents without my stomach rumbling."

"Why is it under there?" Nathan asked. "Were you worried someone might try to steal it?"

Cooper laughed. "No! I couldn't stop thinking about what might be inside last night and I figured 'out of sight, out of mind.' Now I know *exactly* how Pandora felt."

"I bet." Nathan looked as though he'd like to tear the box apart immediately. His eyes were studying it intently and his hands were already reaching for it. Fortunately, Miriam saw him squatting on the floor and interpreted his posture as an invitation to play. She launched herself at his feet, toying with his shoelaces. Moses gulped down the last bite of cat food and then leaped over his sister in order to scale up Nathan's chest.

"Ow!" Nathan chuckled and gently removed Moses's claws from his shirt. "You wanna play rough, huh?" He turned the kittens over and, snatching his scarf from where he'd draped it over one of the chairs, began to dangle it above their eager paws.

Cooper switched on her CD player and hummed along to the songs of *Abbey Road* as she packed meatballs and set them on a lined cookie sheet. Once the meatballs were in the oven, she put water on the stove to boil and began to slice the loaf of Italian bread she'd picked up on the way home. Soon, the tiny kitchen was redolent with the same warmth and comforting smells as Maggie's. Cooper placed her hands flat on the countertop and spent a moment simply enjoying a moment of absolute contentment.

However, both she and Nathan rushed through the tasty meal, eating quickly and talking in spurts. Cooper drank her red wine too fast and felt rather light-headed by the time she'd finished her bowl of linguine.

"So much for a nice, relaxing supper," she commented sarcastically.

Nathan grinned. "Yeah, right! I'm sorry, Coop, but that box is an elephant in the room."

"Let's just dump our plates in the sink and open the thing already."

Nathan leapt up and removed her bowl before she had the chance to move. "I love the Woman of Action side of you. I'll clear this table like Flash Gordon. You get the box and a pair of scissors."

A few minutes later, the open blade of Cooper's kitchen shears hovered over the taped box flaps. Her hand was trembling with excitement and no small measure of trepidation. Nathan moved closer to her. The feel of his warm breath on the back of her neck was a momentary distraction and she almost pivoted so that her lips could find his. Instead, she lowered the scissors point and severed the clear packing tape with a swift, definitive sweep of her arm.

Nathan peeled back the flaps and Cooper reached inside. She freed a file folder containing a few sheaves of oddly shaped, rectangular papers. The folder was labeled *Special Titles* followed by a small mark.

If Cooper had expected to discover a pile of emails from Ivan to Hector containing precise instructions on how to forge documents or conduct illegal drug transactions, she was sorely disappointed. Flipping through the seemingly harmless Department of Motor Vehicle documents, she handed the top four vehicle titles to Nathan.

"What am I not seeing here?" she demanded crossly. "Where's the incriminating video tape? The photographs? Letters? Anything but these car titles!"

"I'm sure if we examine them carefully something will become clear." Nathan slid into a chair without looking up from the piece of paper in his hand.

Cooper grabbed Maggie's Key lime cookies from the counter, placed them on a napkin in the center of the table, and began to pore over the first title on her pile. Absently, she reached for a cookie. She bit into the crisp buttery crust covered in powdered sugar and sighed as a burst of soft, sweet lime and smooth white chocolate chips coated her tongue.

"These cars were purchased from Love Motors. Nothing interesting about that." She rifled through the more than half-dozen titles in the folder and then fell silent, trying to think things through. She stuck her hand out toward the cookie plate and her fingers brushed Nathan's. Looking up, the couple smiled at one another and then resumed their scrutiny of the various titles.

"The cars are all General Motors make, but they're different brands," Nathan stated. "I've got a Cadillac, a Suburban, a Saab sedan, and a Pontiac G8 here."

Cooper read off the cars listed on her titles. "My pile has a Hummer, a Corvette, a Dodge Ram, a Buick, a GMC SUV, and a Cadillac." She took a sip of wine and grimaced. Red wine and lime cookies were not a good mix. "These are not inexpensive cars. I wonder if that's relevant. Two of them have liens but the others were bought outright." She whistled, trying to imagine what it would be like to have enough money in the bank to be able to drive a forty thousand-dollar car off the lot free and clear.

The recorded odometer readings indicated that the vehicles were new when purchased and, after comparing notes, Nathan and Cooper determined that they'd all been bought over the previous three months.

"Why did Maria keep these?" Cooper was exasperated. "If there's a secret here, it's not obvious to me unless the titles are fakes."

Nathan rubbed his dimpled chin in thought. "Do you have your truck title around? We could compare them."

Cooper brightened. "I do! It's in a fireproof lockbox in my closet." She raced into her bedroom, retrieved the lockbox, and popped it open. Tossing aside her birth certificate, a stock certificate she'd received as a gift for her eighteenth birthday, a charm bracelet she'd worn as a girl, and her high school diploma, she came across the title.

"Ha!" She grabbed the paper and returned to the kitchen. Nathan slid his chair next to hers and the twosome huddled over the pair of Commonwealth of Virginia titles. Three sides of each title had a gray-blue border with an elaborate design that reminded Cooper of lace and had been printed on paper covered by the words "VEHICLE RECORD" in shades of blue and beige. Cooper held the titles up to the light, revealing matching watermarks of the State Seal. The light also illuminated only the blue letters and some nearly invisible barcodes. Returning the titles to the table, Cooper and Nathan matched up the information listed on each title line-by-line.

"Maria's looks legit to me," Cooper murmured, pushing the papers away in frustration. "How can a bunch of car titles help the police close two unsolved murder cases? Unless the people who bought these cars are criminals, the cops will laugh in my face if I bring them this file." She recalled McNamara's last warning. "Actually, they won't laugh. I could end up in a heap of trouble." She shook her head. "I can't call them until I have solid proof."

"Wish we had a friend at the DMV," Nathan said with a sigh. "They'd know if the titles were doctored."

Cooper scrunched up her mouth and tried to imagine strutting into the DMV and asking a supervisor to examine Maria's titles. They'd probably think she was a nutcase. Suddenly, an idea sprang into her head. She jumped up and squeezed Nathan's shoulder.

"I may not have friends in the DMV, but I did make a new friend shortly before Miguel was killed." She kissed Nathan on the cheek and then began to dig through the hamper she used as a recycling bin. Flipping through last

Saturday's paper, which was stained by droplets of Dr Pepper and Whiskas Ocean Whitefish, Cooper found what she was searching for.

"Ever been to an auto auction before?" she asked her confused boyfriend. As he shook his head no, she placed the paper in front of him and pointed at the advertisement for River City Auto Auction. "Well, *I'm* going to one this weekend. Take note of this face." She tapped on the photo of a middle-aged woman smiling proudly as she gestured at a row of cars. Several grinning men flanked her, but the sheer happiness of the woman's expression drew the eye right to her face.

"Felicia Hawkins." Cooper spoke to the black and white image of the former secretary as she rubbed her butterfly pin, her fingers tracing the delicate silver filigree on its wings. "You might just be the answer to our prayers."

17

*"A false witness will not go unpunished,
and he who pours out lies will perish."*

Proverbs 19:9 (NIV)

Nathan couldn't join Cooper at the River City Auto Auction Saturday morning as he'd promised to spend the better part of the day doing odd jobs for his younger sister. After that, Quinton, Gloria, Nathan, and Jake planned to install the new computers at the End East elementary school and assist the school librarian in replacing the covers or fixing the loose bindings of damaged books. Nathan was excited to see the elderly woman's face when Quinton presented her with a check for new books. The three thousand dollars Cooper and Edward had won at the pool tournament had grown into nearly six thousand dollars once the congregation at Hope Street had added their donations for the school's benefit. Now, the students would receive healthy snacks each day, but also a fresh supply of books and computer programs. Things were looking up for the East End school.

So while her friends were busy performing good deeds, Cooper spent an hour driving to the complex where the auto auction was being held. Assuming she'd be spending a good portion of time outdoors, Cooper bundled up in her warmest parka, as well as her fleece turquoise hat and scarf. She consulted her map and followed the directions she'd found on River City Auto Auction's website. Luckily, all she had to do was head toward Richmond International Airport and make a few turns once past the airport's entrance.

River City Auto Auction was located in a building that once served as an airplane hangar. The metal structure was surrounded by a parking lot the size of a football field. Dozens of red and white arrows indicated customer parking while another specified an area reserved for River City employees and the disabled.

The website had stipulated that the auction started promptly at ten o'clock, but buyers could preview the cars Friday evening and Saturday morning before the sale began. A complete list of cars to be sold in that Saturday's auction was also available online and Cooper had enjoyed reviewing the photographs and histories of several classic cars.

"Don't get nervous," she assured her beloved red pickup truck as she parked. "I wouldn't trade you for anything."

Outside the spacious building, hundreds of people were walking on either side of a line of forward-facing cars. As Cooper moved closer, a man wearing a red jacket hopped into a Toyota Camry located just outside the building's garage. He started up the engine, drove it inside, and then slid into the driver's seat of the next car in line—a purple PT Cruiser.

Clusters of men stood around chatting and gesturing at cars. Some were reviewing their printouts containing the vehicle history while others were preoccupied making notations, peering under hoods, inspecting paint jobs, and crawling inside to sit behind the wheel. Cooper couldn't recall a time when she had seen so many men looking downright jubilant. With the roar of engines, the scent of gasoline and motor oil in the air, and a row of cars and trucks stretching for as far as the eye could see, the males and a scattering of females were in their element.

"You need help, young lady?" an older man wearing a red River City Auto Auction jacket inquired pleasantly.

"I'm looking for Felicia Hawkins," Cooper answered.

The man appeared quizzical, but then he smiled. "We call her Fizzy! She's just as bubbly as a soda pop. I forget right often that her mama christened her somethin' else." He gestured at the long counter visible through the open garage door. "She's back there, helpin' the buyers collect their tags and such. She's made us so organized we can sell twice as many cars per sale as we used to."

Cooper was surprised to hear that the sour woman she'd met back in January had changed so much that she was now referred to as "Fizzy" because of her perky personality. Still, it was wonderful to realize that unhappy people were capable of change if given the opportunity to do so.

"Thank you," Cooper told the helpful gentleman, and he nodded and turned away to show a man in his early twenties the fancy chrome rims on an Escalade.

Felicia was in the middle of a conversation with a customer wearing a bright yellow sticker on his coat. The number fifty-seven was neatly printed on the sticker and Cooper inferred that it was his bidder number. A glance around the room confirmed this theory.

"If you need to register, you're at the wrong counter," a middle-aged man kindly offered. "You look like you'd be a great match for the five-series up next." He pointed at the silver BMW sedan in front of them. "But you'd better hurry! Merv sells a car about every sixty seconds."

"Wow." Cooper was impressed. She listened, fascinated, as the auctioneer called out prices in increments of five hundred dollars and then one hundred as the bidding slowed. Men waved hands, baseball hats, coffee cups, and newspapers to indicate their bid and several teenage boys shouted as they kept track of the bids. Suddenly, Merv banged his gavel and the Jeep Liberty was driven out through the garage door on the opposite end of the building.

As Merv reviewed the assets of the silver BMW, Cooper felt a hand on her shoulder. She swung around, expecting to see Felicia standing before her, but her expectant smile fell upon Edward Crosby.

"Hello," she said, feeling suddenly shy in his presence.

He dipped his head to acknowledge the greeting, but did not return her smile. "You turn up in some oddball places. Are you buying or selling?"

Cooper put a hand over her heart. "I could never part with my truck. Actually, I'm here to see that woman behind the counter." She jerked her thumb at Felicia. "What about you? Is your taxi cab service expanding?"

"Don't I wish," he growled. "Nah. I'm selling the bike. The cold weather's put a serious crimp in cab fares and we're not making as many deliveries at the furniture store, either. Less tips all around." He shrugged. "Doesn't matter. I was freezing my tail off on that crotch rocket, anyway."

"I'm sorry." Cooper couldn't help but remember how it felt to speed down the dark roads on the red-and-chrome Indian Chief with her arms wrapped around Edward as the wind whipped the ends of her hair and her blood surged through her body. She'd always felt so alive when Edward was near. It was as if his very presence heightened her senses.

A tinge of pink crept up her neck and she looked away from Edward's piercing gray eyes and tried to focus on the car being sold.

"Are you friends with that woman?" Edward asked. "She go to your church or something?"

"No." Cooper quickly explained how she'd met Felicia during a service call and hadn't thought of her again until she'd come across the former administrative assistant's photograph in the newspaper. "I didn't even call her first, but I just need to find out from her if the car titles I've got with me are genuine."

"Yeah?" Edward's tone bordered on disinterest. "Where'd you get them?"

"From a woman who worked as the title clerk at Love Motors. She kept them hidden at her house for some reason and I'm trying to figure out why."

Edward was just about to speak when Cooper felt someone touch her on the elbow. It was Felicia.

"I've been meaning to call you!" she exclaimed after giving Cooper a brief hug. "I owe you a belated thanks. If you hadn't dragged me out to dinner that night, I'd never have had the courage to change careers." She smiled as she gazed around the facility. "I love my job now! It's exactly what I've always wanted to do. I come to work every day with a goofy smile on my face and I don't have to kowtow to another CEO for the rest of my life."

Cooper turned to Edward in order to introduce him to Felicia, but he'd melted into the crowd of men.

"Are you car shopping?" Felicia asked.

"Actually, I came to see you. I need a favor."

Felicia seemed delighted to have the opportunity to help. "Come on back to my office. One of the girls can take over for me."

Cooper followed Felicia down a hallway and into the third office on the right. It was a small room, with only enough space for a desk, a file cabinet, a small bookcase, and a pair of red leather chairs for visitors.

"Should I call you Fizzy now?" Cooper indicated the business card holder on the desktop.

Felicia laughed. "It certainly sounds less stuffy. I *feel* like a Fizzy now, too. But enough about me, what can I do for *you*?"

Removing Maria's file folder from her canvas tote bag, Cooper passed it to Felicia. *I can't think of her as Fizzy just yet,* Cooper thought. Aloud, she said, "This might seem like a strange question, but could these titles be forgeries?"

If Felicia was surprised by the question, she didn't let it show. She picked up one title after another, touching the paper, examining the blue, lacelike border, and holding each document up to the light in order to observe the watermark. "They look legit to me. Trust me, these are very difficult to forge."

Cooper sighed. "Look, I can't tell you why I've got these titles, but they may be the key to solving a serious crime. Is there *anything* about them that strikes you as unusual?"

As Felicia focused on the titles, Cooper cast her eyes around the tidy office. Felicia's shelves were filled with books and manuals on auto parts, appraisal and value guides, and back issues of *Car and Driver* and *Road and Track*. A calendar of classic cars was pinned to the bulletin board above her computer and a row of framed letters from grateful customers covered the wall behind the desk. It seemed as though Felicia had quickly made a home at River City Auto Auction. Cooper smiled. She was pleased that the risk the older woman had taken by changing careers had paid off so well. In fact, she looked and acted ten years younger than when they'd met at the Bank of Richmond offices.

"The thing that strikes me most is that only two of these cars have liens." Felicia pointed to the first papers on the pile. "None of these are inexpensive vehicles, yet all these customers were able to pay cash on the spot?" She whistled. "I'd like a few of them to buy from us!"

"Who fills out the information listed on the titles?" Cooper inquired.

"The title clerk at the dealership fills in the information, but the title itself is printed at the DMV. They're the only ones who can print titles."

So much for my theory that these titles are forgeries. Cooper felt discouraged.

Shuffling the titles, Felicia looked thoughtful. "Maybe there's a logical reason why most of these cars are lien-free, but it seems as though these customers are family members who just happen to be able to afford a fifty thousand-dollar car. See? This Caddy and this Suburban were both sold to the Williamses."

"I didn't notice the name repetition," Cooper admitted.

Felicia laid out the titles across her desk. "The Williams have different addresses, so it could just be a coincidence, but then look at these two. Ryan and Kathleen Sears share a residence and they each bought new cars within two weeks of another. And the Picklers? Two vehicles for them within four weeks. Something fishy here. Do you have any idea where these cars are now?" she asked.

"No. I'd have to get someone at Love Motors to look that up for me."

Felicia returned the folder to her. "That should be a piece of cake. You've got the VIN numbers printed right on the title, so their title clerk or finance manager can pull up the car history for you, if they're willing to do so." She stood, frowning. "I'm sorry I couldn't help you more, but it's unethical for me to look up that kind of information without the owner's consent."

"Oh, I'd never ask you to do that," Cooper assured her with a smile. "And it was worth it to come down here and see you in your element. Fizzy."

Felicia handed Cooper a business card. "I've got to get back out there and issue bills of sale, tags, and promises of title. Please let me know when you'd be free to go out to dinner. This time, it'll be my treat."

Cooper thanked her again and headed back outside. As

she walked past the groups of animated men, she couldn't stop herself from looking for Edward. She also noticed that although there were cars, trucks, and SUVs lined up for sale, there didn't appear to be a single motorcycle in the line.

Did Edward lie to me? she wondered. Brushing aside all thoughts of her former temptation, she unlocked her truck and, after settling inside, quickly dialed Ashley's number.

"Ashley, it's me," she spoke to the answering machine. "I need Lincoln to meet me at the dealership. I've got to ask Alek for some help and she might require his permission, but Ashley, I think some kind of scam has been going on at Love Motors. I'm going to head over there right after I grab a bite to eat. Please call me back as soon as you get this message!"

Cooper fought her way around the Short Pump Mall traffic, marveling for the hundredth time how poorly the exits and entrances to the gargantuan structure were designed. She usually went out of her way to avoid the entire stretch during the weekend, but she had a craving for a grilled cheese sandwich on rye, a bag of crisp potato chips, and a few dill pickles from Jason's Deli, so she sat through endless traffic lights until she finally found a parking space toward the very back of the Dillard's parking lot.

During lunch, she kept her cell phone on the table in case Ashley returned her call. As she chewed the perfectly toasted cheddar cheese sandwich, she jotted down the questions she'd need to ask Alek Jones or whoever else might be available from the Love Motors finance department.

The dealership was mere minutes from Jason's Deli, so Cooper called Ashley one more time before getting back in the truck.

"I'll just have to see if they'll work with me without Lincoln's blessing," Cooper declared firmly.

However, as she turned into the dealership, she spotted her sister's Lexus in one of the visitor parking spaces. Cooper opted for a less prominent spot, being that she wasn't a customer. As she gathered her notebook and purse, she cast a brief glance out the windshield at the sky. It had darkened ominously since she'd left the auto auction and it looked as though Richmond was about to receive more freezing rain. In fact, the instrument gauge on Cooper's dash showed that the temperature had dropped over the last hour, falling from forty-four degrees to thirty-four.

"I can't wait for spring." Cooper held her coat tight at the neck, grabbed her purse, and hurried inside the dealership. Just as she opened the side door, a few needle-sharp raindrops fell onto the pavement.

The dealership was quiet. Cooper knew that the service department closed at noon, and the three salesmen seated at desks around the perimeter of the showroom were languishing. A bored receptionist sat at an elevated desk near the front door, sipping coffee from a Love Motors mug as she studied the pages of *People*.

"I guess they won't be rushin' in to buy today in this weather," one of the salesmen told another. "Let's grab lunch. Harry'll cover for us, won't ya, Harry? He brown-bagged it today."

The third man gave a friendly wave but didn't look up from his crossword. "Bring me something for dessert."

As the two men departed, Ashley emerged from the restroom. She spied Cooper and smiled broadly. "I hope you know what you're doing, Coop. Lincoln's visiting with his daddy and it *wasn't* the kind of visit that could be interrupted." She unwound a pale pink cashmere scarf from about her neck and stuffed it in her Coach hobo bag. "So you get me instead." She removed a slip of paper from her coat pocket. "We've got carte blanche to ask Alek anything we want." She smirked. "After all, Lincoln *is* the boss here. It's like having a note from home telling the teacher to give you recess all day long."

"Thanks, Ashley."

"Is this about Maria's box?" Ashley asked. "You never called to tell me what was inside."

"I'm sorry, but there wasn't a real lead to follow until today." Cooper showed her sister the folder of titles. "The secret lies with these, but we need Alek to look up the vehicle identification numbers on her computer in order to see the history of each of these cars."

"Let's get on with it, then!" Ashley moved forward impatiently. "I'm as antsy as a kid in church."

Following Ashley to Alek's office, Cooper wondered how receptive the finance manager would be when presented with a note from Lincoln requesting that she aid his wife and sister-in-law.

Ashley knocked lightly on an open door midway down the corridor. Alek, who was talking on the phone, indicated they should enter. She wrapped up her call with a few terse but polite phrases, and then rose, eying the sisters with interest. "What an unexpected pleasure," she said, sounding rather insincere. "How can I help you ladies?"

"Could we sit down for a moment?" Cooper asked, warning Ashley with her eyes to let her take the lead.

"Of course." Alek made a slow, regal gesture with her slim hand and resumed her seat. She waited patiently for Cooper to continue, her unreadable blue eyes shifting from one sister to the other.

"I was wondering if you could look up these car titles on your computer," Cooper began. "I'd like to see if any of them have liens or anything . . . unusual in their history."

Alek looked surprised by the request. "If there is a lien, it will say right on the title." But she accepted the folder and flipped through the papers. "Where did you get these?"

Cooper hesitated. She didn't want to mention Maria,

but as she was asking Alek to bend the rules, she figured the woman deserved to know the truth. "From Maria Gutierrez."

"She should not have these in her possession," Alek remarked, her eyes briefly sparking with disapproval. "These are the original titles and are supposed to be in the owner's possession. Not only that, but Mrs. Gutierrez is no longer an employee of Love Motors."

"Perhaps that's why she gave them to me," Cooper answered lamely. "I believe they contain a clue as to why her son was murdered."

Alek seemed to ponder Cooper's bold statement for several minutes. "I'd like to help, of course, but it would be highly unethical for me to look up a vehicle's history without the owner's permission."

Ashley, who had been miraculously silent up to that moment, leapt out of her chair. "Don't worry about that! You've got *Lincoln's* permission. And if Lincoln Love says it's okay, it must be. I do believe the name of this dealership is *Love Motors*, so let's get on with the search." Without waiting for Alek to reply, she unfolded her husband's note and placed it on the other woman's desk. "Can we stand behind you while you search your database or whatever? Otherwise we can't see the computer screen."

Retrieving the note, Alek read it over carefully and then issued a small sigh of irritation. "Very well."

She didn't bother waiting for Cooper and Ashley to reposition themselves and Cooper saw a password screen and another screen flicker by as Alek rapidly typed in a set of VIN numbers. She recited a stream of information in a robotic monotone. "This is the vehicle history on a 2010 Cadillac Escalade. The vehicle was new when purchased. The vehicle was purchased here, at Love Motors, November second of last year. The vehicle was delivered to Love Motors direct from the factory and had 400 miles on it at the time of purchase. Purchase price was $78,900. No lien. The buyer was a Mr. Charles Hancock."

Cooper was having trouble viewing the entire screen. It looked as though there was a note added at the bottom of the vehicle report. "Can you scroll down, please?"

Alek complied. "Ah," she read, her voice belying a sudden interest. "The vehicle was reported missing on December twentieth."

Removing her notepad from her purse, Cooper asked Alek to enter in the next VIN number. It appeared that six vehicles, all costing over fifty thousand dollars, had been reported missing over the past four or five months.

Cooper turned to Ashley. "Didn't you say that sales were unusually high for the months of January and February? The months when sales are usually the most sluggish?"

Ashley nodded. "Yes. Lincoln said some of the sales went to buyers in the same family."

Tapping on her notepad, Cooper thought for a moment and then looked at Alek. She pulled the top three titles off the pile. "Can we find out if Charles Hancock, Sandy Mitchell, Burt Knupp, and the rest of these people were some of those family buyers?"

"It is possible." Alek regarded Cooper with her icy stare. "But what would the reason be?"

Feeling excited, as though she were finally on the right trail, Cooper clasped her hands together to prevent them from shaking the finance manager by the shoulders. "Because they might have committed insurance fraud. And Maria Gutierrez and Hector might have helped them." The picture was becoming clearer now. *And they were working under Albion Ivan's orders.* Cooper kept this thought private.

"What?" Ashley and Alek exclaimed in unison.

Cooper inhaled and then explained her theory as succinctly as she could. "Listen. Hector produced fake IDs and sold stolen Social Security cards as well. Charles Hancock's stolen card, for example. Hector then makes 'Charles' a matching driver's license and 'Charles' comes here to buy a Cadillac Escalade using the real Charles Hancock's credit. He then reports the car as stolen and resells the car. Probably privately."

Alek issued a dry laugh. "You have a vivid imagination."

"Do I? How long does it take for the bank holding the loan to look for a title after the sale's gone through?"

"That depends," Alek answered evasively.

Ashley threw out her arms. "Just give us an estimate!"

"Financial institutions don't really look for the title in the first ninety days," she replied tersely.

"That's a lot of time!" Cooper was certain she was on the right track. "Look, even if I don't have the details or the lingo right, there was a reason Maria gave me these titles. She wanted me to set the record straight, and something's *definitely* shady about half of these cars going missing in less than two months after their purchase dates." Cooper gave Alek a hard stare of her own. "I need to know more about these customers and their relatives or spouses. This could be a major case of insurance fraud."

The finance manager looked at her watch, an expensive gold affair with a gemstone-studded face, and then closed the program on her computer. "We'll have to go back to the file room to view their individual customer folders, but the only records we have in there are the bill of sale, the odometer statement, and the title application."

Cooper said, "And a copy of their driver's license."

Alek nodded. "We moved the files when our offices were getting painted in the fall and we never got around to moving them back. We're storing them in an oversized closet in the service area. Let me get my keys and I'll take you there."

"This is *so* exciting!" Ashley squealed. "You're onto

something, Coop! I can *feel* it! You've got that blood-hound air about you."

"Not bloodhound, bulldog," Cooper corrected. "I'm not leaving this place until I have the proof Investigators Mc-Namara and Johnson need to put that strip-club slime bag in jail."

Alek arched an eyebrow. "I don't know what you're investigating, but I too am intrigued as to why Maria had copies of these titles." She wiggled a bunch of keys. "If you'll follow me."

The three women buttoned their coats, wrapped scarves around their necks, and hunched their shoulders as they stepped out into the freezing rain. The dealership seemed deserted. The only cars in the rear parking lot had sale stickers on the windows and were being coated by a thin but slick layer of precipitation.

Hustling forward to the employee entrance of the dark-ened service area, Alek unlocked the door's deadbolt. She waited for the two sisters to enter and then shut and locked the door behind them.

When Cooper threw her a questioning glance, Alek gestured at the assortment of cars in the service bay. "I'm responsible for these cars while we're in here. After all, it will take some time to sort through a dozen folders."

"Right." Cooper knew that Alek's comment made sense, but it was creepy to be in the empty garage. Their footsteps echoed on the cement and the rain drummed on the metal roof above. Alek walked with brisk confidence to a shad-owy hallway at the rear of the building. She flicked a switch and a weak fluorescent light hummed to life, casting an orange-yellow glow on the gray carpet and the gray-and-beige speckled wallpaper.

"Do you come out here to file things?" Ashley asked. "Seems like a hassle."

Alek opened the door to a small room and turned on

another overhead light. "Someone of a lesser position than mine does that." She made a beeline for the row of horizontal file cabinets covering the longest wall of the room. "The drawers are arranged alphabetically. Feel free to get started. I need to make a phone call and then I will return to help you." She turned and walked away, closing the door gently behind her.

"Let's hurry, Coop," Ashley whined. "It's cold and spooky in here."

Cooper nodded and, because she opened the drawer containing the letter M, began to search for Sandy Mitchell's file. Ashley chose Charles Hancock.

"Look at this!" Cooper exclaimed and rushed to Ashley's side with Mrs. Mitchell's file. "She *did* take a loan out on her car!"

"Then why does the title say 'no lien'?" Ashley sounded doubtful.

"Maria must have changed the title electronically," Cooper replied. "That's what she felt guilty about. She falsified the titles on the computer, and since only the DMV can print them out, they'd be printing whatever Maria inputted into the database. See here? Mr. Ronald Mitchell also borrowed money to buy his Saab, but his title claims no lien as well."

Ashley shook her head. "I can't believe that! She was such a sweet lady!"

"She told me that it felt like she wasn't hurting anyone. All she did was hit a few keys and collect money from Ivan. Hector took care of the forged document side of things and he got paid, too." Cooper laid the Mitchell file on her lap. "If you hadn't found Miguel's body, who knows how long this scheme would have continued?"

The door eased open. Alek entered, gripping something shiny. "Not for much longer, clever Cooper. We only stay in one place for three or four months. It's too risky to continue after that. Someone always gets greedy. Someone always threatens to talk."

Cooper gaped at the woman blocking the exit.

Alek raised the object in her hand and the light glinted off the metal. It was a gun, a very substantial and lethal-looking gun. "Yes, you have figured out a portion of our operation, but not all. Unfortunately for you, you won't have the opportunity to show those pesky policemen just how clever you are. No one knows you're back here and by the time they find your bodies, I will be long gone." She smiled her first genuine smile and raised the gun.

"Oh, please!" Ashley cried. "You can't shoot me! I'm pregnant!"

18

The one who sows to please his sinful nature, from that nature will reap destruction . . .

Galatians 6:8 (NIV)

Despite the fact that a gun was being aimed at her, Cooper turned to her sister. She looked over Ashley's head, however, hoping to spy something on the file cabinet behind her to use as a shield against Alek's weapon. "You're pregnant? Why didn't you tell me?"

There was nothing to use in their defense. Cooper looked at her sister in despair.

Ashley sniffed. "We wanted to wait until we saw the doctor—to make sure everything looks the way it should." Her sapphire blue eyes were wide with fear. "Please don't hurt us!" she pleaded with Alek. "No one needs to know about this. We have money . . ."

Alek laughed and took three steps in their direction, holding the gun in a comfortable, familiar grip. "Money, but no brains. Your husband is the most gullible fool I've ever met! He was so desperate to impress his *daddy* that he was eating out of my hand from the moment I presented him with my fake resumé!" She made a *tsk, tsk* sound with her tongue. "As long as our sales numbers went up, he didn't bother to take a second look at a single piece of paperwork. If he did, he might have noticed that all those expensive cars we sold were reported missing soon after the first payment was made. The banks never saw a second one."

"And Maria Gutierrez falsified the titles," Cooper stated, finally understanding Maria's declaration of guilt and regret.

"For the DMV, yes. Of course, we have someone on the inside there, too. We are very thorough and we pay well." She looked around the sparse room with disgust. "There are so many people trying to start a new life in this country. They are more than willing to type a few little words in exchange for cash."

"You knew Maria Gutierrez when she lived in Norfolk." The pieces began to form a picture. "Double A Autos! *You're the other A!*"

Alek uttered a haughty snort. "We train many of our special employees there. Maria, Nina, Hector, Miguel . . . call them what you will. Except for Nina, they all worked under false names. We've already operated in Roanoke, but I wanted to live near my brother, so I interviewed for jobs with five dealerships in this city." She cast Ashley a look of pity. "As soon as I met Lincoln Love, I knew I'd found the perfect boss and the perfect dealership. Maria got hired first and then I came aboard a few months later. It was so *nice* of the former title clerk to decide to move to California. Like I said, this was the perfect place."

"To be a lowlife swindler, sure!" Cooper snarled and then tried to stall for time as her eyes traveled around the room in search of a weapon. "What happened to the stolen cars?"

"They are exported to my country. To Russia." Alek's icy eyes ignited at the mention of her homeland. "With no lien on the titles, those vehicles were halfway across the world before they were even declared missing. And when these institutions went after Mr. Hancock or Mrs.

Mitchell or any of the rest, they either wouldn't find them or they'd learn that these people lived in different states altogether and had had their identity stolen."

Realization slapped Cooper in the face. She pointed a shaky finger at Alek's face. "That's why you seem familiar! You have the same eyes as Albion!"

Alek smirked. "I should. He's my brother." She smoothed her blunt-cut auburn hair. "But I am the attractive one of the two, no?"

"You're both killers! You took advantage of illegal immigrants in need of money and then disposed of them the second they disobeyed your slightest order! That's a nice gene pool you've got going on! Attractive? You're an ugly, ugly person!"

Ashley whimpered as Alek's lips thinned in anger. Pretending to be unable to meet the finance manager's menacing glare, Cooper raked her eyes around the room. The only potential weapon she could see was a stapler. Other than the file cabinets, the desk, and the single chair, there was nothing else in the room. The desktop was neat and uncluttered, having only a small clock, a tissue dispenser, the stapler, a three-ring binder, a pink memo pad, and a *Far Side* daily calendar on the surface.

"Either way, our Russian genes are more impressive than your weak, American ones," Alek remarked, following Cooper's covert assessment of their situation with amusement. "A trophy wife and a woman who fixes Xerox machines." She huffed. "I haven't killed an American yet, but this is the land of opportunity, is it not?"

Confused, Cooper couldn't help but ask, "Then who killed Miguel and Hector if not you?"

"Those puppets were not real Americans, now were they?" Alek spoke of the two young men as though they'd barely been human. "Miguel was my responsibility, and it was nothing to tie him up and suffocate him. He was such a little man and he underestimated me in many ways. However," she glared at Ashley, "*you* were not supposed to have been given that Cadillac to drive. That was a mistake by one of the idiots in the service department. *You* were supposed to get the white one, but they brought you the one I had used to . . . store Miguel's body in."

"And Hector?" Cooper prodded, still trying to think of a way out of their dire predicament.

Alek sighed, indicating the conversation was becoming tiresome. "Albion took care of Hector. We would have completed the circle with Maria and Nina, had you not interfered."

"Nina," Cooper murmured. "*She* was the person inside the DMV. That's why Maria was still so afraid. Both she and her sister worked for you. They *knew* you'd come for them."

Suddenly, a cell phone began to vibrate from the bottom of her coat pocket. Alek pulled it out and flicked it open. "Where have you been?" she hissed impatiently. "Come to the file room in the back of the service garage this instant! Use the key my brother gave you." Rolling her eyes, Alek began to describe the shape and color of the key.

While the finance manager's focus was diverted by the phone call, Cooper began to slowly edge toward the desk. She wanted to put space between herself and Ashley, in hopes that she could attack Alek and allow her sister at least a chance to escape. Pulling out the chair, she settled into it and then grabbed a handful of tissues from the plastic dispenser. She pressed the soft cloth into her eyes and then gave Alek a tearful glare as their assailant snapped shut her cell phone.

"Why did you have to kill Miguel and Hector? Couldn't you just punish them? Fire them? Did you have to *murder* young men in the prime of their lives?" Cooper asked angrily.

Alek pivoted the gun so that it was aimed right at Cooper's heart. "Hector got greedy. The fool started selling documents to unapproved customers, like *you*. Miguel's problem was also one of greed. His only job was to drive the cars to Norfolk and return with our product. He began to steal said product to sell himself."

"You can stop with the vague talk. I know your brother deals China White." Cooper did her best to sound calm. "So you traded stolen cars for heroin?" It was an educated guess.

"Even with your self-centered American education you must be aware that China is quite close to Russia." Alek shot Ashley a disgusted glance. "Our family has imported cocaine and opium from China for many years. When the Russian economy grew too weak to sustain our customer base, Albion and I decided to relocate our half of the business to this country. We have two brothers overseeing the operation in Russia." She grinned nostalgically. "The Ivanovich family runs the finest car dealership in Kiev."

Cooper felt flattened by the complexity of it all. "An international smuggling ring. Right here in Richmond, Virginia."

Alek straightened her shoulders proudly. "It was so easy. All it takes to fool people around here are some forged documents and a smile. That is why we chose this state. Too many foreigners in New York and California. They tend to be more suspicious. We needed a shipping port in a . . . more naïve state."

"I take it your last name isn't Jones. Ivanovich suits you much better. Though Stalin might be more appropriate," Ashley murmured through trembling lips.

"No, my name is not Jones." Alek seemed surprised to hear Ashley speak. "I have never married. Like I told you at dinner, I am not interested in such things. I take lovers when it suits me, but they are insignificant. Now, it is time

for me to return to Russia and live off the fruit of our labors
for a while. First, I will kill you, and then I will pack."
Her finger stroked the trigger, but a knock on the door
interrupted her. "It's taken you long enough to get here!
Come in at once!" she barked and then gestured at the two
sisters when the newcomer entered. "I believe you already
know my friends."

Cooper's mouth hung open in disbelief as Edward
Crosby slipped into the room, leaving the door slightly ajar
behind him. He stood right next to Alek, surveying the situation calmly. He then gave Alek a slight but subservient
nod and apologized to her for his tardiness.

"I'm sorry to see you here, ladies," he stated flatly and
removed a revolver from the pocket of his black leather
jacket. He held the gun in his left hand and his motorcycle
helmet in his right.

"You weren't at the auction to sell your bike!" Tears
spilled from Cooper's eyes, but the pain of Edward's be-
trayal was overshadowed by the anger bubbling inside
of her. "You're a lying scumbag! Didn't you learn *anything* about honor after your father was killed? He'd be so
ashamed of you right now."

"Good thing he's dead then, huh?" Edward replied
flatly. He chuckled and Alek joined in, her gun jerking up
and down in her hand as she lost herself to a moment of
unaccustomed laughter. It was as though the sound were
emanating from below the earth, like an animal rising from
a dry, dark burrow.

Cooper grabbed the stapler and stood, taking both Alek
and Edward by surprise as she hurled it through the air. It
struck Edward on the forehead and he dropped the gun. As
Alek turned to look at her partner or subordinate or lover—
Cooper didn't care what he was at the moment—she
shouted at her sister, "RUN, ASHLEY!"

Time slowed as Cooper's words floated through the air.

Ashley, white-faced and paralyzed with fear, did not react with the speed necessary to take advantage of the diversion Cooper had created. Her sister's terrified glances darted from the door, to the duo wielding guns, and back to Cooper.

"GO NOW!" Cooper bellowed angrily and Ashley started finally moving toward the exit and hopefully, to safety.

But Alek recovered quickly. She turned her shoulders in order to point the gun at Ashley, but even as she pivoted, Cooper was flinging the clock, calendar, and binder at the female assailant's face. Instinctively, Alek raised her arms to fend off the assault of office supplies and, with Edward preoccupied by wiping blood away from his eyes, Ashley was able to make it to the doorway.

That was as far as she got, however, before Cooper ran out of things to throw. All of the action had taken place in a matter of seconds, and those precious measures of time had not been sufficient to allow Ashley to escape. Alek raised her gun and as Cooper yelled, "NO!" her heart rent by fear for her sister, Edward moved.

In a flash, the arm holding the motorcycle helmet pulled back and then rammed into Alek's gun hand with enough force to knock the weapon loose. But not before it discharged.

The gun went off with a roar. Ashley screamed. Cooper lunged forward, straining to see if her sister was hurt, but Alek's body obscured her view. The finance manager recovered quickly and leapt for her gun, which had come to rest at the base of one of the file cabinets.

Her arm stretched forth to wrap around the grip, but Cooper launched herself upon her enemy as though she was a running back diving into the end zone. She and Alek grabbed the gun simultaneously and the two women began to wrestle for control of the pistol.

Cooper was stunned by the other woman's strength. Alek pulled at the gun and tried to roll away from Cooper, but as she shifted her weight to her left shoulder, Cooper followed the movement exactly, her fingers closing over Alek's as two pairs of arms pointed in the direction of the door. The combined pressure of their fingers released the gun's hammer.

The report of the shot stunned the two women for several seconds, but Alek recovered first, and, taking advantage of Cooper's hesitation, broke free with the weapon in her hand.

"FREEZE!" a deep voice barked from the doorway.

Alek and Cooper both turned. Rich Johnson stood in the threshold, wearing a Kevlar vest and a ferocious glare. "Put the gun down, Aleksandra Ivanovich. It's over."

Cooper's gaze traveled from the policeman to the supine figure on the floor. Edward lay with his face turned toward the ceiling. His skin was glistening with sweat and his breathing was labored. As Cooper rose to her knees, she looked at the carpet and cried, "No!"

Blood was seeping from beneath Edward's body, forming a dark, crimson stain in the gray carpet.

"Drop it now or I shoot!" Rich repeated, easing into the room and lifting the gun so that it was parallel with Alek's chest.

Alek locked eyes with the officer and smiled. "You cannot win." The gun fell with a muffled thud on the carpet. "My lawyers won't let you hold me."

Cooper watched just long enough to witness the policeman kick the gun out of Alek's reach. He pinned her against the wall and fastened a pair of handcuffs on her wrists using adept movements, reciting her rights in an even, professional tone. Alek began to writhe in anger, her shoulders and arms twisting as though she had the strength to escape her bonds. When it was clear that she couldn't get free, she began to mock Rich Johnson by listing all the charges her brother had escaped in the past, extolling the craftiness of her family's legal team, and cataloguing the deficiencies of Richmond's police force. Her voice rose as she spoke, until she was spitting and hissing like a feral cat.

Officer Johnson did not speak a word beyond the Miranda. He gently pushed Alek into the hallway and only then focused his attention on Edward.

"Looks like the bullet went through his lung," he said as he listened to Edward's rasping. "He's losing too much blood. Put pressure on the wound while I call for help."

Cooper shed her coat and scarf. She gently lifted Edward's shoulder from the floor, though her emotions were in turmoil. *How long has he known the Ivanovich siblings? Did he work for them before he went to jail? Does he still?*

"Whose side were you on?" she whispered angrily to Edward while her tears fell. She balled up her scarf and pressed it against the leaking wound with one hand and used the other to slide her coat under his head.

His eyelids flickered, opened. He fixed his gaze on her face. "I'm on your side," he whispered, the words gurgled and slurred.

Fear washed over Cooper. "Don't talk. Help is coming." She placed her palm on his forehead. "Hang in there."

Edward winced, battling with the pain and the supreme effort to draw in breath. "Just in case," he said so softly that Cooper had to put her ear closer to his lips in order to hear him. "Will you say a prayer for me?"

"Of course," Cooper answered and moved the hand touching his face over his heart. She closed her eyes, forcing more tears out. "Heavenly Father, I lift up this man to your care." A calmness flowed into her body as the words welled inside of her. "Lend him Your unsurpassed strength, Lord. He has fought so hard to make the right choices. Please give him the chance to witness how powerful goodness feels." She sniffed. "Allow him the time to continue growing. Please, God. I know he longs to serve You. Give him the chance to do that. You are ever loving, ever merciful. Hear my prayer." She opened her eyes. Edward was alive, but unconscious. "Hear my prayer," Cooper repeated until the sound of footsteps running down the hall made her raise her head again.

"Step away, miss," a bearded paramedic ordered firmly as he removed a long needle and a valve from his case. He tugged Edward's shirt until the bare skin of his chest was exposed, located the two ribs he was searching for, and plunged the needle into Edward's flesh. A hiss of air rushed out. The second paramedic, a pretty young woman, finished intubating the patient. She fastened a breathing mask on Edward's face and then signaled to her partner. Together, they slid him onto a board and then hoisted him onto the gurney.

Rich Johnson reappeared as the paramedics positioned themselves to wheel the gurney out of the room. "Is he going to make it?" he asked.

"We've seen worse," the female paramedic replied, brushing past him. "But he needs blood. We only carry saline."

Cooper stepped after them, not wanting to lose sight of Edward. "Where's my sister?" she demanded without turning to the police officer.

"In her husband's office. She's shaken, but uninjured. Luckily, the stray bullet hit the wall several feet away." The policeman took her arm as they hustled toward the outer door. "Are you hurt?"

"No." Cooper's fear rapidly morphed to anger. "But I *am* confused! How long has Edward been playing both sides? And exactly *how long* were you out in that hall while Alek was getting good and ready to kill us?"

Rich waited for the paramedics to load Edward into the

ambulance and shut both doors before answering. "Not long enough to hear what sounded like a full confession, unfortunately. Please understand, Ms. Lee, I only hesitated until I knew what was going on inside that room. Despite what one sees on television, the police don't routinely burst into every space with weapons drawn. We're actually more cautious than that." He looked pained over not having appeared sooner. "Be comforted by the fact the we've got enough evidence to nail the Ivanovich siblings and shut down their smuggling ring for good. Of course, there'll be half a dozen federal agencies involved, but Albion will *not* slip through the bars of his holding cell this time. He'll be wearing an orange jumpsuit before the ice melts."

As the ambulance pulled away, sirens wailing, Cooper rounded on Johnson. "Why didn't Edward fire his gun?"

"He's not allowed to carry a loaded weapon," the officer answered sheepishly. "Convicted felons cannot own, possess, or transport a firearm."

"So you used him, too," Cooper stated, her anger seeping away as fatigue set in.

"Mr. Crosby wanted to be involved. Against my better judgment, I agreed." Johnson removed his coat and slung it around Cooper's shoulders. "I believe in redemption, Ms. Lee, and that is why I agreed to incorporate him into this investigation. Now," he resumed his authoritative tone. "You've experienced quite a shock. Come inside and join your sister."

Nodding numbly, she did as he suggested. Seeing Ashley seated primly in Lincoln's office triggered the tears again, and the two sisters embraced. Neither one would let go. Eventually, they both broke into a stream of anxious murmuring, repeatedly checking to ensure that the other was truly unharmed. When they finally separated, the sisters gratefully accepted steaming cups of coffee from an ogling salesmen.

"Lincoln will be here any minute," Ashley said in a surprisingly steady voice. "You were so brave!" She reached over and squeezed Cooper's hand. "You saved me! I feel *so* guilty about running away."

"Don't," Cooper scolded her. "You wanted to live. You wanted your baby to live. There's no shame in that."

Ashley placed a hand on her flat belly. "Wait until he hears about this story when he's older."

"Or she," Cooper said with a smile.

"Could you imagine?" Ashley giggled. "Poor Daddy! Four generations of girls!"

Just then Lincoln rushed into the office. He gathered Ashley into his arms and covered her face with kisses. "My darling," he murmured. "Oh, I should have *known* something was wrong with *her*. I should have been with you! Are you okay?" He pushed her away in order to look her over and then pulled her against his chest again.

"I'm fine, sugar. We're just a bit shaken, that's all." She smiled reassuringly at her husband, even though her hands trembled. "My sister saved my life."

Lincoln turned to Cooper. She had been too tired to move and remained seated in the stiff-backed office chair. He fell to his knees and, taking her hand in his, kissed it gallantly. "God bless you!" he whispered with a catch in his voice.

Made slightly uncomfortable by the dramatic gesture, Cooper withdrew her hand. Smiling tenderly at her brother-in-law, she said, "I believe He already has."

19

"Because he takes note of their deeds,
he overthrows them in the night and they are crushed.
He punishes them for their wickedness
where everyone can see them."

Job 34:25-26 (NIV)

Rich Johnson pulled up to the front door of the police station to let Cooper out. She'd been too shaken to drive her own truck, and the policeman was eager to acquire her statement while events were fresh in her mind. Ashley had insisted that she was well enough to give her statement as well, so a reluctant Lincoln had chauffeured her to the station.

"But the second you're done, it's straight home with you. I'm ordering in and you're going to lie down on the sofa and rest. No more excitement for you for the next eight months, do you hear me?" He practically carried her to the car.

Cooper was so tired, cold, and hungry that she barely noticed Nathan waiting for her in the station's lobby. Looking dashing in a navy blue overcoat and a plaid scarf, he set down the brown bag he was carrying and scooped Cooper off her feet, kissing her all over. She wrapped her arms around him and her lips found his. She finally felt safe.

"It's a good thing Batman's parking the car!" Cooper

laughed and rested her head against Nathan's chest. "He might arrest us for public display of groping."

Nathan didn't smile. "I should have been at your side today. I just didn't think a trip to the car auction would end with someone pointing a gun at you!"

"How did you find out what happened so quickly?" Cooper asked quizzically.

"Ashley called me from Lincoln's office. She heard the cops say you'd both need to come down here and I figured you could use a shoulder to lean on." He pointed at the brown bag. "I brought you some food, too. I figured cream of chicken and wild rice soup, a buttered roll, and a cup of hot coffee would give you the strength you'd need to make it through this interview."

Prying open the bag, Cooper almost cried when she smelled the soup and felt the warmth of the coffee cup seep into her palms. "I don't think I've ever loved you as much as I do right now!" She kissed him again and he slipped his arm around her waist.

At that moment, the figure behind them developed a serious throat tickle. "A-hem! Ms. Lee?" Investigator Mc-Namara glowered. "Here I was, thinking we'd made such progress during our little chat in the Kroger parking lot. Yet, once again, you've stepped into the line of fire."

Cooper's neck flushed. "I don't think I compromised anything, sir. In fact, you'll have plenty of evidence to put Aleksandra Ivanovich away and hopefully Albion, too."

"We'll see." McNamara sighed. "I'm going to conduct your interview. 'Batman' has bigger fish to fry." One side of his mouth stretched into the beginnings of a smile, but then was quickly brought into line. He eyed Nathan. "You may join Ms. Lee if you'd like. I can see that it may require some kind of specialized tool to separate the pair of you, and the lobby vending machines are fresh out of crowbars. Candy bars and coffee we've got." He looked back and forth between Nathan and Cooper. "Would you care for some refreshment before we begin?"

"I'm all set, thank you." Cooper showed him the coffee cup in her hand.

McNamara gave it a longing glance. "Ah, the good stuff. I'm trying to cut back a little, so it'll have to be water for me." His eyes flicked toward the lobby doors. "Let's get started. I hear this layer of ice is going to be covered by nearly a foot of snow in the next few hours. You need to be off the roads by dark."

In the stark interview room, McNamara kindly fiddled with paperwork, the recording device, and the thermostat in order to allow Cooper a few swallows of soup before she had to start talking. When her bowl was half-empty, he looked at her expectantly and touched a button on the recorder. He stated his name and rank as Cooper sipped her coffee. He then uncapped his pen and his expression became one of fixed concentration.

It took nearly two hours for Cooper to complete her statement because McNamara painstakingly dissected and reviewed every word she said. When he asked her to repeat her exchanges with Alek in the file room for the third time, she lost her temper.

"I've told you twice! She sends the cars to Russia to be sold, probably by her brothers who own a dealership there, and China White gets imported to the States in return."

"Through Double A Auto?" McNamara ignored Cooper's outburst and tapped his chin with the top of his pen. "The heroin is inside the cars sent from Russia?"

Cooper thought hard. "Alek never clarified that point. I don't know how the drugs get into the country, but Norfolk's a major shipping port and that's where Double A is located, so I'd guess that's what happens, but she didn't spell that out." Cooper sighed, weary to the core. "Alek said they used Double A to train people like Maria and Miguel. She didn't mention where the drugs were hidden."

McNamara made a notation on his legal pad. "Let's go through the sequence in which Ms. Ivanovich's firearm was discharged."

Cooper closed her eyes for a moment. She was so tired that her thoughts were growing muddled. "I can't," she whispered and suddenly all she could see was the blood leaking out from Edward. She stared at her hands, but the vision before her was the stain spreading across the carpet and the sticky, red circle pooling beneath Edward's shoulder. She pointed at the recorder, her lips trembling as she tried to control her voice. "Turn that off. *Please.*"

Complying, McNamara touched the machine. He dug a tissue from his pocket, passed it to Cooper without staring directly at her face, and then bent to study his notes.

"Now *I* want to know something." Cooper was hoarse from talking. Her coffee cup was empty and though she was no longer hungry, the food had only served to amplify her fatigue. "What was Edward's role in all this?"

"He's been an informant for several months now. Edward made contact with Johnson while serving the tail end of his sentence." McNamara capped his pen and laid it down. "I don't know the details, but I believe Mr. Crosby had a profound experience toward the end of his stay at Jail West." He smiled slightly. " 'After the suffering of his soul, he will see the light of life and be satisfied.' "

"Is that a Psalm?" Nathan asked.

"Isaiah," McNamara said. "Edward knows much about the illegal drug trade in this city and he proved to be an invaluable asset. But to be of any help, he had to keep a hand in the pie. His cab has been quite handy in recording conversations and capturing the faces of some the city's most prolific dealers on film. Richmond's specialized drug task force has been working to bust Albion Ivanovich since Edward's release."

"But how did Edward know that I'd have a flat tire the night my sister found Miguel in her garage?" Cooper rubbed her eyes. "Why follow me? I don't know anything about the drug trade."

McNamara shifted in his seat. "I am of the opinion that Mr. Crosby became an informant to impress you. I believe he's been looking for a chance to repay you for giving him the courage and the confidence to change his life. In short, he was following you that night and was thrilled to be there to help you."

Cooper flushed. "Well, if he wanted to do something wonderful for me, he's certainly accomplished that. By hitting Alek with his motorcycle helmet, he saved Ashley's life." She frowned. "Won't Edward be in terrible danger now? If he testifies against the Ivanovich siblings, everyone will know he's been leading a double life."

"After the trial, he'll leave the city. We'll be keeping him in a safe house until then." McNamara stood. "Edward's in surgery now and I've been told the outcome looks good. I'm going to head over to the hospital as soon as I file my report." He eyed his water cup with disappointment. "I'd be glad to call you later with a status update."

"Do you have enough?" Cooper inquired as Nathan held out her coat. "To put those creeps away?"

McNamara held out his open palms. "The case against Aleksandra is strong. Even though she tried to eliminate the people who posed a threat to her profits, she's left a paper trail. Without the testimonies of Maria Gutierrez and Nina Vargas, however, the case still has cracks."

"Because Nina was the crooked DMV employee," Cooper surmised. "She was integral in keeping the scam a secret."

"Correct." McNamara absently rubbed the stubble on his chin. "She turned a blind eye to any questionable titles coming from Love Motors and made sure the titles were sent to the lien holders exactly as Maria entered them into her database."

Nathan shook his head and said, "Two families of criminals. Maria paid a serious price for her duplicity, and, from what Cooper told me, it sounds like she's gone into hiding for the rest of her days. Probably in another country." He put a protective arm around Cooper and gave McNamara a hard look. "I need to know, sir . . . is there any threat to Cooper's safety?"

"There's little danger of repercussion. Albion will be in custody within the hour, and this time, I suspect he won't be let out on bail." McNamara shook his head. "Even if he was set free until the trial, he'll behave like a Boy Scout until the verdict comes in. Those theatrics, several sizable donations to the campaign funds of certain lower-level politicians, as well as a minor detail called insufficient evidence, have helped Mr. Ivanovich avoid any real jail time thus far." His eyes grew dark and the policeman clenched his jaw and jabbed the metal table with his index finger. "But it ends *now*. Either his sister sings or he loses honor for letting her take the fall for him. A loss of face isn't good for business. His days of lording over this city are done."

Cooper thought about the various government agencies who might be involved in an international smuggling ring. "I hope justice doesn't get buried under a mound of red tape."

McNamara chuckled and opened the door for her and Nathan. "You just pinpointed my greatest fear as an officer of the law. I'm not afraid of being shot or of being killed in the line of duty. Just keep me away from the damned paperwork so I can do my job." He walked swiftly toward the lobby, the sound of his heavy boots echoing down the spacious hall. When they reached the set of double doors leading to the outside, he turned to Nathan. "I wish you and this young lady would join a bowling league or a supper club. If you two became overloaded with hobbies, I might not run into her at any more crime scenes."

Affronted by the suggestion, Cooper opened her mouth to reply when McNamara said, "I say this with the deepest respect: Why not devote your extra time and talent to volunteering? Become a Big Sister perhaps? Who knows? If Albion Ivanovich or Hector Gutierrez or Miguel Ramos had had someone to look up to, perhaps they'd have a chosen a better future for themselves."

"I don't think it's that simple," Cooper responded.

"Neither do I." The policeman smiled sadly. "But I'd like you to go home now and stay out of trouble." He gave her a fatherly pat on the back and then marched back down the hall.

"Come on." Nathan pulled her close as they stepped into the falling snow. "I'm going to run you the hottest bubble bath you've ever had in your life."

But Cooper fell asleep on her bed to the sound of the tub filling with water.

For the first time in over a year, Cooper missed church. It wasn't intentional—she merely slept through it. After Nathan tucked her in the night before, fed her crabby kittens, and tiptoed down the stairs to assure the Lee family that both of their daughters were tired, but otherwise physically sound, he drove home.

Cooper woke around noon and swam to the surface of consciousness only because Moses was chewing on her earlobe. Specifically, the feline was tugging at Cooper's small, silver hoop with his teeth while simultaneously digging into the flesh of her cheek with his front legs.

Gently batting him away, Cooper opened her eyes and looked at the clock. Confused, she checked the time against her watch. At that moment, Miriam pounced on her foot and sank her teeth into the skin of her big toe.

"Okay, I'm up!" Grabbing the kittens, she kissed each of them on their pink noses and got up to feed them breakfast. "I'm starving, too!"

Her head was deep in the refrigerator when someone knocked on the door.

"It's just me!" Maggie called out. "I almost used the phone, but then I thought, now that's right silly. I can make my way through a few inches of snow to bring my own child somethin' to eat." She placed two grocery bags on the counter.

Cooper smiled as she observed her mother's church outfit. Maggie wore a peach pants suit, a string of pearls, and a pair of black, knee-high rubber boots. "You look so pretty, Mama, right down to your boots. And here I am, still in my jammies. If you'd come up here ten minutes ago you'd have found me dead asleep."

Maggie shuddered. "Don't you use words like that today, sugar. Your mama simply can't take it." She dabbed her eyes, sniffed, and then enfolded Cooper into a warm embrace. "Your daddy snuck in here 'round ten this mornin'. I made him come up, just to see if you needed anythin'. He said you were gettin' what you needed most and I guess he was right."

"What did you carry up here?" Cooper pointed at the bags. "It's only me." She watched with interest as her mother spooned three-cheese macaroni onto a plate and then added a small mound of peas. "You make a dent in this while I brew coffee."

Cooper dug into the macaroni and sighed with pleasure as she chewed the butter-soft, creamy noodles topped with a crisp cheese crust. "Just what the doctor ordered. What's in the other bag?"

"Cookies," Maggie answered as she dumped measured tablespoons of coffee into Cooper's machine. "Three dozen Magnolia's Marvels Comfort Cookies."

"Yum. I haven't had those in ages. I think the last time you made them was after Drew broke up with me." Cooper speared peas with her fork, thinking of how wonderful it felt to not experience even the slightest pang of sadness when she thought of her ex. Now that she had Nathan, Drew had become a distant memory. "But three dozen? I won't fit into my jeans!"

Shredding a piece of chicken breast for Moses and Miriam, Maggie laughed. "They're not *all* for you! Your friends are comin' over after church. I begged them to get here in time for a meal, but they insisted it'd only be a brief visit." She touched Cooper on the cheek. "They just need to see you with their own eyes and listen to your story, I suppose. We were so grateful to Nathan for fillin' us in last night. Otherwise, we'd have been pacin' the boards until dawn."

Cooper's food stuck in her throat. "I'm sorry. I never meant for you to worry."

Maggie sat down at the table and took her daughter's hands in her own. "When you love somebody and they've made a narrow escape from a real danger, you wanna hold them so bad it hurts." She smiled through her tears. "So you hug those folks hard when they get here, because they truly love you. You've some fine friends, Cooper, and a real keeper in Nathan Dexter."

Nodding, Cooper said, "I know that now. I promise, Mama. I'll never make the mistake of forgetting that again."

"Good." Satisfied, Maggie patted her hand and stood, smoothing the wrinkles from her pants. "I'll see you for supper." She hesitated at the door. "And Grammy wants me to tell you that no matter what nonsense you got up to yesterday, you still have to take Columbus out for his walk."

She left to the sound of Cooper's laughter.

20

"Consider the blameless, observe the upright; there is a future for the man of peace."

Psalm 37:37 (NIV)

A few weeks later, the members of Sunrise Bible Study met at LifeWay to peruse the large selection of studies. It was Nathan's turn to choose and each member tried to influence his decision.

"Let's do *Experiencing God*," Savannah gently suggested. She tapped on the bookshelf where the study was shelved with her cane. "I've heard it's simply life-changing. This is where the clerk said you could find a copy."

"We haven't done an Elizabeth George study yet," Trish piped up, patting her striking houndstooth turban. "I think we should alternate between male and female authors."

Bryant pretended to jab her in the ribs. "I've got the perfect study right here. It's called *The Peacemaker: A Biblical Guide to Resolving Personal Conflict.*" He sighed. "I need to teach Jane's kids a little conflict resolution. I'm not used to all the noise and the violence that defines sibling rivalry. I'm glad I'm an only child."

Jake came forward with his choice. "I vote for *God's Answers to Life's Difficult Questions*. Kinda sums it all up, don't it? I mean, doesn't it." He glanced at Savannah with a smile. Sensing that he was looking at her, Savannah smiled back.

"How about *Christians and Their Money*?" Quinton thrust his choice on top of Jake's. "It covers how to get out of debt, how to invest, how to decide what portion of your income should go to charity. Doesn't that sound fascinating?"

"To a money man like yourself!" Jake exclaimed and placed his workbook back on the top of the pile in Nathan's arms. "I'm a plumber with a mortgage. I'll always have debt, and it's easy to decide what to give away, 'cause there ain't—isn't—much left over at the end of the month to dither about."

"Well, Cooper?" Nathan grinned at her with his eyes. "Have you got anything to add to this debate?"

She shook her head. "It's your turn to choose. I'm sure whatever you pick will be great."

Jake rolled his eyes. "Then side with me, woman, if you don't have an opinion."

"No!" Trish countered. "She'll vote for the female author, I just know it. We girls need to stick together."

Nathan halted the argument before it could get off the ground. "Okay, okay! I've made up my mind. Now, let's go out for pancakes!"

"Good!" Bryant slapped his hands together. "I'm ready for a short stack smothered in boysenberry syrup."

Later, after the seven friends had been seated at IHOP's biggest table, Bryant held out a folded copy of the morning's paper. "I see the trial against the Ivanovich siblings is well under way." He looked at Cooper with apprehension. "Will you have to testify?"

She nodded. "Yes. Even though Rich Johnson heard most of what Alek said that day in the dealership's file room, I'm a more objective witness. Both of us telling the same story should influence the jury."

"What about your sister?" Savannah asked.

"Luckily, Ashley was out of the room and missed many of the key statements as well as Edward being shot. Due to health reasons, Lincoln doesn't want her to appear in court, so they hired a lawyer and Ashley's testimony will be a written statement instead."

Trish seemed stunned by this announcement. "Wouldn't she want to do anything in her power to ensure those two are found guilty?"

"Believe me," Cooper answered, "she'd like nothing more than to do her part, but she truly needs to avoid unnecessary stress right now. Like I said, it's health-related."

"Oh." Trish's expression became sympathetic. "I hope it's nothing serious."

Touching her friend's hand, Cooper replied, "Nothing that can't be treated by rest and a careful awareness of her body's limits. Thank you for being concerned."

Trish smiled and shrugged. "I almost wore a wig to meet you today, but every time I pick up the one with the long, red hair, I picture Jake as Barbarella! If Ashley gets down, just send our two desperate housewives over to her place."

"You're more dashing in a turban, Trish," Savannah said. "I can't see you clearly, but I can tell that you're wearing bright colors and sharp patterns. I can spot you more easily in a room."

The waitress arrived with a carafe of coffee and topped off everyone's cups. "Speaking of finding," Quinton said once she'd left. "Did anyone track down those two women the prosecution needed for the trial? Maria and Nina?"

Nathan spoke up. "Unfortunately, no. Discovering their whereabouts is complicated because Maria's used several fake names since she's been in the States. Nina went by her real name, but she used a falsified employment history to get her job at the DMV, so she's also hard to track." He poured a sugar packet into his coffee. "From what I read in the paper last week, the Mexican authorities are participating in the search, but finding two women in a big country within a month's time can't be easy."

"And Edward? How's he doin'?" Jake asked, his glance keen as two waitresses appeared with their food.

"He's back on his feet." Cooper answered. "At least that's what Investigator McNamara told me. I haven't talked to Edward since that day." She thanked the waitress who'd handed her a plate filled with scrambled eggs, bacon, and hash browns. "I've tried to call him, but his cell phone number doesn't work anymore. I think he's lying low until he testifies on Monday. I'm supposed to go in then, too, so maybe we'll get a chance to talk."

Bryant raised the newspaper again. "According to this reporter, the prosecution's got a really strong case. From what I hear around the station, the informants Edward dug up combined with the paperwork trail *you* found have given the good guys the extra evidence they needed to seal the deal."

"Let's pray that comes to pass," Savannah said with feeling. The Sunrise members bowed their heads as she spoke grace and then devoted their full attention to their meal.

After a few minutes of hearty chewing and the passing of salt, pepper, and various flavors of pancake syrup, Quinton laid down his fork and leaned forward. "Not to keep dwelling on the case," he whispered. "But how was the heroin brought into this country?"

As Cooper's mouth was full, Nathan answered. "Hidden compartments built into used cars. The cars came from the Ivanovich dealership in Kiev and were sold here dirt cheap for their parts. Some government agency seized the last incoming shipment and found the drugs. I can't remember which one because so many of them have been involved with this case. The DEA, INS, local law enforcement—it's a potpourri of guys with guns and badges. Anyway, it was a timely bust for the prosecution."

"I'll say!" Jake exclaimed as he carved into a stack of fluffy pancakes covered in whipped cream and strawberries. "I just wish we coulda been more help to you."

"You are always with me, no matter what I do," Cooper assured him gently. "Remember, this whole thing started in my sister's garage and the criminals were operating out of my brother-in-law's dealership. For some reason, I was meant to handle this challenge more on my own." She shot Nathan a quick smile. "I think I had to go through this ordeal in order to understand what's most important in my life. Now I can check that off my list and get back to normal."

Bryant grunted. "And what's normal?"

Cooper slung her arm around Trish. "Trish kicking cancer's butt, my sister listening to her doctor's counsel, this court case concluding with a long jail sentence for Alek and Albion, peace in the eastern part of the city, and us starting a new study."

"Oh, that's all, huh?" Jake laughed. "No peace on earth and goodwill toward men?"

"Hey, I'm always praying for that," Cooper said and threw a sugar packet at Jake.

"Amen!" Savannah shouted and several of the other diners turned and smiled.

After a long run in the country, in which the sharp, March air seemed to infuse Cooper's lungs with a sense of renewed vigor and health, she prepared to feast on yet another large meal. Lincoln, Ashley, and Nathan were joining the Lees for supper. The next day, Cooper would have to appear in court.

"I'd like a few minutes in the limelight before Cooper

Lee becomes a household name in this city," Ashley had informed her over the phone the day before. "And you're *sure* you haven't let the cat out of the bag to Mama?"

"I haven't told a soul!" Cooper had protested. "Not even Nathan. And you're not *allowed* to get worked up, remember? You're supposed to spend the next seven and a half months in a state of calm."

Ashley had issued a heavy sigh. "I hate being a high-risk pregnancy! I don't mind sitting around or eating a balanced diet or the frequent doctor's visits, but I mind the fear. Every day I wake up half expecting that something horrible has happened during the night."

"You're going to be a great mother," Cooper had said by way of comfort. "Just focus on the present. God will take care of the future."

"Thanks, Coop." Ashley's voice was bright once more. "See you tonight!"

After hanging up, Cooper had dressed in layers and gone out for a run. She'd then changed into jeans and a warm, wool sweater and parka in order to escort Grammy and Columbus out to the field so the hawk could grab himself a late-day snack.

"This is his favorite time to hunt," Grammy said. "Day's meltin' into evening and all the critters are scramblin' to get on home. Not *all* of them are gonna make it back safe, though, hee hee."

Cooper drew her grandmother against her. It was always a shock to encounter Grammy's fragility—her thin frame constructed of light bones, her sharp shoulder blades, and her tiny hands. For a moment, the sun lit her white hair, infusing it with gold, and Cooper caught a glimpse of the young woman who still lived inside her grandmother's aged face.

"I love you, Grammy." Cooper squeezed the petite body and caught a whiff of baby powder and lavender.

"Nearly dyin' makes you awful sentimental, grand-daughter." Grammy scowled, though her cheeks were flushed with pleasure. "Try to keep your nose out of these kinda messes or you're gonna start to sound like one of those *Chicken Soup* books."

Just then, the sound of a car on the gravel driveway alerted the two women that Ashley and Lincoln had arrived. Cooper and Grammy waited patiently for Columbus to devour the rodent he'd captured during his outing, and then turned back to the house.

Another set of tires rolling over the layer of gray-blue rocks announced Nathan, and by the time Cooper had returned Columbus to his cage and helped Grammy out of her coat, everyone had assembled in the kitchen.

Ashley was beaming. Cooper had never seen her sister look so beautiful. Her skin was radiant, her hair was a bright blonde halo, and her blue eyes sparkled like a pair of Caribbean lagoons. She carried a light blue gift bag stuffed with tissue paper in her right hand.

"What's in the bag?" Grammy asked as she got settled at the large farm table. "Is it somebody's birthday?"

Cooper looked from face to face and willed the next few moments to move slowly. Her parents were standing side by side, their shoulders barely touching as they waited for their youngest daughter to speak. Lincoln had his arm around Ashley's waist and was glowing every bit as much as his wife. Nathan stood in the middle of the two couples wearing a nervous smile.

"I hope not," he spoke to Grammy in a loud whisper. "Because I didn't bring anything."

Grammy responded by pinching his cheek.

"We have an announcement to make!" Ashley declared as though Grammy and Nathan hadn't said a word. She handed Maggie the gift bag. "Open it, Mama."

Maggie complied and, after digging through several

reams of white tissue paper, pulled a piece of orange fabric free from the bag. She unfolded the material, revealing the round shape of a pumpkin and holes for a head, a pair of tiny legs, and two little arms. It was a baby's Halloween costume.

"Oh, my stars!" Maggie shouted and immediately started crying. She hugged Ashley and Lincoln over and over again. Earl pumped his son-in-law's hand and then grabbed him in a manly embrace. He then kissed his daughter on both cheeks.

Grammy looked confused, so Cooper leaned over and said, "Ashley's pregnant. I'd say the baby is due right around Halloween."

With a smile that caused a dozen wrinkles to crease her face with joy, Grammy opened her arms. "Come here, my girl! Why didn't you just say so in plain English?"

Ashley bent over and kissed Grammy, tears glimmering in her eyes. "Are we friends again?" Cooper heard her whisper. "Now that I'm giving you a great-grandchild?"

Grammy held onto Ashley's hand. "I didn't want you to have a baby for *me*, you silly child. I wanted you to have one for *you*. And your husband." She included Lincoln in her smile. "All I want is to see my family happy. This is the kinda night that makes it worth stayin' alive for, despite my bad hearin', the aches and pains, my sore teeth, my—"

"Stuff and nonsense, Ma!" Earl waved at Grammy. "You're healthy as a horse. If you weren't, could you have eaten that whole bowl of beef stew *and* a slice of chocolate chess pie besides?"

Grammy ignored him and turned to Ashley. "Now tell me *everything*."

As the family rearranged themselves in order to prepare for supper, Nathan, who was still wearing his wool overcoat, went through the hall to hang it up. He brushed

Cooper's shoulder as he walked by and she felt a rush of warmth flood through her body.

Earl also stepped into the hall, and Cooper could hear the murmur of the two men's voices.

"Honey?" Maggie met Cooper's eyes from across the room. "Can you fetch me the nice salad tongs from the chest in the dining room?"

Cooper nodded and went into the next room to search for the tongs. She rifled through a few drawers in the server until she heard her father say, "Your time will come, son."

Puzzled, Cooper stepped forward just far enough to be able to see Nathan's reflection in the hall tree's mirror. She saw her father's arm reach out and clap Nathan on the biceps.

"You're right, sir." Cooper saw Nathan's hand close over a square, black box. It was just large enough to hold a pair of earrings, a pin, or a ring.

A ring! Cooper retreated, lest her intake of breath and the pounding of her heart give her away. She did a little dance in the middle of the dining room, all thoughts of searching for the salad tongs forgotten.

On the other side of the wall, Nathan sighed, but it was a sigh of contentment. "Yes, my time will come. And I'm not worried. She's worth the wait."

Magnolia's Marvels

RASPBERRY TRUFFLE FUDGE

Ingredients:
- 3 cups semi-sweet chocolate chips
- 1 (14-ounce) can sweetened condensed milk
- 1½ teaspoons pure vanilla extract
- ¼ cup heavy whipping cream
- ¼ cup Chambord Liqueur
- 2 cups white chocolate chips

Directions: Spray an 8×8-inch pan (for thicker fudge) or a 9×9-inch pan with non-stick cooking spray and line with wax paper. In a microwave-safe bowl, combine 3 cups chocolate chips and sweetened condensed milk. Heat in microwave until chocolate melts, stirring occasionally. Be careful not to overcook. Stir in the vanilla extract. Spread into pan, and cool to room temperature. In a microwave-safe bowl, combine cream, liqueur, and 2 cups white chocolate chips. Heat in microwave until the chocolate melts; stir until smooth. Cool to lukewarm, then pour over the fudge layer. Refrigerate until both layers are completely set, about 1-1½ hours. Cut into 1-inch squares.

KEY LIME COOKIES

Ingredients:
 ½ cup unsalted butter (no margarine, please!)
 1 cup white sugar
 1 egg
 1 egg yolk
 2 cups all-purpose flour
 1 tsp baking powder
 ½ tsp salt
 ¼ cup Key Lime juice (in baking aisle)
 1 tablespoon finely grated lime zest
 1 bag white chocolate chips
 ½ cup confectioners' sugar

Directions: Grease cookie sheets (or use parchment paper). In a large bowl, cream butter, sugar, and eggs until smooth. Stir in lime juice and lime zest. In another bowl, combine the flour, baking powder, and salt. Blend into the butter mixture. Add white chocolate chips. (Dough will be sticky.) Refrigerate for about four hours. Form dough into rounded teaspoons (or use cookie scoop) and arrange on cookie sheet. Bake 10-12 minutes or until lightly browned in oven preheated to 350 degrees. Sift confectioners' sugar over cookies while still warm.

COMFORT COOKIES

Ingredients:
 1½ cups flour
 1 tsp baking soda
 ½ tsp salt
 1 tsp cinnamon
 1 cup (2 sticks) softened unsalted butter

⅔ cup sugar
⅔ cup brown sugar
1 tsp pure vanilla extract
2 eggs
1 cup golden raisins
1 cup sweet & tart dried cherries (Maggie uses
    Sunsweet)
3 cups oatmeal, quick-cook or old-fashioned

Preheat oven to 350 degrees. In a medium bowl, mix flour, salt, baking soda, and cinnamon. Set aside. In a large bowl, cream sugars, butter, eggs, and vanilla extract. Gently stir in flour mixture, and then stir in dried fruit. When well mixed, stir in oatmeal.

Drop by the tablespoon onto an ungreased cookie sheet. Bake at 350 for approximately 10 minutes. Cool two minutes on sheet before placing on racks.

*Need to do some catch-up reading with
the Sunrise Bible Study Group?*

Look for the first two novels in the Hope Street
Church mystery series from

JENNIFER STANLEY

STIRRING UP STRIFE
ISBN: 978-0-312-37685-7

PATH OF THE WICKED
ISBN: 978-0-312-37683-3

Recipes included!

Available from St. Martin's / Minotaur Paperbacks